FAMILIAR ACTS

FAMILIAR ACTS

June Barraclough

G.K. Hall & Co. • Chivers Press
Thorndike, Maine USA   Bath, Avon, England

This Large Print edition is published by G.K. Hall & Co., USA and by Chivers Press, England.

Published in 1994 in the U.S. by arrangement with St. Martin's Press, Inc.

Published in 1995 in the U.K. by arrangement with Robert Hale Limited.

U.S. Hardcover 0-7838-1125-X (Romance Collection Edition)
U.K. Hardcover 0-7451-2937-4 (Chivers Large Print)
U.K. Softcover 0-7451-2946-3 (Camden Large Print)

The text of this Large Print edition is unabridged.
Other aspects of the book may vary from the original edition.

Set in 16 pt. News Plantin by Minnie B. Raven.

Printed in the United States on acid-free paper.

British Library Cataloguing in Publication Data available

Library of Congress Cataloging in Publication Data

Barraclough, June.
  Familiar acts / June Barraclough.
    p.   cm.
   ISBN 0-7838-112 5-X (alk. paper : lg. print)
   1. British — Travel — Italy — Florence — History — 19th century — Fiction. 2. Man-woman relationships — Italy — Florence — Fic tion. 3. Young women — Travel — Italy — Florence — Fic tion. 4. Family — England — Fiction.
5. Large type books. I. Title.
 [PR6052.A716F35 1994b]
 823'.914—dc20

94-34501

CONTENTS

'Familiar acts are beautiful through love'.
Shelley: *Prometheus Unbound*

PART 1

East Wood

1

Even when I was very small I was a dreamer. I'd sit by the nursery fire, by the side of Huntington our nurse, who would be knitting socks, and look into the red coals and imagine that the caverns and shapes I saw in them were people and places. When I was not imagining things I'd be talking to my doll, Maryemma. I always found a lot to say to Maryemma and she always listened to me carefully and understood all I said to her. I heard her reply quite clearly in my own head. Often she'd just say things like 'Fancy that', or 'Well I never' — the sort of things that Huntie used to say when she was not really listening to us or if she were being a bit sarcastic. Sometimes I'd have Maryemma on my knee as I looked into the fire, and Huntie would come in and shout — 'Get away from that fire — you'll burn your face to a frazzle!' But that was when she was in a bad mood. Usually she was glad that I was 'out of mischief' for she had a lot of work to do, like ironing Cara's dresses. Cara was my sister and her real name was Clara, or rather Clara Christabel, but we always called her Cara. She was Papa's favourite because she was so pretty, with curly golden hair and white skin and very pale blue eyes. I always knew she was different from me, not only because I had straight brown hair and darkish skin. She did not like doing the things I enjoyed doing. When I was a bit older I'd sit and look at the big, gilt-edged *Little Folks Annual* that belonged to my brother Gregory. There was a story in it about a young man called Sir Percy Vere who loved a girl called Lady Clara and I thought that must be my sister, for the picture looked like Cara. There was something special about Cara that I could not put into words.

I did not spend all my time staring into the fire and talking to Maryemma, or looking at books, for I also enjoyed chatting to our stable boy, Alfie, which Cara never did, just as she was not interested in reading. I got into trouble for talking to the servants, but I knew that if Cara had chatted to Alfie nobody would have told her off. Papa and Mama spoilt Cara. I thought that they were making up with their attention for the years she had not been with us, since she was younger than Gregory and me. It was not Cara's fault that she was spoilt, and I was fond of her, but I preferred Gregory and played with him most. He was two years older than me and, I discovered later, not at all

8

like other girls' brothers who teased them and pulled their hair ribbons or, worse, their hair. Gregory was always kind and I used to pretend that he was Maryemma's father. I was my doll's mother, and Huntington had once told me that brothers and sisters were not allowed to marry. I could not understand this and objected very strongly. 'Why shouldn't I marry Gregory?' I asked her. 'When I'm grown up I shall marry whoever I want.' She laughed and said — 'Don't get into such a passion, Miss Hetty. We can't all do what we want.' I knew very well that I could not do all I wanted, for there were many things which Mama forbade me, such as talking to Alfie or playing with Enoch and Susie, the coachman's children, or climbing trees. Not that I was very good at climbing trees, but I wanted to do what Gregory did. My big brother had dark hair like me, but he was thinner than I was, though I was not as plump as Cara. Everybody said I had a look of Papa because although my hair was dark my eyes were blue. Not pale bright blue like Cara's, but dark blue. 'They'll go grey', said Huntington. I believed her. I usually believed what Huntie told me. Things she said came true — like having a stomach-ache after eating green apples from the orchard.

Papa never took much notice of me or of Gregory. I was about four when the sister after Cara was born, but I can remember that day very well. In the summer, a long time before Hannah arrived, Mama had gone to bed and stayed there; but on

Hannah's birthday it was snowing. Huntie told us that we had another sister. Cara and Gregory and I were playing with the Noah's ark by the fire, but we were bored and restless. 'You've another sister', said Huntie. We stopped our squabbling and were silent. Then Gregory ran to the window: 'I want to make a snowman for the baby so that she can look out of the window and see it', he said. Cara, who liked ordering us about, said: 'I want a snowman — make a snowman for *me!*'

Huntie said new babies could not see out of the window and we must be quiet because Mama was ill. Cara sulked. 'I want my Mama.' Even then I knew how to change an awkward subject, for I sensed that Cara would not be allowed to see Mama that day, so I said: 'Can we see the new baby?' I did not care about seeing Mama.

'When the doctor's seen her', answered Huntie. 'Then you might. Such a fuss', she said. We gathered that they didn't make such a fuss over babies in Huntie's family. Huntie had eight brothers. She was the only girl.

At tea-time we had porridge for a treat with our toast and I scraped my bowl to see which nursery rhyme I had at the bottom where there was a picture. I wanted Little Boy Blue, but it was Little Miss Muffet.

We did see Hannah, after a day or two, but I had the feeling that Papa was not pleased about her arrival. Huntie said that he had wanted a boy. Gregory said; '*I* am a boy', but Huntie pursed her mouth and said: 'You don't count, poor love!'

She often said funny things like that. We were used to them and didn't take much notice at the time, but we remembered.

Huntie seemed always to have been with us, connected with a time when I had been very happy, but I could never remember why. Once I asked her about that time. It was on Hannah's first birthday and Huntie said: 'The poor scrap can't sit up.' I must have asked her how old I was when *I* sat up for she answered: 'Oh, you were a lazy baby — you talked before you could walk.' Huntie had known me from the day I was born. 'It was my Auntie Rosa got me the job with your family', she said. 'I'm a Cockney sparrer born and bred.'

We lived almost in London, in North Kent, in a house called 'East Wood' near Parkheath, a village where the trains stopped for the men who went to work in the City like Papa. The house was big and dark and, except for the nursery, the rooms were cold. The nursery had that nice fire in the grate, with a big guard, where I saw my caverns and people. It was at the back of the house, and when I grew tall enough to look out of the window, which was barred, I could see the paved stable yard and the path that led to the shrubbery at the front of the house and the other path from the big carriage gate at the back that led to the woods. I suppose East Wood was called after them.

Huntie would take us out to the village, me and Gregory and Cara, and baby Hannah in her black pram, and if we had time she would let us watch the trains which puffed along every twenty minutes

11

in both directions. In the station yard Mr Hewitt had his hackney-carriage for those who had no carriage of their own and did not want to walk home. There were many interesting shops in the village, but we never lingered long in them. Huntie would buy aniseed balls for us if we were good, but she never had the money for lollipops.

Huntie was the person who was with us all the time. She could get cross, but she was always fair. When I was older I realized that she looked rather strange with her battered felt hat and her boots and her long apron. Her voice was rough, almost hoarse, and she could be very fierce with the odd-job boy. Even Cook dared not cheek her, though I suppose Cook was older than Huntie. Huntie was ageless. Had there ever been a time when she had looked young and worn her hair down her back and not had her hands all red from washing our clothes? Later I puzzled over why Papa did not have a Nurse for us with a starched uniform, though I was glad he did not. I suppose Huntie was loyal; he certainly cannot have paid her very much. Parlour-maids came and went, but Huntie stayed.

It was difficult for me to love my Mama, who was called Mrs Ella Coppen; after Hannah was born it became harder. Mama did not often come into our nursery but would sometimes take Cara downstairs with her for tea. We were not encouraged to enter Mama's bedroom, Gregory and I, but Cara was allowed to play with the objects on her dressing-table. Once I crept in when Mama was downstairs in the drawing-room and looked at the cut glass bottles and the powder-puff for Mama's rice powder, and the ewer on the side-table, and the small table near her bed with its array of green medicine bottles.

Mama was a 'sufferer'. The smell of her room was a mixture of the scent she wore from Paris and the sweetish odour of flesh and sleep mingled with a camphory smell from one of the bottles. There was a bottle of smelling-salts on the small table, and I sniffed them and sneezed. I was terrified Mama would have heard me and ran out of the room back to the nursery, which was going to be turned into a schoolroom for me and Gregory. Cara was to have a little room of her own and Gregory and I were to go to the top floor to sleep in two attic bedrooms. Hannah slept with Huntie in a bedroom off the nursery which Mama called the Night Nursery.

After Hannah was born Mama would push me away if I tried to get close to her when we were on show downstairs, and I soon stopped trying. Mama had a dreadful temper and would scream and shout at her maid, a woman called Mrs Popplewell, and would sometimes scream even at Cara, though never as loudly or for as long as she would at me and Gregory. Cara always got the best presents too. A few weeks after Hannah was born it was Christmas and Papa and Mama gave her a doll. Another one arrived that day from the postman and the strange thing was that this doll looked just like the one from Mama and Papa. When Cara had unwrapped and showed it to Mama, she went absolutely white and screamed. 'Who sent the child that? Take it away. One doll is enough.' Cara began to cry. Papa was at work and Huntie was fetched to pacify my sister. 'They were twin dolls', I whispered to Huntie later. To Cara I said: 'I wanted to call the dolls Rowena and Rebecca.' 'She's taken it away', said my sister, still clutching the first doll. I thought it was mean — they could have given the second doll to me if they thought two were too many for Cara.

Children do not question the way they live, they think it is the normal way — and they do not think there is anything extraordinary about their parents. It is only when they know other families and have something with which to compare their own household that they realize there are different ways of carrying on. Later, when they begin to reason, they wonder why their own home is so unhappy and strained and why their mother and father do not seem to like them. I did not like Mama; I realized this when I was about four, and I knew that Gregory felt the same.

It was when I was about five or six that another baby came, but did not stay. Hannah was eighteen months old, I suppose, and perhaps it was because I was old for my years, and curiously upset by the 'dead baby' I heard Cook muttering about to the kitchen-maid, that I asked Huntie: 'Why does Mama go on having babies? Hasn't she enough already?' I knew that Papa wanted a boy. Naturally he did not say such a thing to his children, but why had Huntie said when our sister Hannah was born that Gregory didn't count? I remembered those words.

Huntie pursed her mouth. She was darning Greg's socks at the time and she took her time replying. Then: 'If you're married you've no choice', she said. 'There's large families and small — big like mine — though my dad wasn't a gent and couldn't help himself, I don't suppose.' What had Papa to do with it, I remember thinking. I thought that babies arrived once you were married and asked God for them, and I could not imagine Mama asking for another since the ones she already had caused her so much trouble.

Hannah was still neither walking nor talking and she could not sit up without support. 'Poor mite — she's backward', said Huntie. I knew what 'forward' meant because Papa used to say to me, if I spoke back to him when he was finding fault with something I'd done or not done; 'Don't be forward, miss.' I decided that Maryemma was very forward too when I chastised her and she would reply: 'I'll do what I want, Hetty', in a loud voice in my head.

The idea of a dead baby was peculiarly horrifying and I asked Huntie where she — it had been another girl — was to be buried. Huntie did not reply and I heard no more about a burial. I knew dead things were buried because I had seen our gardener, Mr Hopkins, bury Cook's dead canary, and Gregory and I had buried the tortoise which Papa's mother had given him on his seventh birthday. Poor Tippy had never come out of his hibernation. We did not often see Grandma Coppen, who was very old. She lived in Devon, but we had never been to see her there. Mama did not like her. I often heard her telling Papa to tell the old lady to keep away and stop poking her nose into what was no concern of hers. I was an inveterate eavesdropper and in this way I found out many things which my childish mind did not understand, though I had an active imagination. But the dead baby persisted in my head and gave me nightmares for months. The worst time was when I dreamed I saw a little baby being held in the arms of an old man and I screamed: 'The baby's dead', but he went on holding him and jogging him up and down. In the same dream there was a crib with hanging laces and blue ribbons, smarter than Hannah's crib, and the man put the baby down in it and leaned over it, swinging his watch to and fro over the pillow. I was full of horror that the old man did not understand, and woke screaming: 'He's dead! He's dead!' Huntie came in to me. She was wearing the long flannelette nightie that I thought always smelled of toast. She soothed me in her arms. 'There, there, Miss Hetty — don't cry — you were dreaming.' 'There was a blue cradle and a man with a big gold watch', I said. 'And he thought the baby was alive but I told him it was dead.' I began to cry again. The dream had been strangely vivid.

'I expect you was dreaming of Miss Cara's old cradle', she said.

'No, no, Huntie — there were *blue* ribbons', I said. 'A crib with blue ribbons.' I had no memory of *pink* ribbons or of Cara as a baby. I thought Huntie looked at me slyly. After that dream I would pray not to dream of the dead baby again, and made up a long rigmarole to prevent this. If I counted to fifty before I drew another breath, it would be all right, but I must also say 'Our Father' three times with my fingers crossed and Maryemma must sleep in my bed to guard me.

I could count well by the time I was six, for Gregory had taught me, but soon after that there arrived a young lady called Miss Lucy Little who was to teach us every morning in the old nursery, now a schoolroom. Huntie did not go away. She was needed for Hannah who could now stand up, but still could not walk and who never said any word you could understand, just made funny noises and threw her food on the floor when you were not looking.

Miss Little was not little. We giggled over her name. Huntie *was* little, but Miss Little was tall and thin, though quite cheerful-looking. She came every day except on Saturdays and Sundays, and we did our alphabet and our sums and our pot-hooks and she read to us from *Little Arthur's History of England* and Mrs Gatty's *Parables from Nature*. I thought that Little Arthur was her own little boy — and that somehow she meant Arthur Little not Little Arthur. I enjoyed the stories and even the nature tales, though they had long words. 'Will you stay for ever, Miss Little?' Gregory asked

17

her. 'Like Huntington', I added.

'I expect I shall stay with you, Hetty, and your sister Cara', she replied. 'Gregory will soon be going to school, I expect.'

It was the first we had heard of it and filled me with terror. I could bear everything — toothache and nightmares and even tapioca pudding if my brother was with me. He was my best friend, even more than Huntie who I thought was only half grown up.

'Boys always go to school', she said.

I did not believe her.

But other important things happened before Gregory was sent away from me.

First of all, Huntie explained to me what 'backward' meant; and shortly after that another baby arrived. These happenings seem to run together in my head; Miss Little must have been with us for a year when Baby Alice came, and happily stayed, so I had no more dreams for the time being of the dead baby. When Alice was born Hannah was three years old. Yet it must have been when Alice began to walk that I said to Huntie: 'Why does Hannah not yet walk when Alice can?' At first Huntie said: 'Well, Hetty, Alice is very forward indeed in that respect.' But when I persisted, remembering her earlier words, Huntie said: 'I told you Hannah was backward.' 'But what does it mean?' I asked. I was at the table in the nursery; it was afternoon and must have been autumn for I heard the muffin-man's bell outside on the road and he never came before October.

'It means there's something not right', she said in a low voice and looked at the door to make sure neither Cara nor Mama was listening.

'Won't she *ever* walk properly?' I asked her. Hannah could just stand up now and could shuffle along on her hindquarters and she was getting easier to understand, for when she was hungry she made a special sound and when she did not like her food she just turned her face away.

'She may walk soon', was all Huntie said, but the way she said it made me understand that Hannah was always going to be what Mama called 'slow' and Huntie called 'backward'. Mama did not have much to do with Hannah, as she did not have much to do with Gregory or me, but she doted on Alice, and Cara, of course, as she always had. Later, Huntie said, 'Hannah won't ever be as quick as you, Miss Hetty, or Miss Alice or Miss Cara', and I understood she did not just mean in walking. Huntie never said 'Miss' Hannah either as she did about the rest of us girls, but she was always kind to her. As I grew up I realized that although Hannah did not dribble and did not look like some of the children from the orphanage whom we sometimes passed in a crocodile and who all looked alike in their brown smocks, she would probably never speak properly. She began to feed herself as time went on, but Huntie had to wash her nappies for ages. When Mama's friends came to visit, which was not very often, Hannah was sent to the nursery. Slowly I began to realize that Mama and Papa were ashamed of her.

19

'They won't get rid of me now', said Huntie one day. 'They'll always need me for Hannah.'

'Why, Huntie', I said. 'Why should Papa get rid of you? They'd never send you away, they just couldn't.'

I was seven and Gregory was nine when a letter came to Mama and Papa which kept them talking in whispers late at night. I heard them from my attic bed when I lay awake, for their bedrooms were on the floor below and they talked on the landing. I was never a good sleeper.

'He must be welcomed here one day, Leo,' said Mama. 'I have a feeling that if he comes we shall be blessed with a son.'

I did not hear Papa's reply, but shortly after that Miss Little said very solemnly that Gregory was to start at a school in Devon in September and that Papa would speak to him about it. I should explain that Lucy Little did not live with us but came every day on the train from Camberwell where she lived with her aged father.

It was shortly after that, in the summer holidays, which we did not spend at Broadstairs that year, that I met Max.

2

It was a Saturday afternoon in August and I was with Huntie and Gregory in the train which branched off to the next village on the line and then to others where I had never been before. Cara was not with us. We were going further into Kent to a house called The Laurels, Huntie said.

Since he had been told that he was to go away to school, Gregory had been very quiet. He was always a serious boy who kept things to himself, but this time he did not even talk to me.

'Why are we going to this house?' I asked Huntie.

'To see your Auntie Zelda', she replied. This galvanized Gregory, who looked up. 'I remember *her*', he said.

'Is that so?' said Huntie, and looked surprised.

'*I* don't', I said. 'Who is she?'

Huntie took some time replying. Finally — 'She's your Auntie, like I said. My Auntie Rosa worked for her family and that's how I come to know you.' I felt there was some gap in Huntie's logic, but could not quite work it out.

'Why didn't Papa want Cara to come with us?' I asked her after a silence.

'Why should you think that?' said Huntie. 'So

many questions — *I* don't know.'

'*I* know', said Gregory. But he said no more on the subject.

'I wouldn't be surprised if your aunt has a croquet lawn', said Huntie. She looked distinctly ill at ease. I was always aware of Huntie's moods. Abrupt and sometimes bossy, but kind underneath. Huntie, when she was upset, could be read like a book.

'*Boys* don't play croquet, do they?' asked Gregory.

'Don't they?' said Huntie. 'Well, I've been told there's a little boy waiting to play with you.'

'You never said she was married', I said.

'Yes — to Mr de Vere — but he died', said Huntie. She saw that more questions were on my lips and added: 'No more questions now — we're nearly there.'

I looked out of the train window and saw fields and woods and then a line of straggling houses as we approached a station. 'It's the country!' I said. 'Will she have some books, do you think?' The influence of Miss Lucy Little was proving strong for I had become even more of a bookworm. Huntie did not reply. 'Did you say "de Vere"?' I persisted and she stood up as the train drew in to unfasten the leather strap that let the window down.

'That's right', she replied, her eyes on the track.

'That was the name of the man in my book', I said. 'Percy Vere.'

'She's not Vere, she's de Vere', said Gregory

who preferred accuracy.

'It's nearly the same', I said.

We were mildly squabbling — we never argued more than this — as we followed Huntie on to the platform.

We walked behind some ladies as we went through the station waiting-room where a fire was burning merrily in a polished grate. I heard the crinolines under the ladies' wraps making a creaky noise as they walked. I was glad Huntie was a servant and didn't wear a crinoline for I thought grown up ladies' dresses horrible. I hoped I would never have to wear such wide skirts with hoops underneath. However, I was thinking not of crinolines but of the *Little Folks Annual* and Sir Percy Vere as we waited uncertainly outside the station on the cobbled path. Then I thought about the new book given to me by Miss Little at Christmas about a girl called Alice, like my youngest sister. Miss Little said it was very good, and I had started to read it but found it rather difficult. I preferred *Aunt Judy's* stories in the *Monthly Packet*.

'They said there'd be a carriage', said Huntie, looking up the main street of the town. Just then an old man with whiskers came up to us. 'Miss Huntington and the infants?' he croaked. 'There's a fly waiting at the side.' Huntie had on her best boots and shawl but still didn't look like a 'Miss'. I was glad she was wearing the black bonnet that Cook had given her (she told me) and not the felt hat that she wore for feeding our hens in the back-yard. I stopped thinking about Sir Percy Vere and

23

Alice and gave myself up to the journey in the open carriage. 'She didn't send her best carriage', said Huntie when we were seated. 'A good thing we don't weigh overmuch. Remember, the lady's your aunt', she muttered.

After driving through the town and out again we were approaching a drive through an open gate with two stone balls on its pillars.

'I expect her husband was our uncle?' enquired my brother.

'I told you — he passed away some years ago', said Huntie, looking nervous.

I wondered why Papa and Mama had not taken us on this visit. We had never been so far with Huntie before. When we arrived, Huntie rang the bell. A maid opened the door and we saw not one but two boys, before a dark lady with ringlets, wearing a brown silk dress, came up behind them.

'Here are the children, Mum', said Huntie, looking uncomfortable.

'Thank you, Huntington', said the lady. 'You may go round to the kitchen. I'll tell you when they are ready to return.'

Huntie didn't curtsey, but turned tail and went out through the front door again. I looked at Gregory. We were to be left on our own with these people whom we'd never seen before. Perhaps they had a nursery where we could play?

'Follow me', said the lady who must be our Aunt Zelda and we followed her through a large gloomy hall and through a door hung with long curtains of the same colour as her dress, into a big room

with pieces of dark furniture and pictures of buildings and dead birds. The larger of the two boys
marched in with us, but the smaller one held back.
I thought he was about my age.

'This is my boy Max', said the lady, taking him
by the hand. 'I expect you know who I am?'

'You are our Aunt Zelda', said Gregory, his eyes
upon her. I looked up at her in the light from
the leaded panes of the room and had a most curious sensation. I felt I had seen her before.

'Dear little Hetty', she said in a flat voice.

Max shook hands with Gregory and stared at
me. He was a dark child with large brown eyes
and thin legs like stalks from the knee downwards
under his knickerbockers.

'This is your cousin Gregory Coppen', she went
on. 'And this is little Hetty.'

The other boy stood there saying nothing, with
what I thought was an unpleasant smile on his
face. 'I'm Simon Voyle', he said.

'Simon is rather older than you, Gregory', said
Aunt Zelda. I supposed I must call her Aunt.

'Gregory is nine, Aunt', I said proudly. 'And
I am seven years old.'

'I am ten', said the boy Simon.

'Simon is my ward', said Aunt Zelda. 'You may
all go and play upstairs for half an hour and the
bell will call you for tea.'

I was not displeased to leave the big room, for
there was nothing there of interest. A silent maid
wearing a long cap with streamers came to the
door and we followed her upstairs, and then up

another flight of stairs. The 'nursery' was not like ours. For one thing there was no fire and no Huntie, only this maid who sat down and took up some knitting, still saying nothing. We stood there in the centre of the room and Simon said: 'I am to go away to school, Coppen. They tell me it's the same school where you are to go — Lyndcombe' — he spoke in a curious drawling voice as though there was a sneer hidden in it.

'When are you going?' asked my brother, not looking at all pleased at the idea.

'When *you* go, Coppen — in September.'

There was a silence.

The little boy, Max, piped up: 'I've got some soldiers — would you like to play with them?' I thought he might be addressing me, so I replied: 'All right', and he led me to a cupboard which he opened on tiptoe and took out a box. I saw there was a fort tidily arranged in the corner of the room. I left Gregory to deal with Simon and applied myself to taking out the soldiers from the box. They were rather like small dolls.

'Do you have names for them?' I asked Max.

'That's —' and he said a name that sounded funny to me.

'What did you say?' I asked him.

He looked up — 'Oh — I forgot — you don't say it like that in England. He *is* Garibaldi though — he's an Italian. Have you been to Italy?'

I had heard of Italy because Miss Little had done the map of Europe with us the week before. The idea of going to the places she'd showed us on the map had never occurred to me. 'Do you mean you could go there?' I asked in some amazement.

He looked at me seriously. 'That's where we lived — me and Mama — and Simon sometimes — we came here on a train and a big boat, after Natale.' I noticed that he had a slight accent.

'Is your mother a lady from Italy?' I asked.

'Of course Mama is not Italian', he said composedly. 'My Papa was not either, but lots of English people live in Italy.'

'Is Simon your brother?'

'Oh, no — nor even my cousin, as Mama says you are. I will tell you a secret.' He lowered his voice and I looked expectant, but just then the maid with the long cap stood up tucking her needles under one arm — 'Fresh air', she announced. 'Follow me.'

Simon made a face and Gregory laughed nervously, but she turned round to see we were doing her bidding and we followed her down some different stairs, to a green baize door and along a corridor and out again through a door at the back of the house where there was a yard a bit like ours, but larger. She never stopped till she had crossed the yard with us all following and opened a gate in a fence and led us through a shrubbery, again grander than ours at home, and on to a lawn. 'Boys may run', she said and clapped her hands. As I was not a boy I waited, but she took no notice of me, sat down on a rustic bench and brought the knitting out again. I looked back at the house and saw Huntie at a kitchen window. 'May I go to my Huntie?' I asked. But Huntie's face had disappeared again and the maid did not answer. I walked over the lawn. The boys were crouched on the grass looking at a dead bird. One thing I could not stand was a dead bird and when Simon Voyle picked it up and thrust it under my nose, I fled. I heard Gregory say; 'Put it down, you beast!' I shut my eyes and when I opened them saw Simon whirling the little corpse above his head, before throwing it over a wall.

A little voice said: 'He is crude', and I saw that Max had crept up to me whilst I had my eyes shut.

'He is cruel', I said.

'You do not say crude?'

'No, we say rude', I replied. 'Didn't your Mama teach you proper English?'

He flushed. 'I had my *nonna* in Ialy', he said. I was going to ask him how he was my cousin when a loud clapper-like bell sounded over the lawn and the tall maid looked up again. 'Tea', she said briefly.

This was the strangest visit I had ever made in my life, I thought.

Over cups of tea, which arrived on a table with wheels as we sat in the drawing-room as if we were grown up, I said to Aunt Zelda, who had reappeared, though Huntie had not; 'I read a story about Percy Vere. Is he your relation?' I thought I sounded very grown up.

Her eyes were so dark and brooding that you almost got swallowed up in them if you stared

28

at her too long, but eyes couldn't swallow you, only mouths. 'No', she said. 'And it is not Vere but de Vere, a very old family.' I did not try any more conversation and I did not like the sandwiches. They tasted more like flannel than egg. Gregory ate his and I saw Simon eyeing the ones which I had not eaten. Max had not much appetite either.

Shortly after that Aunt Zelda said: 'Well, now you know each other — but you must be going if you are to catch your train.'

Children do not ask the whys and wherefores of the arrangements made in their lives, but I was moved on the way back — Huntie having been miraculously restored to us — to ask why we had gone to meet those strange relations.

'Your Mama did not want you to go', she said. 'But your Papa thought you should. And your Auntie Zelda was most insistent.'

'Don't you remember her?' Gregory said, turning to me. I could not explain the feeling that I had seen her before. It gave me a sort of pain to think about it but I didn't know why. I didn't really 'remember' her. I had the curious idea that she was someone else. But who could that be? Or perhaps 'someone else' had been with her before? I felt cross and tired.

'Simon is her "ward" ', I said, using the word with sugar tongs as I was experimenting with it.

'What *is* that? He's a beast', said Gregory.

Huntie laughed. 'Better keep those kind of thoughts to yerself, Master Gregory', she said.

'Max was nice', I said. I thought, Max looked a bit like Gregory, that was why I liked him. Huntie sighed.

'Well, we've done our duty', she said and no more conversation took place during the journey or even when we got home, for I was tired and Huntie was out of sorts and Gregory was quiet. I thought, he is going away to school and that nasty boy will be there to spoil it.

Nothing was said by Papa or Mama about our visit. That same week I had one of my nightmares again. Not the dead baby but the same feel to it. A screen with birds painted on it and this time Aunt Zelda was there, not the nice old man with the gold watch who belonged to this dream. Aunt Zelda was crying and there was an old woman, who looked like Huntie, but wore a long cap like the maid at The Laurels, looking out of a long window. I woke up. I was not screaming though I felt frightened.

I told Miss Little where we had been on the Saturday and she listened as she always did and looked thoughtful. 'I had a nasty dream', I said. I did not want to bother Huntie with it.

'Put it out of your head, Hetty', she said.

So I did, and when in September Gregory went away to school and I was left with Cara for companion I forgot about Max and Aunt Zelda and the boy Simon and concentrated on making a collection of leaves and sticking them into a scrap book. Cara was given a doll's house for her birthday and wanted me to admire it. 'You need two people to play with it', she said, and I thought it was generous of her. She started lessons with Miss Little and another lady came to teach us to play the piano. Hannah began to walk in a queer sideways motion and Alice played with her. The old nursery was changing, but it was not until I was eight and already feeling I was another person that I learned from Gregory, in the Christmas holidays, more about Max and Simon and Max's mother Zelda de Vere.

When I had asked him the day after our visit to Zelda's house why he had said he remembered her, he had refused to say and I could get nothing more out of him. Now I was to find out. Yet when he came back for the holidays he seemed somehow different. I was so glad to see him that I listened carefully when he told me about the school, and asked him questions about the boys and the lessons, for I had got a bit bored playing with Cara who was not as good a companion as he was, and Huntie was always busy looking after Alice and Hannah.

'I wish I could go to school with you', I said. I knew there were schools for girls because Miss Little said she had been to one in North London, but hers had not been a school for sleeping in.

'Mine's only for boys, worse luck', said my brother.

'Do the boys fight a lot?' I asked him.

'The beak stops that', said Gregory. 'Except when they don't know about the fights.'

31

'Is that boy Simon there — the one we met at Aunt Zelda's?' I asked him.

'Yes — but he's in a different form from me. I see him at recreation, he's not in my dorm.' I learned lots of new words like 'beak' and 'dorm' and 'recreation' from Gregory.

'I didn't like him', I said.

'You'll have to put up with him', said Gregory. 'He says he's going to come and stay with us one day.'

'Here? At home with *us?* But why?'

'*I* don't know', said Greg and looked miserable. 'He says Aunt Zelda is our Mama's sister', whispered Gregory looking out of the schoolroom window. We were alone there. Cara was being measured for a dress since she was to go to a dancing class in town and Huntie was out in the garden with Alice and Hannah.

'Mama's sister?' I echoed. 'Then why didn't *she* come with us to see her that time?'

He was a long time replying. Then he said: 'I think Huntie knows why.'

Whilst my brother had been away Mama had been ill again. I had half-expected another baby would arrive, but it did not. Before, whenever she had been ill, there had been a baby afterwards even if the one before Alice had not stayed. I heard Cook talking to Huntie when Mama was in bed again and I thought they were discussing a lady called Miss Carriage. I never spoke of this sort of thing to Gregory, nor had I bothered him with my dreams; now I wanted to tell him about the one with the little dead baby, but didn't know how to start. Instead I said: 'Huntie told me her Aunt Rosa was nurse to Aunt Zelda once. So she must have been nurse to Mama if Aunt Zelda is Mama's sister, mustn't she? Shall I ask her?'

'No — don't', said Gregory and looked uncomfortable.

'I don't think Mama likes Huntie', I said.

Suddenly he said — 'I *do* remember Aunt Zelda. And *you* were there. You were quite small', he said.

'*I* don't remember that', I said.

'No, I expect you were too little', said Gregory. 'It was when I saw you for the first time, I *think* — in Italy.'

'In Italy!' I exclaimed, astonished. 'What are you talking about?'

He looked shifty again. 'I think I remember Max too when he was a baby', he went on after a pause. 'But Simon was not there.'

Just then Mama came into the room and Gregory said in a high voice as though he had been carrying on quite a different conversation with me. 'Yes, we learn Latin.'

Cara came dancing into the nursery. 'I'm having a real silk dress', she shouted. 'With ribbons and a sash.'

'Are we going to see Aunt Zelda again?' I asked Mama.

'I was just going to tell you about that', said Mama, but then she stopped and went to the window and looked out.

'Gregory says that Simon boy might come to stay with us', I said.

Mama turned round quickly. 'Whoever told you that?'

'*He* did — he says he's going to come and stay here in the holidays', said Gregory. Cara was looking from one to the other as they spoke.

'No, no!' said Mama in an agitated way. 'Not yet. He will stay with his guardian. Perhaps later . . .'

I wanted to say — Gregory told me that you and Aunt Zelda are sisters — but something stopped me. Mama looked so uneasy. I thought she was going to be cross, but instead she turned and said to my brother: 'How do you like him then — Simon?'

'Oh he's all right', replied Gregory not looking at her.

'Max was nicer', I said.

'Who asked you your opinion, miss?' said Mama. I froze. I knew that such words usually meant she was going to shout at me, or slap me.

When she had gone out of the room I said to Cara: 'Well, Max *was* nicer than that Simon boy.' But Cara only wanted to talk about her dress.

That night in my attic bedroom I could not sleep. I heard my brother get out of bed in the room next to ours and waited for him to come and talk to me. It had been a long time since we had talked privately together in bed and I had missed Gregory more than I wanted to let on to him. I wondered if he had missed me.

Now he stood at the foot of my small truckle-bed and said in a whisper: 'I will tell you something if you will promise not to tell anyone about it.'

'Cross my heart and hope to die', I said with a shiver. Huntie had taught me those words.

'My feet are cold', he said. 'Can I snuggle under your eiderdown?' 'Promise?' he said again when he was settled at the bottom of the bed with his feet under the quilt. The moonlight was coming through the small round window.

'I promise on Maryemma's life', I replied solemnly. My brother looked very pale in the moonlight.

'Aunt Zelda knows, because Simon told me she does — and I think Huntie knows', he began. He took a deep breath and I waited. 'Mama here, Papa's wife, is not our own Mama', he said, and the words came out rather louder than he had intended and he clapped his hand over his mouth and looked at the door in case anyone had heard. I gaped at him. 'Our Mama died in Italy and then Papa married — Ella.' I giggled at the way he said 'Ella', which was our Mama's name — or rather now it was not. I tried to understand what he'd said.

'Don't be silly', I said.

'I'm not. It's true. That's why she likes Cara best.'

'But Papa —'

'Oh, Papa is all our Papa's — yours and mine and Cara's and Hannah's and Alice's.'

I was silent and digesting all this.

'Our Mama died', he said again. 'Simon told me.'

'Why didn't Papa tell us then?' I burst out. 'When did she die?'

'Oh, you were only very small —'

I began to want to cry, perhaps because I'd never known that I'd lost someone.

'Don't tell *anyone*', urged Gregory.

'But why is it a secret? People know who their mothers are when they're grown up — they'd have to tell us one day. Huntie could have told', I went on.

'They probably told her not to', said Gregory.

Then I remembered Aunt Zelda. 'Is Aunt Zelda our *real* mother's sister?' I enquired, just to be sure.

'Yes, Simon says that our Mama was her younger sister', said Gregory.

I shivered. Then I said in a small voice: 'I thought I'd once seen her in a dream — do you think it was really Mama?'

'*I* remember Mama', he said. 'I always did — I *knew* my real Mama was in Italy. Huntie was there — I'm sure she was there. I knew our Mama was someone else.'

'Sh-h—' I said. I'd thought I'd heard a foot on the stair. We froze for a moment, but nothing happened.

'Nobody told me she died', he said mournfully.

'Max *is* our cousin isn't he then?' I knew about families — cousins and grandparents — and your mother's sister's child was your first cousin, I knew that. 'Why didn't we know about him before?'

Gregory shook his head. 'I don't know why. But he's been in Italy since he was a little boy.'

'I suppose Simon told you *that* too', I said. I thought, all this story comes from that boy Simon. What if it's what Huntie calls 'a pack o' lies'? But I said: 'We have a cousin and Cara doesn't!' At last I had something she did not. Was Cara still my sister then? Gregory must have been thinking similar thoughts for he said: 'The others are only our half-sisters — Cara and Hannah and Alice.'

I thought about this. But I was still Papa's, and so was Gregory. 'Why can't I tell Huntie? — I could ask her all about it!'

'You promised', warned my brother. 'I promised Simon not to tell anyone.'

'I don't see how *he* knows — it's no business of his, is it?'

'He seem to know all about us', said Gregory.

'Anyway, you're still my brother', I said after a long silence. I wanted to go to sleep now.

'And you're my sister', said Gregory. 'I've got to go now. Promise again.'

'Oh, all right.' He slid off the bed and went pattering to the door. I would have liked to have a long think about it, but I fell asleep and I did not dream that night.

In the morning everything looked ordinary and it seemed impossible that Mama was not Mama. I'd always tried to like Mama, who was, it seemed, not my Mama, and had made special prayers to be good and nice to her even if she was horrid

37

to me. But now I understood why Cara got the doll's house and the dancing lessons. Papa should want me to have them too, I thought. I'm *his* daughter. It was not fair. Why should my Mama have died?

The Mama who lived in our house was what the fairy stories called a stepmother. I rolled this word around my tongue. Stepmothers are wicked in all the stories.

Yet nothing much happened after all that upheaval in my mind except that Gregory went away again for his second term and I was left with Lucy Little and Huntie, and Hannah and my other half-sisters. I missed my brother more this time because we shared this terrible secret. I couldn't help wondering where they'd buried Mama.

3

By the time I had my eighth birthday in December 1867 I had almost become used to my brother's long absences away at school. I missed him when I was not in the schoolroom with Miss Little and had time to myself, but I felt queer when I thought about what he had told me. His absence meant that I need not dwell on it. There were other things though which I noticed more than I had done before, and when I was alone they would come to my mind. I realized that they fitted into this new knowledge of us all.

Papa acted towards me with his customary indifference, and my wanting to please him changed into a sort of sorrow that I never could. If only Papa loved me, I thought, it would not matter that Mama was not my real Mama.

I knew that my pretty sister Cara was loved by Papa as he would never love me, whatever I did or said. She was so unlike me and yet we had the same Papa, and were sisters because of that. Strangely enough I was never jealous of her. Perhaps I was *envious* at that time of her undoubted advantages — being pretty and being Papa's favourite: they were facts I accepted. But her being Mama Ella's real daughter was not an advantage in my opinion. It was at this time that I began to think of Papa's wife as Mamarella. I had always liked making up names — as I had done for my doll Maryemma. Mamarella sounded like Cinderella, though she was the wicked stepmother. I never called her Mama to her face now; I might call her that to Cara and the others, but in my private thoughts she was Mamarella. My sisters Hannah and Alice I did not think of so much as half-sisters. Hannah was now 'Pooranna', which was what Huntie called her, a name I had coined from our nurse's so often exclaiming 'Poor Hannah'. I both wanted to see and dreaded seeing Aunt Zelda again. I felt she would somehow force it out of me despite my promise to Gregory.

When Gregory came home at Christmas he did not mention our secret. He looked preoccupied and sad and I could not find an opportunity to talk with him privately. On Christmas morning however, when I gave him an embroidered penwiper I had made for him and a bag of humbugs, he did smile at me and I knew he knew what I was thinking. I got a penny a week pocket-money now because Cara had told Papa she had no money for presents, and so he decided to give my sister a penny a week and could hardly refuse to give me the same. I saved it to buy the sweets and for the silk to embroider the pen-wiper. Miss Little helped me with the stitches for I was an indifferent needlewoman. To Papa I gave a sheet of blotting-paper and to Mamarella a fir-cone I had silvered with the help of Lucy Little. Mamarella looked at my offering and then at me. Cara had given her the ring which had been in my cracker the year before and which I had given to her. 'Thank you, Hetty', said my stepmother and left it on the table. Afterwards I put it on the Christmas tree.

I gave Pooranna only kisses and played with her a whole morning, which was tiring because she wanted to be held on my lap, where she would go to sleep and I found her heavy. She still had no words and her gait was clumsy and often led to falls. I tried to teach her to understand things like cup and dress and she would look at me silently, but I imagined with *some* understanding. One day in the holidays, when I had her on my knee because Huntie was busy, Papa came into the nursery. I was pointing out pictures to her from a book of Gregory's and she was tranquil for a moment. When Papa saw us he said: 'Where is Huntington? Hannah is not *your* responsibility, Hetty.' I stared at him, but he turned away. I thought that I saw disgust and anger in his eyes directed not at me, but at his slow daughter. 'Papa, Papa — ! She *can* learn if I am patient!' I cried, but he did not reply as he went out of the room.

'Papa does not love me or Greg or Hannah', I said to Huntie that evening when I was drying my hair before the nursery fire. Mamarella still hardly ever came into the nursery except to fetch Cara for a visit in the carriage to the shops or Alice to curl her hair, which my stepmother liked doing.

'Don't be silly, Hetty — of course he loves you', said Huntie mechanically, without much conviction. I was tempted to tell her what I knew, but nobly resisted the temptation.

I suppose ours was a queer family, but it ran very smoothly with the help of the servants, and Papa seemed to have enough money to pay them from his work in the City.

Gregory went back to school without mentioning Simon to me, though I heard Mamarella asking him whether he saw much of him. I was more sad when my brother went back than I had been at first because I felt I had not been able to get near to him. Something seemed to have happened to him, but he had not wanted to talk.

In January, after Gregory had gone away and just before my own lessons began again with Miss Little, Mamarella most unusually called me into her bedroom.

'Would you like to see your Aunt Zelda again?' she began.

'I would like to see the little boy,' I replied, 'Max.'

'*She* would like you to spend a day with them', said Mamarella. 'But it is very inconvenient. I need Huntington here and you are too young to go alone. Miss Little could accompany you, I suppose.' She sighed.

'Will Cara come too?' I asked.

'It is you she wishes to see, not Cara', said Mamarella. I know why that is, I thought, Cara is not her relation. But I said nothing.

The upshot was that Miss Little was asked to take me one day on the train to The Laurels. She said she would use the opportunity to point out the interesting features of the journey. Lucy Little never wasted time and so I was told about the North Downs and the Weald of Kent on the way, though we could not see them. On arrival — the same fly had collected us from the station — Aunt Zelda did not send Miss Little to the kitchen as she had done with Huntie, but made conversation before telling her to collect me at four o'clock. Miss Little looked surprised but said: 'I'm sure there is plenty to see in town, Ma'am.' I supposed she walked back to it for the fly had disappeared. Max was on the stairs and he seemed less small and pale than before, but just as conversationally odd. I wondered why he did not go to school and asked him when we were in the 'nursery', which was just as cold and just as bare as before. 'I am too delicate', he replied, with a long look from under his eyelashes. 'I am to have a tutor soon.'

'I wish you could come and stay with *me*', I said, feeling a bit disloyal to Gregory. 'Miss Little teaches us an awful lot.'

Max did not like the rough games which even Gregory played sometimes. He certainly liked to talk though and began in his curiously accented English to tell me about Italy. He was describing his house in Italy which he called a 'villa' when his mother came in. She sat down and said nothing, just stared at us both and let Max go on talking. She was, I suppose, a very beautiful lady — I had not realized that the first time we had visited her, so intent had I been on absorbing Simon and Max. But now I knew she was my real Mama's sister I paid particular attention to her.

I do not remember whether it was that time or on one of the other visits to her that spring that I began to find my Aunt Zelda both fascinating and mysterious. Anything connected with my real Mama was naturally of extreme fascination to me, but I also felt that Zelda herself encompassed a mystery. I did not think of it quite like that when I was eight years old, I suppose, but I was aware that there was something strange about her. Not only was she exceptionally good-looking — and children are very aware of such things, but she talked differently from any grown-ups I had met. Her voice was strong and her gestures decided and she had this peculiar way of staring at whoever was speaking which made me, at any rate, dry up or stutter. I noticed that she would sometimes finish sentences for people. There was a sort of impatience about her and yet she did not give much away. She treated me as she treated her son, as though we were in some ways grown up, but then she would suddenly lose interest in the conversation and get up and go out of the room. This was rather disconcerting, but Max took little notice.

One time when Max was telling me about his house in Italy, I saw her looking not at him, but staring at me. Had my own Mama looked like her? If what Gregory had told me was true she must have done. Max looked like her, I thought. Did *I* look like my own Mama?

At tea that afternoon, which we took in a small room downstairs, Zelda presiding over the teapot, she began to ask me questions about my own family. I did not realize at first that she was 'pumping' me and was only too pleased to oblige her, at the same time being careful not to reveal all I knew. 'And how are your little sisters?' she asked. 'Cara, isn't it? — and Alice — I heard about them from my ward. Your brother talked a lot about his family to him.' I could not believe that Gregory would have said much to Simon about us and was sure she had other ways of finding out. I had the strange feeling about her that she did not always tell the truth. 'We must meet them, mustn't we, Maxie?' she remarked when I had told her Cara was six and doing her lessons with Miss Little and Alice was a clever girl. After a pause she said: 'And Hannah? I hear she is rather slow?' I was not going to have this new aunt, however fascinating, hearing more from me of Pooranna, so I just said 'Yes', and attacked the bread and butter. The food tasted better this time.

I thought she murmured something like 'A judgement', but I did not understand. I decided to ask a question of my own without giving away anything. 'How am I related to Max?' I asked her. That seemed a safe question. She paused for a moment.

'Oh, I am a sister of your Mama's', she said finally and took a long drink of tea. I supposed

45

she thought I would think she meant Mamarella, and I wanted to say, 'Why does Mama not come to see you then', but dared not.

Afterwards in the garden Max said: 'I *am* your cousin, Hetty, Mama told me.'

I was glad to be Max's cousin, not so sure about his mother, and I just replied: 'I have no other cousins — I do wish you could come to play at *my* house.'

'No, it is not possible', he said, his big eyes upon me.

'Why?' I asked. I was not frightened of little Max.

'I think they quarrelled', he replied, looking uncomfortable.

Both Max and I were, I now see, rather 'forward' for our age in our talk and our interests. Max was encouraged to be so by Zelda, that much was obvious. But nobody, except my governess, had encouraged *me,* yet here at The Laurels I felt I could be myself in a strange way, or at least a self that was not encouraged at home.

I sometimes talked to Lucy Little about it on the way home. She was easier to get answers from than Huntie, but did not appear to know so much about my family and relations. 'Huntie's auntie was nurse to my Aunt Zelda,' I remarked.

'I believe they lived in Ealing', said Miss Little. Now how did she know that?

'Where is that, Miss Little?'

'In West London', answered my governess. 'Queen of the suburbs.'

'Was that near your school?' I asked her. Miss Little's stories of her school fascinated me as much as the history of my Aunt Zelda and the mystery of my Mama.

'No — that was in *north*-west London. Would *you* like to go to school, Hetty?'

'Oh, I should — but I should not like to lose you!' I cried.

She went pink and looked quite happy. 'My father taught me a lot as well', she said. So some girls' fathers taught their daughters, I now discovered.

I realized as time went on that my papa did not want to know about my visits to my Aunt Zelda. I once mentioned her to him. It was an afternoon when he was, unusually, in the drawing-room where I was waiting for Mamarella and Cara to come down since we were all to go to the bootmaker's in the carriage. 'Aunt Zelda thinks Simon might like to visit here in the school holidays', I ventured and was amazed to see my cold Papa's face suffused with red.

'He has not been invited', was all he said before turning away and poking the fire. I wanted to say — Gregory does not like him — but he looked so angry when he turned round again, that I did not.

The visits to Max went on quite regularly that year and when Gregory was home he went with me. Sometimes it was my governess, sometimes Huntie, who took us, never Papa or Mama. And Cara was never invited.

Naturally there were other things in my life apart from these visits, but I was never invited anywhere else and looked forward to them. It was Max whom I looked forward to seeing, for my aunt, after her initial questioning of me, took little interest in me except to greet me and to say goodbye.

'Mama says I am to thank you for coming', Max said one afternoon. It was summer again and we were playing in a deserted summer-house in the gardens, where there was a delicious smell of resin and earth. Aunt Zelda had unexpectedly discovered an old dolls' tea-set which she had given us to play with. It was very pretty with roses in wreaths round the rims of the cups and I could see that there had also been a gold rim to the saucers. Max was quite content to play with me and we invented a family of 'guests' whom we invited and discussed. Max sometimes spoke Italian, and I liked to hear it. 'The cups were Mama's when she was a little girl', he said.

'Was that when they lived in Ealing?' I asked.

'I don't know', he answered and it seemed to me that he really knew very little about his Mama.

I felt closer now to Max than anybody, even Gregory. But when Gregory came back for his holidays, after that period of constraint while we got used to each other again, we got along in the same old way. He did not refer again to our Mama and did not seem to like talking about Simon either.

'I wonder what Max's father was like?' I said to my brother.

'Ask him', said Gregory. 'He was called de Vere, wasn't he?'

Of course, now I remembered, and the next time I went to The Laurels I said to my cousin: 'Did your father die then — "Mr De Vere"? Are you an orphan?'

Max deliberated before he replied. 'I have a Mama, so I am not an orphan.' We were in the summer-house again, but the dolls' tea things were lying on a shelf in the cupboard in the house, for we had decided to play with some canes and pea-sticks and to make bows and arrows out of them with string the gardener had given us when we begged him.

'But your Papa *is* dead?'

'Yes — he was a very rich man', said Max with a frown. 'He died in Italy.' Then — 'Mama wants us to go back there when I am a little older.'

'I hope you don't', I said. 'I like coming here to play with you.'

'We did not think your Papa would allow you', said Max.

I pondered this later. Strangely enough, although for over two years now I had known that my real Mama was dead, I had not connected her in my mind with Papa. Suddenly with a sort of stab I realized that she had been Papa's wife too, not just my mother, and Gregory's. I felt it was strange that Papa had never mentioned her to us, had never alluded to her, not even once, when he must surely have loved her well enough to marry her, loved her as much as he was supposed to love Mamarella, or as husbands were meant to love their wives in books.

I wondered if little Max, who was now eight and looking better and stronger than he had used to, knew more than I did about my mother. I wondered if any of it were really true. What if it were just invented by Simon and told to Gregory to annoy him? I thought that Simon was just the kind of boy who would enjoy doing something like that.

I decided to ask Max a question which was seemingly innocent on the surface and see how he replied. 'Does your Mama know my father and my mother?' I said.

'Well, of course she knows your Papa', he replied. He was attempting to shape the head of an 'arrow' as he said it, his dark head bent over and his nimble fingers that were now not quite so thin, holding the end.

'She knows — my — Mama?'

'Do you mean your stepmother?' he asked, frowning with concentration as he made a fine point to the stick.

I gasped. Everyone knew then! I had never spoken to Max of these matters till now.

'Your Mama died when I was a baby — that's what my Mama told me — and my Papa died too — it was all very sad.'

'You know', I said slowly, pretending to look at my own arrow but feeling nervous and my heart beating with such a thud I thought Max would hear it; 'Sometimes I think I can remember a baby — in Italy — but I wasn't there, was I?'

50

'I don't know', he replied, looking up at me. I saw he was not going to be of any use and I did not want to talk about my nightmare. I could tell him about the watch though. 'There was a man — with a gold watch — and a window, I think. I can remember that . . .' I was thinking, it always makes me happy to think of that, but telling it to Max makes me sad, I don't know why.

'Perhaps the man was my Papa?' he said brightly.

'Will you ask your Mama, Max, if *I* ever was in Italy', I said. 'Gregory says I was — and so was he — but you'd be too little to remember it.'

'I'll ask her', he said. 'It's lovely there because the sun always shines and the people sing a lot. Mama has promised we *shall* go back one day. I have to go to school first though — not to a school like Simon's, but to a school in London — in the autumn.'

'We can still see each other though?' I did not want my visits to The Laurels to stop.

'Of course — I shall insist', he said grandly.

'It was a pocket watch', I said dreamily after a pause.

'I don't remember my Papa at all', he said. 'Come on Hetty, let's try the bows.'

That evening when I got home Huntie washed my hair and as I was sitting by the fire drying it I said on an impulse: 'Huntie — did you know Max's father?'

She looked up quickly. 'Why ever do you want

51

to know that, Miss Hetty — I can't remember.'

'Mr de Vere. You must do — you know his wife, Aunt Zelda.'

'Oh, I suppose I must have seen 'im', said Huntie beginning to comb the tugs out of my long hair. 'Well?'

She said nothing, so I went on: 'Did he have a gold watch, a pocket watch?'

'Lots of gentlemen have pocket watches.'

'I think I remember a man with a gold watch', I said and turned round to face her.

'Let me get through this — it's like a bird's-nest', she grumbled.

'Max says his Papa died in Italy when he was only a baby.' I wanted to say: 'Why was I there?' But instead I said, 'Have I ever been to Italy, Huntie?'

'Perhaps', she said. 'Don't ask so many questions or else you'll get lies told you.'

It was not fair. Even Huntie didn't want to talk about Italy. I resolved to ask Gregory next time he was home whether he remembered Uncle Basil de Vere. But Huntie would have said No, if I had never been to Italy. She was an honest person, I was sure.

4

When I was about nine years old the stable boy told me what men and women did to have babies. It seemed unbelievable until one afternoon I saw Papa's dog Lusty living up to his name, though I didn't know the meaning of the word then, with an unknown bitch in the shrubbery, and made the connection between humans and animals. The knowledge filled me with guilt; I felt I must never let Huntie or Papa, not to speak of my step-mother, know that I knew. But I think it took me several years more to understand that 'it' was not always confined to married people, nor only to the occasions when they wanted a baby. What could bring any woman to allow a man to do such a thing to her unless she were desperate to have a baby? The missing piece of the conundrum fell into place only long after.

Perhaps if I hadn't gone to Italy when I did I should have gone on thinking that women were always victims of a lust they never shared, for that was the impression I had of the whole matter in England.

It is hard to recall how I pieced together various bits of knowledge between the ages of ten and eighteen. I knew from listening to Cook and Huntie that some of the 'orphans' whom we saw walking along near the park in their crocodile were the children of unmarried women, for that was the reason for their 'having no fathers'. But I now knew that everyone had to have had a father at some time. God did not send children to spinsters without some human messenger, though I was worried for a long time by what they said in church about the Virgin Mary. I knew that you were not expected to ask questions about it.

In spite of this enormous Christian exception, which muddied my ideas about men and women, the stable boy and his revelations had knocked on the head for good any idea of connivance by the Almighty in the affair. God did not send babies; fathers and mothers made them: yet they were not responsible for making poor little Hannah as she was!

But I had other things to interest me and was as curious to know the history and geography of the country where Gregory said I had been as a baby as I was to understand the mysteries of human reproduction. I knew rationally that Mama was not Italian, as she was Aunt Zelda's sister, but I felt a mysterious connection to that place since my mother had died there. History and geography, unlike reproduction, were Miss Little's province, but I remember wishing I could talk to her about forbidden topics, although grown-ups never gave you the answers you needed. Lucy Little, delighted no doubt by my interest in Italy, gave me several lessons on that country. Its history was most confusing; everybody seemed to have conquered the place at one time or another — the Spanish, the French, the Austrians — but the geography was easier since the country looked like a leg in a boot.

By the time I was nine I had been taught a little French and I still possess my first French primer with HESTER JOHANNA COPPEN written on the flyleaf in my rather large ungainly hand. Later I was to ask my governess about the language the people spoke in Italy, which was becoming for me a sort of magic wonderland. I rolled round names on my tongue like a spell: Mantua, Modena, Parma, Padua, Ferrara, Firenze. I don't know how I concealed all this thirst for knowledge from my father and my stepmother. I suppose it was because they took little real interest in me that I was able from an early age to lead quite a separate inner life. Whatever the case, Miss Little told me not only that Italians, in her own Papa's opinion spoke the most beautiful language in the world, but that they had also the most beautiful music, called opera. She told me too that Italy had been 'united' and made into a proper country like our own only two years after I was born and that there had been wars and fighting about it.

'Was there a soldier called Garibaldi?' I asked her.

'Why, yes, Hetty — where did you hear that name?' she said in surprise. I thought there was no harm in telling her that my cousin Max called one of his soldiers that.

'Max seems a nice little chap from all you have

told me about him', she said. 'Garibaldi is still alive, Hetty.' I was amazed. So Garibaldi was real — and Italy was real. Somehow I had imagined all Italy as past.

'Mr Dickens wrote a good deal about Italy in his magazine', she said a few days after this conversation. 'It's called *All the Year Round* — we take it at home.'

I begged her to ask her papa if I might borrow that journal and she said she would ask him. My own father did not take it. The only journals which came for him were about money. Even Huntie had heard of Mr Dickens though!

I sometimes talked about books with Max for he loved reading too, but by the time he was ten and I was twelve and still having lessons with Miss Little together with Alice and Cara, he had begun to go to a London day school and was with his mother only on Sundays, not a day one visited. There were always the holidays however when we could see each other if Gregory would take me. Once Gregory was fourteen they let him go on the train by himself and put me in his charge.

Things went on much the same at home as they always had, but some changes were about to take place which make it easier for me to date the years as they passed.

I think I'd stopped dreaming of the man with the gold pocket watch for some time and other nightmares had grown fewer, but I was growing more rebellious in other ways as my teens drew nearer, and I often felt oppressed as well as depressed, feeling that I should never escape to any life other than the day-to-day ordinariness I had known for so long. I did not quite know what I wanted, though I knew what I did not want. I realized, even then, that since Papa didn't much care what I did, I was much more free than many girls — and more open to the influence of a governess. Fortunately Miss Little was a remarkable young woman — as I realized much later. I did not know many girls of my own age apart from my sisters as I did not go to school, and Mamarella did not encourage any visits from girls I might have met at dancing class, where I now had to accompany Cara. My sister Cara was always much more closely supervised, though less often blamed, than I was. I strove for Papa's love until I was about thirteen and then gave up as far as appearances were concerned, but I believe that if he had ever shown me the tiniest flicker of interest I should have responded with all the ardour of my nature. As it was I emulated Miss Little and my only fear was that Papa would one day send her away. Happily for me, and perhaps for Cara and Alice too, he did not. I expect he did not pay her a great deal.

Although I did not dream at this time of those long lost scenes of my very early childhood, I often wondered how Mama had died and resolved to dare to ask Papa when I was grown up. In the end I did tell Huntie what Gregory had told me: that I had once been to Italy. I had longed for years to tell her that I knew Mamarella was not my real Mama, but I had promised Gregory I would not breathe a word of it. Eventually though on one stormy afternoon when all the others were out and I had been confined to bed with a cold, with Huntie to keep me company, I asked her again about Italy. I did not mean to mention my mother, but maybe I was a little feverish and unable to restrain myself any longer. Anyway, Huntie was on my side, I knew that, for I said: 'Max says his Mama *is* my Mama's sister. So he is my cousin.'

'That's right', she replied.

'But he is not *Cara's* cousin', I said.

She looked at me quickly and then deciding that it might be time for the truth, or some of it, to be admitted, she said: 'His "Mama's sister" died in a furrin' country.' She said it in a meaningful way. I stared at her. 'After you was born —' she added.

'You mean Italy, Huntie —'

'That's right.'

'Was I born in Italy — like Max?' I whispered.

'No, you was not', answered Huntie crossly. 'Your Mama went to Italy for 'er health. Stop pestering me, Hetty — ask your Auntie Zelda.' She never said in so many words that Ella was *not* my mother. But another day she said, when pressed once more by me: 'Zelda de Vere could tell you what you want to know — although she might not want to'.

'Why can I not ask my Papa?' I said.

'If you was to do that I'd lose my place, Miss

Hetty —' She looked very distressed. ' 'Cos he'd think I'd been telling you tales', she added.

I felt there must be something Huntie was not telling me. Why should Papa not want me to know about my poor dead mother?

The next time Gregory came home for the holidays I had to confess to him that my knowledge had seeped out to Huntie. 'But she knows anyway', I said. 'I'm sorry.'

'Never mind, Hetty. So long as you don't let on to Papa and his wife.' Mamarella seemed to dislike poor Gregory even more than she disliked me, and my brother had taken to referring to her — only to my ears of course — as Papa's wife. I disliked Mamarella just as much as ever, though as I grew older I managed to make the effort to conceal it. I had the strong feeling that I must not allow her to interfere in my life and therefore she must never know my secret thoughts or my real desires. Cara was growing even prettier and I was proud of her in a curious way. She was never a challenge to me in the schoolroom.

Huntie's time was still taken up with Pooranna, who did not change very much, except to grow larger. Yet she was now capable of a few words. Not sentences, but words such as a two-year-old might pronounce. We all understood her, and she was not ill-natured, though she tried my patience. I was never a patient child, and as I grew older I began to be angry, not with Hannah herself, but with the God who, I had been told, had 'made' her as He had 'made us all'. Why should the God

59

we worshipped in church play such a trick? Papa, unusually did not often attend church and Mamarella was often 'poorly', so we went with Huntie.

Miss Little understood my anger, I think, but naturally she could not say all she felt about my situation. I realized that she had to be careful if she were to keep her post.

'Why don't you go and teach in a school, Miss Little?' I would ask her, for I thought she was wasted on us and imagined she would be better paid in a school like the one she had attended herself. But she said her father needed her to be at home and there were not many posts in schools for young women — and she had not yet finished her own studies. I knew she was very serious about them. Looking back, I believe that she had intended to stay with us only a year or so, but that she actually liked teaching me and would not have cared to have to maintain the discipline necessary in the schools that existed. I did not confess to her all the bad thoughts which sometimes came into my head, but I think she guessed them, for I sometimes wrote compositions where I would, under the guise of an invented person, pour out some of my frustrations. I had stopped wishing Mamarella would die for I knew that if God suddenly asked me if I truly wanted her death I would have said 'No.' My reason told me that it was not Mamarella's fault that she had inherited two stepchildren. She did not seem to care that I avoided her; I believe our feelings were mutual. Now, as I look back on those days, I wonder that a grown woman should have behaved towards a child in a way that may be natural to a child, and perhaps forgivable in one, but not in an adult. She had stopped slapping me, for she had seen that indifference to my character and achievements, such as they were, hurt me far more, especially when it was my father who ignored me. I often wondered if he blamed me for my real Mama's death. That made me feel guilty too.

But Lucy Little was perhaps the cause of my life turning out as it did, for when I was about thirteen she asked permission to take me to her home on a visit one Saturday afternoon. I always had the impression that Mamarella and perhaps even Papa when he was at home — was glad to have me out of the house. If cheap girls' boarding schools had existed then as they did for boys, I'm sure they would have packed me off to one as they had packed off my brother. But those that did exist were, Miss Little said, rather expensive, and not many fathers would waste their money on their daughters. It was easier for us girls to be educated together at home. However, my parents made no objection to my governess's suggestion and this was how I came to be introduced to Mr Adolphus Little, Miss Little's father.

I had had many suggestions about my reading from my governess, suggestions which I always took up with alacrity. I imagined that Miss Little must have an extensive library at home, for she lent me many volumes, and like me she was a bookworm, though I had begun to realize that her interests were scientific rather than historical and literary. I was hardly prepared though for the positive cornucopia which was the Little household's 'library'. The house was not large and not at all imposing, being in a terrace of similar houses off Camberwell Grove, but as soon as the one maid opened the front door to us, I smelt books; books everywhere — in the hall, up the stairs, crawling up every wall and even spilling into the parlour where Mr Little was awaiting our arrival, sitting in a large armchair — and naturally occupied with a book.

'So, this is Hetty', he said and took off his gold pince-nez but did not get up. 'You must excuse my not rising for a lady,' he said pleasantly, 'but I suffer, as my daughter may have told you, from the rheumatics.' I saw that his hands were misshapen and that he turned his head with difficulty. Miss Little brought up a chair for herself and a footstool for me.

'Sit where father can see you, Hetty', she said. 'There.' She looked as pleased as punch to have brought me to her Papa's sanctum and he began to talk to me as though I were grown up, which pleased me greatly. I could see he was a gentleman but there was only the one servant and I guessed that they were what my Papa called 'in reduced circumstances', and books called 'shabby genteel'.

'Lucy tells me you are reading *The Mill on the Floss* — my old friend Clark brought it for me, you know, since I cannot get out and about as I used to. I enjoyed it. Lucy does not read novels', he said fondly and teasingly to his daughter who was looking at him just as fondly, I thought. 'What do you think of it? — Tell me — I like to hear from the new generation.'

I had not quite finished the book, which was not an easy read for someone my age, and said so, but I launched into an enthusiastic paean of praise for its heroine with whom I partially identified. 'I so like Maggie', I said. 'And I think Tom is not so nice.' He led me on to talk of other books which I had been lent, and then of my lessons. He was a most unusual old man — I thought of him as old though he could scarcely have been more than fifty, but he had an antique turn of phrase and spoke in long sentences which I thought were like the sort of sentence I tried to produce in my composition lessons. I could see he was an enthusiast. I knew I was lucky to have Miss Little for a teacher and I liked her father as much. No wonder she was such a fountain of information with a parent like this, who appeared to listen to her as well as giving his own opinions.

'Lucy, ask Ellen to fetch the box of sweetmeats', he said after he had talked of Dickens and I had listened. 'Mr Dickens' death a couple of years ago made the whole of England sad', he said. '*Such a pity* — he drove himself too hard. I went to hear him once doing the death of Little Nell — that was in the days when my dear wife was alive and when I could get about with my stick — and I felt exhausted you know — afterwards — not on my own account, but on his.'

63

The box of sweetmeats arrived on a tray and the maid said: 'There's toast and muffins, Mum, if you will', to Miss Little, who went out to supervise the tea.

I loved sweetmeats and had in the past often stolen them from the glass bowl in our dining-room where crystallized fruits or Turkish delights were often left on the table. These though were sticky butterscotch caramels, and they melted on the tongue like honey. I thought, how unusual to give you the sweets *before* the muffins!

'I shall not ask you any other questions till you have finished your toffee', he said. 'I know how having to talk spoils a good bonbon.' He was unlike any grown up man I had met — I wondered what his daughter had told him about me and my family. He never asked me any questions about them, but when we left after a delicious tea he said: 'Present my regards to your parents and say my daughter is happy to be undertaking the guidance of a young lady who likes to learn.' I thought, I can't say that to them — they wouldn't believe me. I knew that Mamarella thought learning was a waste of time for girls. I was untidy, and 'answered back', and was often accused of 'secretiveness' by her. If only she had known! — but I was aware that I must keep on with my lessons as long as possible; it was no good answering back if that deprived me of time in the schoolroom, for my stepmother knew that I enjoyed my lessons and that to deprive me of them would be a real punishment for me. How I would have loved *not* to be 'secretive', I thought, to be able to talk to Papa in the way I talked to Mr Little, for instance.

I resolved that I should soon confront Papa with my knowledge and ask him the answers to other questions. Who was my Mama? . . . Why did she die? . . . Where exactly did she die? . . . Why do you never speak of her? . . . Why did you not tell me and Gregory that our own Mama was dead? . . . Why do you not love me? . . .

I waited, for I knew the time was not yet ripe whilst being sure it would come one day. I was stubborn, I would force him to answer one day. Then I thought, for the present I will ask Aunt Zelda, as Huntie once said I should. I shall then be able to stop thinking about it all and get on with my life.

It was during the Christmas holidays when I had just turned fourteen that I finally managed to pluck up my courage for the first time to ask my aunt. Max had had chicken-pox, but as I had had it when I was small I was allowed to see him. Zelda was very agitated, I could see, for he was a delicate child, even if at twelve he was no longer as frail as once he had been. When I had done a jigsaw with him, she came into the bedroom and said: 'Come downstairs and take a cup of coffee with me, Hetty.' This was a command. Zelda did not like tea, and made very strong coffee. I had already tasted it on one of my visits. Gregory was not with me that day. He had taken me to The Laurels but gone back into the town to buy some geometrical instruments he needed, and was to call for me later.

I sat sipping coffee like an adult with my aunt in her small drawing-room, the canary in his cage twittering away and a bright fire in the grate. 'My old maid is to come back to me', said Zelda. 'She is to arrive this afternoon.' She sounded excited.

'Is that "Daventry" Aunt?' I asked. 'Huntie told me her Aunt Rosa Daventry was maid to you — and my mother.' Now the opportunity had arisen I could not help but grasp it.

She put her cup down. 'How much do you know?' she asked me.

I pretended not to understand what she meant and said: 'I know her aunt was in Italy with you, but before that Huntie told me you lived in Ealing with your sister.' I thought it was very clever of me to avoid saying 'My Mama' this time. Then I said, to give her the chance to explain, 'But Mama-r-ell—' Hastily I changed this to Mama. 'Mama told Gregory *she* had never lived in Italy.'

'How much do you know?' said my aunt again, fiddling with her teaspoon and deciding that attack was the best form of defence.

I decided to tell her. I could not be bothered pretending any longer. 'I know my Mama, and Gregory's, was your sister, Aunt', I said. 'And that she is dead and that Papa's wife is *not* my Mama.'

'How do you know this?' she asked me.

'Simon Voyle told my brother years ago — but Gregory had always suspected — and I asked Huntie and she could not deny it. She told me, if I wanted to find out things about my mother, I must ask you.'

'Your Mama was a good, sweet woman — but bearing children was too much for her', said my Aunt Zelda. She seemed to be treating me as a grown-up in this matter as in the coffee-drinking. Most ladies would not have said such a thing to a fourteen-year-old girl. But then my Aunt Zelda was not like most women.

'Did I kill her? — I mean, was it when I was born?'

'Oh no! no — but after your birth her mind went. She came to me in Italy with you and Huntie to recover her wits.'

There was a pause whilst she was probably thinking how much she could safely tell me.

'You mean she went mad?' I cried out. I had not bargained for this. Was this why Papa did not speak of her?

'No — not ordinary madness — and anyway she recovered. She died of something else. I could do little to help her. I had just had my son Max and he was a delicate baby, as you know.'

'Max is two years younger than me. Did my Mama live in Italy for long before she died?' I enquired.

'Yes — I told you she recovered from her *crise de nerfs,* but died later.'

'Why did Papa not come to help her? Why does he not mention her name to me?' I asked her.

'I will tell you another day when you are older, Hetty. She is buried over there.' She gave a slight

67

cough and drained her cup of coffee.

'Oh, I should like to go to Italy', I breathed.

'Perhaps you will one day', she said. 'I shall return there when Max has finished his schooling. I prefer living in Italy — but I could not let my son come to school here alone — he needs care.' She got up and said in a different voice, 'I have been very long-suffering, Hetty — *and* in inviting you here after what your Papa . . . but let us leave the subject for the present. Come, I need somebody to take down the ornaments from Max's Christmas tree.' I followed her into the other drawing-room wondering why she did not ask her servants to do this. It was probably one way of stopping our conversation.

I have always been a clumsy person and had to be very careful not to break the spun-glass globes and lanterns, and the fairy on the top of the tree. Poor Max was still upstairs, but at least he had had Christmas before succumbing on Boxing Day. As I was placing the ornaments carefully into a cardboard box labelled *The Laurels/Max's Tree*, I heard the scrunch of gravel which meant that someone was arriving and going round to the stables at the back. I looked out of the window; the carriage had already disappeared. But Gregory was coming up the path and up the stone stairs outside the front door and I waved to him. I'd be sorry to leave with him this afternoon, though I'd not been of much use to poor Max.

Nobody seemed to be about so I ran out to him through the vestibule with its palms and oak

68

stands. 'I think Huntie's aunt has arrived!' I said. 'And Aunt Zelda has been talking to me about Mama!'

'I saw the carriage — don't talk so loud', he replied turning round instinctively to see if anyone had heard.

'It's all right. She knows we know. And Huntie's aunt will tell us what we want to know, I'm sure. You see Mama had a "nervous breakdown" after I was born.' I stopped as Zelda came through from behind the green baize door, followed by a tiny scrap of a woman dressed in black from head to toe with a beak-like nose and wispy grey hair.

'Ah, Gregory', said my aunt. 'How fortunate that you are here to meet my old maid Daventry.' She moved aside and gestured to the old woman.

'Master Gregory — well I never — and little Miss Hetty — who'd have believed it! Oh, Miss Zelda, he's the spit image of his poor Mama', the old woman said, with less of a Cockney accent than Huntie.

Zelda smiled and said: 'Well I promised they'd be here on your arrival, Daventry, but I expect after tea they will have to return to East Wood. They will visit again soon when Max is better. Come now —' And she went up the stairs, with the old woman following carrying a shapeless bag.

'I expect she is going to see Max', I said. The woman had been treated by Zelda almost as an equal, I thought. Later I learned that Rosa Daventry was based in Italy and looked after Zelda's villa in Fiesole, or rather supervised the

Italian servants. Now that I know Rosa Daventry well, it amazes me that for the first fourteen years of my life I never saw her at all except during the first two, which I did not remember, when she and her niece must have kept me alive.

It was always a let down returning home after a visit to Max, even when Gregory was with me. Something about Zelda and Max and their house and conversation, although not cosy or even comfortable, was still freeing to my spirit. Zelda could be critical and even censorious, but not unkind — at least not to me. At home I was still being scolded for being untidy and impetuous and wilful by Mamarella, who reported everything I did or said to my father. 'We are all living a lie', I thought.

Once I had spoken to Zelda and seen Rosa I stopped wondering about my Mama, and did in fact get on with my life, reserving my questions for whenever I should see the old servant again. Then I was sure I would discover more. My curiosity was to return, but Miss Little kept me more and more occupied. I was also learning to play the piano, which my Papa thought a suitable accomplishment for a young lady. In the matter of age I was not yet quite a young lady and had no wish to be one in the matter of quality, but told only Miss Little of my opinion. *She* played the pianoforte most wonderfully, though she preferred the sonatas of Haydn and the fugues of Bach whilst I was determined to master a Beethoven sonata and some Chopin studies. As I grew older, though alas not much better an executant than I had ever been, listening to music began to be more and more important to me and I became more and more affected by it.

My stepmother was forty-four and I was sixteen when she had her last baby, a boy, Felix, who fortunately lived and whose advent released me to a much less anxious existence. Mamarella was wrapped up in her son, and my father went round looking smugly pleased. You would have thought he had never had a male child before. I was glad that Gregory was away at school so that he could not feel the humiliation.

But when Gregory came back from his last term at boarding school, the term after the baby's birth, he did not return alone. When the bell went I was standing on the top landing of the house. Miss Little had just gone home and my sisters were still in the schoolroom. Even Cara had been neglected by Mamarella since Felix's arrival, and she had been sulking during our French lesson and yawning. I heard footsteps clattering on the mosaic of the hall and peered over the banisters expecting to see Gregory, and saw instead Simon Voyle.

Apparently for some reason my Aunt Zelda no longer regarded Simon as her ward — he was eighteen and had left school some time before. 'Your Pater's to find me a job in the City', he told me and Cara when he came down for tea with Mamarella. Gregory was very quiet. I knew that he had disliked Simon from the beginning and I had never liked the little I'd seen of him. Having him staying

with us did not change my opinion. Gregory ex-
changed a look with me as the older boy went
on about the money he was going to make. Then
Cara came into the room and Simon looked at her
with a strange expression on his face. Simon was
to have an office job in the firm of a friend of
my father's, and I hoped the hours would be long
and hard wherever it was for he rubbed me up
the wrong way and sneered at my opinions.

Why should my Papa want to help him? He
was no relation of ours. He teased Pooranna and
made horrible faces at Alice, and I noticed that
he was also very rude to Mamarella. She appeared
to be almost afraid of him and I heard her telling
him to be 'pleasant'. Papa looked disturbed too
when he saw how unpleasant the lad was. All Ella's
pleasure from little Felix seemed, when Simon was
there, to be dissipated, and she was very nervous.

'He should get digs in the City', I said to Gregory
one evening a week or so after Simon's arrival.
Simon was out; he was allowed his own key and
treated as if he was twenty-one, which was most
unfair. It was not as if he was earning very much
for he was only articled. 'He is like a cuckoo here',
I said to Gregory.

My brother no longer confided all his hopes and
secrets to me. I suppose he was growing up and
had his own problems, so I was not sure what
his reaction would be to my outburst.

'Why on earth should he live with us here?' I
went on. 'Nobody likes him. Did you see the way
he tweaked Alice's hair yesterday? And he was

rude to Mamarella — even Miss Little noticed. He's like a child — he doesn't act like an eighteen-year-old.'

Gregory looked at me searchingly for a long time. 'He teases Hannah too', I added. 'I heard *Her* telling him to be "pleasant" yesterday and she sounded quite upset.' I had even felt rather sorry for Mamarella when Simon Voyle had criticized her pronunciation of French one Saturday luncheon. Since Felix's arrival I had been prepared to forgive her past injustices if she would leave me alone. 'She is getting very peculiar', I went on to my brother. 'Huntie says she won't leave Felix alone even in his room at night. Huntie must sleep there if Mamarella is not there and she will not allow even Huntie or Mrs Popplewell or the new nursemaid to wheel him out in the afternoon. She says there are bad men in the wood down the lane, Huntie told me.'

'I expect it's her conscience', said my brother mysteriously. He was white faced and looking the way he'd done all those years ago when he told me Mamarella was not our Mama.

'Simon Voyle is a pig and a sneak and a liar and a thief', he said quietly. 'But he won't be so easily got rid of. You'll find out one day, Hetty — just be careful when he's around.'

5

Simon Voyle did not in fact stay with us very long that time. I was relieved one morning to be told by Gregory that our 'lodger' had had some sort of argument with Papa and left during the night. I hadn't heard anything, but Simon was certainly not at breakfast.

When Papa came in, Gregory said: 'Simon came into my room last night, Papa, to say that he was leaving us for the time being — is that true?' He looked levelly at Papa and I held my breath. I knew intuitively that Papa did not like Simon Voyle either. I had never understood how my Aunt Zelda had prevailed upon Papa to offer her ward a home whilst the youth was starting out in the City in the import-export business.

'That is correct', said Papa coolly, and gave no further explanation, but bent down to his bacon and eggs. I saw a smile flit over my brother's face, a smile of satisfaction. If I had not known Gregory for a kind person I'd have said there was a tinge of malice in it.

Later, as I was preparing to take Pooranna out, my brother passed me in the hall and I said: 'I suppose he will go back to living with Zelda in the holidays?'

'He has no more holidays', said Gregory. 'And in any case he is now free of her guardianship — he didn't like living with her and Max.'

'Where has he gone then?'

'Oh, I expect a place will be found for him', said Gregory casually.

'Thank goodness he's gone', I said again. 'Has he money of his own?'

'Apparently his father is to send him an allowance from Australia.'

'Australia? I thought Simon was an orphan —'

Just then Huntie appeared, dressed in her long coat and flat hat ready to accompany me to the shops, and Gregory put his finger on his lips.

We always took Pooranna with us when we presented our orders in the village to be made up and delivered later in the day by the various tradesmen. It was unusual for a girl of my class to accompany a servant on such business, but our household was not conventional and Mamarella could not spare the time to oversee Cook now that her hands were full with Felix, and she was, she said, exhausted.

Although she allowed the new nurse to tend Felix, it was only under her own supervision, for my stepmother still could not bear to let the child out of her sight and was nervous about leaving the nurse with him at night too. When they took him out for a walk down the path through the woods at the back of the house, a walk which we all knew well, and which Ella had taken for years, she would hurry home if she heard anyone else in the copse. Poor little Felix was being treated like a haemophiliac, metaphorically wrapped in cottonwool every minute of his existence. But if Mamarella wanted me to act as a sort of unpaid servant in order to give her more time to be with her baby, and if she left the running of the house more and more to Cook and Huntie, I still did not mind. It was better than having to endure the sort of 'social' life in which my sister Cara was expected to learn to partake. Mamarella was already grooming her pretty daughter for adult life. Though she was only fifteen she looked two years older.

I rather enjoyed seeing people in the village, and watching Huntie greet her cronies. Also it was an opportunity for us to take out Pooranna and show *we* were not ashamed of her. It was my sister's treat to have a lollipop bought for her on a Saturday.

The morning Simon was found to have left, Huntie saw an old friend of hers in the village, Miss Chadwick, a tall, rosy-cheeked woman who worked at the orphanage, and so we crossed the road by the butchers and the hansom stand to greet her. Usually I never had much time to listen to Huntie's conversations as I had enough to do to hold on to Pooranna who was apt to run off in her queer crab-like way or to shout at horses, or sit down suddenly in the middle of the pavement or even in the road in the middle of horse dung.

This morning, however, the lollipop was absorbing her energies and when Chadwick said 'Good morning', and they began to talk, I stood with Pooranna's other hand in mine as quite a few pitying glances were cast at us by passers by. Few of the woman's words got through to me, but I was only half-listening as I speculated over the sign outside Jeeve and Hopkins' which had lost two letters and now read " 'urniture and 'rapery". I was wondering if I had enough pocket-money saved to buy some red silk there to embroider a pillow-slip for Alice's birthday. I heard Chadwick say: 'Well, it's thine and mine and ours, isn't it? Like it was with my lot at home once?' What did she mean? I'd never heard the phrase before.

Pooranna was never allowed to eat lunch with Papa and Mama and Gregory, though Cara and I sometimes were. But Felix had pushed even the one-time favourite from the pedestal erected by Papa and Mamarella. Poor Cara. Now I was sorry for her; she had never known what it was like to be ignored, and all Mamarella could talk about was the problem of Felix's teething. Of course Pooranna came first with Huntie who could manage her better than any of us, and Gregory came first with me, though I believe he thought I sometimes preferred Max. Alice came first with Cara herself, for she liked ordering around her little sister, who was a practical child. I suppose I came first with Gregory, but there was nobody to put Cara first any more, except Alice.

That day Cara was eating with us and suddenly she said: 'I wish Simon had not gone away. It is so dull without him.'

Mama looked at her sharply but said nothing. Papa, though looked angry.

Simon Voyle had played nasty tricks on Pooranna, had pinched her when he thought nobody was looking — I had seen him do it when I was reading hunched up and wrapped in the curtains of the window-seat and he had not known that anyone was in the room. But he had teased my other sister in another way, nicely tailored to suit her vanity. He had been continually paying her the most extravagant compliments, which at first she had taken seriously, for she was used to receiving homage, but I had thought she had eventually realized he was not sincere and was mocking her. But perhaps she had not, and only I had seen what he was doing, as only I had seen him pinch Pooranna. I had not said anything to him about the way he talked to Cara, for I thought she was old enough to realize what he was doing. I had ordered him to stop tormenting Pooranna and received a twist of the wrist from him which I had told nobody about, not even Gregory. Tears of pain had come to my eyes and I had tried not to flinch. Then Huntie had come in and he had pretended he was looking at my hand. Hannah had stopped blubbing and was staring at him . . . as I remembered all this I realized that Cara had not taken in what type of boy he was. I thought it was surely unusual for an eighteen-year-old youth to attack a girl of my age and a backward child. But the way he talked to my sister Cara was something worse than teasing, though I could not have explained why I thought it so. It was a sort of cold-hearted flirtation — and he was an oaf. I hoped it was an awareness of his cruelty that had sent him away from our house, but I doubted it. My parents never saw what they did not wish to see. Mamarella looked at Cara in a queer sort of way as we continued to munch our roast lamb and Cara said: 'Well, it *is* dull. There is nobody to talk to now.'

I wondered whether to tell Papa what I had seen him do to Pooranna. But I did not want to stir up trouble; it was enough that Simon had gone away. I decided I would tell just Gregory and Cara.

Papa cleared his throat. We had finished eating and were waiting for the parlour-maid to bring in the pudding. I hoped it would be golden sponge.

'His father has taken steps to see that Simon lodges elsewhere', he said and looked over to Mamarella, who did not look up. There was a silence and Cara was just about to say something when my stepmother suddenly rose, saying: 'I believe I heard Felix cry out — I must go to him, Leo.' She threw her napkin on the table and was out through the dining-room door, narrowly colliding with our maid Edwardes, who went over to the dumb-waiter with a martyred expression.

Papa said only: 'Take your elbows off the table, Cara', and Gregory and I were silent.

I had gone on the train alone to Zelda's house one Saturday feeling very pleased with myself for having managed the journey without Gregory, and

79

rather surprised that I had been allowed to do so. It was to be the first of many visits I paid to Max when I was seventeen or so, for I wanted to get out of our house and there was nowhere else to go where I would be welcomed.

We were sitting in the room Zelda called her 'salotto' when I said: 'Mamarella is "in love" with Felix, I think!' and waited to see what my aunt's reaction would be. You could say the most outrageous things to Zelda, I had found, without her batting an eyelid, though she sometimes raised an amused eyebrow. I knew she did not approve of my father and stepmother, though I still had no idea why.

This time she laughed: ' "She" — the cat's mother? Be polite about your elders, Hetty.' There was a malicious gleam in her eye.

I liked to feel that my conversation could interest an adult, though I was sometimes ashamed of capitalizing on my ability. Although not feeling disloyal to Mamarella — for after all what had she ever done for me to feel tender about her? — I did sometimes feel a little guilty and I knew that Zelda unworthily colluded with me.

'Cara is quite put out', I went on. Max was not yet down, since he was in his room doing his prep, some of which Zelda insisted he do before enjoying himself.

I was beginning to find Max a little young for me, though I still enjoyed talking to him about the things that interested him. Gregory had gone to serve his pupillage in chambers so was rarely

80

at home very much. When he was, he spent his time studying more assiduously than Max did, though Max read far more and knew more about unusual things.

'I do wish *I* were eighteen,' I said. Although I felt nothing would ever change, and nobody had ever discussed my future with me, I felt quite desperate to grow up. I had even begun to plan a course of further study for myself so as to be able to take a post as governess somewhere like Miss Little one day. What else was I fit for?

'Have they told you you will come in for a little allowance?' Zelda suddenly asked me, looking carefully at her pearly nails — 'When you are eighteen', she added.

I was surprised. 'Then Papa would *have* to speak to me about my mother, wouldn't he?' I said. 'I expect the money is from my own Mama?'

'Oh, no — the money is not very much — just enough to keep you in ribbons and gloves — but it was left to you by my late husband', she said, and looked up.

I was even more astounded, stared at her.

'*Then,* Hetty dear, I expect your Papa will allow you to accompany me to Florence', she added.

I gasped. 'To Italy!'

Zelda was talking about my old dream as a reality and I could not take it in. But I tried not to appear too amazed for I wanted to give her the impression of a person who was grown up and independent, did not wish to give myself away to her. Some reserve had always held me back from confiding completely in my Aunt Zelda.

'Why? Why should Mr de Vere — leave *me* money?' I asked, seizing on a sensible question.

'Why not? He had plenty and you used to amuse him when you were tiny.'

The man with the gold watch in that room. I knew it must be.

'I shall be eighteen in less than a year', I said dazedly. 'But Papa would never let me go with you.'

'Why ever not? — I should think he would be glad to have you off his hands', she said rather brutally. 'Perhaps I shall offer to take your sister Cara too —'

'Oh, Cara is being prepared for suburban High Society', I said.

She laughed again. 'She could acquire more polish if she were with me for a year', she went on. 'We shall see.'

There were so many questions to which I wanted the answer, but I didn't know where to begin. I had pushed down my speculations for so long and concentrated on living in the present and what Miss Little called 'Getting things in perspective' that this entirely new attitude of Zelda's threw me.

'I *shall* write to him — and perhaps quite soon he will see me about it', she said idly. Then, rising and walking over to the mirror in the room and looking at herself critically in it before turning to me again, she said, as if to close the conversation, 'Rosa will talk to you about Italy'. Did she mean that Rosa Daventry was ready to tell me more about Mama too?

'I was thinking', I said quickly as she made to leave the room once more. 'I was thinking that perhaps I could become a governess one day like Miss Little — would Italy help me do that, do you think?' It was her turn to look astonished. 'I have to become independent', I said. 'I can't go on living at home when I am grown up. They don't think of me as they do of Cara.' I meant that they wanted Cara to marry well, but had not thought of marriage as anything that would ever happen to me. I would be the spinster daughter tending their old age. I shuddered.

She stood there patting her hair. 'You may change your ideas', she said. 'But they will let you go with me, I think. Don't say anything at home yet. I shall prepare the ground.' I could hear Max in the hall talking to Rosa. He used to tease her by speaking in Italian. She adored him, I could see.

When Max and I went out into the garden — for it was a warm sunny day and he said he needed fresh air, which was an unusual statement for him to make — I told him what his mother had said to me. 'Oh I wish I could go back now', he burst out. 'But I have to finish at Westminster first. It's such a bore. Mama is going to open up the villa. I shall have to wait till I am eighteen myself to live there permanently again.'

'She says that she might take my sister too', I said.

Max had never seen my sister Cara. I was so used to my 'other life' with Max and Zelda that I'd stopped thinking of it as odd that only Gregory and I ever visited them and that they were never invited back.

'I shouldn't think she'd want to travel', I went on, thinking of my sister. 'Perhaps your mother meant just for a holiday.'

'I should like to meet your sister', he said.

Cara was still out of favour, though that did not mean that anyone but my baby brother was in it. Felix was kept with Mamarella all the time for she was now frightened that he might be stolen by gypsies! 'Poor Cara is quite squashed now', I said to Max. 'Even Papa finds fault with her.' My baby brother was growing into a sunny little boy in spite of being fussed over, and was proving more adventurous than any of his sisters had ever been, which may have accounted for my stepmother's vigilance. 'Mama was like that about me', said Max. 'But I went to school — they will have to let your brother grow up, won't they, and go to school? It's different for girls.'

'I don't see why it should be different for girls', I said mutinously. 'My stepmother is foolish about him.'

'Because she loves him', replied Max looking at me with his big, soft brown eyes which were so like Gregory's.

Did I wish that someone loved *me* like that I wondered, as I went in to see Rosa who was in a small room where she sewed and mended and

84

where Zelda wrote her letters.

Love. The word intrigued me. I had read too many novels from the Littles not to know that 'falling in love' was dangerous. Though I longed for that sort of love, I had thought it might never come to me just as I had never had love from my parents. I loved Huntie and Gregory, and even Max — and Lucy Little — but not with the passion that I felt stirring in me when I read poetry or listened to music. Perhaps it was only in books? But I knew I would be capable of feeling it, though I had never been adored as Cara had been and Felix still was. There was something waiting in my nature, something ready to unfold, that I did not connect with domestic relations which were also called 'love'. We used the same word in church too for God. I felt my vague stirrings were more like religious rapture — and yet they needed an object, for I had not been able to 'love' God. A sort of worship it would be, but mixed with excitement too. I felt love for the idea of Italy as well. Had my Aunt Zelda loved her husband in this way? I felt there was a passion somewhere in her.

'You look desperate', said Max, who missed nothing. 'I'm sure your Papa will allow you to have a holiday, at least, with us.'

'I want to earn my living, Max', I said. Then I should be free, I thought.

'Did Mama tell you about the legacy?' he asked as we went indoors again — 'From my father. Are you not pleased? Then you may not need to earn your living!'

'Your mama says it is only enough for ribbons!' I replied.

'Oh, Mama is extravagant', he said calmly. 'I expect *you* would make money go a long way, Hetty!'

I went in to talk to Rosa who, in spite of the many times I had tried to find out what she knew of my Mama, had never offered more than I already knew. I felt that I must avoid mentioning Rosa to Papa, though why was a mystery too; as far as my parents were concerned they probably did not even realize that Rosa Daventry was back in England.

'I do wish somebody would tell me about my Mama', I said to Max. 'Tell me *properly* — and why it is always so strange at home and why they let me come here but never talk about you — and why they had Simon Voyle to stay — and why he went away — and why your mother sent him to Papa . . .'

'Oh, she did not — she was quite annoyed about that', said Max frowning. 'It was his own idea — and your parents seemed quite resigned to having him — he told me he was welcomed at your place.'

'Gregory said his father is in Australia — have you met him?' I asked.

'I remember him from Italy', said Max. 'I expect he was once a business associate of your Papa's or something like that.'

Clearly there were many things Max did not know, or had not been told.

86

Rosa was more amenable that afternoon — her mistress must have told her to talk to me. She had intimated more than once that Gregory looked like our Mama, but said nothing about *my* appearance. Yet whenever I was alone in a room with her I had the disturbing feeling that she looked at me covertly and that a lot was going on behind that sharp little face and beaky nose.

I chatted to her now whilst she was making special fruit-cakes from dried fruits of all sorts. She was not the official cook, but was allowed to take over in the kitchen when Zelda's cook had her day off. I think Zelda would have liked Rosa to do all the cooking as well as the sewing. My aunt was clearly more indulgent to her than she was to any other servant, including the strange maid we had met the very first time, who did not live in the house but came daily. That woman had never said more to me than on that first day long ago.

'My Aunt Zelda is hoping that my Papa will allow me to accompany her to Italy next year', I began.

She looked at me but said nothing, nodded her head.

'She might take my half-sister Cara too', I said. At this she put down her spoon and stared at me. 'She is my *half*-sister, as *you* know', I said.

'I have not met her, *Miss*', she replied stiffly.

On an impulse I said: 'Did *you* ever know the Voyle boy? Max says his father is in Australia.

Why was he made my aunt's ward, Rosa?' I must have sounded rather nosy and wheedling. She cleared her throat.

'His father asked her to look after him when he went away.'

'Is his mother dead?'

At this she bridled. 'Don't come nosing around, Miss Hetty — it doesn't concern you —'

'Well, Papa had him to stay with us last year you know, and then he suddenly went away — Gregory and I don't like him, so we were pleased. He tormented my little sister.'

'Which little sister?' she asked me, now busy weighing sultanas. 'You have three, I believe.'

'Oh, well, he was nasty to Pooranna.' (I had told Rosa my name for her). 'And even nastier to my sister Cara — but in a funny way — making her think he thought she was beautiful and she thought he meant it.'

'Making up to her you mean?' Now she looked interested and yet sort of scared too.

'What does that mean? No — as if he hated her. She *is* pretty, Rosa — it's just that it's not good for her to be told she is.'

'If he pesters her again you must tell your mother', she said.

'Well, he's gone now. And you mean my *step-*mother, Rosa. *You* know my father's wife is not my Mama.'

She said nothing to that, but started to cut up some tiny pieces of peel with a special pair of long silver scissors and then popped the tiny pieces into

88

a bowl of flour. I thought, well my bridges are burned now and I must just see how she takes it. Instead she changed the subject.

'How is that niece of mine?' she asked. 'Still as stubborn as ever?'

'Huntie sends you her love', I answered promptly and primly and popped a piece of peel into my mouth. I was perpetually hungry. Rosa did not stop me tasting her ingredients, but went on: 'Not got herself a young man yet then?' and went off into a fit of wheezy laughter.

'Huntie doesn't like young men', I said, realizing for the first time that this was true. I smiled and waited for the wheezing to stop.

'Just as well then.' I waited. 'How's Master Gregory — and your dad?'

'Do you know my Papa well?' I asked her.

'I should think so, Miss Hetty. But those days are over. He was a good-looking young man, your dad —' I waited again, with bated breath. Perhaps now she would say something more about Mama. There was no hurrying her. She was as stubborn as Huntie and if she thought you were bullying her would refuse to continue the conversation. But as she said nothing more I could not resist a further question.

'Did he *love* my mother?' I burst out, before I'd realized what I was going to say.

'Miss Hetty, what do *I* know about love? It was all long ago — like I said.'

'Not *so* long ago — Gregory's only nineteen — Papa must have married my Mama about twenty years ago — you worked for my grandmother, didn't you? Do tell me — you knew my Mama and Mrs de Vere, didn't you — in Ealing?'

'Yes, I was maid to your grandma — God rest her soul. Miss Maria married young — well they both did. Like as two peas they were, but the weakness wasn't in Miss Griselda — ah, it's no use harking back, Miss Hetty. It won't bring *her* back — if you want to know about your mother you'd better ask your dad. Why don't you? Or ask my mistress.'

'Oh, *she* won't tell me what I want to know and Papa doesn't even know that I know his wife is not my Mama — I'll be eighteen at the end of the year — surely he'll want to tell me then?'

'It's not my business,' she said, but the way she looked at me was not unkind. She was, I suppose, circumspect enough to realize that she must not indulge herself in idle gossip with a girl my age and must appear respectful even if she did not feel it.

'Miss Daventry,' I said, in my best schoolroom tones trying to sound like Lucy Little, '*please* tell me about my mother. You knew her. You were with her when she died, were you not? Tell me — I need to know — I'm not a child any more. Why does Papa dislike me so — and Gregory too? What had my Mama done to make him so strange?' I took up one of the small weights from the table that were neatly piled in front of the iron scales and fiddled with it.

She sighed. 'Miss Maria was a sweet girl', she

said, but in a mechanical sort of way. 'She didn't deserve what happened to her — but she couldn't help her nerves, Miss Hetty.'

'Does Huntie know all you do — about Mama — and Papa?' I asked. It was all so frustrating.

'Just remember, Miss Hetty, that Elizabeth Huntington is on your side,' she said, but not replying to my question. I'd never heard Huntie's Christian name before. 'But if she ain't loyal to her master she'd be sent packing.'

'They need her for Pooranna', I said.

'Buffy wouldn't want to leave you', she said. 'But it ain't her place to tell you all you want to know.'

I sighed. 'Do you think I'd like Italy?' I asked her.

'You might.'

I thought, neither does she want to lose her position here with my aunt. I shall have to find someone else to ask. Rosa was so obviously faithful, and my aunt's mixture of laxity and amusement towards her and yet firm expectation of service was not something I could emulate. Neither she nor Huntington were *my* servants to order about. I wished she'd open up about Italy though.

'My aunt says I can stay in her house in Fiesole', I said. 'If they let me go with her.'

'Oh, Miss Zelda — Mrs de Vere — is very generous', she said.

'But Papa may not let me go.'

'I expect he will if Mrs de Vere asks him', was all she said, and busied herself breaking up butter into small pats and mixing it into another bowl of what looked like cornflour.

'You and your sister could "come out" in Italy', she said as though she had thought it all out long before.

'Come out?'

'The Season, Miss — they start younger than here in London.'

I had never thought that we belonged to the sort of society from which débutantes emerged and must have looked surprised. 'Your mother did in London', she went on. 'And your Aunt. A picture they were, the two of them.' I felt a shiver go down my spine. At last she was talking. 'But that won't be possible here for your sister', she said.

'Oh, *I'd* never thought of going into Society when I'm grown up', I said hastily. 'I want to study, you see — but I'd like to travel too', I went on.

She took a quick sidelong glance at me.

'My sister is being prepared for polite society here in London', I said. 'She has dancing lessons still — and only does French and needlework with our governess. But I have no desire for polite society myself.'

'Do you remember Mr de Vere?' she asked me, suddenly changing the subject.

'Yes — I can't have been very old, but I do remember a man with a gold watch — and there was a cradle in the room — but that may have been another time.' I did not mention the legacy.

'He was fond of you, the old man', she said

with a faraway look in her eyes. Then, more briskly: 'That would have been Master Max in the cradle — a delicate baby he was —'

'It had blue ribbons', I went on. 'There was a long window and the sun coming through — and a lady — could that have been my Mama?'

I was not going to tell her how this memory was mixed up with the nightmares, for I had stopped having them and did not wish to remember them.

'I expect it was your Aunt', she said carefully. 'Your Mama was delicate —'

'Did she die of consumption then?' I whispered. If only Rosa would just sit down and tell me the whole story from the beginning. She did not answer my question so I went on: '*Was* the man Uncle Basil? He was nice.' Suddenly I seemed to remember sitting on a man's lap, a memory I couldn't recall having had before. But was that Max's father?

'He did have a gold watch, yes. He was fond of you', Rosa Daventry repeated. 'Poor gentleman.'

'Was my Papa there then, if Mama was ill? In Italy?'

'Certainly not', she said briskly. 'Now I must see to my raisins. Just go on with your studying, Miss Hetty — not long now till you are eighteen.'

'There's such a lot to do before that', I said. 'I want to play the piano better and learn more Italian and —' I stopped. I had been going to say, 'Make my Papa proud of me.' I hadn't known either till then that I wanted that. I felt suddenly sad. He would never care, and I must not care either.

I went upstairs to Max and knocked on the door of his room. He always had an incredible amount of prep to do, though all he really cared about was collecting beautiful things and talking about pictures. But I helped him sometimes with his French, a language he said he did not like — in exchange for his talking Italian to me. He said I had a good ear. He learned Latin too, which I had never been allowed to learn. Miss Little said that it was not regarded as a language for girls and Papa did not wish me to learn it.

I went home that day full of all my aunt and Rosa had told me and determined to spend the next year profitably. If one day I could accompany Zelda de Vere to Italy I was sure that the solution to all my questions would lie there. I would find Mama's grave. Perhaps I'd find work there too as a governess to some expatriate family. Zelda said there were many English people there. Me a débutante! Stuff and nonsense, I thought.

My father continued in complete ignorance of my knowledge of my own mother. He must have thought me very stupid. Had Gregory had it out with him? Was that why my brother was hardly ever at home now? Often I wondered how I could go on in a twilight world of half-truths. There was as yet no return visit of Simon Voyle, for which I was thankful. Papa never whispered a word about my 'legacy' from Uncle Basil. Did he know I knew?

Pooranna got rather fat just as Mamarella seemed to grow thinner daily. For my own part the quaint child who had given a new name to her stepmother and communed with her doll and named her little sister Pooranna had disappeared. The process that had begun gradually gained momentum and in a few months I looked grown up and put up my hair. I wanted to embark upon a course of intensive reading, but I was in agony those weeks just before my birthday, wondering whether Zelda had yet approached Papa about my projected stay with her.

I could tell nothing from his demeanour for he was usually silent and remote. Mamarella often had red eyes, but whether it was from staying up with an ailment of Felix's or from some attitude of my father's I had no idea. I knew from the girls I had met at dancing class and other pupils of my piano teacher that neither did *they* speak to their fathers about important things, though most of them had more indulgent male parents than mine. Only Lucy Little has a father who treats her as a human being, I thought. But what use would Mr Little be if I confessed my uncertainties to him? He knew nothing of my parentage or the strains in our family. If he was ever to visit us he would see only Papa and Mama walking silently together across the lawn and would mistake the silence for comfortable mutual security. If he talked to my brother it would be to a promising and hard-working future young barrister. He would make allowances for Pooranna since he would know that children like her were born in the best of families. He would smile at Alice and Felix and see Mamarella's fussing over him only as the normal anxieties of a young mother. If he saw Cara he would see just a lovely young girl who at sixteen already had the face and figure of a siren. Perhaps it was all my imagination, and we were a happy family, and they had never spoken of my Mama because they wished to spare me pain? I had passed the age of combined disillusion and impatience with grown-ups, and grown less irritable with myself. I had had a good education with my governess; the world was before me and there was a possible trip to Italy and the prospect of a small allowance. Yet I felt by turns torpid and sluggish and then unbearably distracted in those autumn weeks before my eighteenth birthday. Even my reading suffered, and everything felt stale and unprofitable. But soon, I thought, the day of reckoning will come and I shall rise to the occasion and demand that I go with Zelda; I shall have a full explanation of my mother's life, will be treated one day as an adult by this Papa of mine when we confront each other at last.

I spent hours in the conservatory in the warm, soil-scented air, feeling that I was suspended in a limbo not of my own making or choosing. We were all, except for Miss Little, living a lie, or lies, I thought, and I was the fly suspended in the spider's web existing from day to day in the hope that the web would be cut down or the fly released. In all this I noticed more and more how wretched my stepmother looked. I hoped she was not going into a fashionable decline. But if I did not like her I would be glad that she was wretched, would I not? I realized I was sorry for her and that the birth of her longed-for son had led her into the most awful anxieties. I thought of all she had gone through — still-births and miscarriages and pregnancies. She still looked dissatisfied and miserable, and I, a woman too now, began to realize that my father did what she wanted whilst she did what he wanted. I was so used to her nerves that I would offer to play with Felix if Huntie was busy, or if he were ailing at night to sit with him — the nurse had gone to another family by then — to allow Mamarella to get some sleep. Mamarella accepted my help, but would keep coming into the night nursery to look at him. Often it seemed to me she was about to say something important to me — but she never did.

6

Towards the close of the year which would end in my eighteenth birthday I was beginning to feel quite fond of Felix, though I often wished he were not so spoilt. He was an engaging child, handsome and very active, and playing with him was an excuse to indulge myself with his toys, the sort that had never been bought for me and not purchased in such quantities even for Cara or Alice. Gregory had had a kaleidoscope with which I'd amused myself for many a long hour until Pooranna had thrown it across the room and it had broken. But Felix was bought the new praxinoscope and even Papa used to amuse himself with it, revolving the figures on the cardboard wheel very quickly in front of a mirror which made the horsemen and horses go round when you looked at them through the tiny holes. We still had our old Noah's Ark, but Felix was bought a miniature butcher's shop from the Soho Bazaar. He already had a drum which he much enjoyed banging as he strutted up and down, making Mamarella's head ache. Although she was afraid to let him out of her sight she had no patience, not even to help him build towers which he could then knock down. He had many bricks — which Pooranna also liked to throw around — and shields and swords and spears. But the toy I liked best of all the treasures bought for him was a toy theatre. It was far too old for him and had been sent by Grandmother Coppen for his fourth birthday. I believe she had been the sender of the 'twin' doll all those years ago, a doll which I now believe had been intended for me. Dolls had had no interest for me for years, though I still kept Maryemma. I wished Grandmamma had sent *me* a theatre when I was small. After all she was my grandmother too, though she still never came to visit. The antipathy between her and my stepmother was mutual; Papa never invited her to stay in his house. But I enjoyed playing with her present to Felix, though I was 'grown up' — or would be on my eighteenth birthday, according to Zelda.

I made up a play for Alice and she and I, and sometimes Cara, would take the parts and act them. Moving the cardboard figures was finicky and fiddly work, but Alice was nimble-fingered. Felix would soon become bored listening to us and, if we were not careful, he would escape into the kitchen and out through the back door into the shrubbery where he kept his wooden wheelbarrow and several carts. When she had her headaches Mamarella no doubt thought that three sisters could keep an eye on him, and one of us always had to go after him. I would lure him back to the nursery with his humming top, and once he was back would often try to teach him his letters from the picture alphabet, a set of pretty little hand-coloured cards in a wooden box which Gregory had once owned and with which he had taught me my alphabet.

I wondered, as I tried to instruct Felix in the apple and the bee and the cow, or rather the a, b, c, what *I* should be doing when Felix was as old as my own full brother was now. Felix was more interested in the things represented by the pictures and would ask for an apple or look for a bee and would be out of the room once more if given a chance. I thought I might make a tolerable teacher one day — at least I was having some practice trying to teach one little pupil his letters.

I was beginning to take more interest in clothes, though never to the extent that Cara did. Mamarella adored finery but never looked so chic as my Aunt Zelda with her stylish dresses of darker hues than the ones Ella favoured. But there was so much draping and pleating and fuss now about hems and ribbons and bustles — I wished I were a man and could wear knickerbockers and check jackets and boots like Gregory and father! Zelda never appeared to spend as much time over her toilette as my stepmother. Had my own real Mama once been a fashion plate? 'I dress very simply in England', my aunt once said to me. 'Naturally in Italy I had to dress for Society, though they change less often in Florence than here in London.'

'But you do not change very often here, Aunt', I said.

'I do not go to formal dinners or to the theatre

here, Hetty — I am a "hermit", you know.'

I thought how boring it would be if I found that I had to spend time abroad considering my toilette.

'Oh, you will find your style', she said laughing at my expression and guessing my thoughts. 'Young women have to cut their clothes according to their cloth. We shall get you a decent day dress and white ones for the evenings.'

She spoke as if my travelling to Italy with her was already arranged, but would not say whether she had spoken to Papa about it.

I liked to curl up in Aunt Zelda's conservatory with a book just as I did at home, but with fewer interruptions. It led out of her small drawing-room that had a green striped sofa, round mirrors with swags and swirls of gilt, and urns on high columns. But she said that it was not a patch on her Italian house where the mantelpieces were of marble and the ceilings high and white. She glowed when she spoke of Italy to me. I thought how rich she must be to own two homes which she could decorate as she wished, for she had altered The Laurels since my childhood, except for the big sitting-room which she had left pretty well as it was.

But Papa and Mamarella's conservatory was where I would sit on summer evenings when the younger children were in bed. I read Mr Trollope's *The Prime Minister* there that summer. Mr Little had enjoyed it, but was not sure that I would. Although Trollope had probably as great a knowl-edge of the human heart as the author of *The Mill*

101

on the Floss, I really preferred the lady writer and had read her *Adam Bede* with great admiration and pleasure. But could *I* ever settle for a tranquil, rural existence? Nothing much happened at East Wood except in my own head. I felt I was cut out for something more elevated. Yet I did not like this idea of 'Society' and Mr Trollope's books were all part of that. If I ever wanted to move in English Society — not that it seemed likely — I had better know who *my* grandfathers and grandmothers were, as he said was necessary at the beginning of his book. I was not even supposed to know who my mother was! I suspected that Zelda and my mother had only just managed to scrape into polite society from their Ealing home and that it was Zelda whose ambitions had led to a rich husband, even though he did live in Italy. But if all I knew of the world was from novels, I was not going to be very well prepared.

I can see us all now in the conservatory at home, whose iron chairs were green instead of Zelda's white ones, can feel myself back there on summer evenings when the sun cast long shadows. Why, we almost looked like an ordinary family: Mamarella with the tapestry work that she never finished, Cara looking idly at her hands and Papa reading his *Times*.

My eighteenth birthday dawned frostily, the sun in a clear blue December sky. The evening before, Papa had said casually as he bade me goodnight — 'I believe it is your birthday tomorrow, Hester?'

102

'Yes, Papa', I answered and looked him full in the face. He will have to tell me now about the legacy, I thought, even if he will not speak of my Mama. But *I* shall speak of her and if he is angry I shall go to Zelda's. My mind was quite made up. 'Come up to my study at twelve', he said.

Gregory was in the hall and heard this short conversation. Papa went back into the drawing-room and I went upstairs slowly. Gregory had his hand on the banister at the bottom of the stairs and whispered: 'Hetty —' and I turned. We had not spoken for years now of our secret and he no longer visited Zelda and Max as I did. He seemed to have become spiritually distant from me, but there was a gentleness in his face as I waited to see what he wanted. I had not mentioned Uncle Basil's money to him, thinking it tasteless before it was actually mine. His own last birthday had not been celebrated with us — perhaps he had preferred it that way for he was seldom at home now.

'I have something to give you that Papa gave me', he said. 'But don't open it till tomorrow, will you?' He came up the stairs and put a tiny package in my hand. 'I'm sorry I can't afford much myself', he said. 'There will be only a book and I shall not see you till the evening. Tell me then what he says to you. But do not speak of this present.'

Usually the birthdays of Cara and Alice and Felix were celebrated at tea time with a cake, and my sisters had always given me presents on mine, though Ella had only allowed me a cake because she had found that for the last few years Huntie and Cook had made one for me without her knowledge and she had had to pretend she'd ordered it. I took the little parcel from my brother.

'You know Zelda wants to take me to Italy?' I said.

'You want to go?' he looked surprised.

'Of course I do — do you think *He* will make difficulties then?'

'You must take care, Hetty — think it over carefully.' I thought, perhaps he is jealous knowing that I am the favourite at The Laurels and wishes himself to go with my aunt? My brother was a puzzle to me; he was so grown up and reserved in manner.

I made to go up the stairs. 'Don't open it in front of Papa', he said, and was gone. I had the impression that there was something else he'd wanted to say, but had thought better of it.

I went down to breakfast at eight o'clock and found a pile of presents on my plate. 'We thought you would like it better', said Cara. 'You are too old for nursery tea and cake.'

It was a Saturday and Papa and Mamarella never breakfasted with us on a Saturday. Pooranna was in the kitchen with Huntie, and Felix still upstairs with Mama. No sign of Gregory.

'Gregory has had to take the early train — he said he'd see you tonight', said Cara.

'Aren't you going to open your presents?' said Alice, young enough not to hide any excitement

104

she might feel over birthdays.

I put on my plate the tiny parcel Gregory had given me — I had not wanted to open it alone, I don't know why. There was already something waiting there from my sisters.

'Mama says she is giving you one of her dresses', Cara observed as I began to open the parcel, 'but it is still hanging in her wardrobe so as not to crease.'

Perhaps Ella and my father had already spoken of my going away abroad and the dress was to be a travelling one?

'What is it?' asked Cara as I drew out a thin gold ring on a velvet ground from its small heart-shaped box. Gregory had written a little note that was wrapped round the box. 'This was our Mama's wedding-ring. Papa gave it to me for me to give you. He does not wish you to speak of it to him. From myself, dear Hetty, you have all my love.'

At last Papa had acknowledged he had a first wife! I could not help the tears welling into my eyes. 'It is a present from Gregory', I lied. 'It looks like a wedding-ring', pursued my sister.

'Yes, it was an ancestor's ring', I fibbed, though that was partially true at any rate. 'I must open your presents', I said gaily and tore open the neat wrapping of Alice's gift under which was a pair of cherry-red bedroom slippers, knitted by herself. It was a kind gesture. She was observing me closely. 'They are lovely, dear', I said. 'How kind and industrious of you to make them for me.' I kissed her.

'Open mine', Cara commanded me.

Just then Huntie came in with Pooranna, who was holding a box in her thick little hand. Cara's present turned out to be a book about whose purchase she had consulted Miss Little. A book I really wanted, Arnold's *Culture and Anarchy*. I exclaimed: 'It is just what I wanted to own!' and she was pleased, though she could not resist saying: 'Miss Little found it for me on the sixpenny stall.'

Then I had to open the box Pooranna was holding, though at the last moment she did not want to relinquish it. Huntie had bought an artificial rose for her to give me from both of them. 'It's from me *and* her', Huntie insisted. A lovely, pale pink, plush rose. Pooranna wanted to stroke it and did so. Sometimes she appeared quite sensitive.

'Oh, Huntie', I said. 'How lovely.' I thought, shall I show her mama's ring later when the others are not here?

I had to go into Papa at noon and my stomach was already churning from nervous trepidation — I intended to have it out with him once and for all. Every time I thought of an opening to our conversation some difficulty arose. In the end I decided I would leave it to him to start our conversation. My questions were burned in my head through many a sleepless night of this year that had led me to my eighteenth birthday: Why did my Mama go to Italy? Why did she die? Why will you never talk about her? Why have you never even acknowledged that I had the same mother as Gregory, but that it was not Ella? What happened after I was born? Why do you not entertain my Aunt Zelda and cousin Max here? Why has my stepmother never hinted in words that I am not her daughter?

Yet when the grandfather clock in the hall struck twelve and I walked slowly down the stairs from my room, having ascertained from Cara that Papa was indeed alone in his study, I suddenly became calm. I must concentrate on getting to Italy. Perhaps Gregory would tell me what I wanted to know if Papa had gone so far as to give him Mama's ring. I had not dared to put it on my hand. First I must see how the land lay.

'Come in', was the answer to my knock, and when I entered the room he was sitting at his large desk, bent over papers as he so often was. He was just beginning to go a little grey — I noticed it for the first time. His side-whiskers were seeded with little silver hairs which stood out from the dark brown ones. He looked up as I stood there looking at him.

'Ah, Hetty', he said as though I were one of his clerks. Then: 'Many Happy Returns — I believe it is your birthday.' As though he wasn't sure! But then I saw that it was a sort of joke and that my Papa, my stern, unloving, unbending Papa was nervous.

'You wanted to see me?' I said coolly.

'Yes — sit down, Hetty. You and I have a few matters to discuss.' I waited. 'I believe you have been invited to stay with your Aunt Griselda de Vere in Italy?' he said, looking out of the window.

'She has approached you, I imagine?'

'Yes, Papa,' I said, my heart now thudding uncomfortably in my chest, 'but of course I should need your permission to accompany her.'

'Yes indeed', he said and then turned and looked fully in my face. 'You are aware of the relationship', he said in frosty tones, as though discussing an investment.

'Papa —' I began, but he waved his hand in front of his face with a curious gesture as though brushing away a fly, saying when he had regained his composure: 'Your brother will enlighten you further.'

'I know it all', I said and he dropped his eyes as I continued. 'Well, not all — but that your first wife, our Mama, died. There is so much more I want to know.'

He looked up. 'Let us discuss your plans to accompany Mrs de Vere to Florence.'

I thought, if I insist on finding out what I have determined to discover, my whole plan of escape from his house — and from England — will be in jeopardy. I had better keep my mouth shut for the moment.

'You are to be informed that a small legacy has been left to you by your uncle Basil de Vere.'

I said nothing. Zelda had not told him I knew already then? I tried to look amazed — and succeeded, I think.

He looked relieved that I did not ask why. 'And your grandmother will see fit to give you a small income, when you are of full age.'

I did look surprised at this. 'How much money shall I have altogether then, Papa?' I asked.

'One hundred a year invested for you from my mother eventually and the legacy of two hundred and fifty', he said, looking away again out of the window. He must have been rich, this Basil de Vere! It seemed a lot of money to me. 'The two hundred and fifty your aunt will hand over to you to bank for all your expenses in Italy — and after.' He seemed, I thought, to be casting me off. Then he said stiffly: 'Your home will be here — if you wish it to be — after your stay in Florence. You will be able to contribute to the household expenses on your return.' He was not casting me off then, but he would expect me to pay for my keep! I did not know whether to be glad or sorry.

'I intend to take up work as a governess, Papa', I began. 'I have spoken to Miss Little and when I return she has promised to aid me in finding a post.' It was his turn to look surprised. 'Then I shall no longer be a burden on your household', I added. His cheeks went pink. 'Both Gregory and I will earn our own living', I said.

'You seem to have everything nicely arranged', he replied sarcastically.

'I know you have many expenses in the family', I said coolly.

'That is true', he said, and paused. I thought — Now I must ask him — Why will he not talk to me as a daughter? — but he said, before I could formulate a question: 'I have very good reports from your governess, Hetty. I am sure that if it were necessary you could emulate her example, but I don't think it will be necessary — if you are careful with your little fortune.'

'I want independence', I said unthinkingly. 'Mama' — [and I meant Mamarella] — 'will wish, I am sure, that I earn my living as my brother does.'

'I believe Mama has the present of a dress for you', he said. 'Your aunt will help you purchase what is necessary for your stay with her —'

'Papa', I said interrupting him, and it all came out in a rush. 'Papa — why did Mama go to Italy? Why did she die? — and why do you not speak of her? I have waited years to ask you — I have known for a long time about her — why do you not entertain my Aunt and cousin here? Was there a quarrel after Mama died?'

He looked uncomfortable and there was something else in his eyes when he looked up. I thought it was guilt. But he said: 'I don't think there is any need to prolong our discussion.'

I knew I was dismissed. Then he said again, with a forced smile — 'Happy Birthday.'

'Thank you', I said. I got up and went out.

When I closed the door he was looking out of the window.

Mamarella gave me a travelling dress, which she said she had hardly ever worn. It was quite a good shape and of a dark green, a colour I did not dislike. I intended also to be measured for two more dresses straight away, which I would pay for with

110

the money that was to be mine. I had pondered these outfits ever since I knew that Uncle Basil had left me a little money, and I wanted a lilac dress for afternoon and a dress of cream lace for evenings. Cara was ecstatic over my plans, on the way to the Littles to take tea in Camberwell where she had never been invited before. There was a little cake waiting there for me from Lucy, with one candle to stand for the eighteen. I thought, if only I could go back to the day of my birth and then forward a few years — the years I was too young to remember — *then* I might solve the mystery of my mother. But I tried to be sociable. As far as I knew Cara had no inkling of the fact that I was only her half-sister and I was not going to tell her or Lucy Little yet.

As we sat in the little parlour with Mr Little in his chair by the fire, an organ-grinder passed in the street and stopped before the window.

Cara clapped her hands. 'He knows it's your birthday!' she exclaimed.

A little tune came through the curtains, which were still drawn back. I listened as if there was really a message for me in it, and we were all silent for a time.

'It is *il sol dell'anima*', said Adolphus Little with a reminiscent smile. 'From *Rigoletto*. That opera is so full of lovely arias — how lucky you are to be going to Italy, Hetty.'

'Oh, I wish Papa would let *me* go', exclaimed Cara, and looked very mournful.

'Maybe when you are eighteen you will be able

to join Hetty there', suggested Lucy as the tune died away, the maid having opened the street door and given the organ-grinder a coin.

Cara went on — 'I don't think he will — it is so dull at home — and will be duller when Hetty has gone.'

Lucy Little said, 'I expect they have plans for you, Cara — your Mama said to me there will be dances next year for you — I shall soon have only Alice to teach.'

'And Felix', I said. '*He* will need your firm hand!'

Cara pouted. 'Why does this Zelda woman not invite me to her house? I have never even met Max!'

'You had better ask Papa', I said. 'Tell him you would like to meet them.'

Mr Little looked puzzled. He broke the short silence that followed by saying: 'I haven't given you my present yet, Hetty. Here it is.'

I unwrapped a book bound in green. It was *Daniel Deronda*, and I was delighted — George Eliot's latest book which I had not yet read.

'And here is mine', said my erstwhile governess, giving me a parcel that looked as though it would also reveal literary treasures.

Cara said — 'I asked Miss Little what you would like — you liked *my* present, didn't you, Hetty?'

'I love them all', I said and found dear Hardy's *Far from the Madding Crowd* inscribed to me 'from Lucy Little with best wishes for your future'. 'My "bibles",' I said, and Mr Little laughed. 'The other was Matthew Arnold — from Cara,' I explained.

'I wonder which you will enjoy most, Hetty — you must take them to Italy — you will have time to read, I hope, in the midst of your busy life in Florence!'

'She could not exist without a book to read', said Cara. 'I believe she would rather have a book than a new dress.'

'Well, I am to have those also', I said. I couldn't help feeling that just for once my position as eldest girl was being acknowledged. 'Never mind, Cara. You will have lots — and just think of the dances you will go to next year.'

'Your sister looks as old as you', said Lucy's father, pleasing Cara no end.

As he had no carriage my sister and I took the horse bus back to New Cross and then a train to Parkheath. I was looking forward to seeing Gregory at supper. I was still far from knowing all the truth about our family.

At supper, eaten together by Mamarella and Papa, and Gregory, Cara and I, Cara tackled Papa about her own future. 'I wish you would let *me* go to Italy with Hetty. Mightn't I go next year?'

'Hetty does not know how long she will be staying for', said Papa. 'It will depend on her aunt.'

'Is she not *our* aunt too?' asked Cara and there was a long pause before Gregory replied, tactfully, since Papa just looked down at his plate — '*I* do not see much of her either. Perhaps you may visit Max one day?'

'You're always talking about him', grumbled

Cara, and her mother headed her off by talking of a fitting at the dressmaker's. I thought — it ought to be Cara going to balls in Florence, for I'm sure, lace dress or no, I shall not fit into that sort of life. But nevertheless I was longing to leave.

There had been a letter from Zelda waiting in the hall from the third post when we arrived back from Camberwell. In it she detailed the day of our departure after Christmas and asked me to go over to see them on Boxing Day so that we could discuss travelling arrangements and my future wardrobe.

I managed to talk to Gregory in his old room in the attics after supper. 'He would tell me nothing', I whispered. 'Except acknowledging he *had* had another wife! But I didn't want to give him time to change his mind about letting me go with Zelda, so I didn't pursue my questions. What do *you* know, Gregory?' I took my ring up and looked at it again. 'What did he say when he gave you it for me? He never even asked me if you had given it to me!'

'He was embarrassed', said my brother. 'He has told me very little — but I have discovered it for myself since I left home. She was sent to Italy for her health — as Zelda told you. But he knew Ella before our Mama died.' I was silent, digesting this. 'I can't tell you more now — I shall try to come over in the spring after my Bar exam, Hetty. Our Papa is a weak man, I think, but not a *very* wicked one. Try to forget the past — and go and enjoy yourself.'

114

'Will you tell me when you find out more? I promise I will tell you what I discover myself — I'm sure the answers are in Florence.'

'Take care if Voyle should reappear, won't you', he said suddenly. He seemed anxious, so I said I would. My mind was too full of the excitements soon to be mine to worry overmuch about that nasty young man. Zelda would hardly encourage him to visit her abroad, I thought.

Huntie was the one who said she'd miss me most. 'You'll be here when I return — I don't know when exactly, but you'll always stay with Poor-anna?' I said to her. 'Stay for ever, Huntie.'

'We'll see — *I* ain't got no invitations to Italy —'

'*She* couldn't manage without you — with Felix — and Hannah', I said. Huntie knew this, I suppose, for she smiled. 'Unless you get wed', I added.

'I'm like my Auntie', she said. ' "You do as I did, doll", she said to me years ago — "and you'll never want". I don't fancy fellows if you want the truth!'

'But you like babies, Huntie! Wouldn't you like one of your own one day?'

'Liking 'em ain't the same as having 'em, Hetty', she replied. 'Don't you worry — I'll look after little Hannah — and Master Felix too — it's nearly sixteen year since I come back from Italy with you —' She stopped. 'I was only eighteen meself', she went on after a pause. 'I'll miss you, Hetty.'

'And I you', I replied and gave her a big hug. But I knew I had in many ways grown away from my old nursemaid and she recognized that.

'That "Lucy" will miss you too', she said. 'Write to me when you write to her, won't you?'

I knew that Huntie could not read very well and this was her way of asking me to keep in touch. She liked Lucy Little who had no 'side' and was the same with the servants as she was with us. It was unusual for servants to like a governess.

My new dresses were made by Zelda's dressmaker and I was fitted for them over Christmas. I wondered whether it would be the last Christmas of my life I would ever spend at home. We were to leave England on Twelfth Night.

PART 2

Stars in my Eyes

7

I stood on the outside balcony of the cavernous drawing-room, or *salotto*, of my Aunt Zelda's villa on the hillside a few miles from Florence. I looked out over misty fields and vineyards trying to see the city that lay brown and blurred in the distance. It was raining, but just for a moment the clouds parted and a shaft of sun lit up the Duomo that rose up from the view like an open umbrella, next to Giotto's tower.

Mr Dickens had once said that the streets of Florence were magnificently severe and gloomy, and from what I had seen of them so far I agreed with him. They were also dark and smelly; at the time of which I write, the heart of the medieval city with its market and twisting alleys had not yet been ripped out in the name of Progress and the cathedral façade was bare and crumbly. I had not minded that the weather had been atrocious when we arrived there, for our journey to Italy had been long and exhausting — mentally more than physically so far as I was concerned. I had been glad of a few days' rest at the Villa de Vere to think over the previous week. We were not to stay there for long; Zelda sojourned outside Florence only in the summer months, but her own town apartment was not ready. The American family who had been renting it was, on account of some muddle that vastly annoyed my aunt, to leave it only during the week following our arrival. The villa, whose original name was Villa Fortuna [I discovered this from the servants], was certainly not the place for a January stay, being constructed for warm days and nights. I did not mind the cold, though I had not expected it. I was a little apprehensive about moving back to Florence. It had indeed looked very dark and forbidding when we arrived at night after our long journey — the crossing from Dover followed by the long rail journey from Paris through France and Switzerland and across the Alps before two more long days by rail and road. I knew that I had not yet seen the 'real' Florence which, according to a book I was reading, possessed more masterpieces to the square metre than any other place on the globe. My Italian education was to begin when we moved on the following Tuesday into the city, and would last until late April.

My new lilac-striped dress was too thin for sitting indoors, so I was wearing my old woollen gown and cape as I stood looking out from the balcony. Suddenly a rainbow sent its dazzling arc over the fields, ending somewhere in the city. It lightened my spirits, which were always more dependent on the weather than they should have been. My offer to help Zelda arrange the few rooms in the villa that were opened up had been refused. 'The servants will see to that, Hetty', she had said.

There were not many here as yet — the permanent ones would be engaged later for the spring and summer — and Rosa was busy ordering about the two rather rustic-looking domestics in her curious Italian — or in English if words failed her. The people of Tuscany around Florence were said to speak the best Italian of this newly united nation, but I doubted that I could learn much from Zelda's servants who did not speak the language I had begun to learn in England, but an almost impenetrable dialect. I tried to talk to them even so, for I was eager to understand 'real' foreigners. Giuseppe and Serafina were their names.

The rainbow disappeared as swiftly as it had come and I went in to finish my letter to Cara which I had begun and left off many times since starting it in pencil in the train from Paris to the Alps. I had so much to say, though I wasn't sure whether Cara really wanted to hear of my reactions to the places through which we had travelled and my tumbling thoughts about everything under the sun. 'Abroad' appeared to have uncorked my mind, so that I was full of notions and imaginings, as well as delighted reactions to the new and strange. I'd be better off writing to Lucy Little but some loyalty dictated I write to Cara first. East Wood seemed millions of miles away, and I was not homesick for it. I would eventually share my raptures with my former governess whom I missed more than anyone. It wasn't fair that Lucy would never be able to travel, unless as a governess with a rich family. I marvelled that I had that money in the bank, a fortune indeed to me and one I did not intend dissipating too swiftly. Zelda herself did not seem to lack money; her husband must have left her very well off. But money could not always buy efficiency, as I saw with her dealings with the Tuscans. The house was very grand but needed repairs and several licks of paint. It stood in cultivated fields, closed off from them by a high wall, and had extensive gardens edged with little box-trees that had grown straggly. At the bottom of the garden was a pool for fish and I had already wandered there and leaned against the ivy-covered walls and decided I would sketch the baby cypress tree that grew by itself some way from the pool.

From the winding white lane through the farm-land you could see the villa's central tower, and as you approached the main entrance you saw old cypresses and ilexes clustering round the buildings, and the large barn and stabling. The fountain was not playing at present, but Zelda promised it would when we returned and that I should see the lemon trees in blossom in their tubs on the large terrace that had two flights of steps down to the garden proper. I could see that it would all be very beautiful in the warmer seasons of the year. At present it looked neglected.

The actual house was noble in its proportions and very old. There were four storeys, with a roof of dark red tiles, and the balustrades of the two flights of steps that led up to the front door were of marble. There were one or two marble statues indoors too, which had surprised me, and many — mostly broken ones — in the garden, along with large reddish jugs that looked like the one that adorned the pictures in Max's Latin history books. At the top of the stable wall were a weather-cock and a crucifix together — an odd juxtaposition I thought, and there was also a painted sun-dial on the inner wall of the yard. There had not yet been any sun for me to test its veracity. When you stepped inside the house from the terrace it was like entering Kew Gardens, for there was a profusion of palms and plants, as well as various antique-looking busts in special niches. They all looked very dusty and I could see that there would be work for an army of servants and gardeners. The plaster, especially, both indoors and outside, needed expert attention. I had no doubt this would be seen to, for Aunt Zelda was an extremely efficient woman. I wondered why she had ever left her paradise; that Max had needed to be educated did not preclude his being tutored by the many young men I heard lived in Florence. But she had probably wanted him to be an English gentleman.

She was busy this rainy morning despatching her own letters to tradesmen from her room next to the dining-room as I settled down at a beautiful little desk in the smaller *salotto* to write my letter to Cara. I had no doubt that various tradesmen and artisans and gardeners would soon move in when we moved back into Florence.

The only non-Italian I had met during this first week was a tall, healthy-looking young American girl whose parents had a villa nearer the city than ours and who had driven over to see me. The Pontravens had lived for some years in Italy, I gathered, but Eleanor had little Italian and was chiefly glad to meet me because I spoke English. I had peered with her at the immense shuttered rooms with their marble floors and grand air, and marvelled at the space of it all. Zelda must have felt quite constricted in her Kentish home! About my aunt, in spite of her crossness and busyness, there was an indisputable feeling that she had in all ways 'come home'. But when she was not ticking off her peasant minions or listing the repairs and arrangements, she was audibly worrying to me about her son and what mischief he might get up to before Easter when he was to come out to us.

'Max will not get into any mischief Aunt', I said. 'He is a good young man — and will be too busy at school for that.' Max was lodging now in Westminster with a school usher and his wife. I wondered, although I did not let my aunt know, whether Lucy would take my sister to visit him one Saturday, as I had suggested. I thought she was too protective of her son and he ought to be allowed to make his own friends. He had always expressed a wish to meet my sister.

I took up my letter to Cara. There was so much to say. I knew it would run to twenty pages once I tried to finish it.

'Dear Cara' — I began afresh —

I enclose the pages I wrote to you during our journey here. I expect by now you will have heard from our telegram that we are safely arrived in Italy. We are at my aunt's villa only for a week or two however, for soon we shall move into our apartment in Florence and return here only when the better weather arrives. I don't know why the houses here are not made comfortable for winter and confess I miss the cosiness of our nursery with its fire and curtains, though everything I have seen here entrances me. The people are handsome and dark and very voluble — I like their manner of expressing themselves by opening their mouths wide and saying what they feel. I noticed this immediately on the journey here. They must think us very repressed, for we are not apt to make a to-do in public if the soup is cold, though I'm told by a new American friend — Eleanor, to whom I was introduced a few days ago — that the English and Americans will complain loudly when they are not in their own country, but in their own language! Eleanor herself says she does not speak Italian well, but I can't imagine her becoming rude in public, for she is very gentle. My aunt however speaks Italian in a loud voice and is quite 'at home' here, is indeed a very tempest of volubility when speaking to the natives!

Our villa will be very beautiful in summer, but at present we are 'camping' in it. The gardens are fine but neglected, with cypresses and pools, and other trees that never lose their green — ilexes, I think — and there are many marble stairs with urns, with a wall enclosing the property from the fields. I can see in the distance the empty poles of vines — or maize — that will be covered in summer. So far though I've seen no 'smart' Italians and am glad that for the moment I needn't go abroad as a 'lady' in my new clothes. *You* would enjoy that, I'm sure, but if you are ever to come here you must learn some of the language. I do not intend to act like a *turista* myself. I am looking forward to some sunshine and for the fountains to play and the statues of rustic beauties or goddesses to awake . . .

. . . For your information and Miss Little's, the King here has just been crowned "King of Italy" — Umberto the First. The Florentines are sceptical — what do they need of Italy when they governed the jewel of the country, Tuscany? Tell your governess too that my "bibles" are much with me — I kept *Daniel Deronda* wrapped in a silk scarf throughout my journey, but took him out to read when there was a lull in our arrangements. I told you about

France — indeed I think I should love that country almost as much as this one here. I think I felt for the first time I was "abroad" when we sat before French coffee steaming in big white cups, with the smell of tobacco and cologne . . . I felt it too when we saw dawn over the mountains of Switzerland and the whole land awoke with people beating their mattresses on the balconies of chalets . . . Oh, Cara, it is all so beautiful! — I began this letter on the train, but was too interested in the passing scene to finish it or even give my reading a thought. There's a confession, for what is Hetty without her reading? [you will say].

There is a pianoforte here, but it needs tuning. Aunt says there is a better one in Florence and I shall be able to practise there, though I know I shall never make a decent player. Rosa has just come in to tell us that our simple meal is ready — I am very partial to the food here and will need my new dresses let out if I continue to eat as I am doing at present. Such delicious soups and "pastas". Have you yet thought of visiting Max de Vere? I am sure he would be pleased to see you. Perhaps you and Miss Little might sally forth one Saturday to a museum and gallery and call on him — take him out to tea and muffins? He would be glad to have a respite from his studies for I'm sure the family where he lodges have kept his nose to the grindstone. There are so many paintings and sculptures in the galleries here that they say one could live seventy years in Florence and visit one a day and still never come to the end of them all, what with all the churches too and "palaces". I feel very ignorant, I must confess, but my artistic education will commence as soon as we move into the city apartment. Give my best regards to Papa and Mama, and to Alice and Hannah and Felix and yourself a kiss each. Tell Huntie I think of her and wonder what she made of Italy all those years ago when [you may not know] she accompanied her Aunt Rosa as maid here. It is a secret she keeps rather well.'

I did not feel the time was yet ripe for me to enlighten Cara as to our semi-sisterhood, but wished that she *could* somehow know before we saw each other again. Maybe Max or Huntie would tell her and then she might tell Papa. My sister, though more worldly than myself, was apt to say whatever came into her head. I thought it was about time that secrets were uncovered in our family. Distance had made me feel bolder. Perhaps Huntie would tell her more. I signed and sealed the letter — Eleanor had said she would take mail to be posted in Florence.

I did finally prevail upon my aunt to allow me to help in washing the porcelain and cleaning the silver before we left for Florence and I had to accustom myself to yet another new place. I felt quite sad we were to leave the Villa Fortuna for four months or so, but once I had rested I looke forward with a mixture of excitement and drea about being in a place where I knew for certain my own mother had been, a place where I imagined I was to be tested and tried, not only as a complete beginner in the connoisseurship of painting, but also as a woman in 'society'.

The minute I set foot in the apartment in Florence I knew I had been there before. The Browns, the American family who had been so reluctant to leave it, might have left traces of themselves in the comfortable cushions and stacks of American journals and newspapers and the new stove they had left for us, and all was clean and fresh, but it felt very un-American to me. Perhaps it was the faint scent that clung to the hangings that reminded me, or the view of the little piazza from the long windows — but I said nothing to Zelda. At first it continued to rain for days on end and I was glad I had packed my 'bibles', for Zelda was now busy going back and forth from the apartment to the villa and so I was left much alone. Eleanor Pontraven and her mother called for me once or twice in their carriage and accompanied me to a few 'sights' — many churches — but until the weather improved we went only to places nearby. Mrs Pontraven however was as voluble as her daughter was quiet and I found I could not concentrate upon 'beauty' with her voice continually in my ears. I had time to become accustomed to the apartment, and I was no trouble to Zelda who remarked that I seemed to know how to amuse myself.

127

The curtains at the long windows that looked out on to that small square with a fountain in its centre were of dark blue velvet, and I thought they smelled of mimosa. Every morning I woke in my large bed in the small room on the same side of the apartment as the smaller sitting-room, and heard the street cleaners and the sellers of fresh bread and flowers and cakes on their way to open up their little stores. Bells tolled interminably, all jangling together, but not too cacophonously. There were children everywhere and crowds of pushing humanity in the over-narrow streets once you turned into the via from our small piazza and made your way towards the river or in the direction of the Duomo. The Arno lay still and dark-green, crossed by its many bridges, waiting for the sun to shine on it.

At first I would sit by my window in the morning looking out across the square, watching the people scurry to and fro and glad that Zelda was not yet released from directing her manifold chores. For a week or two at least I could breathe the city in alone. I watched the people and saw how easy it was to pick out the 'foreigners', for in their tallness and the length of their strides they were so very obviously not Italian. They also moved in twos and threes, usually with a guide-book and a puzzled expression. I don't want to be like that, I thought; one day I want to be accepted as an inhabitant. I had to make my personal acquaintance with Florence before Zelda threatened me with my first 'tea' with an English family, for once we were settled in the apartment and she had seen that her workmen knew what they were doing, I was to be taken to meet some of those English who lived permanently in the city and whom she had known quite well. I did not want to spend the rest of my life reading or looking out of windows or writing long letters to Lucy Little or even accompanying the admirable Eleanor; I wanted to meet Italians, and yet Zelda's friends — so far — all seemed to be English or American. Eleanor frightened me with all her knowledge of painting and sculpture which came out so quietly and diffidently in her kind, friendly tones. To improve my own knowledge — nay to start to learn of all I did not know — I needed to walk around the place by myself.

I was unprepared for the impact of all those buildings, all those paintings, all those statues, when one morning I set out alone on the pretence of meeting Eleanor, whom I knew was safely at home with a cold. American girls went round in groups, English ladies not so much — but I wasn't a lady. What harm could come to me in crowded galleries? I suppose I was at first too innocent to wonder what those Italian words meant which were sometimes murmured in my vicinity as I walked along the busy streets, pressing myself into the sides of buildings to avoid carriages, and people coming from the opposite direction. Armed with Mr Ruskin and my guide-book I began to look at statues and paintings in the galleries, wanting to see the masterpieces for myself. But without the books I felt my own responses too puzzled, too ignorant. Then the next day I went to the Accademia and saw Michaelangelo's *David* — whom they had moved only a few years before from his place in the open air — and marvelled. Lucy had once told me that Michaelangelo had died the very same year both Shakespeare and Galileo were born. Had God wished to replace one genius immediately with two? I already worshipped Shakespeare, and I decided Michaelangelo gave me the same feeling. Just as everything here — houses, buildings, squares, seemed larger than in England, though Florence was much, much smaller than London, so this gigantic statue said to me: This is what a man should be like. This is a representative of humanity. I returned to it many times. Florence had many pearls, but I felt I was the proverbial swine on whom they would be wasted unless I learned to look carefully for myself. I found I could not respond to so much at once without mental indigestion. I would walk by and glance for a moment as most tourists did, but I had not 'looked'. Yet how should I know what to look for? I decided I would choose one or two paintings I liked and would look at them every day. Slowly I managed to begin to pick out a few from the many which I could appreciate and try to study, so as not to feel like a barbarian. I could truly find nothing for my imagination to work on from the Ghirlandaios enthused upon by the rest of my compatriots, but before Botticelli's *Primavera* I found tears come to my eyes. Tears of joy — and yet of sadness — for I suddenly had that feeling of 'tears in things' when I thought of beauty caught for ever in time, from some real young woman who had been dead hundreds of years and yet spoke of life to us. I knew it was not a very 'aesthetic' response, but it was my first. I spent the following day between that picture and the same painter's *Venus Anadyomene*. *I found the same face too in Filippo Lippi's Madonna* and wondered whether the younger Botticelli had seen it. I was enchanted by *Primavera*'s flowers and by the girl's dress — but it said to me what real flowers also said when they were in profusion in meadows and gardens. Never mind, I would just enjoy myself among these paintings and forget the guidebooks for a time. They had said that his *Venus* was the first female nude to be seen since the Romans — the perfection of female beauty, as *David* was the perfect male. I compared the two in my mind. It was the first gift bestowed on me by Italy — the sight of two naked human bodies in all their splendour.

I enjoyed the earlier paintings in the Uffizi for their pinks and blues, but they did not speak to me as Botticelli did. In Bronzino's *Elenora de Toledo* I thought I saw the face of my own new friend Eleanor; in Perugino's *Giovinetto* and Franca's *Evangelista Scappi* I lingered on the dark eyes, seeing them as beautiful and natural as flowers, for once I gave myself up to enjoying the colours and the paintings I liked instinctively, I felt as if a burden had slipped from my shoulders. I could study the dates and the copious information from the books and the commentaries another day; for the time being I would not feel guilty at my ignorance.

One day I asked Zelda where Mama had been buried — was it in the Cimitero degli Inglesi? She was busy that afternoon interviewing women for the post of maid, for she only had Rosa in Florence and Zelda wanted a woman to buy the food and cook and serve our meals, sweep the floors, open the doors and serve tea when we entertained. Then she might accompany us later to the villa in spring.

'Oh, Hetty — that is further away', she said evasively in answer to my question. 'But go to the Cimitero here and you'll find Mrs Browning and old Mrs Trollope — I know you read their works.'

I knew the Villa Trollope was still in Florence; it was not the Trollope whose *Prime Minister* I'd enjoyed, but his brother who still lived in Italy with his second wife. I thought, I'll go to the cemetery one day but not yet. I went back to the galleries, especially to the Uffizi, and found the later painters easier of access — Rubens and Rembrandt and our own Hogarth. I still felt that Titian and Raphael were too far removed from me by the centuries, and I could not truly understand religious paintings, though I saw many 'foreigners' respond to them with ecstasy. I would study them one day; my responses were too personal, I knew. I saw Rossini's tomb in Santa Croce along with Machiavelli's and Michaelangelo's, but could not connect their tombs with their lives. I felt I was waiting to be moved by something, I knew not what. Would I feel the same when Zelda took me to my first opera?

The day came when I was to accompany Zelda to the tea-party given by the Smith's, an English family. I dressed in my mauve striped dress, thinking my new green silk too grand for tea, and felt nervous as our carriage took us over cobblestones to the ochre-coloured palazzo. It did not seem like a palace to my eyes but rather a blank-faced barracks behind an inner courtyard. Inside, the large downstairs room was warm and stuffy and the visitors were more like those of a vicarage tea-party than a fashionable gathering. 'All you have to do is to answer questions politely and make a cup of tea last half an hour', Zelda had said to me beforehand, explaining that the Smiths were highly respectable and useful for keeping in with if there were ever 'difficulties' with Italians, Mr Smith having some diplomatic post and his wife being the daughter of a Protestant clergyman.

It seemed homely enough to me, but I hoped not all such parties would be so deadly dull. 'My niece Hester', — 'Pleased to meet you, Hester. You must meet my daughter Rose.' And so on and so on. They were mostly English and American and past their first youth. To my eyes the women were overdressed and far from chic, and their talk was as dull as their dress was fussy. Maybe my prolonged immersion in looking at great paintings was spoiling me for real people. But no, when I looked at the native Italians in the streets, at the fountains, or even at the new maid Maddalena in our kitchen, I knew that I had begun to criticize my compatriots and to find many of them ugly. One lady at the tea had so many ribbons and bows on her dress on the shoulders, at the neck and down one side of her skirt that she looked like a maypole, and she was not young either. She kept saying I must meet Harry without explaining who Harry was, her husband or her son — or perhaps her dog? But I tried my best to be polite among the lace and gloves though I felt the women were all animated lampshades.

Zelda laughed about them when we got back. 'They are decidedly *not* smart, Hetty, but it is always a good idea to be accepted among the philistines.' I wondered why. 'There are many less gloomy people', she went on. 'Soon you will meet some.'

I realized that most of the Anglo-Florentines were middle-class and rather censorious of the Italians. They never bothered to learn Italian either — to whom would they speak the language but their servants or people in the shops? Where was that smart society of Italians and English Zelda had spoken of and of which I had read in the forbidden Ouida? Not that I wanted to mix with the aristocracy, English or Italian: what I wanted was to meet the present-day equivalent of the Brownings and the Botticellis!

But just occasionally, as I stood alone in the *salotto* looking through the double doors to the smaller room where Zelda sat with her accounts or embroidery [I never saw her finish anything], I had that strange feeling of having been there before which I had had when I arrived. Something was different about the rooms, but they were the ones of my dream, of that I was certain. I had said nothing more to Zelda about that old nightmare and nothing further about my Mama. Once we were settled and I felt myself ready, the subject would come up naturally, I thought. I wondered if my Papa had ever been here in this house. He had bade me farewell with his usual cold composure the day Zelda's carriage had come for me to take me to The Laurels whence we should begin our journey. Even then he had not seen her or she him; the whole matter had been arranged as if one of them had the plague and the other was fearful of catching it. Had Papa enjoyed travel in his youth? Had Mama? Had either of them ever been entranced as I had been by my first sight of 'abroad', not to speak of Italy?

Maybe it was just a trick of the light or the smell of Zelda's pot pourri which she had been freshening with lavender oil, but one day I had a sudden memory — or vision? — of two women, or rather of skirts that belonged to crinolines. I 'saw' pink silk as if I were a child looking up from the floor and when I shut my present eyes I seemed to remember being lifted by one of the crinolines and smelling lavender on a bare neck that rose from a bodice of pale green and pink. I remember sniffing the roses on the bodice as if the perfume came from them and then somebody laughing and my thinking they were laughing at me, and my feeling ashamed. Try as I might I could not recall the faces of those women, but I thought I remembered a fan held in the hand of one of them. I had never remembered this before, but it had happened in the same room as the one where I now stood and where the old gentleman with the gold watch had also been. I knew that if I was remembering my mother and my aunt they would be wearing their hair parted in the middle with ringlets each side and a bun at the back, for I had seen pictures in books of the styles of sixteen years or so before, but I could not 'see' them. I let my mind go blank, hoping that something more would return, but all that swam into my head at first was a silver-buckled belt, and I could have seen that anywhere. Had someone worn a bonnet with flowers and someone else a sleeve with a bead design on the wrist? But that did not seem to connect with the women whose presence I remembered more than their actual bodies. If I remember my Mama now, I thought, it is only as a dress, a scent, a fan, and what good is that? Why should such details be held in a child's brain when a once beloved face is not?

'Listen to the tick-tock', was the phrase I thought I remembered from the old gentleman. Perhaps I was making it all up; I knew I had always been taxed with an over-lively imagination. Yet as I stood in Zelda's *salotto* on that day when the sun came through the shutters for the first time

136

in March and when the scent from the velvet drapes was with me again, for some reason it was English voices I thought I remembered. Both Max and Gregory as children had been in this apartment in reality, never mind my dream. The fact was strangely comforting on the days when I felt rather lonely, for Zelda made no pretence at confiding in me; our conversations were strictly to do with her present difficulties or about future receptions.

I had wondered when I eventually went for the first time to the opera whether I should respond to beauty with that terrified recognition of ignorance I had had at first with the great paintings, which I was still visiting whenever I could, sometimes now with Eleanor Pontraven. Florence was not, they said, the best place for opera; not all the first rate companies came there. Second rate or not I was to find with delight that there was no aesthetic difficulty this time. My romantic soul, which I had half-shamefully realized I possessed, was to feel at home immediately, and the music bore me away on a tide of longing and pleasure. I believe those memories of the distant past were still half in my mind that evening Zelda took me, along with an Italian gentleman of her acquaintance, Count Belotti-Donatoni, to the performance of Verdi's *Ballo in Maschero* in the gold and white theatre. Fashionable Florence was swirling, clotting, round the entrance to the little theatre, 'Courage,' I said to myself, 'now you must begin to know the world.' I cared more to hear music than to ogle 'Society', though that was not the case with most of the audience who were treating the evening as an extension of their own personal dramas and social obligations. As we sat down and the music began, I thought, my memories are like this — masked and perhaps not even true. But I was soon transported out of myself. I did not know the music, had never heard it before, but there was one air that was repeated in other parts of the opera that ravished me. Some of the people were chatting even as it was sung, but it got several 'Bravo's' so I knew it must be well-known. I was sitting in a small box with Aunt and the Italian gentleman who had only bowed stiffly to me and made no conversation as we made our way into the theatre. I could not resist whispering to my aunt as the clapping died away: 'What are those words, Aunt? What is he singing?'

'Oh, it is a famous air', she said and turned to her companion to ask him. *'La rivedrà nell'estasi'*, she reported to me in a whisper. I hoped it would come back again. The tenor who sang it was quite good-looking, but it was not the man I was listening to, just the music. In the interval Count Belotti fetched ices and bowed to me — saying in Italian: 'It is a pity that Orsini is not here tonight. They say he was detained and so the understudy sings.'

I had to write to Lucy after this first visit. The impact of the music had been overpowering. Had everyone in the audience felt the same? There had been enthusiastic clapping — and yet people were talking of their own concerns in the interval and showing off their dresses and staring at others with haughty looks, whilst I just wanted to sit and hear the music again. It did not worry me this time that I did not understand the 'technique', that I knew little of Verdi, or of harmony, for the subjective impression had been so strong that all I wanted was for it to be repeated. If only music was like painting and you could stand and take your fill of it for hours motionlessly, as people did when they swooned over the cinquecento in the galleries! In the fashionable crowd, despite my feeling of rapture, or perhaps because of it, I felt an outsider in a different way. I was not aristocratic — though my aunt was accompanied by a count; I knew I was intelligent — yet I could not summon up the small-talk necessary in such a gathering. I heard it all around me, especially from the foreigners, and they were half the audience and in the dearest seats. Where was *my* society who I would know was feeling as I was? I pointed all this out to Lucy in a long letter.

I had escaped to Italy to be free of my family and to live in a freer society, but so far I had not found Zelda's acquaintances as fascinating as I'd imagined they would be. I was probably judging too early. She had been so busy with 'arrangements' that we had yet scarcely touched on her usual life. She knew *some* Italians at least, which was more than such as the Smiths did. I'd not found the Count to be quite what I'd expected either, for he seemed to be interested not so much in ideas as in talk of his investments. Oh well,

I was nobody, so nobody would care what friends I made! With this comforting thought I prepared to be bored whenever I was in company. I mentioned to Eleanor that we might go together to the opera in the cheaper seats, for I was determined to hear the music again and I did not think Zelda would raise any objection — she seemed to want to cultivate Eleanor's parents.

I had taken Eleanor to look at that *Portrait of Elenora* and she had smiled and said I was a flatterer, but not been displeased at my comparison. She and I were soon to go with Zelda and Mr and Mrs Pontraven to a reception for the new American Consul, my first real party, for I did not count the tea-drinkers. Zelda was beginning to relax a little now that she had found workmen she could trust in the matter of plaster and paint and so I managed to convey that I should be going to the opera in future with the Pontraven family. I intended to hear that air again; I had tried it out on the little pianoforte in the apartment. That week after my first visit to the opera I began to feel very happy: the combination of spring weather and the prospect of listening to more music, I suppose. I would spend some of my own money on the purchase of tickets for the opera. At the end of April we should be back at the villa and I did not want to waste my time. I was slowly getting my tongue round Italian now and had more understanding of what I heard.

The grand reception for the Consul came and went and I did not disgrace myself. It was quite easy to talk sweet nothings, though it amazed me they were taken at face value. Afterwards my aunt said: 'You did very well, Hetty. Several people asked me who you were.' This made me feel uneasy as though I had been a guest on false pretences.

These were then my first impressions of Florence before I began to go regularly to the opera with Eleanor, sitting in cheap seats, and less regularly with Zelda, sitting in expensive ones. I did not feel the Outsider when I sat in the balcony, where I need not make the sort of conversation that went on in the grander seats; did not feel myself to be such a nobody. I disliked the frivolity of others of Zelda's friends to whom I had at last been introduced — a mixture of Americans and Italians — but I also felt awkward with the 'respectable' English. Should I never fit in in any society but my own? I would prefer the champagne to the tea-urn but did not need champagne or the wearing of fashionable clothes to excite *my* senses!

They were not to play the *Masked Ball* again until the beginning of April, but we saw, or rather 'heard' *Luisa Miller* and *Rigoletto*. Eleanor also introduced me to several other young Americans of her family's acquaintance and I found them agreeable and more open in manner than the English. They found my English accent 'quaint', and I teased them about their attempts to speak Italian. When they did try, their inability to imitate the Italian accent made all they said sound so American. They did not understand you cannot *drawl*

141

Italian with your mouth closed.

But April came at last and with it *Il Ballo in Maschera* once more. This time the tenor role was to be taken by Orso Orsini, the one whom the Count had missed that first time. Zelda had decided to take me, along with two of her friends, the Countess Guccioli and Mrs Warburton, who were in fact sisters, and I could hardly refuse a seat in the stalls. We arrived rather late as the Guccioli coachman had apparently been in a brawl the night before and a replacement had had to be found. I noticed that Zelda enjoyed her friendships with people she had known for years and that they also enjoyed her company and were quite deferential to her opinions. I was presented as 'Niece' and I thought a swift glance went between the two ladies when Zelda said my name.

We arrived in our seats when the orchestra had already begun the overture — but many people did that. I heard the air weaving its way into the overture and sat down with great excitement. I had looked at the score since my first visit to the opera and had carefully studied the libretto, yet I was still of the opinion that the plots in opera were an excuse for the music and one need not take them too seriously. I knew that opera was often represented as a revolutionary art and that many a political allusion had been smuggled into an innocuous story — why, even this one had been objected to at first because a king had been killed! So I tried to forget my companions, the Countess in her white satin and ostrich feathers, and her sister in blue silk. My aunt was in plum red velvet that set off her magnificent skin and colouring — she really was a very handsome woman.

Once the scene opened I *did* forget them, for I heard a voice of such sweetness and power that prickles went down my spine. It was Orsini, a tall, dark and [I thought] handsome man with a big mouth and flashing dark eyes and much 'presence'. I waited for the air I loved, sure that this time I would love it even more. It was short and would be followed by a chorus. I shut my eyes, but at the words *La rivedrà nell'estasi* I opened my eyes again in surprise, for this time the music, beautiful as it was, seemed to meld itself to the words so entrancingly enunciated, so strongly pronounced, that I took in their real meaning which had escaped me before. Orsini sang to the end — and then the audience began to clap for him to sing it again, though the other singers were waiting. I felt tears come to my eyes — such lyricism and such strength together in one voice I had never yet heard, though by now I'd heard two or three other singers of renown from the balcony. This voice would reach there too — it would reach all over Florence, I thought, even when Orsini almost whispered, for it had such resonance and passion in its intense silver tone:

> *La rivedrà nell'estasi*
> *Raggiante di pallore*
> *E qui sonar d'amore*
> *La sua parola udra, sonar d'amore,*

O dolce notte, scendere
Tu puoi gemmata a festa
Ah! Ma la mia stella è questa
Che il ciel non ha!
Quest' è mia stella . . .

I don't remember exactly at what point my absorption in the opera and the rapture I felt at that tenor voice was interrupted by Zelda poking me in the ribs and hissing gently: 'You see that woman in the box up there with the man with an eyeglass — *she* knew your mother!'

It was such an odd thing to say for she had not spoken of Mama since my enquiry about the grave and for several minutes I had been transported to quite other feelings, but I obediently looked up at the box, knowing that the opera on stage was going to end badly with misapprehension all round.

'Who is she?' I asked, intrigued in spite of my other more intriguing feelings.

'Mrs Holroyd', she replied and then transferred her gaze to the stage as though to say — Now I have done my duty. I registered the name and saw a man lean proprietorially over her shoulder and then raise his binoculars to the stage. I saw that the theatre provided these small opera-glasses in a little niche in front of the seats, so I unhooked one myself the better to see Signor Orsini for myself before he disappeared again.

I noticed on his face the tell-tale creases at the sides of his eyes which I recognized as laughter

144

lines. He was very dark; he was comely; he was excessively sympathetic. As I watched his face it was time for his first aria of this act. His soft voice carried to every corner of the theatre, soft — and yet it was so powerful. I put down the glasses, amazed at the strength of that voice which seemed to glide so effortlessly out of the throat, and I suddenly wanted to weep. But I was sufficiently rational and sufficiently aware that I must modify my raptures; keep them to myself to luxuriate in later. I was used to hiding my feelings — I had had plenty practice in my father's house after all. But if anyone asked me what I thought, how would I be able to help myself from showing my enthusiasm?

When the interval came I followed Zelda and the Countess and Mrs Warburton to a small room where some of her friends were already drinking champagne.

'Zelda, dearest one!' and to the Count — 'At last you are back!' 'Wasn't he just too marvellous!' 'So this is your niece. How do you do? Are you enjoying our opera?'

'Yes — it's lovely —'

'Did you see La Holroyd, Zelda — and our old friend Peter?'

Zelda parried this question from a sharp-looking woman, and a man came over to join us and then some more men and another woman, and they all began to talk of themselves with an occasional: 'Wasn't he marvellous?' and then I heard — 'He'll be coming to Mathilde's farewell party next week

— are you invited?' Could they be speaking of Orso Orsini? How well did these people know him? Did he move in their circles? Did everyone find his voice had a powerful effect upon them? I was pondering this, wishing I could go somewhere quietly to hear that voice in my inmost ear, though I doubted I could recreate it, when a thin, fair man came up to Zelda. He was wearing a monocle in one of his brown eyes.

'Good evening', said Zelda politely but frostily as he came up and took her hand and kissed it. I was obviously with her, though just about to turn away with Marjory Warburton when Zelda said: 'May I present my niece — Hetty Coppen — Peter Voyle.' Good Heavens! — was this Simon's errant father?

He extended his hand to me and I shook it. 'Miss Coppen,' he said, 'I believe I had the pleasure — many years ago —' He had a queer, harsh voice.

'Hetty will not remember', said my aunt with a touch of nervousness, I thought. 'Are you staying in Florence?' she asked him.

'No, I think I shall return — home — soon,' he said.

I wanted to say, I have met your son — if that were really the case, but something stopped me. He did not look much like Simon Voyle — perhaps he was his uncle? But he reminded me of someone else. I could not think who. Not the face or the height, but something in the eyes. 'I expect we shall meet again before you go', she said, and bowed.

We were on our way to our seats when I asked her: 'Is that Simon's father?'

'Oh — yes', she said. 'We used to know him years ago, but he went to Australia.' She gave no further explanation. Mr Voyle went out of my head when Orsini appeared on stage again and I gave myself up to the ecstasy of hearing a perfect voice.

The next day and the next kept being visited by a sudden feeling of joy — there seemed to be no other word for it. 'Does Orsini sing here often?' I asked my aunt and she replied: 'Tolerably often — but he is a great favourite everywhere.' A favourite of all these smart women I thought. 'They say he will be even more famous one day — though he has not been singing long — he will join a better company — you enjoyed the opera, did you not?'

'Oh, immeasurably, Aunt', I replied, thinking I *must* find when he will sing again, I *must* hear that voice. It was perhaps strange that a voice that had sung of sad and impossible passion should yet remain in my memory as joyful. Had I been so used to feeling neither happy nor sad that the emotion aroused in me should be so sharp and strong? Though the paintings had given me feelings of quiet satisfaction, and even reverence, they had not touched me so. Only the *David* had given me an inkling of the same beauty I found in the music, and the voice that sang that music. I could not distinguish between the two now, yet the first time I had heard that opera I'd certainly wanted to hear the music again. I tried to imitate the way he had pronounced those words *'La rivedrà'* with such a swelling on the last syllable and then the soft lift of the voice towards *'nell'estasi'* and a lingering on the word. If this was not passion incarnate in a voice it was nothing. I loved, in any case, the sound of Italian, which gave an additional musicality to music itself; I had always loved sounds. I had once invented 'Mamarella' and 'Pooranna' and what were they but approximations to the sounds of Italian! It was then that I wondered — had my Mama loved an Italian and was I perhaps not my father's daughter? This would explain Papa's coldness as nothing else would. But I could not ask Zelda who saw very well that I had been seduced by a voice and from whom I wished to hide any further evidence of my infatuation. I would keep it to myself, hug it to my bosom, and if I ever met this tenor at a reception or party — and it seemed we might — would be as cool and English and bluestocking as everyone thought I was. If they were all in love with him, if 'Society' had made a pet of him — which Zelda hinted — well then I would not be one of them. He was only a man, I thought during the day. But at night I knew he was a genius and that this was the sort of man I could fall in love with if I ever loved anyone.

To Eleanor, who wanted to know how I had enjoyed my second *Ballo* I said only: 'The tenor was much better than before — I have never heard singing like it.'

'Oh, that would be Orsini', she replied. 'All the women are in love with him.'

'Really?' I answered. 'How old do you think he is?'

'About thirty I should think — last year he was only beginning, but since then he has sung all over Italy — they treat singers like princes here, you know.'

'I met a friend of my aunt, a Mr Voyle', I said, to change the subject, though I would gladly have gone on talking about Orso Orsini all day. 'Have you met him? I think I once knew his son Simon in England.'

'No, I never met a Mr Voyle', she replied.

'I thought you knew just about everyone from the English colony!'

'All those who stay, not the birds of passage, Hetty. I hope you will not be a bird of passage yourself?' She was so nice that I wished I could confess the powerful emotions that had swept through me at the sound of Orsini's voice. But I was not going to ally myself with 'all the women' — certainly not! Such feelings might also alarm Eleanor. How could I say to her, standing there by me as we paused in the square before walking back to my aunt's, that his voice had been to me like sunshine suddenly flooding a dark cave and bathing every fissure, every grain of sand — and every crevice of my soul — with a sweet golden light? I would go to hear him again in *Rigoletto* before we left for the villa and see if the magic still held.

The idea of a forbidden love, mixed up with my mother and with the story of the *Ballo*, began to haunt me. Had not Orsini been singing of a forbidden love, of the way he imagined 'She' would speak to him, when he sang that delicious aria whose very music was a *suono d'amore?*

'Oh, he is elusive, that one', said Zelda once when they were talking of a soirée to be given by another friend, the one I called the Principessa, though she was really a Countess. It meant that they would not catch him and flatter him, that he escaped their nets. I hoped she was right. But even if she were, such acquaintance with genius was not going to drop in the lap of an unknown young Englishwoman. I would have to stick to those dreams which half-shamed, half-terrified me. At least my emotions helped me to understand now the feelings of Gwendolen Harleth for her Daniel Deronda, and I finished the book feeling somehow older and sadder. Gwendolen knew her own foolishness and had no hope her adoration would be returned, but it made her a better person. I would have to content myself with that. Men did not in any case like girls who evinced passionate yearning or worship; they were foolish who wore their hearts on their sleeves. I knew all that but I could not help dreaming.

A week or two later I went with Eleanor to hear Orsini in *Rigoletto* in which he was to play the wicked Duke of Mantua. The Duke was given such lovely music to sing that one really could not believe in his wickedness. I could not help wondering whether all young virgins were so gullible whilst I sympathized with poor Gilda. When they sang on the balcony I remembered the organ-grinder outside the Littles' house in Camberwell, and when Orsini sang along with that soprano, a small woman with long fair hair, I believed in their love, for it was as sudden and impossible as I felt my own was, nurtured by music, seduced by it — mournful and ecstatic at the same time. Eleanor saw I was moved.

Next time I went to the galleries I looked for Orsini's face among the many faces painted so many years ago and caught a glimpse of it in the picture I'd liked at the very first, that portrait of *Scappi* by Francia, though Orso Orsini's face had looked happier, even as it was the cause of such heart-piercing melancholy in me. As I studied the portrait I felt my previous ignorance had changed to exhilaration for I was now seeing the painting through a haze of heightened emotion. I had not as yet drunk champagne very often but the effect had been the same, except that Orsini affected me more strongly than wine!

By the time I went to my first 'society' party I felt both younger and older. I was elated and excited — what if Orsini were to be there? There was just a slender chance and it kept me going and enabled me to hold my own, until I realized he was not to be there after all, and calmed down.

The weather had suddenly turned warm and we were to move back in a few days to the Villa

Fortuna — or 'de Vere' — where Max was to join us for Easter. Before we did, something quite extraordinary happened.

I had long wanted to see the parts of the city where the ordinary Italians lived. It was not enough to talk to servants and shopkeepers if I wanted to understand Italy. Accordingly, I had decided to go out one morning at dawn before the house was astir, to walk over the bridge to the San Frediano district. I managed the first part of this adventure, my thoughts far away for once from music or singers, and leant on the parapet of a bridge looking at the sky that was all pink and gold. The soft early spring air was on my face and the water was a pale blue, reflecting the cloudless sky. Then my attention was distracted by another dawn walker who came to stand near me. I hoped I was not going to be accosted, for it was not the done thing for a young woman to go out walking alone, though all the shop girls I saw hurrying across the bridge made that journey alone every day. I was wearing my old cape and skirt, for I wanted to look as inconspicuous as possible, and I was carrying a book of poems, intending to look for the Brownings' house when I crossed the bridge. Nobody knew I had gone out and I hoped to be back for breakfast. It was going to be such a lovely day and I already felt I should miss the city when we went to the villa.

'It is a beautiful dawn', a voice said to me in Italian and I turned, half-annoyed, half-glad, to practise my language.

I could not believe my eyes, for Orso Orsini was standing there in an old coat, hatless! I was sure it was him. My heart leapt in my chest and I had to swallow before I could reply. I must not let him know I knew who he was. I felt instinctively that he wanted to remain incognito.

'It is indeed beautiful', I replied in my best Italian. 'But the whole city is lovely — the place is as interesting as its paintings, I think.'

'You are not Italian.' he said, disappointingly. But of course young Florentine maidens would not go out alone at dawn, or find their own city beautiful.

'I am English, signor', I said. 'I am on my way to look at the Casa Guidi before the crowds arrive.' I showed him the book.

'You are not afraid to walk alone? Ladies are usually accompanied by their servants', he said.

'I do not have servants', I said. 'Not of my own. And I am used to walking in London, though I have never seen dawn over the Thames.'

He laughed. 'Then I will leave you to walk in peace', he said and smiled. I did not want him to go — oh, how I did not! — but what could I say to detain him? He said *'Addio'* and walked away and I turned back to my perusal of the sky and water. I found I was trembling and no longer desirous to see the Casa Guidi. Instead I walked on in a dream and eventually found myself near the Pitti Palace, but it was shut. Perhaps Orsini had gone to the Boboli Gardens for a stroll? I could hardly follow him there, though I wanted to. I looked down at Dante's 'cursed ditch' near where the poet had met his Beatrice. Life was no longer like that. Your heart's desire did not worship you from afar; it was women who seemed to do the worshipping. I walked back home just in time for breakfast. Zelda was chatting to Rosa, who was doing her hair whilst my aunt supped her coffee. I had spoken to him! If one day I grew to be an old lady I could tell my grandchildren that the great tenor Orsini had spoken to me on a bridge in Florence.

The next day dawned rainy, but Zelda was still decided to move ourselves and our belongings to the villa at the end of the week.

'There is a letter for you', she said when I knocked at her bedroom door to see if there was anything she needed. 'Drop in at Doney's for some cakes if you don't mind, Hetty — Mrs Warburton is coming to tea. Read your letter first — they don't open till ten.'

I slit open the letter which was from my sister Cara. I recognized her large garlanded hand. How far away she seemed. What would she think of her sister dreaming of impossibilities? I scanned it quickly. Apparently Simon Voyle was staying at East Wood again for a week or two. I was surprised.

'Aunt', I said. 'That man you introduced me to at the opera — Mr Voyle — you said he was Simon's father?'

'Yes — but he did not bring him up, Hetty — why?'

'Just that Simon is staying at my father's again. I did not think they would want him back. He is not a pleasant young man. My sister writes to me about it.' She turned round from her toilette.

'Your father can always send him away', she said rather coldly. 'The boy hasn't had much family life — that is why he is — awkward.'

'Why does his father not receive him?' I asked her. 'He said he was going to England soon.'

'Oh, yes — I believe he did. Well, I'm sure he will get in touch with Simon once he is there.'

'But why does Papa entertain Simon, Aunt? I don't understand it at all. He was unpleasant to Cara and to Alice — he even teased poor little Hannah you know. Oh I wish Cara could come and stay in Italy with me', I added impulsively.

But it was Max who arrived the next day, dear Max who had grown since we last saw him and who was beginning to look like an English gentleman — until he opened his mouth and expressed himself in perfect Italian to the 'natives'.

'Dear Hetty — isn't this ripping? — I've seen your little sister you know — did she write to tell you?'

Cara had mentioned this to me, but her letter was more of a lament about her boring days at home and the nuisance of having Simon Voyle visit.

'Did she say that Simon Voyle was staying at East Wood?' I asked him.

'No — I saw her two weeks ago with your ad-

155

mirable governess — your papa does not even know we have met. Isn't Cara a beautiful creature?'

It was no use arguing with him in this mood, but I felt worried about Cara and puzzled at the hold young Voyle had over my father. There was something extremely fishy in it all.

When Max had gone out that evening to visit an old friend whom he had known from a little boy, Zelda said to me, without preamble: 'You asked me once why your Papa never mentioned your Mama's name to you, Hetty.' I waited, sat down. We were alone together, about to play a game of cards, for Zelda loved any game and I was the only partner till Max condescended to play with her.

'You are going to tell me that my Mama had a lover — and that I am not Papa's daughter', I said before I could help myself for that was what I had been thinking ever since the opera evening.

'No! No! Hetty — of course not! Your Papa is *ashamed* to talk about her with you. One day you will know the whole story.'

I thought of the guilt I'd seen on his face on the day of my birthday.

'He found a "substitute" very quickly, Hetty. They married as soon as your Mama died.'

'You mean he knew Ella when my Mama was ill here?'

'Precisely — Ella. You went back to them with Gregory who had been sent to see his Mama. You were already with her. We still hoped for a cure, but it was not to be. He lost no time in marrying again.'

'Oh, I see', I said feebly, not at all sure that I did. Did she mean that Mamarella was already living with my Papa before he was free to remarry? Living with a man who had an invalid wife? It seemed sordid, but I understood that if it were true he would not want anyone to know about it. Gregory probably knew, but did not think it suitable knowledge for me. 'Your father is, in a manner of speaking, "indebted" to Peter Voyle', she went on. 'So he feels he must help him out with Simon.' She did not pursue what connection there might be between this indebtedness and my mother. I would rather like to have had a romantic Italian father, but I believed my aunt when she denied the possibility and she did not allude to the matter again. About Peter Voyle too she said no more. Yet they had seemed to know each other well. About the whereabouts of my mother's grave I knew she would still be uncommunicative. I intended to discover it for myself.

But I tried to put all these sad thoughts of the past away from me for I was going to enjoy a perfect Italian summer, even if I had to repress my imagination, filled as it was with a growing passion for an Italian.

8

When the time came for our move to the villa I was in that curious state of mind which is the result of too much daydreaming, a mixture of voluptuous sadness and excitement. I could now hardly believe that I had actually spoken to Orso Orsini on the bridge. How I longed to hear him sing again. I knew I was only one of many who found his voice entrancing, but I nurtured the sweet illusion that I alone appreciated and understood every nuance of his caressingly silver tones. I knew I ought to stifle these foolish fancies of mine, which were partly for a voice, partly for a personality which I sensed was unlike any I had ever met. What better than a change of scene to put me back in my right mind!

Aunt was ready to entertain. She had always entertained at the villa, she told me, rather than in Florence where her apartment was only large enough to give small intimate parties. I decided that once at the villa I was going to make the effort to 'grow up', to try to become more worldly. I might possibly learn more about my own nature.

I was not prepared for the enormous difference the season had made to the gardens and grounds. It hardly seemed the same place, now that spring had brought all its flowers and scents and foliage to delight me. When we arrived, dirty and dusty from our short carriage journey, the new maid, Maddalena, with us, the fountain was already playing. Zelda's 'organizing' had paid dividends. We now had a gardener, a coachman, a groom, a cook, and two maids of all work. The groom was to deputize as footman when necessary [footman!], and the coachman, Giuseppe, was to be butler, since he was married to the cook, Serafina. The kitchens and the servants' quarters were on the garden floor of the villa, not up under the eaves in the attics as they would have been in an English country house, and I often heard the servants singing as I walked in the gardens.

I occasionally used to wonder why my Aunt Zelda wanted me in Italy with her at all, for what could I, with my English gaucherie, add to her existence? I came to the tentative conclusion that a niece entrusted to her care gave her a respectable air, though why she needed to look respectable I was not sure. My rather ordinary attributes also set off her own immaculate dress and bearing. She was a sophisticated woman, but not without flaws of character. I imagined that she thought I might help her if I became acquainted with the younger members of families with whom she might wish to be intimate, acquaintance that would naturally culminate in more visits. For a woman who had as far as I knew hardly entertained or visited when in Kent, she was a veritable tornado of sociability. She was to have her At Home on Thursdays, and

Max and I would be expected to help her in the business of hosting it.

In his seventeenth year Max was no longer the little spindly-legged boy I had first known, but a tall, nice-looking youth with dark hazel eyes. He was still a little too thin, still inclined to irony in his conversation, had a manner far older than his years, but he was good fun. What Max did not know about furnishings and bibelots and statues and paintings was not worth knowing. How had he acquired such extensive knowledge? I asked him when we were arranging Zelda's reception room, placing the silver and the flowers in strategic positions to impress the first visitors.

'How do *you* know all you do about books?' he asked me in return.

I considered. 'It's because they interest me', I said finally. 'I've never found it an effort to know about poetry and novels.'

'Precisely', he said. 'You were born like that. *I* was born with perfect taste!' I laughed with him.

'Cara doesn't take much interest in books', I said. I was eager to find out what further impression my sister had made on Max. He had said only that she was beautiful.

'No — she's not a bit like you', was all he said then.

Zelda told me that 'real' Florentine society, that of aristocrats both Italian and British, contained only about a dozen *principessas* and *contessas* and honourables, with twice that number of courtiers, young men from great old families who were passed over now that the Tuscan court was no longer the seat of power. They were there to dance attendance on some of the ladies who never visited lesser mortals. But the men were welcomed in slightly lower ranks of society, such as ours, and among some of the Americans, who were mostly, but not all, rich.

'Many of the Americans do not bother at all with the Italians', Zelda explained. '*We* get to know the more interesting ones. Most of the English too keep to themselves — only English like ourselves care to know Italians.'

'The English who "keep to themselves" — you would call them "middle-class" — like the Smiths?' I asked, only half-innocently. 'They wouldn't be invited here, I don't suppose?'

'Oh, I might invite them, Hetty, but they don't have villas outside the city. There are several professional men, and some married ladies and widows — even some divorced ladies — whom I entertain, since they live up here in the hills.'

'Mrs Wilberforce is divorced, is she not?' I enquired.

'I believe so', replied Zelda, not inviting further discussion.

Later I discovered that divorced ladies' daughters could not be presented at the English court and so their Mamas came to Italy with them. Some of our friends had, I suspected, come down in the world, but as I had never been up in it I held them in no less respect.

'Some of the English are like us', Max explained. 'They prefer Florence to stuffy old England — soldiers or retired Navy people — they can be quite fun — there's a doctor or two as well, and some writers, artists . . .'

'Musicians?' I enquired hopefully. 'They come to your mother's salon too?'

'Oh, yes — but there is also a sculptor who never sculpts and a lady who spends her time copying Michaelangelo —'

'You make them sound like the worthy Smiths —'

'No — some of them belong to *la vraie Bohème*,' he said gaily. 'Mama's real friends are not usually poor, Hetty, but I believe there are quite a few talented people around here who are not *rich*, whom I expect we shall meet.'

I wondered how much he remembered of his early life here — he seemed to have it all nicely sorted out. Max was never rude to people — he treated them all the same and did not seem to worry about the social degrees of our various guests. But you could never tell when he was being ironical.

It seemed to me that, whatever she said, my aunt preferred rich people and was happy to entertain and have among her friends a contessa or two who might prefer her company to that of 'real' society. I knew the names of the most famous hostesses — two titled Italians and two titled Englishwomen — and I imagined that Zelda hoped to be invited to their parties eventually but was playing it cool. She had been a long time away from Florence and would, if I understood her rightly, proceed carefully and without too much ostentation to re-establish herself. I knew that one or two of her old friends had died, but that Mrs Warburton and her sister, Countess Guccioli, were very old acquaintances. It would not be Zelda's way to dazzle with displays of over-spending but to gather a few discreetly fashionable women — and men — so that the word would spread that she was worth cultivating. Of course she had money too, though I was never sure how much. She was careful with it, I knew that, even a little cheeseparing when it came to servants' wages. But it was not my place to criticize one of the few people who had ever shown any interest in me. Aunt was giving me opportunities, and it was up to me to sink or swim. She was not exactly my 'guardian', had no more responsibility towards me than the aunt who had befriended her dead sister's daughter. I had the impression though that she would not have cultivated me if I'd been stupid. She might speak dispassionately of the most glittering society, but I was sure she'd enjoy it if offered. I don't think I gave the impression of a clinging poor relation, though I might give her the opportunity of appearing generous in public. The awful suspicion occasionally troubled me that Zelda wished to match me with some rich young count — but then my common sense told me that I was not that sort of girl, did not look like a conventional young charmer and never would.

Cara on the other hand . . .

A few evenings after our arrival Zelda was talking about the artists who lived in some of the villas which were dotted all over the nearby countryside. 'You must meet Jacobsen', she said to Max. 'He has a great "nose" for the genuine — you can still find bits of medieval frescoes in people's barns you know', she went on, turning to me. 'And Max might help him to catalogue his collection.'

Max looked not at all gratified, but said: 'Yes, Mama,' in a meek voice, winking at me. I thought, Max would be clever at scenting hypocrisy or the fake, in people or ornaments. I trusted his judgment instinctively, more than I trusted Zelda's.

'Hetty has been telling me about the operas she has heard', he said with a mischievous look at me — 'Are we not to have some musicians at your receptions, Mama — they tell me that musicians and singers are great flirts and good as guests at parties . . .'

'Oh, all the women here adore singers', said Zelda as if she were not one of them. My heart missed a beat.

'Now, Mama, we are to have tea and sandwiches from Doneys, and Marsala later, is that right?' Max went on.

They went on to discuss our first At Home, Zelda saying that she hoped to give a few dinner parties too when she was settled.

'Our first party will be just to test the water', said Max to me later. 'I shall die of boredom if

I have to talk about frescoes with some of those old frauds.'

As it turned out our first reception was a great success though no musicians were among the guests, and I spent some of the time talking to Eleanor and other Americans in the gardens as it was such a lovely day. Various other guests drifted out and I was invited to the picnics which were being planned for May. Zelda seemed pleased with the arrangements since one result was that we were all invited to a large garden party the following week at the Villa Bodini which was owned by one of those ladies who are half in half out of 'Society'. 'Because she is rich and also because she is divorced and does not give a fig', said Zelda.

Max said: 'Will Eleanor be here?' and I thought he must be a little smitten with her.

'No, the Pontravens do not visit Mrs Paravicini', answered Zelda. We seemed, I thought, precariously balanced between the respectable and the faintly raffish.

Spring was suddenly turning into summer and not only ilexes with their sea-green leaves were smothering our property now when you looked at it from a distance. The first roses opened, and lilies, when the lemon blossom had fallen. Magnolias, yuccas, oleanders, followed them and there were dense thickets of myrtle, the pale pink stars of banksia, and clematis climbing everywhere. As the sun grew warmer the scents were indescribably lovely to one who had had as yet few hot summers in her life. When the flowers opened the butterflies came in all hues and every morning when I looked out of my second-floor window over the garden, the sun's light was like a benison, and the smell of summer before it passed its zenith as entrancing to me even as music. I used to make my breakfast of coffee and bread with Max sitting by the stone pond that was now filled with goldfish, and little frogs used to hop out of the marble basins that fed it. There were other flowers whose names I did not know and Max did not either — his expertise did not stretch to 'Nature'. I wanted to paint it all, do something with all this beauty which seemed to flow over into me. Max came into his own indoors when he showed me the things Zelda had collected, now brought out of dusty high cupboards; miniatures which he said were genuine, old china with gold and blue patterns, some drawings acquired years ago at auctions which he said were priceless. When I was enthusing over a nightingale heard from the balcony he was indoors advising his mother as to the colours that should be painted on the walls that had not yet been done: pale green, he said, for what had once been the ballroom (and stretched over half the ground floor, at present used for receptions); gold and pale blue for the dining-room when it was restored. He would point out to me the Louis Quinze furniture that had been shrouded for all the years of their absence, and the Venetian writing-table she had purchased when he was only a little boy because he said it was 'pretty'. It was my job to gather flowers and arrange them, and this I loved. When

Max enthused over ceilings or furniture I would go into rhapsodies over the flowers. I used to hum the airs I had heard Orsini sing, though I had tried not to betray to Max my passion for that voice in particular.

'Mama has no tapestries — it pains her', he would say. 'My Papa once had some', and I would only half take in his descriptions of past glories. Max would have been an inexhaustible guide to my early days in Florence, but I was glad he had been absent and I'd discovered things for myself, even if my knowledge would never match his.

The day came for the grand reception at Villa Bodini. 'From 3 to 6' it said on the silver-bordered invitation. That party was to be a turning-point in many aspects of my life, though at the time I thought only of what it meant to fall in love, and whether you could love a voice, detached from the man who 'owned' it.

There was already a large crowd when we arrived shortly after half past three. Italians, Zelda explained, never arrived on time. These first arrivals were mostly American and British, and I had already met some of them. Mrs Warburton came in with us and went into raptures over the banks of flowers that were heaped behind the long table at the far end of a sumptuous salon. They looked like hothouse flowers. On the tables were silver teapots in honour of the English, and bottles of wine on ice — the sparkling wine they brought over from the Emilian Plain, Zelda said. And there were silver salvers of tiny sandwiches, and pastries looking too beautiful to eat, and early fruits, and ices of all colours and textures. I eschewed the wine at such an early hour and took a plate of goodies. I looked out at the garden which stretched out from the long loggia windows into the distance — a lawn like an English one that must have taken half the water supply of the commune to keep green. Our hostess, Mrs Paravicini, was of mixed American and Swiss descent and her dead husband had been Italian, I learned. After being introduced to her and having made a few polite remarks, I was glad to go out under the long pergola where a few others were already chatting, and several new arrivals joined us. I saw young men with beards and long hair who I thought must be painters, and one or two superannuated poets, old men who were apt to demand a great deal of listening from you. There was a British admiral, Max said, and some young American men — none of Eleanor's friends. A faded English couple looked as if they would have fitted in more suitably at the Smiths, but Max whispered to me that the lady on the arm of her elderly companion was not actually married to him, though she shared his home, he having another wife in England — 'And many debts', added my cousin. I wondered if Max approved of a quartet of two young Italian's and two young women who sat near us, the girls fanning themselves dramatically. They looked like actresses. Then I thought I had better go back into the *salotto* and mingle a little, or Zelda would think I was not doing my duty.

It was then that I heard his voice. I had just decided to eat an ice and drink a little wine — it was now five o'clock. The voice was saying something in reply to the tones of rapture in which an English lady past her first youth had fluted: 'Ah, maestro — such an honour!' and then there were more voices from ladies in a little knot round a man who turned as I turned, and I saw Orso Orsini, dark and glowing in the midst of this bevy of beauties.

'This is *the* singer, I believe', said Max at my elbow. 'They say he is a great flirt and loves being "adored" ', he added, with a malicious glint in his eye.

'They are certainly adoring him', I said, for these society ladies were clustered round him like bees round a honeypot and Orsini did not look displeased to be petted. Why should not such a man be frivolous and enjoy himself receiving the adulation which was his due? I said to myself — but secretly I'd have liked him to look disdainful — serious. What was the real man like? Was Talent, or Genius, so different from the Ordinary that those who possessed it carried on their private lives differently? You might be a great singer and have little to say for yourself, I thought. I followed Max out again with my ice on a little silver tray. We sat down again and a few of the younger ladies who had come with their Mamas were introduced to us by Zelda who then disappeared again with the Countess.

'You have to work very hard to be such a good

169

singer', I said to Max, to show I was not a fool.

'They say Orsini comes from the People', said my cousin, licking his spoon and looking at me with that penetrating glance of his which I knew of old. I did not want to be mocked by him so I said: 'If you have great talent I suppose your fame may go to your head?'

'Why? The English are always worrying about "getting above themselves" — "showing off" — I see no harm in it', he said.

'Neither do I', I replied. 'I would not like to be famous myself — but it is worse to be a failure, isn't it — like some of the other people here?'

'Failures? My dear Hetty — of whom can you be thinking? The old poetaster there is an ornament in society — they wouldn't know what to do without him at their parties. The admiral was actually a successful admiral! Ladies, of course, don't have to be successes except in the matter of small talk and flower-arranging.'

I saw he was teasing me. He liked calling me a bluestocking, and his poking fun at some of my radical notions was not serious. Max liked people who had something to say for themselves and I certainly had that, sometimes to my own discomfiture. The little crowd round Orsini had now moved to the lawns and others had joined in the worship.

'Come, Hetty — I must introduce you to the Contessa Belleza's nephew', said Zelda's voice bearing down on us. I put down my ice and followed her towards another knot of guests. The party was crowded, but there was plenty of space and one did not have to push through the wall of humanity as one did in the galleries or as Zelda had told me you did at London gatherings. 'Oh dear — he has gone', said Zelda. We were now nearer Orsini and his worshippers. One of them caught sight of my aunt and came up.

'Have you talked to him?' she said excitedly. 'A divine man — I suppose you heard him this season?' They both moved towards the singer, I in their wake. He turned then and I stared at him. I could not help it, though I felt foolish.

'May I introduce Mrs Zelda de Vere?' said her friend to him and he shook hands.

Then: 'My niece', said my aunt shortly and introduced me. She was not the sort of woman to swoon over artists or singers herself. Would he recognize me, and if he did would he say so? I bowed to him and he smiled, but looked a little puzzled. The women were all talking at once now. Then, 'Did you see the Casa Guidi?' he asked, turning to me. I started with astonished pleasure. He had remembered! My heart once more seemed to leap out of my chest. Now was my chance to impress myself further on his memory — and yet I scorned to simper and look adoring.

'No, I went to the Pitti instead. Somehow the Brownings no longer fitted the morning', I replied at random.

'I so loved your Duke', said a feminine voice to whom he turned and bowed.

'I am to sing for my supper here, you know', he said.

He was to *sing*? Here? I could not stop my excitement betraying itself in my eyes.

'You thought I only went for walks?' he said to me. The woman looked cross and uncomprehending.

I did not answer his question but said: 'I preferred Riccardo in *Un Ballo* to the Duke of Mantua.'

'Ah', he said. 'A nicer man, yes?'

We were talking in Italian and for once I seemed to find the words, though I felt so dry-mouthed I don't know how I enunciated them. The American ladies there did not speak it and began to speak among themselves, but the other ladies who did drew him cleverly into their conversation. I could not help looking at him, feasting myself upon his face when he was looking away. Max came up to me.

'He is going to sing later', I said. Orsini was now talking about Verdi and the Risorgimento. The ladies were looking blank.

Max giggled. 'Opera is a revolutionary art', he said, just loud enough for Orsini to hear.

The singer turned. '*È vero.*' There was something a little similar in their eyes, I thought. Both looked mocking, and reserved something of themselves. But Orsini was used to adulation and so it did not matter what he said, for everyone wanted to be able to boast they had met him and spoken to him. For that it was essential that they say some-

172

thing piquant themselves: '*I* said to him', and his doubtless charming reply. Just then our hostess came up, and bore him away. I had felt I could get on very well with him as a person, singer or no. Perhaps the singer *was* something quite apart from the man — but I liked the man too.

Orsini was not to sing quite yet. For this another *salotto* was being prepared, with a grand piano on which several tall vases of pale lilies were placed. Max and I peeped in to look. Orsini had disappeared. I felt a little like a child at a party. That was how I would be seen, I supposed. I wished I could say something to him that was arresting and fascinating. But possibly such a man only knew women to seduce them, and there were plenty around — taller, more assured, and more beautiful than myself.

I considered this as we passed into the villa again and sat down with Zelda and her friends, who were now exchanging gossip of the highest order. My aunt looked quite at home. He had looked passionate, I thought, a passionate man. Well, naturally he would be. You could not sing as he did if your veins ran with milk and water. There had been laughter in his eyes, but shrewdness too.

There were several other men now around us: in their thirties, men to whom I was introduced by Max, whom they all appeared to recognize . . . some were good-looking, most were easy mannered; not one of them was Orsini, and they bored me, though I tried not to let it show.

I was determined not to make a fool of myself.

173

Who was I that He should notice me? But he had remembered our meeting on the bridge! — I could treasure that at least. I wandered out on the terrace again, suddenly wanting to be alone and away from the hubbub. Then I heard from a window next to the loggia a liquid, lyrical line of music — he was trying out his voice. I lingered. One of the ladies joined me. 'They say he is off to St Petersburg and Madrid this summer', she said.

'Like all the best singers, I suppose he has the entrée to society?' I said in my best intelligent brisk 'English' tone of voice.

'Oh yes, my dear — but more in Italy than at home, you know. Our own court is not exactly one for artistes.'

I looked at her more closely. She was a lady in her early forties with a sad-looking, pretty face and a pleasant manner of speech.

'Are you not coming to listen? You *are* Mrs de Vere's niece, are you not? I once knew your mother', she went on. I thought she would say, as I had already heard a few times, 'Such a dear creature — such a pity', but she did not, added only: 'You do not look like her. Your cousin has more a look of Maria, I think.'

'Here he is', I said as Max appeared from the loggia saying: 'Come along, Hetty — they are soon going to begin!' The lady smiled. Max bowed to her. 'Mrs Holroyd', he said, and kissed her hand. He made to introduce me, but she raised her hand in what looked like a little benediction, and I went in with my cousin. I was eager to see Orso again

174

— but I affected a slight indifference.

Once in the music-room and among the rest of the party, who were seated on little gold chairs that looked as though they would bend under the weight of some of the older gentlemen, one or two of whom had their eyes closed, I found a seat at the side with Max and waited. Mrs Holroyd had found a seat near the admiral.

Orsini came into the room with great aplomb, bowed, dusted an imaginary speck of dust from his collar and announced, in his light voice, so light that you wondered later where the resonance came from, that he would sing first an aria from *Luisa Miller*. His accompanist stood, bowed, was applauded, and then silence fell. *Quando le sere al placido* was the aria he sang first, in which the hero is under a misapprehension that the heroine does not love him. I shut my eyes, wanting to detach the voice from the surroundings, from the glitter and the guests and the atmosphere of worldly charm. His voice, which I realized he was adapting to the room — for he could have sung three times more loudly — floated over us. It had such richness that voice, such reined-in power controlling the sweetness, and yet the impression was one of naturalness, of simplicity. It soared up at the end of the aria and lay among the gilded putti of the ceiling and there was a silence which I did not want broken. It was soon broken though by claps and bravos and requests for more — and he came back and sang some airs I had never heard before — from Donizetti, I later discovered. First,

Com'è gentil that enraptured me with its silky sadness, and then from *La Favorita*. Max poked me in the ribs — '*Magnifico!*' he exclaimed. I smiled, for it was, and that voice had to be shared. I wished he would sing *La rivedrà*, but one could not have everything. Shortly after his last encore he was off, some said to Paris, some to Russia. Mrs Holroyd was nowhere to be seen and we left at half past six, Italians being just as dilatory in their leave-taking as they were in their arrival. I had much to think about.

It had been an exciting afternoon, but I was glad I had not known that Orsini was to be there. His appearance had been so sudden that I had had no time to feel nervous. What did I feel about him now? As I had when I heard his voice for the first time? No, even more intensely. The man fascinated me — and yet I was glad that he was to go away, that he would not be round some corner in the city or at some villa soirée, so that wherever I went I should hope to find him. Let him go and flirt with Russian noblewomen or Spanish grandees' wives if that was what he liked. Yet could such a voice belong to anyone but a superior example of mankind? Even if, as I heard a gentleman say to another about Verdi — 'It is music for the *bordello!*' [He had not known I was in earshot.] I had time now to elaborate my ideas of Orso Orsini's personality. There is always some mystery as to what attracts us first of all when we are young and impressionable — and even goes on attracting some people all their lives. Others might speak of him — and did — and of other singers too, though of none with the hushed awe with which they spoke of Orsini as a new phenomenon.

I saw that he was only at the beginning of real fame. He would be idolized, and I might be one of his idolators, but I would have preferred to know him in an ordinary way. If I worshipped, it would be at a private shrine — and I vowed again that I would not make myself foolish. Thinking it over as the days passed I realized that I was able to feel far more detached about the other young men to whom my aunt presented me. I could be natural towards them because I could never love them. I was in love with a voice and there was no space for another voice in my ear, so I could even give a passable imitation of worldliness since it cost me nothing.

My other interests did not pale into insignificance because of my preoccupation with Orsini. No, everything seemed more worthwhile since it existed in a world that also contained him.

Max said once, in his own worldly way, of a painter with whom all the women were in love, another 'charmer' — 'Oh — all these men have families at home, you know — wives who look after them and give them a tisane when they come home with indigestion. They know about the way their husbands carry on but they have the "real" man and his children.'

I thought, great dazzling ladies could carry on *affaires du coeur*, not young nonentities like myself.

177

Dreams would have to be enough for me, dreams and other burgeoning ideas culled from my reading. Was there a conflict between my passionate adherence to these 'ideas' and my equally passionate idealization of Orso Orsini? I hoped not.

Gradually, as I talked with some of the people, chiefly men who knew Zelda, and began to be invited out on my own account, with Max as an odd sort of chaperone, I saw that there were two sides to my nature. They did not at present conflict, but they were a stark contrast. That a young woman who had read John Stuart Mill's *Subjection of Women* should feel that this subject was no longer such a pressing concern was disquieting! Did passion, when it came into play in the lives of men and women, mean that common sense and reason took second place? I had read of ladies who chafed under the yoke of marriage and were angry at the position of women in society and I had thought I'd be one of them. Yet a glance from a pair of dark eyes and a thrilling voice were enough to unsettle me . . . Between the independence which I had planned for, and the love I felt already in me, there was a deep chasm. Choosing between solitude — when I felt most myself — and joining that frivolous but not unintelligent society would inevitably lead to conflict: Italy and beauty had too much power to seduce my northern soul. I longed to experience passion more than I wished to read all the books in the world. Yet I owed the books, the ideas, the radical thinkers — and Lucy Little — a debt. It was they who had set me out on my individual road and I should be unfaithful to my highest ideals if I allowed myself to be seduced by sun and music — and that voice, those eyes — Oh, I don't suppose I put it to myself quite so clearly that summer, but the realization was there. One day I might have to choose. Women who loved were so easily ruined; I knew that. Only those who put self-interest first survived, even in Florence, even among the rich and easy-going. The Contessa and Mrs Warburton, perhaps Mrs Holroyd, certainly the actresses, and, who knew, even my Aunt Zelda, had had at one time to look out for themselves. My poor Mama, I began to think, must have died from love; some lover had lured her to Italy, though Zelda denied it. Maybe I inherited her nature? Life was easier for men. They were the seducers, not the seduced. I knew of all these things, though I had not been brought up to know of them. If 'love' was just a game people played, I'd lose it, for I would always have my feelings as forfeit.

I learned from one of Zelda's friends that Orso Orsini was regarded as a fascinating mystery and that nobody knew if he was married. He was gossiped about a good deal — but I pretended not to listen.

One hot day in June Max and I were talking in the garden under the shade of the ilexes. 'You should not want to be a man, Hetty. You would have to work for your living unless you were rich and you would have to find some heiress to marry if you did not want to work!'

'I shall work, Max,' I said. 'I want independence!'

'And who is more dependent than a governess?' he enquired.

I was silent.

'And, you know, if you were a man you would not have all those nice young men paying you attention!'

I would not be able to dream of Orsini, I thought. That would indeed be sad!

I laughed, and Max suddenly began to talk of his father. 'I was only a baby when he died', he said. 'I wish I had known him.'

I thought, my brother Gregory lost his Mama, and Max lost his father — and I lost my Mama too. Did these events exert a power over our futures? Had my Mama loved my cold father once? Had *he* loved *her*? How little we knew of what was to be our fate. I shivered. I had managed to assimilate my past by making another world, a little cocoon for myself, from my studies with Lucy Little, and now Italy and excitement were changing me. I did not want to die young like Mama or be widowed like Zelda or divorced like the Countess. I did not want to fear the future. But would I be for ever consumed with yearning for an impossible pair of brilliant black eyes and an angelic voice that seemed to be speaking to me alone?

We had been on several picnics and I'd been introduced to the Contessa Belleza's nephew, and the Countess Guccioli's son Bruno, and I'd talked to several young men — and women — and yet they all seemed unreal when I heard a phrase, a snatch of music, in my mind's ear. I could not will it to come; it would arrive without warning and I'd stop to listen to it as though I'd had a hallucination. However hard I tried, I had to listen to it when I 'heard' it.

Max was often surrounded at these parties by a bevy of sixteen-year-old Italian beauties who knew of his fortune. He was always unvaryingly polite to them, but he knew that it was not for his looks or his personality or even his brains that they flocked but only, dutifully, because their Mamas had told them to. He had little small talk of the banal kind, was apt to launch for fun into a long description of some painting or view, and they would look discomfited and a little frightened. But then he was so charming and made them laugh when he imitated the English accent of his compatriots when they tried to get their tongues round Italian. Yet I sensed that Max was not especially happy. He would leave Westminster School soon and need have no money worries, but I thought he was looking for a direction to his life. I suggested he might study for the Bar as my brother had, but he held up his hands in horror. 'And yet you are English too', I said. 'Your parents are both English — you will not want to live in Italy all your life?'

'Who knows, Hetty? I imagine that my expertise — about which you flatter me so — would be of more use to the London auction houses than here in Italy. But can you see me going to work every day with a furled umbrella?'

He was so grown up this cousin of mine, such a man of the world.

9

Every night before I fell asleep I tried to recall Orso Orsini's face, but just as his voice came to me only in involuntary snatches I could not put together his features behind my eyes when I wanted to.

One afternoon, a week or two after he had sung at Mrs Paravicini's at home, it was too hot even under the trees and I was reading in my chamber with the shutters half-closed. I loved to hear the sounds from the garden, the bees and the little creak of the cicadas, and savoured my solitude. Suddenly I heard my aunt's carriage coming up the lane across the fields. She had gone to Florence that morning to order delicacies from Doney's for we were soon to entertain once more. This time however she did not expect many guests since several of her friends had gone north on account of the heat; one or two were by Lake Como where it was deliciously cool.

When I heard Zelda come into the vestibule I almost went down to greet her, but was too lazy, and disinclined to move until the cool of the evening. I listened to her footsteps on the marble with only half an ear for I was immersed in a new book that one of the English colony had lent me —

Mornings in Florence by Mr Ruskin. I found it rather hard-going, though necessary to the reduction of my ignorance. Such books were rather likely to disintegrate into daydreaming. Italy had changed me; I felt less driven, less inclined to work, more content to enjoy life as it came. Perhaps it was just the weather.

But after a few minutes Rosa knocked at my door. 'Mrs de Vere says will you come down to the *salotto*', she said. 'Were you asleep, Miss Hetty? There's news from home, she says.' My heart missed a beat. I would forget 'home' for days on end, but now suddenly I felt guilty, and hoped the news was not bad. Alice and Miss Little kept me up to date, and even Cara wrote — in fact I'd had a letter from her only that week and been rather disturbed by it, but put it to the back of my mind when I should have time to think it over.

Zelda was still in her carriage clothes and her hat with its plumes lay on the sofa beside her. A letter written on thick white paper was lying on the table by her. I recognized Papa's usual writing-paper.

'Your father has written', she began. Oh, please God not to ask me to return, was my only thought. Zelda glanced at me and then took up the paper. 'He wants your sister Cara to come here to stay with you for a time', she announced swiftly and then looked at me for my reaction. Relief that nobody was ill or that I was going to be asked to return was quickly followed by surprise and, I must admit, a feeling of annoyance. I could not believe that Papa would want Cara to join me and I knew I could not wholeheartedly welcome my beautiful sister to a place I had made mine. I was ashamed as soon as I had the thought. Zelda was looking at me a little warily and I detected a certain excitement in her voice when she said: 'Well, what do you think of that?'

I gathered my wits; I was not entirely surprised, for Cara's letter had told me that the unpleasant Simon Voyle was still staying at East Wood. Lucy Little and Alice had written of this too in their last missives — sent together to save postage and probably as a sort of exercise for my little sister, who would not have written without some external encouragement. Lucy had mentioned that Simon had told her he was now a partner in some import-export business, adding as she knew only I would see the letter: 'I think that young man *loves* money'. Alice's letter had been even more frank, for at twelve she was young enough not to hide behind fine phrases. 'Papa has no time for him but Mama lets Felix play with him — I think everyone is falling in love with Cara — the butcher's boy whistles when he sees her and Simon compliments her all the time but she says he is a nuisance . . .'

I looked directly at my aunt — 'Is it because Simon Voyle is staying at East Wood?' I asked her. She knew my feelings about the untrustworthiness of that young man and I imagined she shared them, but she had never liked long discussions of character or motive as Max and I did.

She looked down at the letter again, then looked up at me and sighed.

'I must declare I am surprised your father has written to *me*. He says only that Cara, who is "old for her age", is anxious now to go abroad and needs a change of air —' She coughed slightly. 'He tells me your brother Gregory would bring her out here if I were willing. He also encloses a bank draft.' Suddenly she gave an ironic 'Hm', half-contemptuous, half-amused.

'I am not surprised, Aunt, that Papa wants Cara out of the way if he persists in extending his hospitality to Simon Voyle', I said. Why could he not just send the man away, were my unspoken words.

Zelda however did not rise to the bait. 'Shall I agree, Hetty? It is up to you. I do not owe your father anything — quite the reverse in fact.'

I thought she must be referring to my staying with her, but she went on: 'Your sister is no flesh and blood of mine, Hetty', as you are, and it would be up to you to entertain her. There is room here however for a whole phalanx of sisters.'

'Max likes her', I said suddenly. 'They met when my governess was accompanying Cara to the Science Museum and called on him. Did he not tell you?'

'Possibly', she said. 'Naturally Max might help to look after the child . . .'

'Is it because of Simon? Does he not mention him?' I asked her again, thinking, Cara is not a child.

'I could introduce your sister to people here', she continued, still not answering my question. She meant young men, I knew.

Max came in just then and overheard her last words.

'What is it, Mama? Why are you looking so agitated?'

'My father has written to your mother asking us to have Cara here with us for a time', I replied flatly. Max's face took on an expression of intense boyish pleasure. He rarely showed his feelings, except in the matter of porcelain or bookbindings, but I had already come to the conclusion that Cara had made another conquest.

However this did not seem to be worrying Zelda. She rang for Rosa and ordered some China tea. 'He ought to have written also to *you* Hetty — it is with you he wishes her to stay — that it is in my house is of course taken for granted!' I waited, sure there would be more. 'Has your sister written to you complaining of the Voyle boy?' she asked in a different voice, ignoring Max who stood there expectantly.

'Yes — a little. She does not like him — I told you before — but my little sister Alice also mentioned that he was staying at East Wood — she hoped Papa would send him away again! Why *does* he put up with him?' I asked her. But she had not answered that question before and I thought she would not now.

'It is all very difficult for them, I suppose', she said, and looked undecided — not a normal expression for her. 'Your father in this matter is too soft-hearted!'

I had never heard Zelda say a good word for my Papa in all the time I had known her, and to call him soft-hearted amazed me. I had never found him so. I knew there was some mystery centred on Voyle of which my aunt was cognisant — that was clear. Perhaps he was my father's bastard child? Don't be ridiculous! I said to myself.

Max said: 'Oh, do invite her here, Mama — she is a very sweet girl — I will show her Florence myself!'

'Cara is not interested in monuments and pictures', I said truthfully but cattily.

'She might *become* interested', he said.

The tea came and I drank a cup and then went out into the garden. Max went off somewhere else, probably to swing in the hammock he'd put up under the trees in the shade.

Through the window I heard my aunt say to Rosa: 'Of course they still haven't told her. They ought to — then there would be no awkwardness.' Of whom was she speaking, Cara or myself? Rosa's voice murmured something in answer and then Zelda said, 'The "replacement" would naturally find no ill in him —' and laughed.

That evening my aunt said that she would accept my sister as a paying guest for a few weeks. 'It is always nice to be able to help someone who does not approve of you', she said enigmatically. She would telegraph her affirmative answer.

'I'm sure it's because of Voyle', I grumbled to

Max. 'Why can't they just get rid of him? What obligation are they under to entertain him?'

Max hesitated. I thought he was nearly about to say something, but then thought better of it. I considered my sister Cara. I had wanted Max to like her and she him, but I still felt a little apprehensive about her arrival amongst us all. At the bottom of my heart, though I had never been jealous of Cara's type of beauty, I did not want her to meet Orso Orsini! Why could Peter Voyle not have his son to live with him? If he was in fact his father, as Zelda said he was. So many questions went through my head. Had Simon been 'misbehaving' with my sister? Surely if that were the case Papa could easily nip it in the bud?

Cara's arrival would include Gregory too. My kind grown-up brother had been treated by Papa worse than myself. Did Gregory know the answers to my questions? Max certainly seemed to be hiding something.

It was Gregory whom I first saw alighting from the carriage one cloudy afternoon a week or so later. Then he turned and helped out my half-sister Cara, hatless, her lovely hair shining in the sun like molten gold. We all went out into the courtyard near the stables where the carriage had stopped. Giuseppe was smiling and all the servants came out to stare till Zelda told them to go back in.

'Hetty!' cried my sister. 'Isn't this wonderful! I'm so excited! And Max!' Max bowed in a most gentlemanly way. Cara looked happy and I was ashamed of my silly fears. Gregory however did not look too happy, though he smiled at me. His manner was, as usual, quiet; he spoke little at dinner beyond answering, rather perfunctorily, Zelda's questions about their journey.

Once introduced to her, Cara kept telling Zelda how she wished they had met before and how kind it was of her to invite her, and kept telling *me* how thrilled she was to see me again. 'Hetty looks quite Italian', she said.

'And *you* could not be anything but English', said Max. I reflected that from him this was usually not a compliment, but it might be this time.

I had no occasion to question Gregory about Voyle till after the meal, when Cara was unpacking her trunk in which she had folded practically every item of clothing she owned. I took him then into the garden where the empty hammock was swinging slightly in the evening breeze.

'If you listen carefully you may hear the nightingale', I said. He looked sad and preoccupied. 'Cheer up, brother', I said as we both leaned against a large stone urn at the bottom of the path. Usually it had water but had dried out in the heat. Gregory said nothing for a time, then he roused himself.

'I'm glad to see you looking well. Italy — or the sun — suits you, Hetty', he said.

'Will you stay? I hope you will — so does Max. You've come a long way. It's lovely here.'

'Our Aunt Zelda looks well too — I don't think

she'd welcome another uninvited guest — Cara thinks she was invited, by the way. Anyway, I have to go into Florence in the morning about some business — it may take a few days — for a client before I return home.'

'Oh, Gregory, can't you leave your work at home? You need a holiday. You look tired.'

He grimaced. Then he said: '*I* had to persuade Papa to allow Cara to come away for a time. Cara never said anything to him about — you know who — but she complained to me. I knew it was no use saying anything to Mamarella, so I told Papa.'

'It *was* Simon Voyle then! What happened?'

'Oh, nothing happened, but I saw the way the wind was blowing. Papa likes him even less than our half-sister does.'

'Then — why?'

'— does he not send him away? Because of Ella. I think he must have promised her — if she had a son —'

'Ella? What do you mean? — don't talk in riddles, Gregory —'

'If I tell you the truth you must promise not to breathe a word to Cara.'

'She doesn't even know we are not full siblings, Gregory.'

'She might be told that soon', he conceded. 'But the other matter — not yet anyway —'

'I can be discreet', I said. 'What is it all about?'

Quite innocently Cara had brought with her some of that unhappy atmosphere and tangle of emotions I'd lived with all my childhood and hoped to leave behind for ever in London.

'Did you find Mama's grave?' he asked.

He was changing the subject so I answered shortly: 'Not yet — Zelda says it's not in the Protestant Cemetery. Then, surely Cara must guess something about us, Gregory? I hoped Max would enlighten her, you know. I told Lucy to introduce herself to him and visit his lodgings — and she took Cara with her. Cara isn't a baby — she's almost seventeen — I think she ought to know we are only half-sisters, she and I.'

He looked so downcast that I put my hand over his larger one. Mine was sunburnt, his paler. 'What is it, Greg? Have you discovered something about Simon? I saw his father, you know — Zelda used to know him. But I think he's gone back to England — she says he was living in Australia for some years —' I stopped. I thought he looked suddenly angry. But it was not with me.

'Hetty', he began. 'When I say I have business here it is not unconnected with your questions.' He gritted his teeth. 'You can tell Cara if you want about Mama. She ought to know. But since you keep asking about Voyle junior, I'll tell you —' He took a deep breath and turned towards the setting sun which was now all pink and gold in the still, deep blue. 'Simon Voyle's mother was divorced by her husband', he began.

'Was she?'

'That husband', he went on, 'was once married to our stepmother, Ella.'

192

It took me a moment or two to understand what he was driving at. Then — I drew a sharp breath. 'He is Ella's *son* — Simon? — then that's why Papa allows him? — but I don't believe you! It's preposterous. If it were true his own Papa would not want him to stay with his rival — and our Papa would not want to . . .'

'Oh, Papa does not wish it. He can't stand him. *She* prevailed upon him. Her poor motherless boy. She is a fool, but guilty about the child she abandoned for our father — abandoning Simon to his. Which Peter Voyle said he wanted. Then he promptly gave him to Zelda, a woman he could trust to look after him. I don't think *he* cared for him either.'

'Then Simon — poor child, *nobody* wanted him —' The full import of what he had said began to dawn on me. 'Mamarella was *divorced* — you mean she was married to that Mr Voyle I saw and fell in love with Papa whilst she was married? —'

'If you like to put it that way, Hetty — since you are so romantic — and broad-minded.'

'But where was our Mama? Papa didn't divorce *her*. She was ill — it was after I was born when she came to recover here in Italy —'

'Precisely — she was conveniently away — recovering as you say from giving birth to you. She went to her sister. To Zelda —'

'But Papa couldn't divorce her! She hadn't done anything wrong —'

'No, he could not. They had to wait till she

died to marry. Voyle divorced his wife, but Papa had no grounds, even with the new divorce laws. Simon knows all this, so of course he knows that Cara is his own half-sister. Unfortunately Cara does not know. They are so frightened of their children discovering their mother lived in sin with Papa that they would even risk Simon "making up" to Cara. They're too deeply ashamed to tell her, and also because —'

He stopped. I was staring at him. It all seemed unbelievable — yet it made sense, made several of my own observations slide into place.

'They will not tell us, any of us, because it would mean going into — details — and then there are the little ones you see, though it won't affect Alice in the same way, or Felix.'

'What do you mean, Gregory?' My big, grown-up brother actually blushed.

'You see, Hetty? I tell you this because you are sensible — Cara was born before they could legally marry. They moved away, came to East Wood — but she is still what our world calls a — well you know what the world calls a child born out of wedlock! even if its parents marry later —'

'It isn't Cara's fault', I said hotly.

'No, of course not. But the world hasn't had the benefit of your education with Miss Little.'

So that was why Cara couldn't "come out" in London — and now she was nearly ready to do so. Was that the real reason for sending her here — because she was illegitimate? Poor Cara! I hoped she would never discover. It was not the sort of thing one was supposed to mention in polite society, and would also hurt my sister personally — more than it would have hurt me who had always felt excluded and unwanted.

'I think Papa is hoping you will look after her — he has a high opinion of you, Hetty, you know!' I looked at him in amazement. 'They'll hope she will marry a man who knows nothing of her misfortune', he said.

My mind was whirling. 'Why did he allow Simon in his house? He can't have much love for him.'

'No, but Ella has. She adores him. It was a thing I heard them talking about years ago — he promised her if she had a son he would allow her other son to visit her if he wanted to when he was eighteen.'

'So you've known all this for a long time.'

'About her divorce, yes. Not about Cara though. That was only because I have a lawyer's mind, Hetty, and did a little searching amongst dates at Somerset House.'

'I shan't tell her anything', I said. I had decided suddenly. Let Cara enjoy herself. I wouldn't even tell her we were only half-sisters.

That night I could not get to sleep. I kept thinking of that cold man, my Papa, and how I had always thought of him as a strong person who got his own way. I thought, in the face of love perhaps he was weak? He must surely have once loved my mother enough to marry her — a handsome man he had been, Rosa had said . . . And he must have loved Ella too — enough to take her from another man. From Simon Voyle's father. Poor Simon — taken away from his own mother — or had she abandoned him? — and handed over like a parcel to Aunt Zelda. But how had my aunt known Voyle? Had he too gone to Italy when Ella had abandoned him for Papa? It seemed odd to go to the very place where his rival's wife was recovering from a nervous illness . . . It was all a puzzle that did not seem possible of solution. I tossed in my hot sheets trying to find a cool place for my legs — and a cool, rational place in my mind so that I could explain things to myself. The trouble was that I could not believe my unapproachable Papa had ever been in love. I tried to imagine Mamarella as a young woman with a husband and child, risking everything — respectability certainly — for love. I could easily believe there was some sort of stigma over Cara's birth — oh yes, I could believe that! for why else had they spoiled her so, my pretty little sister?

But what had happened to my own Mama? It seemed there could have been no grounds for Papa to divorce *her*, whereas there had been ample grounds for Voyle to have divorced his own wife. I thought of Voyle, that thin, fair man and tried to believe he had once been Ella's husband. He would have been glad to have shamed her, wouldn't he? To have divorced her as a scarlet adultress? I knew that divorce brought shame in our society, if not always in the society of Florentine expatriates. It should have been my father and stepmother who came to live in Italy! I supposed though that they had left Ealing because of the disgrace, and moved to East Wood. I had read enough novels — the sort of which Lucy Little did not approve, secret mysterious novels about bigamy and guilt and shame — to know how a woman was regarded who had broken the marriage bond. I had even read some of them at Zelda's, for she had read novels when she was in England and I had purloined them when I was bored. But Papa was not a bigamist; he had not married Mamarella until my own mother was dead, if what Gregory said was true. How convenient it had been that my Mama had died so young! Just before dawn the thought came into my head; was my Mama murdered?

It was cooler now, but the sweat trickled down between my shoulder-blades. I tried to put the thought out of my head — it seemed ridiculously operatic — but I could not. Finally I put Orso Orsini into my head instead, to banish other ideas, and fell asleep as dawn broke.

When I woke, late, the garden was already bathed in sunlight and my fears and suspicions seemed mad. But what Gregory had said, I believed. I would leave it to my brother to find out the truth about Mama and I would still say nothing whatever to Cara. I would live from day to day.

Gregory had already gone when I came downstairs but Cara was being shown round the villa by Max. That morning, alone in the garden, I resolved to try and forget the past, not to make any more attempts to rake around in it. I was young; Cara was young; we had our whole lives before us. Whatever had been the situation between my father and Cara's mother, it was all past history. My childhood had been over long ago; I could not alter it now. I might certainly want to see Mama's grave before I left Italy, but there was plenty of time. I felt I would never want to leave Italy. I would introduce Cara to all my new acquaintances in Florence and Fiesole and would begin that very afternoon with Eleanor Pontraven so that when Zelda had a party Cara might already know some of the guests.

I found my sister talking to Max in the courtyard in the shade of an evergreen. The fountain was playing at the front of the villa and the sky was deep blue and cloudless, the sun stippling shadows on my sister's bright hair. It was not the time then to talk to her alone, but I finally got to speak to her that evening. 'How nice Max is', she began, when we were sitting in my bedroom, myself on the dimity-curtained bed, which I always thought rather an incongruous sort of furnishing for the place, and Cara in my big chair by the window. I looked at her sharply when she said that, for I was sure that Max reciprocated her sentiments. They had almost nothing in common, I thought, except that my sister was beautiful and he loved beautiful things.

'I'm so glad you've come', I said, trying to feel sincerely pleased. 'I'm surprised Papa allowed you —'

'Oh, it was his idea', she replied ingenuously — 'Of course he knew I wanted to.'

'Was the Voyle young man still there when you left East Wood?' I asked, trying to sound casual.

'No — I think he was soon to go off abroad for his business — he'd returned to London. I believe he's some relative of Mama's, you know, whom she feels obliged to help. He was an awful nuisance to me, Hetty — I told Gregory to tell him to stop pestering me —'

'I should beware of him', I said.

'Oh, he was just a nuisance — I'm old enough to deal with him now', she said complacently. Then: 'I can see I'm going to enjoy myself here — Max says he'll take me into Florence this week —'

'And there's Zelda's party too', I added, glad to get off the subject of Simon, whose name I'd felt obliged to mention before we could forget about him. I told her about the sort of people who came to Zelda's At Homes, and then we went up to the room where she was sleeping and looked her clothes over.

'Papa gave me some money to have a new summer dress made here', she said. 'What do you advise?' I was rather touched that she now regarded me as an arbiter of fashion and in truth she was treating me rather respectfully. I suppose I must have looked at home in the place. She said she liked my lilac dress and my ribbons. 'You've changed, Hetty', she said as we went downstairs to the garden to enjoy the evening coolness.

'Oh, one has to adapt', I answered, thinking how Cara would adore the sort of society I found so tedious when there was no Orso Orsini to look forward to seeing again.

Gregory was not to return to the villa. His business would take him a week or two and then he was to go straight back to London.

'He's doing well now he's a barrister', Cara said. 'He hardly ever comes home — he's so solemn though, isn't he? He thinks I'm just a flibberti-gibbet.'

I wondered what sort of 'business' my brother was executing, suddenly remembering that he had said it was to do with the Voyles, but turned my thoughts away from that path and answered: 'Yes — he's always worked hard.' I had thought my brother had looked both strained and excited. He had given me the impression of someone with a grievance and I did not like to think of him like that. I felt that perhaps Gregory had suffered more than I had from our family tensions. I looked at Cara as she sat swinging in the hammock and thought how dreadful it would be for her if she knew of the secret of her birth. She was obviously looking forward to meeting a man who might fall in love with her and marry her out of the school-room. She looked older than me, as Mr Little had once remarked, maybe because she had a fuller figure and was taller. I thought again, *I* would know better how to bear it if I suddenly found out it had been I who was illegitimately conceived. Once more I turned my thoughts away from that unprofitable path and bent my energies to entertaining my sister. I had been invited to several picnics during the following weeks and wrote to those who were giving them to explain about Cara's arrival. Naturally they would invite her — new young ladies were at a premium — even if they had not yet set eyes upon her.

Indeed when we went to the old amphitheatre at Fiesole one afternoon with a group of Americans, including Eleanor, and with the Contessa's son Bruno, Cara was the centre of attention. I liked sometimes to observe others without their noticing and I enjoyed watching the way the young men manoeuvred themselves to pay their attentions to my pretty sister. People fascinated me as much for their differences from myself and for their occasional indifference towards me as for the mystery of personalities who were socially adept, stylish, rich, and yet (it seemed to me) deficient in the kind of knowledge I had myself, though I had had it mostly from books. I saw Max watching Cara too. She looked radiantly happy. I hoped both Max and Bruno would continue to show interest in her. So long as she never met Orsini! I was superstitious about that. I knew that Italians were very fond of blonde women — even Botticelli had liked them! With her pink cheeks and fair wavy hair, Cara looked a bit like a Botticelli model.

'I can see that your sister is going to be a great success', Max said to me as we walked back over the fields, having sent the older people in dogcarts home. Especially with young men, I thought. Poor

Max was smitten with Cara, but it would do him good to see that he was not the only pebble on the beach! I nearly told him what Cara had said about him — that she liked him — but thought better of it. Instead, I said: 'She's a very sociable girl — she'll have lots of admirers, as my little sister Alice tells me she already has at home. But I don't think her head is turned — yet.'

'Listen to Grandmama!' he said.

The next day was Zelda's At Home. Cara was excited. Bruno Guccioli was invited, and Eleanor, and Laurence Merryweather, a friend of her cousin, and *his* friends who were Americans 'doing' Europe and taking a long time over it. I felt quite free and light-hearted since I knew that Orso Orsini was not in Italy. They said he was to return early in October to perform a 'Benefit' for a hospital for poor sick children of which many of my aunt's friends were patrons. I hoped it was true. There would however be no music at Zelda's At Home, unless someone was prevailed upon to play the piano towards the end when the older folk had gone home.

I looked at Cara who had come down in good time to help receive the guests. I'd advised her on what she was to wear and had chosen amongst the dresses in her trunk a white one in fine lawn which went well with her fair skin and hair. It had a pretty pink sash and I thought she looked like the heroine of *Rigoletto*! How incongruous it was that Cara was in the centre of all my tangled emotions about my father and stepmother, emotions of which she herself seemed so blithely unaware.

Zelda came up to me as I looked at her. 'I expect she is your Papa's dearest possession', she said in a strange tone of voice.

'No — I think Felix is that', I replied and turned to look at her. 'My stepmother certainly puts her son first now.'

'Then it would be a good idea if Cara married young', replied my aunt. 'I imagine your father hopes she will meet a suitable 'parti' over here, though he has never approved of my circle.' I thought she was going to start reminiscing and I was at last going to hear more about mother's young days, but she went on: 'The Paravicini boy would do, I suppose.' I knew he too was the son of divorced parents and thought that was why she suggested his name. She had never mentioned marriage to me in such terms before. I supposed she thought I was a lost cause. She did not appear to have noticed that her own son had already made it quite clear he found my sister attractive! But I remembered her saying that Max would not marry until he was thirty. Whether this was meant as a forecast or as a prescription I was not sure.

She was about to move towards the door as we heard the scrunch of wheels on the gravel drive, but I said quickly: 'Have you invited Mr Voyle?' She turned quickly back towards me.

'He is not in Florence', she replied rather frostily.

I hoped that the father was not to bring the

son out to Italy. My father's fears would have more justification if Simon Voyle was free to torment my sister when she was away from the parental nest. It would be much better if Cara could make many new friends here who would keep an eye on her. I knew that my aunt was wary of the Voyles; there had been something indefinable in her manner towards Simon's father that night at the opera, but I could not tell whether the emotion was one of anger or fear, for her feelings had been covered by a sort of complicit banter.

Zelda said no more, but went forward to receive her guests. One of these guests turned out to be Mrs Holroyd and she came up to me as I sat on the terrace with Max and Bruno Guccioli and Cara and Eleanor. Cara was the cynosure that afternoon. It was not that her conversation was sparkling or that she flirted even slightly with the young men who came up to her. She was in fact always rather quiet in company, but she looked as though she had interesting thoughts; a slight smile was playing over her lips today and an enigmatic expression in her eyes that I knew would attract men. I wondered whether she did it on purpose, and decided she didn't, that it was her nature to know how to look mysterious, even though, as she had told me before we went down to the party, she felt quite nervous of meeting new people. I wasn't sure whether to believe that. Now, as she smiled, the corners of her mouth turned up and her dimples showed.

I introduced Mrs Holroyd to my sister and that

lady took a chair next to mine. 'My brother came over with my sister a few days ago', I said, just for something to say. 'Cara has never travelled before.' I, of course, had travelled as a tiny child, as I was sure Mrs Holroyd would know if she had known my mother.

'Oh, I'd love to meet your brother — is he here?' she replied.

'No — he had business in Florence, and then Rome, for a client — he's a barrister.'

'You're not at all like your sister', she said in a low voice when Cara began to talk to Eleanor.

'Well, no — Cara looks a little like her mother', I said pointedly.

Bruno was talking to Cara now and she was looking up at him, her lips parted slightly as though he were the fount of all wisdom. Max looked sulky and barely listened to poor Eleanor who was trying her best with him. I thought Cara looked more than ever like the seduced virgin in *Rigoletto*. Somehow she managed to arouse my protective instincts.

'You must come to my own last At Home', said Mrs Holroyd. 'I don't see young people as often as I'd like.' I wondered what sort of parties she would give, not having forgotten that the first time I'd seen her was when Peter Voyle had been around too. Probably the sort where the women wore white satin and fake diamonds and waved white fans. But Mrs Holroyd was dressed discreetly — why should I think she'd know the demi-mondaines? My imagination was running away with me once more. There was the sound of animated conversation from indoors where Zelda held her court. The Countess and Mrs Warburton were there — I could hear the peals of Mrs Warburton's merry laughter, as famous in Florence as the Campanile. I felt suddenly lonely, and this made me ask without thinking: 'Did my Mama die of a broken heart, Mrs Holroyd?'

She looked astonished, and then sad, and paused before she replied to me. 'No, my dear', she said in a low voice. Then: 'If you want to know more about her, Hetty — I'll tell you one day — not today — one day when we can have a quiet chat.'

'Promise me!'

She looked disturbed. 'Walls have ears', she said. 'I am your friend, Hetty, as I was your mother's', she added in a soft voice, almost too soft for me to hear it. 'She was beautiful', she said. 'Better looking even than Zelda —'

'Then I don't look like her', I replied, knowing she would agree. She looked closely at me. 'You have fine eyes — and good cheekbones — you are too young yet for your kind of looks.'

I thought, but Cara is younger than I am and everyone says *she* is pretty!

'So young', she said with a smile. Not too young to fall in love, I thought.

Then: 'Did my mother like opera?' I asked, wanting now to escape her scrutiny. 'I believe she herself used to sing a little?'

'I never knew her in London', said Mrs Holroyd. 'And she did not go out a great deal here. You enjoy it yourself?' she asked politely. We talked of the opera season then, even of Orsini, and I did not bat an eyelid!

But I did venture to say that all the most ravishing parts were written for tenors.

'You think that because you are a woman', she said with another of her smiles. 'The sopranos excite the men most!' She spoke quite matter-of-factly. I thought, I could not have this conversation even with Zelda. I spoke of the music I liked best and she said: 'You are an *exaltée*, Hetty. Not like your mother in that.' I thought Mama must have been a very down-trodden sort of person. But as she got up, the admiral having hoved into view, she said: 'Remember, my dear — you won't always have youth on your side.'

I pondered that remark as she smiled at the admiral who then came up and gallantly offered her his arm and they went off to look at a picture of a battle at sea which Max said might be a Turner, exciting the admiral immeasurably.

Mrs Holroyd did not look to my eyes the sort of woman who had shamelessly indulged herself in that sensuality well-brought up girls were not supposed to know about or feel. She looked to me a sad woman who had had a difficult life. How well had she known my mother? I knew I had not embarrassed her with my questions.

Later that evening, when there were only a few remaining guests talking quietly to each other or walking in the garden, I heard her say to the Countess as I stood behind them chatting with Eleanor: 'Of course, in Basil's time they went to Rome and Venice a good deal — England has calmed her down.'

If that were true, then my aunt must have had a very different personality from her sister's!

Max was now with Cara as the others came up to take their leave. When they had all gone and I had said goodbye to Eleanor and gone back to the hammock in the garden, he came up to me without her. 'Where is Cara?' I said. 'She looked as though she were enjoying herself, didn't she?'

He said nothing and I added: 'You ought to get to know Eleanor better, cousin, she shares your interest in paintings and bibelots.'

'One does not always have things to say to a girl just because she shares your interests', he said huffily.

'Well, it's a good beginning', I said.

'Friendship does not need reasons', he added. I knew he was thinking of my sister and was sure he had fallen in love with her. I don't think I would have minded, even if I had not had other dreams to dream, for I had always regarded Max as a sort of brother and nursed no romantic aspirations towards him. But I saw that though he was so young Max had already a man's desires; he was interested in other things besides connoisseurship.

'I think you are alluding to *friendship*', I said daringly. His dark eyes looked at me with the old penetrating look and then he laughed and I knew the danger was over for the time being.

208

'Did you hear my mother pumping la Holroyd about Voyle?' he asked. 'But she gave nothing away.'

I had not heard that. Was Mrs Holroyd supposed to know his whereabouts?

I had a lot to think about after this party of my aunt's. I was revising my estimate of Cara — and of Max — and even wondering about Zelda's own past, and I was coming to the rueful conclusion that so far as I was concerned young men did not find me attractive. I went down to the kitchens the next morning and found Rosa there getting a tray ready to take up to her mistress who had, she said, a slight headache after the exertions of the previous day.

'Let me take it', I said. It was a long way up to Zelda's bedroom and Rosa was not young. I might as well use some of those energies that young people were supposed to have. 'Did you know Mrs Holroyd before — at the time I came out to be with my Mama?' I asked on an impulse as Rosa followed me up the stairs, protesting ineffectually the while.

'I might have done', she replied in her usual maddeningly mysterious way. I had always thought Rosa was too much under the thumb of my aunt to tell me anything Zelda might prefer me not to know, but I did wonder also whether her reactions were also to some extent self-protective. The less people thought servants knew, the less they could be blamed.

I followed her downstairs, having allowed her

to take the tray from me at the door of Zelda's boudoir.

'Who was Mr Holroyd?' I asked her. 'Did he die too?' I emphasized the last word. So many of these women's husbands were dead. Perhaps that was why widows haunted Florence, looking for new husbands. She did not choose to answer that. 'Most women marry, don't they?' I said after a pause. She was now sitting on a wooden chair shelling the magnificent peas Gabriella had brought from the market at Fiesole. I had a pang of sympathy for her. She was getting old and maybe Zelda kept her on from pity?

'I'll expect *you'll* marry one day, Miss Hetty', she answered. 'To one of those Eyetalians, perhaps.'

'I'm not thinking of marriage — yet', I answered. She'd noticed that I liked talking to the Italians we knew.

'All young ladies marry as soon as they can — else how can they live?' she said. 'They don't work — like we do.'

Had Rosa been told about the money Basil de Vere had left me? — the difference between poverty and a small gentility for a year or two, a fortune to Rosa. 'I want to teach one day', I stated, aware that I might sound less than enthusiastic. 'I intend to become a governess.'

'Here?' she asked me, her bright eyes upon me.

'Perhaps — certainly if I ever have to return to England.' At the idea of returning to my native land my heart did sink.

She considered for a time then she said: 'Working girls don't have time for "love". All love does is bring you babies like my poor sister Fanny who had a good position before she married.' And Mamarella, I thought. And my own mother. Both of them never well in body or even in mind, and yet they had only done something 'natural'. In our family love seemed to lead only to misery. The children must be the real compensation. I ought to write soon to my stepmother. Did she know I knew that she was not my real mother? What did she and my father talk about?

'Papa's wife is always nervy and headachy', I said, taking a peapod and shelling it, the green sap going under my nails. I thought, Ella's son Simon only tormented her when he came to stay. How much did Rosa know about him?

The old woman stood up stiffly. 'I must get on with my work', she said severely.

Only another month now before we returned to Florence! The days had been dissipated in picnics and parties, at all of which Cara had been fêted and flattered. She had flirted a little, but not excessively — she did not need to try to attract young men for they came up to her in any case. Bruno was always at her side and one day my aunt asked me if I thought Cara liked him.

'She likes most people', I replied.

'It would be a good match', murmured Zelda.

'I don't think she is thinking of marriage quite yet', I said rebelliously.

'Is she not?' said Zelda with a slight smile.

Max though was genuinely infatuated with my sister and I wondered whether his mother realized this. He was adept at hiding his feelings from her and she chose only to see what she wanted to see. Max had one more term at school in London and was then to leave and return to Italy for good — if he had anything to do with it. Cara was basking in Max's admiration just as she did in that of others, but I resolved to find out whether she had any particular feeling for any of her beaux.

Alice wrote to me and said Simon Voyle had not come back. 'Felix is to start lessons with Lucy in the autumn and Papa wishes him to go to a preparatory school when he is eight,' she added. Would Papa want Cara to return soon? He might send Gregory over once more. I did want to see my brother again.

I went into Cara's room one afternoon when I knew she would be taking a siesta before sallying out in the early evening with a group of Americans. The Americans always took one or two old aunts with them when they visited each other's villas and they were supposed to be adequate chaperones. Eleanor had told me that American girls always stuck together and were never in danger of a too rapid seduction. Cara was as popular with the American aunts as with their nephews and nieces for she was not an argumentative girl; all trace of her former imperiousness seemed to have disappeared.

I sat on her bed and after chatting about some

of our acquaintances I said: 'There's nobody I especially like among them' (which was true). 'Do you like anybody in particular — I thought you seemed interested in Laurence when he was talking about New York?'

'Laurence? Oh, you mean the one they call Teddy? Yes, he's nice — but so are they all. After East Wood, Hetty, I should think one's head might be turned quite easily.' I saw she was mocking me and knew perfectly well I was trying to find out if she nurtured more than normal comradely feelings towards any of her swains. Max called them 'Cara's swains', I suppose to make a joke of it.

'Americans are nice', she went on. 'They don't, you know, "try things on" like the Italians do. But they are sincere when they tell you things, I think.' What had they told her? I dared not ask if any of them ever tried to kiss her, for my sister had been for long in many ways a stranger to me and it seemed indelicate to ask more. But she said, as she sat up and pushed her hair back over her head, 'Not like that slimy Simon Voyle.' I waited, sure that she had never told anybody the complete extent of his unpleasantness. 'He tried to kiss me in the garden once! I didn't tell Gregory that. He said he meant to marry me one day too. Ugh!'

'But he *can't* marry you', I said before I could think.

'I can't stand him', she went on, not noticing my choice of words. Now was the time to tell her of the relationship, but I just could not. What had

Mamarella been doing whilst all this was going on? Worrying about Felix probably. Or having a headache.

'Huntie was angry — she saw him', added Cara, 'and she told me to tell Gregory. But I didn't tell Greg anything except Simon pestered me. It all seems *so* long ago — I hardly knew anyone then.' As only two months had passed since this scene it was hardly a long time. But Cara had grown up in these last weeks. 'I would certainly tell him off myself now if he tried to kiss me', she said. 'And as for proposals, they're two a penny.' I laughed. If Simon Voyle came to Italy with his father he'd soon find out Cara had plenty young men to send him packing.

There was genuine horror in my later reactions to her 'confession'. Simon Voyle knew quite well he was half-brother to my sister and so his conduct was meant only to hurt. Unless he was a trifle mad.

I had wanted to ascertain my sister's feelings towards Max. *She* probably thought of him as 'just a schoolboy' with an inconvenient calf-love for herself. Max was not just any young man but someone I was fond of. Not a flirt either.

Later that day when I was in the garden and Cara was waiting for the carriage, she added: 'Huntie was a brick you know. But she has funny ideas — said she'd been to Italy herself and to beware of Mrs de Vere!'

'She *has* been to Italy — she was here with her own aunt — Rosa Daventry — I told you, didn't

I?' Cara had obviously not read my own letters with much attention. Huntie had never warned *me* against my aunt! 'How curious', I said. But I couldn't tell Cara that Zelda was not her own aunt, though she was mine. Cara assumed she was a sort of distant cousin and was called aunt only for politeness's sake.

We had had the villa piano tuned and during my last weeks there I played and practised two hours a day in the room that led off the 'ballroom' which was cool and reasonably out of earshot . . . I played the tunes I had heard Orso sing from the *Masked Ball*, *Rigoletto* and *Luisa Miller*, and luxuriated in a sadness I knew I had not earned. The 'idea' of Orsini replaced the real man, but the music brought his face back to me, dark and shining, and with it a memory of that voice of honeyed rapture. I would often try to reconstruct the way he had been that day of the party at the Villa Bodini, with his wide mouth, his black eyes — the laughter lines at their side — and the strong broad nose. He was not a delicate-looking 'romantic' sort of man at all. I had in a few minutes seen so many expressions flit over his face that I did not know which was the most habitual one, but imagined he had in repose a face different from the one when he talked with women; and yet another when he sang. I pretended that my feeble attempts to play the piano were changed into a beautiful execution which drew his admiration. Oh, many were the daydreams I had that summer as it changed slowly into an Indian one. I saw Orsini, tall, extrovert, and friendly, a thousand miles away from Italy and from me, a man who would never know of the emotions he aroused in a young woman whose first experience of unrequited and secret passion this was. If I had been older, if I had been famous for my own talents, I would have shamelessly sought him out. But I was not poised or shameless enough, and too young to be taken seriously. Mrs Holroyd had seemed to think there was some advantage in being young. I knew of none. Thinking of him was a relief from those other thoughts which made my mind often like a treadmill however much I had resolved to forget them.

I daydreamed about the forthcoming 'benefit' in October when we would have returned to Florence, and was a little worried that my dreams would collide with reality when I saw him again on the stage and met people who knew him. I could touch only the edges of the cosmopolitan life of the adults in Florence. How I wished I were older, more experienced in the ways of the world! How I even wished that I was a young man and that my hero was a woman — and then I should be permitted to seek her out. It was not fair.

As I played I felt pulled in two directions. However disturbing my *grande passion* was for a man I hardly knew, there was more that was disturbing about my parents' past. I had resisted the temptation to probe Rosa or Zelda for further details; I wanted a future that had nothing to do with my father and mother and those glimpsed imagined mosaics of all our pasts — of my mother, Maria, and Ella, and Zelda with her old husband, and Max — and Peter Voyle and his son. They seemed to belong to a different world and one I knew I ought to leave. I must seek my own fortune — and hope to meet one day in the distant future a hero with Orso Orsini's face and bearing who would sing to me of his love.

10

I'd be sorry to leave the Villa de Vere when October arrived, even though the sun, still bright, had become less warm, and the evenings shorter. But when we did leave my feelings were mixed. I'd miss the sight of the orchards with their apricots and peaches, plums and greengages — but I'd see the trees in blossom again on our return the following spring. I'd miss the shrubs and flowers, the smell of herbs and eucalyptus and lavender, the vine-clad slopes and the silvery-grey olives and the glow-worms lighting up the villa terrace when dusk fell. I'd miss the bluey-green fir trees and the cypresses at the bottom of the garden by the high lichen-covered walls, and the late roses; and the box-hedges — for the gardeners had performed wonders and the place looked very well ordered in contrast with its earlier dishevelment. But if I could look forward to seeing them again, these emblematic memories of summer would stock my imagination. I'd never forget this first Italian summer, when I had found everything so beautiful — but I was ready for autumn. Perhaps I'd even had enough sun, and needed streets and rain and crowds. Although I had never before missed London I did think sometimes of London now, for I think England is at its most beautiful in autumn, and in all my years before, that season had meant new books to study and the schoolroom opened up again, and soon after that the scent of garden fires, and chrysanthemums in the gardens. Whatever the reason, when we returned to the city of the *giglio* — the Fleur de Lys — and not to grey, smoky London, I was vaguely excited, looking forward to meeting once more the green-and-ochre coloured Arno and making the acquaintance of new pictures, new sculptures. I also wanted to explore more of the city on the other side of the bridges, the Oltrarno. And I hadn't yet discovered where my mother's grave was . . .

When we came down from the hills, and I saw the houses of Florence with their distinctive colours, which I always thought of as dirty orange and lemon, and once we had got the carriage through the narrow streets, having to go the long way round since so many of them were not broad enough for a carriage to pass, I felt I was coming home again. Naturally my feelings were not unconnected with the fact that Orso Orsini was soon to sing again in the city at that 'benefit'.

Cara was not to leave for home until just before Christmas since Gregory could not come for her before then, so I should have my sister as companion most of the time, but I determined that I would snatch some hours alone. I had always needed to be by myself for at least part of the day, and Italy had not changed my preference. Cara had grown up a good deal and I mildly enjoyed her company, but I always felt a little constrained when I thought of all I knew about our family that she did not. She had enjoyed her time at the villa — no wonder, for her life, like mine, had not been very exciting at home in our London suburb, though she had always gone out with Ella and Papa more than I had. Here in Florence there were far more interesting companions than her parents. She was immediately delighted with the aspects of life in that city to which I myself had grown accustomed. She liked the food as much as I did, and now we were back in Florence she could enjoy the brown loaves and rolls the 'English baker' left at our door early every morning and the milk and cream and butter brought along a little later. We had missed such luxuries at the villa where 'foreigners' were too dispersed for one seller to visit them all daily. 'We can send out now to the *trattoria* for a hot meal if we want', I told her. 'It arrives in a tin box with a pan of coals to keep it warm, all carried on the head of a boy!'

'It sounds most convenient — just think if one lived here one could dispense with servants — and Mrs Beeton!' she said.

I agreed. The enormous expenditure of energy it had always taken my stepmother to tell Cook what to cook, to supervise it and then grumble about it, was one of a housewife's domestic tasks, endlessly repeated, that had always filled me with gloom, although nobody had expected us to cook the meals. In retrospect English meals were either too heavy or too tasteless. I remembered rice pudding and greasy mutton and undercooked boiled potatoes. How pleasant to send to a restaurant for one's needs. I forebore to remind my sister that all these things that made life so pleasant cost money, and that it was cheaper to have an Italian cook than to send out for meals, for I liked the idea myself.

I took Cara to the market where I'd been once or twice with Maddalena and Rosa, and to the confectioners where we bought our loaves of *pane santo*. One thing though which she never got used to was the wine. I was by now quite a wine bibber and loved the Chianti Classico which came in a bottle sealed with olive oil. Nobody drank the water in Florence for it was very hard, even worse than London water. Wine and olive oil were the staple products of Tuscany about which Cara had once been instructed by Miss Little but, as my sister said, 'Geography never seemed real before.' Our lamps too were fed by olive oil. Cara exclaimed in wonderment when a fire was lit not with coal but with little briquettes made from ground-up pine-cones that smelt marvellous when they burned. 'I'll never get used to London again', she confessed. I'd not expected her to like it as much as I did, but my sister's tastes had been indeterminate before and were now being formed by 'abroad'. One thing she did not eat as much of as I confess I did myself was the delicious *pan forte* from Siena, for which I had a weakness. Cara said it spoiled one's teeth and would also make me fat. I supposed she was right. When we were at the villa she had spent a lot of time regarding her neat waist — and making sure that freckles did not mar her white nose — whereas I had forgotten my waistline, and loved the sun, which I thought improved my own sallow complexion. Cara was now looking forward to shop-window gazing too and dreaming of new clothes.

She had a passion for flowers and would buy whatever the man at the door offered her. He came regularly in the morning with his basket of autumn blooms and ivy, and Maddalena, who was used to bargaining with him, was no match for Cara who went into ecstasies over his offerings. I went out by myself those first mornings of our return whilst Cara stayed in flower-arranging and doing things to her hair, having got up late. Eleanor, who had also returned, thought my sister very pretty and intimated to me that Bruno had confided in her about his feelings.

I wondered if his mother the Countess would be quite so enthusiastic. Should Bruno's feelings be serious ones, or at least taken seriously, would my Aunt Zelda feel obliged to inform her old friend that Cara had a stigma attached to her birth? I prayed not, for I did not want my sister to be unhappy and there was no need for such revelations when the Countess herself was divorced.

Eleanor had told me that there was a new 'circulating' library for English books in a sort of shop behind the cathedral, and so I went alone one morning to sample its wares, feeling a need to read in my own language after a summer of reading such books as the Villa de Vere provided in high, dusty cupboards, which had belonged to the owner from whom Basil de Vere had bought the villa many years before. I walked in the direction of the cathedral with a spring in my step, breathing in the morning smells and hearing the street vendors' cries with renewed pleasure, for Florence, in spite of its summer heat and winter rains and crowded streets was so civilized, was indeed one of the places where our own 'civilization' had begun. Once I'd managed to locate the library, and borrowed a novel by Ouida for light relief after Mr Ruskin, and *I Promessi Sposi* which I wanted to read in Italian, I did not feel like returning home immediately. I wanted to sit down and begin my books. Women could not sit alone in cafés, and the gentlemen had their chic clubs, but I had heard of a new 'ice-cream' salon — or *Gelateria* — what a perfect place to sit with my novel! Perhaps they might serve coffee too. I knew it was frequented by Americans and even that two English ladies of indeterminate age had gone into it alone so I plucked up my courage and went in the direction of the Accademia for I knew it was somewhere in that area.

When I found it I saw there was a shop and a dim marble-topped interior, at whose tables a few American ladies were sitting, one of them with a sulky looking child. I supposed that on Sundays the place would be full of Italian children brought by their grandparents for a treat. This morning

I felt like a child myself when I saw the delicious goodies in the window display. Yes, I'd go in alone and consume an ice. I sat down thankfully once I'd opened the interior, for my boots were hurting a little, not being made for long walks. I'd better buy another pair. How pleasant it was to know I could afford it.

While I was waiting to be served at a table at the back I saw there was an Englishman across the room eating from a tall glass of ice topped with cream and fruit. Perhaps a man felt a little out of place for a change in a place where the customers were mostly women and children! I need not feel self-conscious myself on my own account. When my ice came it had fruit crushed at the bottom of the glass too and I looked at it as I would a work of art. It seemed a pity to eat it, although that would not stop me. It was a novel sensation being able to walk alone and sit down alone; I had never been able to do it in London. A few people had stared at me when I walked in, but having decided they did not know me had resumed their degustation. The Englishman never once looked up but consumed newspaper and ice together. I was sitting near a screen that half-divided the tables at the back and I opened my novel but then shut it and applied myself to the ice. Occasionally I tried to look as if I were waiting for a friend, and consulted my watch, but the pantomime was lost on the other customers. It was not the done thing for a lady to sit alone but I had never had the desire to be a lady. Neither would Italian girls ever venture out alone either, unless they were working girls, who would have had no money for luxuries. My *gelato* was topped with cherries and I ate it slowly. Two middle-aged men came in and sat on the other side of the screen behind me, one tall, the other fat and greasy-looking. They took no notice of me as they passed my table.

I know that Italians in general thought that English and American women were a trifle mad for I had heard remarks from Italians who did not realize I understood their language, since they never expected an *Inglese* to do so. Most of the English speakers did not, so I was rather at an advantage. It was obvious however that I was not Italian since I usually went around with a book and had never perfected that Latin way Italian women have of gliding around with small wiggly steps.

I took up my book now as the delicious confection slid down my throat, and it was as I was reading that I heard the muttered conversation those two men were having behind the screen, oblivious to the fact that not only could I hear what they were saying but actually understand most of it. I have always had especially good hearing as well as an especially good sense of smell — although a poor visual imagination — and I had made enormous strides in understanding Italian. Suddenly my attention was caught by the word 'Beneficio' and I pricked up my ears. Anything remotely connected with Orso Orsini had me immediately on the alert. Then —

'He *will* be surprised', said, in Italian, one of the voices unpleasantly.

'You're sure that Torelli won't make a mistake? Are you *sure* Orsini's decided to do that scene?'

'Torelli's information is always correct. And only our friend touches the glass — he's the only one to drink — and he always sings that aria for the ladies' "benefit".' They laughed unpleasantly.

I strained my ears while appearing to concentrate fiercely on my book and thought I heard the word '*velen*'.

'So our nightingale's song will cease!'

'For a time — what a humiliation!'

'Perhaps for ever!'

I was angry, then aghast, and my hands were trembling. I put them under the table on my lap as I strained every nerve to hear further. They were speaking like conspirators; they *were* conspirators, I was sure of it. And they were talking about a scene I knew well from *Luisa Miller* and one I was hoping Orso would sing. The tenor is always the rebellious young lover and in this opera the young man who loves beyond the bounds of class drinks from a glass of wine on the table. I remembered it well. The men went on to discuss what sounded like a business contract and I could not understand all their words, which were to do with money. Then I heard chairs being pushed away as the men got up. They passed by my table where I was desperately 'reading' whilst managing surreptitiously to look at them out of the corner of my eye. They appeared quite unconcerned. The fat man looked quite like a sergeant run to seed and the tall thin one was a lugubrious, droopy-moustached type. They certainly had not been aware that I could hear them and went out of the door of the parlour with a curt *Grazie* to the woman who was behind the counter at the front of the shop.

Had I been deluded, and had they been discussing something quite innocuous? Had my infatuation for the singer actually persuaded me I had heard something different from what they meant? Had I half-made up their conversation? I was not yet completely fluent in their language, and it was easy to make mistakes. What a strange venue for such talk — an ice-cream parlour, a place for women and children and foreigners during the week, certainly not for businessmen — that must be why they had come here. I was sure now I'd heard the word *velen*, which could only mean 'poison'. I knew I had heard the word nightingale — *usignuolo* — for I had just recently had to look up the spelling of that word in the dictionary. And I had certainly heard *umiliazione*. What else *could* they have been talking about? My blood did seem to run cold when I thought over what I'd heard — a sort of prickly sensation I'd never had before, a mixture of fear and disbelief, and horror.

What should I do? I got up, trying not to appear agitated, and went out after paying my bill. Perhaps I ought to have followed the two men straight away to see where they went, but it was too late. I thought I might have seen the fat one before, but couldn't think where.

As I walked along I thought that I ought to go to Orsini — they would tell me at the Opera when he was to return, or I could leave a message. But what kind of message? It would sound ridiculous and melodramatic if I said I'd overheard a conspiracy to — what? — not kill him it seemed, but stop his singing. And how silly I'd look if I went personally to Orsini with my story and it turned out I'd been mistaken. Even worse would be if he thought I was trying to become acquainted with him and making up some cock-and-bull story to get him to listen to me. I was besotted with the man's voice, but I did not want to be like those lady followers of his who swooned all over him and whom he probably despised.

But I did know him in a way. I'd spoken to him twice, and he might remember me still from our chance words on the bridge. What was certain was that I wasn't going to tell anyone else what I heard, or thought I'd heard. Might I send him an anonymous warning? No, I despised anonymity as much as I despised flirtatious forwardness, and he wouldn't take any notice of what might sound like the ravings of a madwoman. But they had been plotting against him, such things really did happen, away from books and melodramas! Somebody must hate him. I walked back, finding myself eventually near one of the bridges, which was out of my way, but I wanted to think and

I gazed into the shallow, summer-dried Arno.

What if I had not gone into that *gelateria?* Was it the hand of destiny? I shivered. That seemed ridiculous too, though it went with the sort of music Orso sang. Maybe opera aroused such emotions in rival singers — or their agents and managers, for the men had not looked like singers.

When you are young you are always waiting for Something to Happen and I had had a long, lazy summer in the country whilst dreaming privately about Orso Orsini. I'd been sociable, gone to parties and picnics and done a good deal of reading, but it was true I'd stagnated a little since I'd met nobody else who made my heart beat faster. I had thought that 'growing up' was about discovering social ease, fitting in, making new friends, having 'opinions' one was not afraid to voice — and I had done all these things. But now I was confronted with a choice — to do nothing, or to do something to avert what might be a tragedy. If the men had been discussing putting the singer into jeopardy, who knew but that what they plotted would not have far-reaching effects upon a career which I sensed was just taking off? If Orsini had to miss engagements, could not sing — and that seemed to be what it had all been about — he might lose the chance for ever, or his voice might be permanently affected. I thought I knew how singers regarded their voices, those instruments they carried around with them, for during those long summer nights after meeting Orsini for the second time, I had imagined how *he* might feel, when I

229

had tried to analyse why I felt about him as I did. I didn't think that Orsini without his voice would ever have aroused those first stirrings of pleasurable pain that told me I could love the voice's owner.

I had never before been faced with such a strange situation or decision. True, I had had to decide for myself whether to tell Cara about her birth, but I shared that secret with Gregory. I knew nobody whom I would want to advise me in this matter, certainly not Max or Zelda, partly because I did not want them to know my feelings for Orsini, which would make me a silly victim of *Schwärmerei* in their eyes — and partly, I must confess, because I wanted to act alone. I wanted to get to know Orsini, though I must never let him know that — men were conceited enough, I had found, without additional encouragement from young women — and now I had been offered a way of doing so.

I knew that the benefit was to be in ten days, and so Orsini was unlikely to be in Florence before another week had passed. If I left a message at the theatre asking him to meet me on a certain day? — so long as I could trust the messenger. But perhaps they were all in it, all plotting to murder that voice, if not the man. Orsini would see it as murder, I was sure. I went over and over what the men had actually said and veered from complete scepticism about my understanding of Italian, and complete disbelief! — people did not plot poisoning in ice-cream parlours — to a conviction that he was truly in danger and that I could save him, or at least warn him about not drinking from whatever innocuous-looking glass of water was on stage during his rendition of Rodolfo's aria. As I neared Zelda's apartment I decided that I had in fact overheard intrigue on behalf of a jealous rival or agent, and that I had not let my imagination run away with me. Whatever they were going to do, he should be warned. It could not hurt to warn him. My only misgiving was still that he would not believe me and that he would spurn my message or laugh at me. Well, I would not mind being laughed at if it spared him future humiliation. I'd rather be humiliated myself.

There was an equinoctial storm the next day and a smell of autumn in the air, and after that it became a little cooler. In the privacy of my room I wrote and rewrote a note that would alert Orsini and not be dismissed by him. He would not remember my name. How should I sign it? I decided on 'The girl you met on the bridge'. In the message, which I intended to hand in at the theatre, I would say only that I had something of importance to his work to communicate to him and suggest a meeting place. Then I would search out those men who sit in the offices of theatres adding up receipts or selling tickets, and trust to luck. I sealed the note and went out the day after the storm.

They were already putting up the bills for the benefit. 'Almost sold out', it said and I pushed open the door of the stalls entrance where I had

231

often been with Zelda and her friends. I had a gold coin ready to bribe whoever I could find to take the envelope. I hoped my Italian would be adequate. What if I saw one of those two men from the *Gelateria* and they overheard me? I tried to forget the snags and dangers and went across to a little door behind the booking office where I hoped someone would be working. There was no answer to my knock at first. If only Orsini himself would suddenly appear — but he would still be far away. I knocked again and the door was opened by an old man in breeches and with a pair of steel-rimmed spectacles perched on the end of his nose.

'Signor', I began, feeling my heart thudding under my grey poplin dress. He looked enquiringly at me. Oh God, he was deaf! — for he held a hand to his ear in a supplicating way. 'May I speak to you?' I said.

He hesitated, then ushered me into the small office. Fortunately there was nobody else to over-hear me. 'I have an important message for Signor Orsini', I said and showed him the envelope on which I had written Signor Orso Orsini in large, clear capital letters.

'He is not here', he said in Italian and leered at me. I realized he thought I was a girl friend of the singer. Perhaps the place was full of ladies bearing anguished messages to their idol?

'When he arrives', I said, and then repeated: 'When he arrives — will you please give him this message?' What if he, the old man opened it? He would not gather much from what I'd written. I showed him the coin. 'I will give you this, if you will promise to deliver this personally to the maestro — and another (I tapped it suggestively) when I hear that you have done so.' In the note I had put that I would meet Orsini in Santa Croce at noon on the day before the benefit, being sure that he would be there for rehearsals by then. I only hoped that the old man would not decide to come there himself. He took his glasses off to inspect the letter and then to my infinite relief nodded and held out his hand. I gave him the envelope and the money and he chuckled.

'It shall be done', he said in a half-pompous, half-suggestive way. '*Bella voce*', he said and pointed to Orsini's name again.

'*Bellisima*', I replied and bowed stiffly.

'See, I shall put it here in my book', he said. 'I shall not forget.'

I seemed to have chanced upon the right person for messages, for he pointed to a sheaf of envelopes and papers. 'Already they write to him', he said. 'You are coming to the benefit?'

Zelda had already bought tickets for us all, including Cara, and so I said: 'Of course.' Then I bade him goodbye and left my little envelope in what I trusted would be his safe keeping.

Until the next week I was on tenterhooks.

I told nobody at home about my adventure and tried to remain calm and collected. Zelda herself appeared *distraite*. She was a different person in Florence, more anxious, it seemed to me. She would half lie in her long wicker chair with its scarlet cushions arranged behind her head, and Rosa would look round the door every evening before we retired and suggest a 'Nice tissy-anne.'

My aunt always replied: 'That would be perfect, Rosa,' or 'Daventry', on the days she was in a less good mood. Then Zelda would idly turn the pages of a fashion magazine and comment upon it to Cara. She had struck up quite a friendship with Cara and they enjoyed such discussions. Sometimes though she would stand at the window and look out over the dark square or bend her head and flick at imaginary irregularities in the weave of her silk bodice. I wondered what she was thinking about; I could never guess, for Zelda was a mystery to me in many ways. She was never exactly in low spirits, but looked preoccupied and I used to think that perhaps she had financial difficulties. But surely if she had, she could not live the life she and Max did, which if not opulent was extremely comfortable.

When she looked broody I would wonder what the late-lamented Mr de Vere had been like. I presumed he had been a connoisseur and that that was where Max had got his aesthetic interests from, and from whom Zelda had some of her own knowledge. As a widow Zelda was popular with the other sex; she never lacked a companion and there was a tight little circle of old-timers who had known each other years ago, including Mrs Warburton and her sister and the Count. I often thought the Count would have been happy to settle down and marry my aunt. Though he always acted perfectly properly in public, I had seen them, heads together, murmuring in private. Zelda however was used to managing her own affairs and very independent. Once or twice when she had mentioned my mother — which was not often — she had looked disturbed, always alluding to her as 'Poor Maria' or 'My dear sister', and once she said: 'Your mother was a bit of a Dora Spenlow', knowing I would catch the allusion. I was sure that Zelda had always been the stronger of the two both physically and emotionally.

I had still not asked her again to tell me where Mama's grave was. I don't know why, except I felt she would tell me in her own good time, and during the week I was waiting to see Orsini I thought little of the past.

If Max joined us they usually gossiped about acquaintances. Max enjoyed gossip; he was old for his age. If Cara joined in such conversations Zelda would quiz her about the young men she had met at the villa and which ones were organizing parties now in Florence. If Cara and Max chatted together I would sometimes surprise a strange expression on my aunt's face that I could not decipher — regret? wryness? slight amusement?

'Her face is her fortune', she said to me more than once about my sister. I thought she was probably thinking that *mine* was *not* — and one afternoon I asked her if she and Mama had looked alike. 'We had the same height and colouring, though your Mama always wore her ringlets at the side', she replied. Although she was now over forty Zelda was still a handsome woman.

Max was to return to London for his last term. 'We must protect him from fortune hunters', Zelda said to me the day he was out registering his trunk for the journey. 'Young men should sow their wild oats before settling down.' I thought, she does not know her son so well. Max was quite determined not to remain too long under his mother's thumb.

On those evenings when Rosa did not bring her mistress a tisanne it would be China tea and *pasticcinos* at nine o'clock, for we dined early *à l'américane* if we were not to go out. Zelda ate little, fearful I expect of spoiling her waistline. However well I had got to know her since we came to Italy I still felt there was a lot I did not know about her — and about my mother too. So I told Zelda nothing of my adventure for I did not quite trust her, in spite of her kindness to me. She usually had good judgement about people, but I wasn't going to risk opening my heart to anybody and spoiling the rainbow bubble I had blown for myself round the handsome head of Orso Orsini.

The day dawned when I should see Orsini if he had received my message. There was now no time to be lost. What should I do if he did not turn up? The benefit was for the morrow. I had passed the Opera a few times since my visit to the little old man but never seen any singers. In my note I had asked the singer to meet me by the tomb of Rossini — it seemed a suitable venue.

I was extremely nervous when I entered the great, high, marble-floored church where so many great Florentines were buried. It was such a vast place with its beautiful windows; in the middle of the crowds of *turisti* who were always there visiting it, I thought I should pass unobserved. I went straight to the tomb, though I was early, not even going to see the Giotto frescoes as I usually did. Even with all the groups of people walking about, the place looked vast, and echoed with their footsteps and voices. But nobody took any notice of me. I'd covered my head with a black scarf as I intended to pretend to pray in one of the side chapels where I might speak to Orsini. If he came. I looked around. No sign of him yet. It was nearly noon. He probably had better things to do than make assignations with mad girls.

I waited a few more moments near the tomb pretending to study it. A few nuns passed, and one stayed for a time and then went on as most people did to the sanctuary windows. Suddenly, when I had thought I was alone, I heard a quiet voice behind me, and turned. Orsini had slipped to my side from behind a tall pillar. I started. Now or never! I gathered my wits, and looked him full in the face. How big and handsome he was, his eyes so dark — and looking at me I thought, quizzically. Then he made a bow to Rossini and his tomb, and that made me smile.

I said in my best Italian: 'Thank you for coming. I have something to tell you — it is not concerned with me', I added, lest he should think I was about to throw myself at his feet in worship.

'The girl on the bridge!' he said. 'Come, we will sit down — over here I think.' He took charge and I followed him to a chair in a side aisle. What if he refused to believe me? All my carefully prepared explanations seemed to go out of my head as I sat next to him. He did not pretend to pray but said: 'Well, Beatrice — what is the matter?'

I knew he was referring to Dante and his lady and the bridge, but I could not let him begin to flirt with me however much that might please my lowliest instincts.

'Thank you for coming here,' I began. Then as he waited, a half-smile on his lips, 'It is a matter of life and death', I whispered. 'Life for your voice, I mean.'

Then I began, in my halting Italian, to explain what I had heard and where I had heard it and I ended up saying: 'Please believe me — I know I do not speak your language well, but I understand it reasonably well, you see —'

'What did they look like? Tell me again', he commanded. His face had grown pale and serious. I tried to describe the fat little man and the tall thin one, using my hands in my endeavour, as Italians do. 'I know nothing of your plans — nothing of what you are to sing', I finished. 'But I knew they were talking about you — at the benefit — and if you are to sing from *Luisa Miller* — that was what they were talking about — *if* there is a glass of wine you have to drink? —'

Now he looked very thoughtful. But he said nothing till I had repeated my story ending with: 'Do you have enemies? I am sure of what I heard, but forgive me if it turns out I was mistaken.' My mouth was dry with my repeated explanations.

For answer he took my hand very solemnly and said: 'You were right to tell me — yes, I think I have enemies — but I did not know Alfieri was so — never mind . . .'

'It is your voice', I whispered, 'it is your *voice* they want to silence.' Your lovely voice, I thought, and for some reason — a reaction I suppose to all the emotion of the past few minutes, never mind all my agonizing over the past ten days — tears began to form in my eyes. I hardly knew him; he was a stranger; if I knew him it was only as others did, as a singer, and I was only one of the thousands who paid him the compliment of listening. But as I sat on and he looked searchingly at me, it seemed that I did know him. But I was determined not to say anything that might lead him to think I wanted intimacy or special consideration. 'There — now you know,' I said huskily. 'I felt I had to let you know. You will know what to do? I must go.'

'No — stay a moment — you have not told me your name — at the party they said it but I forgot. I remember you very well — how clever you were to know what they were talking about — *Dio Mio!* that they would do *that!*'

'It *was* about something to make your throat

wrong?' I said, not quite finding the words in another language.

'It is easy to scald a throat — stop a man's voice for ever', he replied.

'For ever? — I thought it was just to make you look silly tomorrow.'

'No — it will be more serious', he said.

'Then you do believe me — truly?'

'Yes — I believe you, truly — but tell me your name. Then I shall go and find my friends and they will help me.'

'Oh, it is Hetty', I said. 'Hester in English, really — Hester Coppen.'

'Ester — Then, Ester, you will come to hear me sing tomorrow? I promise you it will be better than when I sang for my supper in summer!'

'Of course I shall come', I replied, hypnotized by those eyes. His voice was light. I guessed he often spoke quietly, not wanting to spoil his voice for singing. Then I said: 'If they murdered your voice they would murder *you!*'

I hadn't meant to say that, but when I did, he took my hand, and kissed it. Then he said: 'You make me a small prayer here? I will go out, and you can follow later — if they recognize you with me . . .'

I thought he was being unnecessarily careful and I said: 'They did not see me — and I am nobody — but I will pray for you if you like.'

'I have no more time now', he said. 'Rehearsals in half an hour. Promise you will come tomorrow, and afterwards there will be people in the salon

— you must come there and I will see you.'

I knew that Zelda and her friends were to stay on afterwards to be presented to the singers who would then present them with a cheque for their hospital, so I said: 'Yes — I shall come with my aunt — I will be there. *Please* take care.'

He stood up and turned once more towards me and he said: 'It was very brave of you to come — I will thank you later. Afterwards —' Then he was gone and I remained sitting there alone. I shut my eyes for a time and felt as drained as if I had just recovered from a fever. Not my mission, but the presence by my side of the man I had worshipped so long. I only hoped that he had no inkling of my feelings. I had done my duty. I got up after a few more minutes during which I prayed to some strange god that it would all be resolved and that no harm would come to him and that if I saw him again I should be able to preserve my equanimity.

As we entered the opera house the next afternoon — for the benefit was a matinée — I was in a gut-turning fever of dread. What if he should by some error drink from the glass those two had prepared for him? What if? But it was no good agonizing. I just hoped he had sorted it all out for himself. There were two items to begin with, sung by an enormous soprano, and then it was to be Orso in his first piece, a song of Bellini's: *Vanne O Rose Fortunata*. As soon as I saw him I knew it was going to be all right. His bearing had nothing nervous about it; he was in fine voice — there was tension there but it added only to the intensity with which he pronounced the words with his great rolling r's, the voice suddenly opening out when he wanted to convince whoever it was to whom the song was addressed. I looked at the programme. Yes, a song from *Luisa Miller* after some duets from a baritone and a mezzo whom I hadn't heard before. There were to be no intervals.

Suddenly, at the end of the duet, a man with a small beard came to the footlights and stood there for a moment waiting for silence. 'Signor Orsini has slightly altered his programme', he announced. 'He will be singing from Bellini's *I Puritani* and from *Rigoletto*.'

That was it then — no *Luisa Miller!* Thank goodness I should not have to watch what I was dreading — the appearance of a glass of water or wine on stage. He must have settled their hash. I hoped that he had been able to *prove* there was something wrong, not just that he had decided to sing arias where there was no possibility of glasses of liquid appearing. Perhaps I'd never know what had happened.

I forgot all that when he came on again in a series of songs that each, in its way, showed what a maestro he was; from the delicate, lyrical — and yet powerful — *bel canto,* to the elemental impact of *Ella me fu rapita* sung by the wicked Duke of Mantua. He sang words with no appearance of effort, the result of incredible technique. I felt it was wasted upon some of the patrons who would have preferred something more sentimental, less elemental.

I saw the beads of sweat on his forehead as that fabulous voice, so expressive, so exciting, and yet with a sensual appeal not lost on me, soared and swooped and rang out the notes of human suffering and human ecstasy. I believe it was then I began to realize for the first time what a physical thing singing was, almost an athletic feat. In some of the phrases there was a driving force behind the voice that was the man himself, powerful, large. When he had finished the Duke's song, one of the older ladies near me was murmuring: 'Ravishing, truly ravishing.' I agreed with her, though I would not have said it aloud. The applause was deafening and he took three bows before going off and giving way to another woman, a coloratura who was to sing a duet with him later. She was excellent, but I did not think you could pour your soul into such high, sweet music. Romantic it might be, but not so appealing to me. When Orso Orsini sang it was as if he was using music both to express feelings which I understood, while at the same time as lending his voice as a servant to music. A violin might have expressed some of it, but the human voice made me feel more human myself, made me feel that life was an adventure, solemn, and thrilling, and worth living. Many tenors sang their top notes as falsettos at this time; Orso never. However high the notes he sang they came from the chest — where was his heart —

and were thus given that power which moves other hearts. Another thing I noticed that afternoon, as outside the sky faded and we sat in our ridiculous finery as though it were night, was that when Orso sang he seemed to be enjoying himself. In spite of all the effort needed to sing like a god, he was enjoying himself! But I was sure that enjoyment, however genuine, came also from years of self-discipline.

Whilst listening to him and thinking these things as others sang or played, I forgot my fears for a time and began to wonder whether I'd been mistaken and imagined the whole episode in the parlour. Yet he had altered the pro-gramme . . .

Max, whose last day it was in Italy until Christmas, was seated next to me, and I felt he was observing me with those sharp eyes that missed nothing. However hard I tried to remain unmoved and not to betray the turmoil of longing and ardour aroused by Orsini and his singing, I could not help forgetting myself to the extent of clasping my hands hard in my lap and half-rising from my velvet chair. But Max said nothing. On the other side of my aunt, Cara was looking a little bored. I knew that when we all met in the salon the society women would be fluttering their fans round Orsini and I almost wished he had not asked me to speak to him then. I had no wish to call attention to myself. What chance had I with all the glittering talent around him? Did they speak sincerely, in spite of their wealth and sophistication and the numerous *affaires du coeur* they doubtless conducted?

The time came for Orsini's final appearance. Two arias, one a duet with the coloratura singer and the other from Act II of the Ballo in Maschera which I knew would recall to me the first time I had heard and seen him. I settled back for the Bellini. I had never heard this before and was to be captivated. When they sang together, he and his soprano partner and supposed lover, I wished *I* could sing with him, for the voices mingled ecstatically, and when he sang the *Viene Viene* I could not help the tears in my eyes. I should have to take hold of myself. If I went on feeling this passionate sadness and longing I'd destroy my old self that had been content with escape from home and never looked further than an independent life.

On the high, eerie 'Ah!', which I had not expected, the audience began to clap but I remained motionless, a lump in my throat. I would like time to have stopped with that note. The audience seemed in a frenzy. What a success he was having! I wondered if those two shifty-looking men were here, or had he unmasked them publicly? The audience demanded a repeat and Orsini sang part of it again. It was not just the music that made my heart beat faster and my own throat tighten, as though mimicking his. His voice seemed to have two different tones — one high and honeyed, mellow, tender, light, every word enunciated clearly even when the voice almost whispered, with those 'r's rolling magnificently; the other when he came to the end of a repeated stanza or sang a different kind of song. Then he rose in a passionate ascent higher and higher, reaching the top notes with thrilling power and staying there apparently effortlessly. After what seemed an age he descended in cascades of failing liquid sound or suddenly cut the sound off abruptly when it would echo on. I never wanted him to stop singing, though sometimes I felt he might die on those top notes. His voice had seduced me long before I ever spoke to him, but that afternoon it was not only his voice that I loved.

'He is a *force naturelle*', Max said and I turned to him.

'It is art too', I whispered, but pleased at what my usually critical cousin had said. Orso Orsini was the most gifted person I was ever likely to meet; if I had in some small way helped him I could feel only humbly grateful. I looked at him as he received the plaudits of the audience and then they finally fell silent and the *diva* disappeared and he was alone on stage once more for his last song.

But Orsini was about to say something before the conductor of the small orchestra could raise his baton for he raised his hand for silence and the conductor waited. In a quiet, light voice, the voice I had heard in the church the day before, he said: 'I always think when I sing my last song to you that it is the voice of Dante who speaks to his Beatrice.' I shivered, remembering that he had jestingly called me Beatrice. It did not mean

246

anything of course, was only a gesture to the Italians of Florence, but when he began to sing: '*I shall see her in ecstasy*', I imagined he was singing to me! I pulled myself together again when the benefit finished with a rousing chorus, and after a few speeches and flowers I filed out after Zelda and Cara with Max bringing up the rear. 'I'll see you all later', said Max. 'I can't stand this sort of crush and I've got a few things to sort out.' He looked at my sister as he said this, but she said nothing and he turned away and went off.

We went into the special room reserved for friends of the hospital where some of the artists were already being presented to the old representatives of Independent Tuscany. Bruno moved up to talk to Cara, and Zelda was chatting to her Count. Mrs Warburton was as usual accompanied by her sister but there was no sign of Mrs Holroyd in the melée. The champagne was already being poured and for a moment I lost Zelda and Cara and the others and remained standing by a white-napped table, the music still in my ears. Then I saw Orsini at the other end of the room with the soprano. I looked over at him carefully as he smiled and acknowledged those who were presented to him and bowed low to the dignitaries to whom he was presented. I did not belong in this sort of society.

He was tall, certainly tall for an Italian, though not a giant, and he looked relaxed and happy. Such large, bright, black eyes! Did his own singing move him? Then I lost him in the crowd as I sipped the champagne I'd been handed by a lackey, and wished everyone but Orso would go home. That fount of feeling in me which the music had made me realize already existed, was choking me. I did not know how he could appear and look so at ease when he had just poured out that music.

A man came up to me just then as I was deciding I'd better find Zelda and try to be sociable. In my purse I had the gold coin to give to the old man who had delivered my message and I intended, after a few moments' chat, to make an excuse and find him, unless he had gone home. But, 'Signorina', said the man who had come up to me. 'Signor Orsini is waiting to speak to you in the antechamber if you are Signorina Ester — a small young lady, he said, with plaited hair. It is you?'

I started, 'Yes, I am Hester', I replied.

'Then follow me.' He led me through a door behind all the tables and chairs and I followed him round the corridor until we came to where another door was open leading back to the crowd opposite another door that was shut. The man opened it and bowed and I found myself inside a small room with two chairs and a curtained alcove. The alcove's curtain parted and Orsini appeared to me.

'Grazie, Grazie!' he said and took my hand and kissed it.

'Is it all right then — what happened?' I asked confusedly.

'Only that you saved my life', he said, and released my hand and looked suddenly away. I was determined to appear cool and collected, though I had never felt so full of inner turmoil. 'I knew who it was — never mind their names — I challenged them behind the scenes when the glass was already filled and the scenery ready for my first aria,' he said. 'So they could not deny it for I asked them to drink from the glass —'

'You mean, just before the performance?' What style!

'Yes — I had to do it then or they would deny it. They would not drink so I threw the contents of the glass in their faces. *Quale odore!* — a smell of ammonia, I think —'

'But are you not going to have them arrested?'

'They will deny it — Never mind, I am on my guard. I shall take the dregs to the pharmacist.'

'Who can hate you so?'

'Ester — a singer's life is dangerous when there is much money and jealous managers — it is all horrible — sometimes I wish' — But he stopped and gestured me to a chair, sat down himself. 'It doesn't matter . . . I only wanted to thank you from my heart. Tell me where I can find you — I am to go to your country next year to London — to Covent Garden, but before that to many other cities. Will you see me before I go? There is no place suitable here to talk — and I have to go and be polite. You liked the concert?'

He looked at me as though he really awaited my verdict just like any ordinary man of thirty or so who was uncertain of his reception. I wanted to say — you were wonderful — but said only:

'You must know you are a great singer, signor — you do not need an ignorant English girl to tell you that!'

His eyes flashed. 'Yes I *do* need that. They will clap me whenever I reach a top C — you know — I have sung Arturo better — but *La Rivedrà* never better —'

'The song for Dante', I said shyly and smiled.

'Ah, yes — and for Beatrice', he said. A large smile enveloped his face. 'The world is a cess-pool,' he said, 'but also a paradise. Tell me where you live — and whether you will stay in Florence. I hope to return here after Parigi and Londra — and then I shall thank you again.'

'You *have* thanked me', I said. 'I am on *Via Manzoni*', — I gave him the number, — 'but I live with my aunt Mrs de Vere who will be wondering where I am — you must go to your admirers, signor.'

'Yes, I must', he seemed to sigh. 'But before I go to France I might walk again by the bridge at dawn — as I did before — or in the Boboli Gardens.'

I knew it was an invitation, but I was not sure what he planned. He could not possibly feel for me anything but gratitude and I did not want to encourage an ordinary sort of flirtation, so I said: 'October dawns are cold, Signor Orsini.'

'Ester! — you will call me Orso — or I shall be cross', he said. 'Go back to your people and I will do my duty. But you will call me Orso, please!' He was jolly now, seemingly having forgotten the risks he had taken earlier that afternoon. Like all Italians, I thought, he lives for the moment.

'*Addio, Orso*', I said. 'You sang like an angel.'

'*Addio, Salvatore*', he said and kissed my hand again and then opened the door, and I went back into the room with all the crowds and could not help thinking, this is the best day of my life, even though I do not want him to be in my debt for I am in debt to him and the world he has opened up to me.

I found Zelda, and a few minutes later I saw Orso, as I must now call him, chatting and laughing and the centre of attention. Cara was with Bruno and they were both presented to the singer by the Count, but I did not go up. I saw him say a few words to my sister, who looked ravishing. I imagined his glance lay on her rather longer than on other less pretty young women. But I turned away, clutching to myself all his words. I must begin to see him as an ordinary man, not an angel, or a god, or the owner of a voice in a thousand million, but a man, the only man I had ever wanted in all my young life.

I had still not repaid my 'messenger' for I had to leave the theatre with Aunt Zelda and her party, and a carriage was waiting for us in a side street.

'He has a reputation, that Orsini', said my aunt as we drove home. She had not noticed my short absence from the party.

A sort of joy, the feeling of having been in the

251

presence of a benignity, stayed with me when we returned. But how could I ever know the man normally? *He* had not written the music that enraptured me; he was only the vessel for it. I had been brought up to distrust emotion and passion and irrational desires, all things highly unsuitable for young English ladies — and yet — had not my own family also sacrificed themselves on the altars of love? Was I already marked out for blisses and agonies because those feelings had been no strangers to my parents either?

11

The day after the concert I was in my room when quite by chance I overheard Zelda's Count and a friend of his talking about politics. The men I knew did not normally discuss ideas with young ladies; with older ones they might occasionally discuss political personalities. They were waiting in the sitting-room for Zelda to appear since they were to accompany her to a 'tea' at the British Embassy. I had pleaded a headache and suggested Cara went with her, for the idea of listening to trivialities whilst my mind and heart were overflowing with the remembrance of the previous day's excitement was anathema. I hardly ever absented myself from social occasions, so Zelda was sympathetic. Our apartment was not large and my own room led off the alcove where we usually dined — which was separated from the common sitting-room by double doors. Today the doors had been opened by the woman who had been cleaning the rooms in the morning and she had forgotten to shut them. Zelda would be with the men soon from her boudoir but whilst they waited I caught the word 'revolution' and 'anti-clerical'. I pricked up my ears when I heard the name Verdi, for anything to do with that wonderful composer fascinated me. Without music written for them to sing where would the greatest singers in the world find themselves? Singing to the goats, I supposed, or casting their rendering of folk songs to the Venetian waters. The two men said nothing interesting after that; soon afterwards I heard Zelda's voice, and the conversation became its usual mixture of Italian and English. I wondered whether Orso was a Catholic, and whether he agreed with the opinions of the man whose music he sang so beautifully. But practitioners of the musical art, not being men of ideas, needed to express only what the songs might mean to them personally. I knew I was myself a woman of ideas, though mine, such as they were, seemed to flee from my head when a more powerful interest put me under an enchantment, but men did not like girls with opinions — they were 'unwomanly'. Men would rather have women in love than women capable of thinking rationally. I had better beware. Yet I wanted to 'be myself' with Signor Orsini as far as opinions were concerned. I would never tell him of my other feelings!

I sat at my table and was idly opening a book once the others had gone. Cara had put her head round my door to say goodbye, all glowing in a pink gown she had had made by Serafina's sister who was a mistress of sewing and embroidery. She looked happy, even though Max had gone early that morning. I could not help feeling sorry for anyone who was in love with her for they would have plenty of rivals. I heard the door-bell, and

Rosa answered it. Shortly afterwards she knocked at my door. 'A note for you, Miss Hetty', she said and stiffly handed me a small white envelope.

'Who came with it?' I asked, getting up in my excitement.

'A boy. I said "I'm not promising to give it her — give it to her yourself". But he ran off.'

'Oh, I expect Eleanor is wanting to arrange a visit to a lecture at the Accademia,' I said, hastily improvising. She looked sceptical but went off, closing the door with a bang. I must keep Rosa on my side, I thought, as I opened the envelope whose only addressee was Signorina Esta at Via Manzoni 7/2. The note was brief: 'I shall be walking in the Boboli Gardens this afternoon unless it rains. Can you meet me there at four o'clock?' The signature was two Os, one inside the other.

I hastily gathered my bonnet and cloak and went into Rosa. 'Eleanor wants me to see her about a party', I lied swiftly, 'I need some fresh air — I shan't be long.' I did not have to justify my comings and goings to Rosa, but I felt I ought to tell her where I was going. 'We are to take a stroll in the Boboli', I added. 'It is not raining, so I thought I would go —'

'Take care — traipsing about Florence by yourself', she grumbled, but I don't think she suspected anything.

'It will do my headache good', I said, unable to prevent myself embroidering on an untruth. As I went down the outer stairs and through the front door I wondered at my own capacity for fibs.

The Boboli Gardens, which stretch out behind the Pitti Palace on the other side of the river, are extensive, but there was an entrance from the palace end, not a very long walk from our apartment. The gardens are laid out on a hill, and that afternoon quite a number of people had decided that the sun was to stay out long enough for them to enjoy a stroll. In the distance there were many geometrically arranged paths and there were statues scattered everywhere.

I went on to the terrace of the Palace overlooking the Fontana dei Carciolo and saw Orsini already there, standing looking at the splendid view. He was dressed in a pale grey jacket and grey trousers and I paused a moment, just looking at him as he stared out over the gardens; which I would have called a park. Then he turned, and I went up to him.

'Oh, I'm so glad you could come, Ester', he said in Italian. 'It was such a business yesterday — and I am going away this evening.'

My face must have fallen however much I tried to dissimulate. I said: 'I told them I was meeting a friend.'

He took my hand and then thought the better of kissing it, I think, for he said: 'Shall we walk a little in the gardens?'

'The benefit was a great success?' I suggested feebly, waiting for him to say something about the danger he had courted.

For a time he said nothing, but we walked on until he saw a small fountain near which there were chairs for visitors. Then: 'It is better that you know little of our intrigues', he began, as we sat down in the benign autumn sun that had suddenly reappeared that afternoon. Because it had rained so recently the earth smelt rich and carried with it a perfume which I shall always connect with Florence. It came from the box-hedges and the various herbs that had soaked in sun all summer. There were orange and pink flowers in the neatly maintained beds; the gardens stretched a long way down the hillside with their statues and the formal patternings of 'walks' leading right down to the Porta Romana. I had never yet visited them. I took a deep breath and shut my eyes for a moment in the sun. When I opened them he was looking at me. 'You saved my reputation — and probably my life', he said in that light voice that so belied the power of his singing. 'It amounts to something', he said.

'I was happy to be able to do so', I answered formally, my heart beating as I cast surreptitious glances at his large hands and broad shoulders and the black — oh so black — eyes. His gaze lingered on me then and I dropped my own, feeling quite overcome. His every pore seemed to me to exude Italy, and beauty, and love — and humanity. 'Anyone would have done as much', I said after a pause.

'No, they would *not*', he said in a decisive voice. 'Why should they? In any case, who would have understood what those two were discussing? It is hardly the sort of thing one expects, is it?'

'Not in a *Gelateria*', I answered, and he laughed.

'And they would not have understood, your compatriots. *You* speak my language well. That you understood was perhaps divine intervention!'

I supposed he must believe in God then, but I wondered if he was also a Radical, like Verdi. '*They* would not have *listened!*' I said — then 'You have thanked me enough, Signor Orsini —'

'Now, I told you you must call me Orso', he said reprovingly.

'Orso', I rolled out. 'It is a curious name — why did they call you that? The Great Bear', I said in English. 'It is a star', I added in Italian. (Like you, I thought.)

'Oh, I was christened Luigi', he said. 'I took the name for euphony and perhaps I *am* a bear, you see. Quite patient and good-tempered unless I am attacked.'

'What are you going to do? — they might try something again.'

'I had the dregs analysed. It was a poison to scar my throat. But I do not think they will try again. The manager and the répétiteur do not know exactly what happened — it was all too quick — but the man you saw — the fat one — has gone away and is nowhere to be found — probably gone to see his tall friend. He is called Bugatti — the fat man — he is an agent of my rival.'

I gasped. Surely people did not go *so* far to unman the opposition?

'They still fight duels here, you know', he said conversationally. 'Though it is forbidden — and I do not believe in duelling. That lamp-post of a man you saw — he is connected also with the police, you know.'

'With the police! Good Heavens!' The idea of a London bobby having criminal connections would be preposterous, I thought. Now that Italy was a modern united country, democratic institutions would prevail, wouldn't they? I had heard of the Mafiosi and knew that you could not get very far in this country without greasing someone's palm, but that a plot should be encouraged by a guardian of law and order! Remembering palm-greasing called to my mind the little old man in the opera office, and I brought out my gold coin. 'This is for the man who sits in the office and sells tickets — he promised to give you my letter — and I forgot I'd promised him a little further perk if he did. Please give it to him, will you — it is not always easy for me to get out alone. I have my sister now with me and so until she leaves I shall be accompanying her — and my aunt of course.'

'Your sister is the *bella bambina* in pink who was presented to me by Count What's His Name?' he asked, and I laughed.

'Yes, she is very pretty, Cara, — but I don't want *her* to get mixed up in anything. Do you think they have any idea how you knew about their plan?'

'None at all. Before I threw it at them I just sniffed the famous glass and said it smelt atrocious. You should have seen Bugatti's face!'

I shuddered. I so wished he were not going away,

but I could not go on continuing to impose this debt of gratitude. It was an artificial reason for meeting — but then, I hadn't invented the circumstances.

'You said anyone would have done the same', he pursued. 'But no — you were brave.'

'Please do not be in my debt', I said stiffly.

'Are you to stay here in Florence for the rest of the year? Your aunt — Mrs de Vere, she lives here?'

'Yes, she used to live in Florence years ago and returned last January. I suppose I may have to return home one day, though I would rather not. My own mother is dead. And I prefer Italy. But I want to work, you see.' I found myself telling a sympathetic listener about my intention of teaching.

'You must improve my English', was all he said when I'd finished. 'Will you give me your address in London so that if you return to England and I do not come to Florence for some time, I can see you?'

I was certainly not going to give this wonderful man the address of Papa's home and I answered with Lucy Little's address in Camberwell instead. 'I could be reached there', I said. 'But it is a world away from the sort of place you will want to know in London.' I was overjoyed that he had asked. He took out his pocket book and wrote the address down at my direction, which I spelt out alphabetically in Italian.

'The money now for the singers is in America',

260

he said as he put away his diary. 'I shall go there, I expect —'

'You have fame before you', I said solemnly.

'You think so?'

How could I explain what I felt about that voice of his, sitting there decorously on a little spindly chair in that peaceful park? Never perhaps to see him again. I concentrated in my answer on music and he listened to my stumbling attempt to describe my reactions to opera.

'But I love — other sorts of music too — it is just that singing is the closest to heaven', I ended, having found one could say such things in another language. I felt reckless.

'You are a woman of spirit', he said and looked very serious.

'It is true I am serious-minded', I answered after a pause. 'But if I could sing like you I think I should not want to do anything else. It must make you very happy?'

'Yes', he said. 'In spite of all the effort and work and the exhaustion — yes, it is the most wonderful feeling to be able to sing and to have the world listening — that also is wonderful. It is happiness', he added. 'Like *fare l'amore* is happiness. But my singing is not quite so natural.' He said all that quite directly without the sort of simper I had noticed on so many men's faces if they referred to love. Not that anyone had ever said anything so direct in my hearing before. This man was not ordinary. Even if he had not had a divine voice he would have had a magnetic personality. Without

the voice what would he have been? I was thoughtful. So many things were said to be 'natural'. If
you had to train your voice, did you even so also
have to learn how to love?

'Do not be shocked', he said.

'I am not shocked', I replied. 'But wanting to
destroy may also be natural!'

'Indeed —' he answered gravely. I thought,
there has not been much of the right sort of love
in my family. Or was it an excess of passion that
had led to my mother's death? Women were not
supposed to be passionate — and neither did I
want to give him the impression that I could easily
abandon myself to him, but I wished I too could
be 'natural'.

'I am sorry you are leaving Florence', I managed
to get out. 'But I must go now — I am supposed
to be with an American friend.'

'It is a pity, for I should like to walk with you
in the Giardino del Cavaliere. It will be for a future
time? I know I am not following the *convenances*
— though they say that English ladies are sometimes allowed to behave — "naturally".' He gave
a big laugh.

'Not in England', I replied. 'But I am not a
lady — at least I don't want to be one. I despise
smart society. I don't like flirtation', I said boldly,
then hoped he did not believe I thought his own
manner flirtatious.

'Ah, it is a dangerous world, is it not?' he said
with a slight smile.

I looked round at the clipped walks as we

wended our way back to the Pitti Palace, and thought our English gardens were more natural. Orsini told me that he had never yet been to 'Londra', it would be his first visit there in the New Year, and so I warned him of the dirt and squalor as well as the majesty of the city.

'Don't forget to give the messenger my little coin', I said as he bade me farewell. Then he took my hand and turned it, and kissed the palm. It made me shiver. I looked into his large, black eyes and wished I dared kiss his wide, generous lips.

'I will not forget — and may God go with you', he replied, and he raised his hand and was off round the corner of the Palace. We had crossed the road together and for a moment I did not know where I was, felt dizzy with a great surge of love and desire — and anguish that he had gone.

I thought I was under no illusions about Orso Orsini. I had seen he was a kind man and also a man most sympathetic to young women and I thought, well, I have had my adventure. But the tumult of my feeling for him amazed me. I longed for his presence. Nobody remarked upon my absence, for Zelda was back late and Cara was full of her meeting with some young Englishmen from the Embassy who were, she said, less tiring to talk to than Italians. I saw Eleanor the next day, but said nothing to her about Orsini. I guessed she would have advised caution.

It was the day after that when a little boy came running up to me. Cara and I were leaving the house in the afternoon for a visit to a *galleria* for I had promised to acquaint her with some paintings. Cara had gone back for a wrap since it was chilly and the child pressed a small package in my hand and then ran off. I found myself later opening a small box in which reposed a silver coin inscribed on one side 'MIZPAH', and a card inscribed 'OO'. I realized then that it was possible that Orso Orsini might truly like me for myself rather than as the 'saviour' of his reputation. And I knew that if he did I should throw caution to the winds. But he had gone away.

In the solitude of my bedroom I looked up my Bible Concordance and found Mizpah in the book of Genesis. 'The Lord watch between thee and me', it said, 'When we are absent one from another'. I could not believe he had sent it! It was a declaration of some sort, but should I trust it was sincere? It would have taken an Englishman a year to dare to send that to a young woman.

Later I looked up the word 'love' in my English-Italian dictionary. Under 'Amare' I found both 'to feel profound affection for' and 'to be in love with'. When he had forgotten my helping him, when other prettier women had made his acquaintance, Orso Orsini would forget me, I thought. But just for practice and not without a wry smile I wrote in my journal: *'Ti amo'* and *'Ti voglio bene'* and wondered which had the stronger meaning. I crossed out both phrases and tried to confront 'reality' rather than dreams. Reality had harsher aspects, as I was soon to discover, though I could not arrest the flow of my feelings for a man who could probably possess any girl to whom he took a fancy.

The weeks passed and I was already thinking of my first Christmas in Florence. I was told that some people gave presents on the first day of Advent and that others deferred to the northern custom of Christmas Day, but that the Mass on the eve of Christmas was the great celebration. I wondered how Orsini was getting along in Paris, and scoured the French newspapers, but there was nothing. Perhaps he was rehearsing.

Gregory was to come for Cara before the middle of December just after my nineteenth birthday. My sister had become uncharacteristically quiet. I knew she wanted to stay longer in Italy, but the danger of Simon Voyle must have passed, for Papa had sent for her and told her he was arranging for Gregory to fetch her. He had never written to me; indeed I believe he had 'written me off' and I felt relief tinged with sadness. I saw that Cara dreaded his letters and hardly replied with more than a short note.

'But you can see Max in London. He is to stay into the New Year. Papa will not stop you seeing him, I'm sure, if that is what you want', I said, not too sure whether it were true. Papa would not want his favourite daughter marrying his first wife's nephew, however far in the future. Max though would one day be rich. I don't think that Cara had thought of this. However, other things were troubling her.

'What do you *do*, Hetty?' she began one day when the others were out, Zelda having gone with Rosa to her more fashionable dressmaker. 'What do you do when a man says he loves you, and you like him, and he is a — well, from a good family — and you reply that you are only seventeen and then he says he can wait but wants to get *fidanzata*?' She pronounced the Italian word with a certain hesitation.

'Is it Bruno?' I asked her directly.

'Yes — but he is to go in the army and he wants us to have an "understanding" for when he is free.'

'Well, do you love him — or he you?'

'He says he loves me, but it is a secret —'

'If he wants to marry you it can hardly remain a secret', I said drily.

'Oh, well, you see his mama wants him to marry someone else.'

'A rich girl, I expect?'

'Yes — it seems that they are not rich. But I don't mind about being rich, Hetty. It's not that!'

'You don't love him?'

She paused for a long time and looked so wretched I took pity on her.

'How can you know?' I said. 'One can like a whole host of young men — but marriage to one of them is rather different.'

'Oh, Hetty, you are so sensible. You see I *do* like him and I think I do want to marry *soon*, but —'

'If there are any "buts" ', I said sagely, 'you

266

should not commit yourself, Cara.' I did not suggest she asked Mamarella's advice as I was beginning to think my parents had made rather a mess of their lives. But who was I to speak?

After another pause she said, 'Really, you know if Max were not so young I think I could be, well — quite fond of *him* — he is amusing, isn't he? and he does not say silly things.' I wondered what silly things young Bruno had been saying.

'Tell Bruno you can decide nothing till you are eighteen', I said. 'If he is fond of you, he will wait.'

'I think you are right', she answered, her face brightening. 'And I shall soon be home.'

'Don't say anything to Papa or — Mama, then. But don't hide the fact that you have enjoyed Max's company. Why not ask him to take you to Covent Garden?' I thought they had better be prepared in case one day Max's suit was preferred in earnest. Being too young would be against him, but the de Vere money would not. What a schemer I was!

'Max will be a rich man one day', I said to my sister casually.

'Yes, I know', she replied. 'I will ask him to visit. Gregory or Lucy Little could chaperone us if Max did want to invite me to the theatre.' Later, after reflection, she said: 'Will that singer you so like ever be singing in London?' Yes, I thought, both you and he will be in England and I shall be nearly a thousand miles away.

'He might', I answered shortly. It seemed I

hadn't succeeded in covering up my feelings —
or my little sister was more pespicacious than I
had imagined!

I was annoyed that I had had to try to appear
cool and collected before Orso himself but had obviously let some of my real feelings appear when
I spoke of music. What sort of world was it where
women could never express what was in their
hearts without men imagining they were therefore
easy game? I had to try to dissimulate, but the
reason for caution was not that I cared what others
thought of me but that I cared what Orso Orsini
might think of me. Italians were happy to conduct
flirtations with young — and not so young — foreign women who responded to their charms, but
the same response from their compatriots, especially if they were young and pretty, would be
regarded as shameless — at least until they were
safely married to someone else! Marriage appeared
to be the only way a young woman was allowed
to grow up, and marriage meant losing your freedom — as I well knew. I'd rather be a 'free'
woman, but the only way of joining *that* company
was to lose one's reputation. Unless one was an
'artist' or a 'genius'. George Eliot lived with a man
to whom she was not married — but she was a
'genius'. Serious young ladies were the last people
expected to behave in an unorthodox manner. I
tried to put all this out of my head, and succeeded
for a few hours at a time, but sometimes I thought
that the way things were was rather unfair on men
too, for how could they know a woman's true na-

ture unless she was to reveal her innermost thoughts? When my mother had married Papa, how well had they known each other? Rosa had hinted at a great romance, but had Mama been truly in love with Papa? Had she even shared his tastes? If it had been such a love match why had he allowed her to go without him to Zelda to recover after my birth? When I was born they had been married only three and a half years and Mama was still only twenty-two, not much older than I was now. Papa was ten years older than Zelda, that I did know, so Mama had been nineteen to his thirty-one when they wed. I thought Papa ought to have been old enough to know his own mind by then. He could not have expected to fall in love with Mamarella; what magic had she wrought upon him? What spell had she lured him with? Yet now they were a conventional married couple.

I was considering these matters when I should have been preparing for Eleanor's visit to our apartment, and I could not get them out of my head. Why should I believe that Mamarella had planned what had happened any more than had Papa? People did fall in love 'unsuitably'. I knew that now! And if Simon Voyle's father had been anything like his son I did not envy Ella her first husband. Had he dealt cruelly with her that she should have fallen so quickly into Papa's outstretched arms? She must have loved Papa to be prepared for the social ostracism a divorced woman was sure to receive. If I were true to my principles of 'love', I ought to admire Ella instead of detesting her. For the first time in my life I began to try to see things from Mamarella's point of view, and as I waited for Eleanor to arrive I even began to see Papa's. They had probably not meant any of it to happen. They might have intended a clandestine affair until my mother came back recovered, but the imminence of Cara's birth must have made everything more urgent. I tried to look through the mists of the past and to understand what had happened to them all. As I did so I began to think more deeply about Orso Orsini. Was a man like Orso ever able to show his own natural self any more than could a young woman? Only in his art perhaps could he be himself; those who are adulated must be sorely tempted to act a role in society that might have nothing to do with their real selves. If I ever felt that Orsini was showing me his 'real' self I'd show him mine. He would have to take the first step; men could not so easily be compromised. But what if Orso was not the kind of man to want a rebel for a friend? (I dared think no further than 'friend' in spite of 'MIZPAH'). Nor might he want an emotional woman like myself for more than friendship. Neither had I seen anything of happy marriages — though Zelda always spoke of hers as ecstatic. Marriages ended either in death or recriminations, it seemed to me. I thought of Lucy's father. *He* would have been a good husband. So, was a man like Mr Little the sort who would make me happy? Should I look for a gentle, scholarly man, not dream about his opposite? Anyway, I thought rebelliously, why should I ever marry? What had that to do with love?

I read again the letter that had arrived that morning from England, since Eleanor was late and further speculations were profitless. Huntie had dictated a note and Alice had written it down for her. 'Your mother's nerves are worse. Please tell my Aunt Daventry I think she is frightened that someone is spying on Master Felix.' Well, that was nothing new, and what could Rosa do about it? Alice had not mentioned it herself but spoke only of the bonfire they were to have on 5 November and how there was the rumour that a school for girls was to be opened in the neighbourhood. 'If it does, perhaps Miss Little may teach there and I be her pupil!' she added. There was nothing from Lucy and nothing yet from Gregory about his arrangements for accompanying Cara home. It was nice of Alice to write. She always finished her letter with 'Hannah sends her love' and I often wondered if thoughts of me ever went through Pooranna's strange, slow, brain. I'd give Rosa the message from her niece that evening.

Eleanor came in rather breathlessly when I'd already started a letter back to Alice. Cara was looking out for her from the big window in the sitting-room and let her in.

'I'm sorry I'm late — I guess we just overlooked the time', said Eleanor, but she blushed, and I was sure she'd been with the handsome Laurence who was soon to return home to Massachusetts. We spent the afternoon chatting and playing cards since it was raining again. Was I to spend the rest of my life waiting for rain to stop and having undemanding conversations with my sister and my friend? Even in Florence, ordinary existence turned out much the same. Eleanor stayed to dinner, at which Zelda announced she'd had a letter from my brother Gregory. 'Your mother needs you for Christmas', she said to Cara and Cara pouted a little and shrugged her shoulders. 'He will arrive on 11 December', she went on. As she was talking I remembered Gregory telling me not to put my trust too completely in Zelda, so I said nothing to her about Huntie's little note but sought out Rosa in her own small quarters when Zelda had retired to bed and Eleanor long gone. I said nothing to Cara either.

I read Rosa the note from Huntie, but she insisted on putting her spectacles on and perusing it for herself. Somebody had once taught Rosa Daventry to read. Finally she looked up and I thought she looked worried.

'My stepmother is always imagining things', I said.

'Buffy would not write unless she was worried too', was all the answer I got.

'What can *you* do? Why does she bother you?' I asked, rather rudely.

She did not reply and after a moment I said: 'Do you think that the Voyle boy has anything to do with her fears?' I had given her an edited version of Cara's complaints about Simon Voyle. She looked up sharply, but still did not speak. 'You do, don't you, Rosa? He's never forgiven his mother for preferring my Papa to him!'

She pursed her lips. I wondered how much of all this would get back to Zelda. I'd never seen Peter Voyle since that evening when I first came to Florence, it seemed years ago. Had Zelda? Suddenly Rosa said: 'She didn't want to leave him his Dad took him away!'

'I should think that my brother Gregory could settle Simon Voyle's hash', I said.

'Buffy wouldn't have wrote unless there was something new bothering her', said Rosa again. I thought, something else she doesn't want to tell my father about. Had Mamarella been seeing her son Simon in secret? With the morning post the next day Cara had a letter from Max, but there was nothing for me and nothing for Zelda — I looked.

Cara looked up from her letter when Zelda had gone into the kitchen to sort out the day's meals with Maddalena who had returned from the market bewailing the price of the *zucchinos* she had bought early that morning. 'He says he will come to Italy as soon as he can and stay there for ever', she said with a sorrowful face. 'And *I* shall be in London.'

'Well, he can do as he wishes when he is of age', I said. 'You'll see him soon when you go back home.'

'I've missed him, you know', she confessed.

273

'Write him a nice letter back then — he hates school, doesn't he?'

'He says that there is nothing worth looking at in London — and that he wants to spend his life collecting beautiful things.

I thought, if he has said nothing more personal than that perhaps he has recovered from his summer feelings for my sister. Men were strange creatures; they had other things in their heads but love, and seemed to be able to manage a balance between their work and their emotions. But Cara might not tell me if there had been anything more personal in his missive!

'It will be *so* dreary at home', Cara said now. 'I wish I need not go back — there's Alice who is only a child and Hannah who will never grow up and Huntie always cross and Felix spoilt and Mama ailing and Papa always busy —' It did sound dull.

'I'm sure Mama and Papa have lots of things planned for you', I said. I wasn't going to mention Huntie's fears. Cara would discover them soon enough. All I said was: 'Help Mama to look after Felix — you could make him more obedient, I'm sure. Huntie has her hands full with Hannah.'

'Oh, Hetty, it's you he likes best', she said. I wondered if that were true. I hardly ever thought about them all in East Wood and felt I would never belong there now. I was sure that Cara would get used to them again, especially if she could see Max now and then and if Simon Voyle was banned from the house.

'Have you said anything yet to Bruno?' I asked her.

'I shall tell him what you said — when I see them all tonight at the Torcellos.' Her face brightened, not at the prospect of telling Bruno Guccioli to bide his time, but at the idea of a party where she could wear her pink dress.

'I'm not worrying about it any more — I want to enjoy myself', she said, and smiled.

'You do that', I answered. 'Make the most of Florence — you can come back next summer, I'm sure.'

Cara always took parties and social occasions at their face value, whereas I was still struck by the thought of all the huge parts of people's lives that were hidden under the talk and the laughter and the little plots and amusements.

I had mildly enjoyed the evening party the night before at the Torcellos, the family of an Italian lawyer, and was up rather late the next day, though I had promised to help Cara pack her trunk and to give a small Italian boy, Paolo Serra the nephew of the Count, a lesson in English. Zelda had mentioned it casually and not expected me to want to take up the suggestion, but I had agreed with alacrity for I felt restless and needed occupation that was not reading or dreaming or looking at pictures. The opera season had not yet started up again, though the pillars outside were plastered with forthcoming attractions — no Orsini there. I felt an extreme reluctance to go to listen to anyone

275

who was not Orso.

When I was drinking my coffee, Rosa came in and, looking round the door to see nobody could overhear her, said: 'He's coming here —'

'Who?' I asked, half-asleep. 'You mean the Serra boy?'

'No — Mr Voyle', she said in a low voice and put her fingers on her lips nodding her head in the direction of my aunt's room.

'Who asked him?'

'Oh, she used to see him from time to time and it happens he's coming to Florence next week — I thought you'd like to know, Miss Hetty —' She looked at me with a sort of challenge in that cockney sparrow gaze.

'Do *you* know him?' I asked her curiously, for she seemed excited.

'Oh, I've met him — years ago —'

'You knew his son too, I suppose, when he became your mistress's ward?'

'Haven't seen him since he was a nipper —'

'Well, I hope his father is nicer,' I said. 'Because — the son is horrible —'

'Sh-h.'

'Is my aunt going to tell him about Simon, do you think? I mean, to tell him that my stepmother is frightened of him?' [Or is frightened of something and dare not think it could be her son of whom she is frightened, I thought.]

Rosa looked shocked. 'Your stepmother wouldn't be frightened of her own son! — I don't think Mrs de Vere would mention a thing like that — he wouldn't want to know anything about your stepmother, I'm sure —'

'He must know that Simon stayed in our house?'

'I don't know if he ever sees that child of his. She says he hasn't been back to England though he said he would return one day.'

A funny sort of father, I thought. But he didn't let Simon stay with his mother. He wouldn't want him seeing her, would he, even though he had abandoned him?

'All I know is that Mr Voyle is coming to see your aunt', she went on. 'She says — better keep your sister out of the way.' So that was the purpose of telling me of the visit! 'It doesn't matter about you — but Mrs de Vere thought your sister could visit the dressmaker that afternoon so she's made her an appointment.'

'And I don't suppose she wants Cara to know Simon's father is to visit us?'

'She leaves it to you', said Rosa.

Zelda must realize that Cara had no idea about her mother's first marriage, trusting in my discretion. Why did people always assume I'd keep my mouth shut?

But I wanted to see the man; I was curious.

'Come to that he wouldn't be too pleased to see much of *you*, Miss Hetty — seeing it was *your* Dad.'

'I was introduced to him at the Opera in February', I said. 'But I won't obtrude myself.'

Cara was delighted that Aunt had asked the dressmaker, Serafina's sister, to make her a little cape for her journey back home. 'She's so kind', said Cara. 'It's to be my goodbye present from Florence!'

I went to work in my room the afternoon Voyle senior was to visit us. I'd had one lesson with little Paolo for whom I intended to prepare a questions and answers game. I needed a few brightly coloured illustrations which I was cutting out from an old scrap-book. Paolo was then to learn the English names for colours and objects and I would use them for a sort of 'snap' which he would win if he could say the word in English. Cara had looked in on her way to the dressmaker's as I was doing this.

'How industrious you are, Hetty', she said as she bade me goodbye until the evening.

For a time I worked on, rather enjoying myself, for I did enjoy teaching a biddable child. I had hoped there might be some little girls too who might profit from my labours, but Italian mothers seemed less enthusiastic at the idea of their daughters learning anything at all — they were all sent to convent schools as soon as they were seven from which they emerged at fifteen ready to find husbands. I wondered if Orso had any sisters and if he approved of girls acquiring more than the skills of embroidery and dancing.

Eventually I heard the outer door shut, and a murmur of voices, and pricked up my ears. If they went into the sitting-room rather than Zelda's boudoir I might hear something of their conversation.

I knew I was a shameless eavesdropper, but hadn't my overhearing the plot against Orso Orsini been an intervention of Providence? The door was shut between the anteroom and my own room, though I could hear an occasional murmur. I opened the shutters and stepped on to the balcony, which ran along this side of the house and where the servants kept geraniums in urns for my aunt's delectation. I know I should not have done it — it gives me no pleasure to report my own nosey-parkeyness. But I wanted to see the man again, and if I peered round the window of the sitting-room — that long window which I had remembered so often in my early childish nightmares — I might hear something. Zelda often opened a small part of the shutter at the top to let in fresh air unless it was a cold day, and today was not. I saw her sitting on the sofa when I peered through the slats of the shutters, half open as they were. The man was standing nearer the window with his back to me. I could hear nothing Zelda was saying, though I did hear what I thought was a rather mirthless laugh from her. Then he said something like: 'Yes, I know you kept it', in that harsh voice of his, and she got up and went to the table with her back to him. Was she looking for something?

'I certainly did', she said in a loud voice. Though I could not see her, she sounded cross. But it did not seem she was looking for anything for she resumed her seat and he sat down now in the big easy chair the Americans had left. I could see him clearly now. He was wearing mustard-coloured trousers, and a bow tie of the same colour, and a loose jacket. On the little table by the door there was a curly-brimmed bowler hat. Voyle crossed one long leg over the other and with his blond head tilted back looked in charge of the situation. I wondered what they were talking about.

'I told you you could have the other one for your own purposes', he said. 'But the situation might change.' She said nothing, and then he said — taking up a paper-knife from the table, a knife which we used for opening our letters, and pointing it at her. 'You've more to lose than I have.'

'Wait till he's twenty-five', she said. 'Then we'll see.'

He put down the implement and yawned. 'I'm getting impatient in my old age', he said. He looked older than I'd thought he was that first time. Were they talking about his son Simon?

She said: 'There is a draught — let me shut the shutters,' and I darted back as quick as lightning to my own open window. I was trembling, dared not try to hear any more. It was clear that they too were plotting something. I shut my window and bent myself once more to my self-imposed task. But their words went round and round in my head. They didn't make any sense, but I had had the distinct impression, even though I had only just caught their words and had had to strain my ears to hear anything, that my aunt and Peter Voyle were not talking as mere acquaintances, and that Zelda was not pleased.

Zelda never called me in to meet her visitor and

he departed at about four o'clock. She knew however that I knew he had been there and I wondered why I too had not been sent away. Was she perhaps frightened of him and needed another woman in the house who was not a servant? But that seemed far-fetched. This second and voluntary eavesdropping brought me, like the first involuntary one, no peace of mind. Cara came back from her fitting and things went on as usual that evening and for the next few days. Gregory was soon to come for her and I looked forward to that.

Part 3
The Sins of the Fathers

12

Gregory arrived to take my sister Cara home to England on one of those deceptively sunny December days when the sky looks summery but the branches of trees pointing up towards it are bare. I thought my brother thinner than when I'd seen him at the Villa de Vere. He had not corresponded with me since, and I was longing to ask him what he'd been doing. It seemed years since I'd seen him; my involvement with Orso Orsini had caused everything else to seem lost in the mists of time.

Gregory never seemed to do anything but work. He was only twenty-one but already looked careworn, an unusual adjective with which to describe a young man, but nevertheless true. He had always been kind to me — was invariably polite to everyone — but I thought I now detected a slight irritation in his manner, a sort of impatience, not with me especially or with Cara, but with life in general.

After dinner my aunt went out and Cara said she wanted to go to bed early when she had finished packing for the journey. When Rosa had given us our coffee, Gregory and I remained together in the sitting-room. He got up and shut the door and then looked to see if it was properly shut. 'I want to speak to you in private', he began. I thought the pantomime of door-shutting was rather overdone, but then recalled the two occasions upon which I had heard conversations, once from behind the dividing doors and once from the balcony.

We drank our coffee and then he put down his cup and I waited.

'Did you tell Cara about her birth?' he began.

'No, I did not — I couldn't see what good it would do, though I expect she'll have to know one day . . . She's had lots of beaux over here, you know — she'll find East Wood very dull!'

'Has she had proposals?' He looked excited, if that is not too strong a word.

'There is a young Italian whose mama is a Countess — but Cara has told him to wait . . . that she's too young to decide what she wants. Actually I think she prefers our little cousin Max.'

'Trust Cara to see to the main chance', he replied, I thought unkindly.

I said, a little distressed: 'She's not a fortune hunter, Gregory — she's nicer than she used to be. Being away from home has made her grow up. It wasn't *her* fault Papa and Mamarella spoilt her when she was little —'

'And does Max reciprocate? — or want her for his collection of *objets d'art?*'

'As a matter of fact I think the interest was on his side to begin with. They get on well together and he does know about matters of taste — and things like that now interest Cara. She knows she is pretty but she's not really vain. Max was a bit jealous, I believe, when other young men made a beeline for her, but he tried not to show it. He's very young — he leaves school at the end of this term.'

'What will he do then, do you think?'

'I expect he'll come here — he prefers Italy. He's such a nice boy, Greg — he reminds me a bit of you, though he's more critical about *things* than *people*.' I hoped this was not too barbed a reply, but it seemed to me that my brother was more complicated than of old, less inclined to take people at their own evaluation, more cynical.

'So long as Simon Voyle keeps away', said Gregory. 'He's never been near East Wood again, you know — our stepmother has just had to put up with it — perhaps even she realizes that he was a bad influence.'

'His father came here not long ago — he knows Zelda quite well', I said. 'I've the feeling he might once have known her very well indeed.' I did not want to confess I'd eavesdropped on their conversation, and paused. But Gregory said, 'I didn't want to talk about the Voyles — I wanted to tell you something quite different.' He looked round again to make sure we were not being overheard. Then: 'Did you ask Zelda where our Mama was buried?'

'No — somehow I never felt it was quite the moment — I thought she'd tell me when she felt like it.' I didn't say I'd wanted to feel free of all our miserable past — Mama and Papa and everything — but I added, 'I expect I *shall* ask her one of these days.'

'You don't need to — I've found out', he replied, his eyes on me.

I got up in my excitement and agitation — 'Where? Oh, do tell me —'

'As a matter of fact my discovery is connected with some of the business I was doing when I was here last', he said quietly, his eyes on my face. He spoke deliberately, choosing his words. 'Where she was buried is in the graveyard of a little village by the lakeside — Lake Como.'

'Not here in Florence at all then! But how did you find out?'

'Never mind how I did, Hetty — better you don't know all the ins and outs for the present — I copied the headstone for you. Here.' He handed me a leaf torn from one of those little sketch-books you see girls going round with in galleries when they are trying to copy great paintings. I looked at a picture of a gravestone with a carved top, and at the words written on it.

'It's exactly as I found it', he said as I stared at it.

IN LOVING MEMORY OF MARIA COPPEN
DIED SEPTEMBER 30TH 1862
IN THE 26TH YEAR OF HER AGE,
AND OF HER INFANT SON
BORN AND DIED SEPTEMBER 30TH 1862: RIP.

I looked up at him, upset and puzzled.

'But Zelda never mentioned a baby! — Neither did Rosa. Mama didn't die in childbirth, they said — and she's still got Papa's name! — but it couldn't be Papa's baby —'

'No, of course it could not', he said gently. 'But I don't think either Zelda or Rosa would mind your knowing about the grave now.'

'Gregory — what *do* you know? Tell me. You've always known more than I have about Mama.'

'I told you Hetty, as a budding barrister I make it my business to discover the truth. Though as a matter of fact I'm thinking of chucking it in and training instead to be a solicitor. Never mind that, though.' He paused. 'It's better at present that you know no more than the fact that Mama was buried near Como and that her gravestone has an unnamed infant in it.'

'Whatever she did — don't you think now that bygones should be bygones, Greg?'

'It depends on the bygones', he answered drily, but I could see from his expression that he knew a lot more than he had told me and that he was obsessed by our sad history.

'Gregory', I said. 'Why rake it all up now?'

'I have to discover the truth', he said again.

'I can't stop now —'

'But what else are you looking for? We know Mama was deserted by Papa. We know about Papa and Mamarella and Cara — and the Voyle boy — can't we just forget about the past and get on with our lives?' I spoke more loudly than I intended and he put his finger to his lips.

'Hetty — if there is an injustice to put right, if there has been past wickedness — never discovered — do you not think it should be brought to light?'

'I suppose so, but — wickedness? — what are you looking for?' He did not reply directly to my question.

'You must know that nine-tenths of the world's miseries come from the invention of money, and the other tenth from the curse of our animal nature. Lawyers have to know about money, and so I have to know about certain wills, and certain lies, and certain — omissions. Sometimes, you see, it is what is *not* there rather than what is, that tells you something you were not meant to know.'

I was frightened at his expression and remembered my dream of a few months before about Mama being murdered. But Mama had never had any money. 'Mama never had any money!' I said aloud. 'And what she had, Papa would take — is that what you mean?'

'No — not that. All I can tell you —' he lowered his voice — 'is that I am looking for a peculiar form of confirmation of a suspicion I've had for a long time. But proof is hard to come by. I'm looking for a will and for two death certificates.'

'Two?' I repeated. Mama's must be one of them, I thought.

'Yes, two — and I don't think I shall find them!'

'Gregory, either tell me more or stop talking in riddles!' I thought he looked grim and unhappy.

'It's what one does not find, Hetty, that often puts one on the right track', he repeated.

'Oh, Gregory, don't bother with it all — what business of ours is it? I want to think about the future, not the past.'

He leaned over and took my hand. 'I'm sorry, little sister — but I must see this through. You see, the past goes on affecting the present.'

I thought, that's true enough. Gregory has been irretrievably hurt by Papa's attitude to him, whereas I've got over it. When I think of Orso, all this past fades away. As if divining my thoughts he said in a brighter voice: 'I'll talk of it no more. I never asked about *you* Hetty — what have you been doing? I expect you have as many beaux as Cara!'

I knew that I had secrets too now, but I said lightly, 'Oh, nothing much has happened — I've just been happy, that's all, reading and having that wonderful summer at the villa — and listening to music', I concluded lamely. 'No proposals', I added, after a pause. 'Greg — I've been thinking — I shall soon want to work. You know if I could start a little — well, not exactly a school, but have a few pupils here, teach English to some Italian children — I've got a pupil already — it might turn into a school one day!'

'You mean to stay in Italy?' He was surprised.

'Well, at first I used to think I'd be like Miss Little. I do admire her, you know . . . be a governess, or train to teach — there are colleges for young women now — but I've been thinking recently that I'd rather stay here. My allowance goes further here, you see, and I could gather some pupils together. Zelda knows lots of people —'

'Don't you want to marry one day?' he asked me.

'Well, perhaps one day, but not yet. I want to be independent.' I thought, but did not say, what good did marriage do Mama or Mamarella? — and I didn't want to marry a rich man as Zelda did.

'I admire you, Hetty, you're very — honourable', he said.

So are you, I thought, but you have grown a steely carapace over your honour so you can no longer be hurt by anyone. Perhaps it was Mama's death rather than Papa's conduct that has made you like this. *I* had been too young to know what I'd lost when she died. I knew my brother was very intelligent and I was sure he would succeed in whatever he did since he was such a compulsive worker. But I did want him to be happy too and he didn't look happy.

'Don't worry about anything I've said today, Hetty', he said. 'I promise I'll tell you if I do find what I'm looking for. Nobody else knows what I'm doing.'

'And what about *you?* — have you found a nice

girl to fall in love with?' I asked him.

'No — unfortunately poor girls need rich husbands and I'm not rich — and rich girls don't look at poor young lawyers.'

'You should come here for a proper holiday and meet some of our American friends', I said. 'Some of them *are* rich, I believe, but all they want in a husband is a willingness to work hard, and enjoy leisure.'

'If you are here next year I might come', he said, and smiled.

'Can I just ask you one thing?' I said after a pause. He waited. 'Is that Peter Voyle connected with your "enquiries"? — I should imagine he's a man who needs money and goes where he can find it.'

'He might be connected with it in a manner of speaking', replied Gregory carefully.

I said, 'I didn't like what I saw of him — and I had the impression, I don't know why, that he was talking about his son Simon — but I've never seen Simon Voyle out here.'

'Simon is an oaf', said my brother, 'and yet — none of it is *his* fault —'

'No, he lost a mother', I said. 'Like we did — except his wasn't dead, which would make it worse.'

He looked at me searchingly and then dropped his eyes. 'Let's talk of something else — did you do any sketching or painting whilst you were at the villa?'

'Why, yes — but they're not any good. I enjoy

painting, you know, because I know I'll never be any good at it, so I can relax.'

He laughed and for the rest of the evening until I bade him goodnight he looked at my little sketches of the Villa de Vere paying particular attention to my attempts to paint the wild garden and the little cypress trees at the bottom and the lichened walls. I managed not to talk about opera, and the name Orso Orsini never once passed my lips.

It was after my brother had departed next day with Cara and we had seen them off at the station and I had gone to bed early feeling rather depressed now they had gone and I was alone once more with my thoughts, that I dreamed the dream of the dead baby again, and woke with my heart thumping with terror. Had I really known Mama's little dead son? But he had not lived more than a day, might even have been born dead — and I was sure I'd never been to Como. I tried to put it all out of my thoughts, but Gregory's words had disturbed me. I decided the only antidote was work, and when I felt a bit better I would challenge Zelda over Mama's grave.

I needed someone to instruct me in Italian, to improve my grammar and teach me a bit about Italian literature, and was lucky in finding a Mrs Lambert. She was an old lady who had been married to an Oxford Professor, but had returned to Florence when he died. Zelda said she was a bit mad, but when I entered her dusty apartment on the other side of the river I did not find her mad, just very unworldly. She was related to Mrs Warburton's long dead husband and it was through her Zelda had found her. The Count was amused that I should want to spend my time learning and reading, but he was a tolerant man and excused me on account of my being English. I went twice a week at four o'clock to Mrs Lambert and the three mornings I was not studying continued to instruct little Paolo in the anteroom at Zelda's. She did not object, though she was puzzled. 'You have enough money not to work, Hetty', she said.

'Yes, I know — I am lucky — but my money will not last for ever and I don't work just for that', I replied. I'd not mentioned again to my aunt my ambition of actually starting a little school of my own one day.

The time passed agreeably, or as agreeably as it was possible for it to pass for me when there was no prospect of seeing Orso. Cara wrote but added in her letter that there was nothing on at Covent Garden or Her Majesty's. He must still be in Paris, I thought. I did not expect him to write, for I knew that men were not great letter writers, but I did worry that he might be in danger, that those awful men might have caught up with him somehow.

I thought quite a lot about Gregory too as the New Year came and went and I heard nothing from him either. I decided that Gregory despised our Papa, whilst I did not. I didn't condone what Papa had done to Mama, but I thought I might understand better than my brother how Papa had fallen in love with Ella Voyle. But I did not want to believe that I might act as cruelly out of infatuation or passion.

Then one day at the end of January Zelda told me she would soon be leaving Florence for a time to travel with the Count Belotti. They were to go to Rome, and later in the season to Baden and Homburg and perhaps Monte, ending up back in Italy, in Venice.

'Does that mean I cannot stay here?' I asked her.

'No, Hetty — Rosa will not be accompanying me and it is a good idea to have you here in the apartment. I shan't open up the Villa though till June this year.'

How the seriously rich live! I thought. The Count goes where it pleases him. If I had that amount of money *I'd* rent a palazzo in Venice. Suddenly I had the mental picture of myself leaning out of a window in Venice with Orso singing to me in a gondola underneath the casement, and I smiled in spite of myself at my romantic dream. But I wouldn't want to go to Homburg or Monte — though I'd like one day to go to Rome.

'You won't be lonely living here for a time with Rosa and the other servants?' my Aunt asked. She did not think it odd to leave a nineteen-year-old to her own devices and I thanked my lucky stars she did not. Zelda was no conventional woman to think about chaperones and respectability. But then she said to me one day a week or two later:

'I expect you will want to return to London — perhaps in the autumn — unless of course you meet someone who wants to marry you over here!' So she hadn't quite given me up as a marriageable quantity.

'I am grateful, Aunt, that I have a home here with you', I said quietly. 'I would not want to live at Papa's any longer, even if I returned to England.' I cleared my throat. 'I'm not thinking of marriage yet — I'm hoping to enlarge my circle of pupils, you see, and perhaps rent a little place myself eventually and make a little school here.'

'You seem determined to be independent', she said. 'But would you have enough if you didn't live here with us? The money required for rent and food and heating and — schools — is not a small sum.'

'No, I know — but I hoped I might earn it', I replied.

'Well, there's no need to do anything yet', she said and I saw clearly that my Aunt Zelda was 'on the move' herself and might be contemplating a more permanent arrangement with her Count.

'I never thought of taking your hospitality for granted for ever', I said. 'You've been very kind to me, but when I am of age — it's less than two years now — I shall have a little money from my Grandmama, Papa's mother, and with enough pupils I'm sure I should be able to manage.'

'You seem to have thought it all out', was all she said, but I thought she looked rather quizzically at me.

Cara, it appeared, after the upheaval of returning home, was far from content. She wrote that our Papa did not like her going out with young people, that her parents wanted her to accompany them now and again to boring parties. She had managed to see Max though, had persuaded Lucy Little to go with her to visit him. 'Max wants to come and see me here', she continued, 'but Papa frowned when I spoke of it'.

I had not answered this letter before another came. I knew that Max was now to stay in London whilst his mother was on her travels, and that even she did not think it seemly that he should stay in Florence with me whilst she was away. Poor Max, he would be angry. He had left school but was still lodging at the usher's whilst (he told me in a letter) he haunted salerooms and was actually looking for work there. I was impressed that he was not wasting his time regretting that he could not come over yet to Florence, or pining after Cara.

In her next letter Cara explained some of this, which I already knew from Max himself, and added as a postscript, 'The man whose singing you liked is to come to Covent Garden at the end of March'. My heart gave a great lift. Orso must have been in Paris till now. If only I were a man and he were a lady and I could go and find my beloved! Yet even if I were a man I could not presume on someone's reciprocating my feelings. I treasured the little 'MIZPAH', and slept with it under my pillow at night and kissed it before I went to sleep.

Rosa was not at all pleased that her mistress was to abandon her for a time. She had been so long with Zelda, and this was apparently the first time, apart from when Zelda had gone to London, that her presence had not been required, and she was jealous. I decided one day when Zelda was out at a fitting for her travelling dresses to ask Rosa about my Mama's grave. Maybe she'd be more forthcoming to me if she were cross with her mistress. I acted sheerly out of instinct when I said to her — going into the kitchen where she was sitting sewing — 'Rosa — I wonder if you can help me?' She looked up but she did not put her needle down, held it poised in the air as if to signify interruption. 'Shall I make you a cup of coffee, Rosa, before you get on with your sewing?' I asked craftily.

'What do you want, Miss Hetty?' she asked as I put the pan on the spirit stove without waiting for a reply to my question. I got the flame going and then I turned.

'You can tell me where my Mama is buried', I said without hesitation or circumlocution, for a surprise might jolt an answer out of her. This time she did put her sewing down. 'It's not an unusual request, Rosa — after all she was my mother! I've a right to know.'

'Hasn't that brother of yours found that out yet?' she said. Now I was confused so I told a half fib. 'Yes, he says he knows but he won't tell me.' I was aware as I said this that I really must stop myself telling half truths — it seemed I was just too good at it. 'He did say it wasn't in Florence', I said after a pause. I set down the coffee cups — I might as well have a cup myself. All cosy. How could she refuse me? And she did not.

'Your mother went to the north — to the Lakes, they said — to recover from her weakness.'

'Who said that? and what weakness?' I enquired as I poured out the coffee. 'I mean, I thought she had recovered from her first illness from what my aunt told me?'

'Your aunt said she needed to get out of Florence — she wasn't eating and was always tired — I believe they thought her lungs were affected.'

'A doctor said that?'

She looked up at me. 'I expect so. Miss Zelda always looked after your ma right well, Miss Hetty — no cause for you to start thinking she was neglected.'

'No, I never thought that', I replied. 'But are you sure it was her lungs — wasn't it perhaps that she was going to have another baby?'

Rosa's hands flew to her throat and she dropped her sewing and looked up at me with a curious expression on her face, half-pleading, half-defiant. 'Who told you that?' she enquired huskily.

'Gregory hinted it', I answered composedly, feeling sorry for her.

'Yes', she said after another long pause and she looked down at the sewing which was lying on the table.

'Have your coffee', I said.

'Yes, she was going to have a baby, but don't

297

ask me any more about it. The fact is, the poor child was born dead and it killed *her* too.' I waited. 'My poor Miss Maria', she whispered. 'She had no luck.'

I wanted, of course, to ask whose baby it was, but somehow it seemed indecent to be asking Rosa such a thing about my own Mama. She answered my unspoken question though.

'Those Italians loved her — she was more popular than your auntie even', she said. 'But she had no common sense. There, I shouldn't be saying such things to you — and it's all long past.'

I had heard all I needed to know, I thought. Mama had liked an Italian man, had possibly even loved him. Like me.

'*I* didn't see why you shouldn't know', she said and finally took up her cup. 'I told Mrs de Vere' — she always said Mrs de Vere when she wanted to sound solemn and formal — 'I told her — Miss Hetty ought to know about her Mama — what harm would it do now? After all, the baby died and there was no scandal.'

No scandal, I thought! Is that all they care about, even Zelda de Vere who always disdains respectability? No, it was Rosa who would care about scandal.

'But didn't the father — I mean my mother's lover — didn't *he* know or care?'

'Oh, they don't stay around, some men, when they've got their ladies into trouble', she said. He wasn't a gentleman, I decided. Italian or English, he wasn't a gentleman.

I left it at that and tried to turn the conversation round to more ordinary matters. But before I left her I said: 'Tell my Aunt I know, will you? And that I'd like to see Mama's grave one day — I've waited long enough to ask.' She nodded and looked at me for a moment with an indecipherable expression. 'It won't get you into trouble, will it? I mean, I asked you and you had to tell me the truth.'

'No', she replied. 'Miss Zelda said, if you asked, to tell you.' So although in no hurry to enlighten me, she had expected I would ask one day.

Zelda departed and I stayed to welcome another spring. There was no sign of it yet, though I felt restless. For the first time since I'd come to Italy over a year before, I felt I'd like, just for a few days, to be back home again. Or rather, I'd like to see Lucy Little and talk about bookish things; I'd like to hear Orso Orsini, who was now far away from me about to start a season at the Garden; and I'd like to see my sister Cara — and Max. But I was not going to return home to be treated like Cara and 'not allowed to go out very much'! I wished I could stay with Lucy in her cosy house in Camberwell if I ever returned to London.

Zelda had telegraphed us when she knew her address in Rome. Apparently she was not staying at the Count's family home. I supposed his mother must still be alive and he had a bachelor apartment not suitable for my aunt. Was she his mistress? Somehow I doubted it. I thought she had decided to be his wife and was therefore playing it cool. Anyway, they'd soon be on their way to one of the fashionable spas.

Although I toyed with the thoughts of a short holiday in England whilst Zelda was away — though she had never suggested it — I could not stop thinking of Orso. Why had he given me that little medallion with its sentimental message and yet never written a word to me? I hadn't expected him to, but was it true as Rosa seemed to imply that Italians loved their women and left them? Not that he 'loved' me, but he had liked me, I was sure of that, apart from the accident of my unveiling the plot against him. And I so liked him, apart from my love of his singing and my overwhelming need (which I tried not to think about) to be held close in those big, strong arms of his and looked after, and loved. I did not deny my feelings, but I was wary of them. Perhaps I'd hear him again when he next visited Florence, but I must keep my longings to myself and concentrate on teaching. And yet . . . and yet . . . It is hard when you are young to teach and study when the air bears with it all the promise of another spring and distant intimations of something better, some possible joy with which fortune might bless one. Youth is so optimistic.

So when one morning a boy rang at our door with a yellow envelope addressed to me, a telegraph from INGHILTERRA, and I opened it with a sinking feeling of dread, the horror with which I read it was also compounded, I confess, a moment or two later, with a sudden feeling of destiny, of hope. The message was short. It was from my sister: 'FELIX HAS DISAPPEARED. PLEASE COME: CARA.'

Not from Papa or Mamarella or Gregory, but from Cara. That decided me. I was needed. I packed immediately, sent Rosa out for a ticket and a timetable, explained the situation to her and sent a message to Mrs Lambert and to little Paolo, and next day I was in the train that would take me to the frontier, to Switzerland and to France and after a choppy sea voyage, to my old home — to England, to London, and to East Wood.

13

As the train rattled its Morse Code — de-de-de *der* — under my feet there was no doubt in my mind that if Felix had disappeared Simon Voyle was behind it. And there was no doubt either that although I was going home to support my family and do what I could, I was also with every mile I traversed nearer to Orso Orsini's present whereabouts, for he was soon to sing at Covent garden I was tired, for I had not slept, borne along by these twin considerations. It may sound heartless when I confess that in all my anguish over Cara's message I was also thinking of Orso.

I did not know what to expect when I reached home — I'd asked Rosa to telegraph my arrival. Would I be welcome? But as there was nothing I could possibly do whilst I was in Italian and Swiss and French trains and on the Channel *paquebot*, and finally on the familiar London train from Dover, I gave myself up to extracting all I could from the pleasant sensation of independence which I found travelling alone gave me.

When I arrived at our village station it was foggy. I had begun looking for a hackney-carriage when I saw Enoch, now a fully fledged coachman, coming over the cobbles of the station yard in wisps of fog.

'There's the old hoss and cart, Miss', he said. 'Been waiting ever since three this afternoon.'

The 'old hoss and cart' was his way of referring to Papa's second-best carriage, more of a trap or governess cart really, and I smiled. Enoch and I had been friends when I was little and I still felt easy with him. 'She's here too, your sister', he added as he took my bags.

'Is there any news?' I gasped out as we walked across the yard where I could now see several carriages lined up awaiting the arrival of Papas from the City.

'No — gorn into thin air 'e 'as. Mind you — 'e'll turn up. A little scamp, your brother', said Enoch.

Then suddenly out of one of the carriages stumbled my sister Cara and flung her arms around me. 'Oh, Hetty! — I've been waiting all afternoon — thank goodness you've come!' she cried. We squeezed ourselves into the back of the small equipage and she began to tell me all that had happened. It reduced itself to quite a simple story. Felix had been playing all afternoon in the garden on the Monday previous — Cara's telegraph had arrived in Florence on Tuesday evening, and now it was Friday — but when Huntie went out to get him for his tea he was nowhere to be seen, though Mamarella had seen him at about three o'clock when she returned from some shopping in London. They'd looked for him everywhere — it was not at all misty or foggy that afternoon — they had searched the garden and the wood nearby

303

and gone up and down the village and to the station, but there was no sign. Papa had arrived home to find the whole house in hysterics with Huntie being blamed for not checking every two minutes where Felix was. Poor Huntie — as if she didn't have enough to do without watching a six-year-old child play in his own garden. She'd kept saying: 'I saw him after the mistress came back — and next time I looked he was gone.'

I thought, even now, Papa does not see fit to welcome me at the station. But still, he was not the one who had begged me to come back.

'Gypsies', said Cara now. 'They all think it's gypsies!'

'And do you?' I asked her.

'No. But *you* will find him, Hetty. I *know* you will. I just had to ask you to come.'

I didn't say anything then to her about Simon. When we arrived home, the atmosphere was a mixture of hysteria and gloom. Mamarella had insisted on getting up, though she had not slept properly since her son's disappearance, and was lying on a sofa in the drawing-room with her smelling-salts. Papa was standing nearby, his face white too with loss of sleep, and anguish writ all over him. Huntie clung to me in the hall and then wept into her apron, and Alice was quiet and heavy-eyed. Only Hannah, my Pooranna, gave me her usual welcome — almost knocked me over with delight and stroked my clothes saying 'Hetty! Hetty!' over and over in her gruff voice. Huntie eventually led her off to bed, and Alice went too.

Nobody was hungry, it seemed, but Cook gave me some soup and toast in her kitchen and after that I went into Papa. I could see no point in trying to do anything till the next day and I had to get some sleep myself. I did ask Papa though where Gregory was, as he was obviously the person who could be of most help.

'He's been to Charing Cross every day looking for him — we think Felix may have run to the station and got on a train and be wandering round there — Gregory's coming back here Monday evening.' He paused. 'It was good of you to come — though there was no need', he said, and cleared his throat.

I did not know whether to suggest to Papa that Simon Voyle had something to do with Felix's disappearance. I must think things out.

'Miss Little has kindly helped us search', he said. 'It has been in the *Kentish Times*, and notices have gone up. The police have been, but they tend to agree that there have been gypsies in the area and Felix might have gone off with them — or rather been taken by them.'

This gypsy idea was just too convenient. 'Have the police tracked them down then, these "gypsies"?' I asked him.

'Nobody knows where they've gone. Further into Kent, they think, if they were here Monday, but there's been no sign, though several people have said they saw them last week. There's nothing *you* can do.' He added — 'There will be a special prayer in church — your mother asked for it.' He looked worn and old. Did it not even occur to him or my stepmother that her eldest child might know something about all this?

'He's *my* brother too — Felix', I said after a pause. 'I had to come and help.'

'Gregory has thought of everything', he said, and so I could not help myself saying then — 'Papa, don't you think that perhaps — Felix's other brother might have taken it into his head to perform a vanishing trick on the child?'

I saw him register that I knew about Ella and her son, and then another expression, one of fear, showed plainly in his eyes. But he said: 'Oh, nonsense — he is abroad. Gregory *did* ask at his old lodgings in the City, I believe, but he had not been there for some time.'

So the idea had occurred to Gregory. It must be Simon, I thought to myself. I thought, why does Papa not face it? Is he frightened of suggesting it to his wife?

'I refuse to believe that young Voyle could take my son away', he said, then: 'I think you must go to bed, Hetty'. He refused to contemplate any involvement by his stepson because he felt guilty on his account. I saw that clearly now.

I went upstairs, where my old bed was now occupied by Cara, but another had been made up in the attic where I used to sleep when I was small. Cara came up to say goodnight. 'You think it's Simon, don't you?' she whispered.

'It could be — but I must think it all over in the morning. Has anyone told Max about Felix's going missing?'

'He owes me a letter', confessed Cara. 'But he's away somewhere in the north of England — there was a sale of old things from some castle there and he went to look at it. Did you know he's started valuing things for a big auction house?' I did not know, but I saw that Max was not wasting his time. 'Papa doesn't know we correspond', she said. 'It was all right till about a fortnight ago and he let us meet, if Miss Little went with me. But then he suddenly turned queer about him — I don't know why. I think it was a letter that came for him from Italy — but he's said nothing about it.'

'From Italy!' I exclaimed in surprise. Was Zelda warning my father off the idea that anything could ever happen between his daughter and her son? Or had Cara been mistaken? Naturally he would not relish any formal alliance between Cara and his first wife's nephew, yet by allowing them to see each other he might slowly allow the two families to become more friendly.

What was important was that I tried to put myself into Simon's shoes and think where I would take a six-year-old child I had 'kidnapped' from his parents' home. What did Simon think he could get out of it? There had been no 'ransom demand', or letter, or any communication at all, I was sure, or Papa would have told me. What did Simon want with Felix? The idea came to me suddenly when I woke in the night, that Simon did not want anything but to cause unhappiness to his mother. Huntie had felt it, and told Rosa in that letter from Alice — but I had not yet spoken to her about it. We spent a miserable Saturday; that the situation was desperate even the police who visited us again seemed to agree. I woke more refreshed on Sunday and tried to eat a good breakfast. I must go somewhere alone to think. I was looking forward to seeing Lucy Little who might have some ideas on the subject since Felix was her pupil. I went to find Cara to ask her if she had any idea of any other place Simon Voyle might have stayed recently.

'I haven't seen him since before I came out to you in Florence', she said, looking scared. 'Gregory went to his lodgings in Stepney and to his workplace — but didn't Papa tell you he'd gone abroad? Mama doesn't even know Gregory has been to look for him!'

I went into the old schoolroom. Felix's copybook was on the table with some not very well-formed pothooks. Poor Lucy — she would be just as distracted as the family. I sat down at the table. It was only an ordinary schoolroom, but how it brought back the past! All my childhood; the tedium of a child's life. I tried to think calmly. Where would I have taken Felix if I'd wanted to hide him away and cause maximum grief? Somewhere nobody would think of. Not abroad, or into London where people swarmed, but somewhere nobody bothered about.

It came to me suddenly. An empty house. The Laurels, where Simon had lived with Zelda and Max. If only Max were in London to consult. But I knew there was nobody living there, for Zelda had told me it was all shut up. Should I voice this idea to Gregory? But Greg wasn't coming to East Wood till tomorrow and I wanted to do this by myself. Perhaps if I could find him I'd make both Papa and his wife look at me with new eyes? That thought was in my head, though I tried to pretend it wasn't. I wanted their approbation. When had they ever heeded *me?* If I succeeded in finding their precious son they might be sorry for the way they'd always treated me. Yes, that thought did occur. But more than any of these ignoble considerations was my dislike of Simon Voyle — and a curious feeling I had that if I caught him and punished him I'd be avenging my own Mama. But I would not carry out my idea from home. I didn't want them interfering and arguing and preventing me. No, I'd go to Mr Little's and from there I could catch a train further into Kent. The railway from Peckham went into that part of Kent where Zelda's old house lay. The fleeting idea that I should ask Lucy to go with me did occur to me then, but I dismissed it. I wanted to do this alone. But I'd hint to her I might just take a look.

I got ready to go out, taking with me only my purse, a bag which I stuffed with apples, and a book. Then I went into Papa's study. The thought of sitting through another meal with them all, listening to Mama's tears and trying to cheer up the others, did not tempt me. I'd do this alone, and if I was wrong and Simon Voyle had not taken Felix there, then nobody would be the wiser but Lucy Little.

'Papa, I'm going to the Littles', I stated. 'I'll come back with her tomorrow. He did not even ask me why. I was out of his jurisdiction now and that pleased me. 'Tell Gregory where I've gone if he comes back this evening.'

'He won't be here till tomorrow', said Papa, looking away.

'I just want to talk it over with Lucy', I said. And I was quickly out of the room before he could say anything else. I met Cara in the hall. 'I'm going to Lucy's now', I said. 'I've had an idea. Don't worry — I'll be back tomorrow.'

'Can't I come too?' she asked. For a moment I hesitated. But no, the fewer people who knew my plan the better, and Lucy was the most intelligent person I knew.

'Leave it to me, Cara', I said. 'I can't stay here — it's too gloomy and we all make each other worse. You can tell Mama where I've gone, — and Huntie,' I added.

I was off and on the way to the station yard where there were horse buses that went to New Cross and then Camberwell. I hesitated again. Why not go straight to The Laurels by myself? But I was a cautious person in many ways and I had to tell *someone* where I was going, and so I made my way to the Littles' house that Sunday morning with all the church bells ringing and the fog gone, but the air cold and damp, so unlike the winter air of Italy which, even when it rains, seems to say — 'It won't last long. Soon the sun will come out'.

Lucy was surprised, but pleased, to see me. Our pleasure in each other's company was naturally cut short by the seriousness of what had happened to her small pupil and we promised each other long talks when all this was over — if it ever was. Lucy was not one to mince her words. Her father was not up so we sat in the parlour with a bright fire and I told her who I thought was responsible.

'Oh, surely not!' she exclaimed. Then — 'Hetty — have you not thought? Little Felix he might not be alive? Horrible people do exist who take away children and murder them.'

'I know, Lucy — but I don't see Simon Voyle as a murderer, rather as a bitter and twisted person who was jealous of us all.' Then I explained who Simon was and why he hated his mother. 'What better punishment could he inflict than to steal her favourite child?'

Lucy looked amazed at my revelation of the relationship, but said sensibly: 'What could *he* gain by it? He'd have to give him back one day.'

'He could torture her with uncertainty. What I want to know is, would Felix go with him quite happily? He knew him — was there ever any talk between the two of them? Papa refuses to believe that Simon is capable of such a thing — but that's because he doesn't want to believe it. Is Felix easily led, do you think?'

'I'm afraid so — and he used to talk to Simon when Voyle was here last year — Simon played marbles with him, I remember. I think Felix liked him.'

'Then he's the only person who ever did', I said. Simon Voyle would love having a small boy to tell him he was wonderful.

'But where would he take him?' asked Lucy, wide-eyed.

'I've been thinking, Lucy. You remember The Laurels?'

'Where your aunt didn't invite me in — and I tramped round that one-horse town and finally found a bookshop where I read till it was time to collect you?'

'Oh, I'd forgotten — how rude of her! — well — The Laurels is uninhabited at present. It's where I first met Simon — the same day I met Max. It's where he lived as a child in England when he was Zelda's ward — and incidentally there's something fishy about that — but he knows the place. People wouldn't think twice if they did see him there. You could "camp" nicely there — if you got some fuel in for a fire. And Max left all his toys there — and probably Simon too — Felix is most likely having the time of his life, don't you think?' My voice trailed away. I didn't like to think of what Simon's reaction might be if nosey Hetty Coppen, whom he'd always disliked, interrupted his plan.

'I never liked Simon', said Lucy suddenly, 'I told you there was nothing he liked better than money, didn't I?'

'Then you think he'll keep my mother guessing for a bit and then ask for money?'

'I don't know. What I'm frightened of, if you

312

are right and he *has* taken him, is that things will go wrong — the child will want to go home eventually — and maybe the money won't arrive . . .' It was Lucy's turn to leave a sentence unfinished.

As we talked, that gulf of years which had once separated pupil and teacher seemed to have vanished. Lucy was the perfect confidante; she took my ideas seriously and then applied her brain to them. I nearly told her about Orso, remembering guiltily that I'd given him her address, but now was not the time for such confidences.

'What shall you do then?'

'Just go and look — it gets dark about seven o'clock at present. I want to do this — go there — alone. You stay here and if I don't return by late tonight, tell them to look for me there.'

'Hetty, I can't let you run this risk! — he might be dangerous —'

'I could just go and look — see if there is anyone about, and if Felix *was* there, then go and find someone to help in the village.'

'Will it be locked up?'

'Zelda once gave me a key', I replied triumphantly. 'And it's on my châtelaine — it was for when I was going to stay with her that time we left for Italy. She was to be in London and might not have got back in time and Rosa was out running final errands. I didn't need it, as it turned out, but I kept it.' I showed her the key to the back door of the house which led to the kitchen. I was impatient to go now, and stood up.

After a pause Lucy said: 'I'd always wondered

313

why that young man was so jealous — especially of Gregory — it didn't seem natural.'

'I'll tell you more about all that later', I said. Lucy would advise me what to tell my sister. 'Papa was married before too.'

She looked at me gravely. 'Is Mrs Coppen not your real mother? I always had the idea she was not — oh, Hetty, she treated you so badly!'

'And Gregory too', I said. I wasn't going to go into details, but Lucy said: 'She was married before then — and her husband died? But why did your father not take Simon to live with him when they married?'

'She was divorced by Simon's father', I said. 'And her first husband forbade her to see him. My aunt brought him up — don't ask me why, for I don't know why. Lucy, I must go and see if he's there!' I had still not told her about my own Mama's death.

In any other circumstances this talk would have been momentous, but I had to go now to The Laurels. There would be time for me to unburden myself later to my old governess.

But Lucy said, as if she still wanted to get things straight — 'He will be especially jealous of his mother's only other son. Oh, Hetty — it could be dangerous — does your Mama — I mean Mrs Coppen — not see *why* he might be jealous?'

'She is very blind to feelings of that kind', I said. 'She adored her first son, I'm sure, but once he grew up and was allowed to stay at Papa's I suppose she thought it was all nicely sorted out.

Except he annoyed my sister —'

'I know about that', she said. 'Even more reason for you to send someone else to look for him!'

'I might be completely wrong and Felix has been captured by "gypsies" ', I said. But I did not think that was the case and I could see that my ex-governess did not think so either. 'Remember — if I'm not back — there is a late train which arrives in Peckham about midnight — send for help.'

'Oh, I'll wait up, Hetty — let us hope you find him', she said. She kissed me goodbye, with many admonitions to take care.

I was lucky and caught a train that went straight to the town a mile or so away from The Laurels. I pretended that I was just out for a country walk. I walked away from the station where another world ago I had arrived that first time with Gregory and we had argued about our Aunt's name. But I was thinking as I walked not of my mission but of the Littles' house in Camberwell and how happy they were and how all the trouble in the world came — according to a French writer I'd read — from men being incapable of sitting peacefully in one room and reading and studying. I wondered if Lucy knew how fond Max was of Cara and whether he had said anything to her.

But as I came to the drive that went off the main road out of the small town I began to feel a little frightened. Tall coniferous trees made the drive dark. There were hedgerows on each side

315

and I guessed that it had once been just a country lane and The Laurels had replaced an old farm. I tried to think of Gregory, and of Max. If I succeeded in finding Felix, then I would allow myself to think of Orso. Since arriving home he had become dreamlike to me. How could such a lovely man exist in the same world as kidnappers and poisoners?

Max was the one person who had never seemed bothered by Simon. He'd had to share his home with him when he was little, but he had not had to go to school with him at an age when a bully enjoys bullying, as poor Gregory had had to. Had Simon ever bullied Max? I couldn't see Zelda ever allowing that. Simon had never expressed any interest in Max and Max never mentioned him if he could help it. I thought of my little cousin and how we'd played together in the very summerhouse whose weathercock I could see now rising above the trees as I went further down the drive towards The Laurels. It seemed much longer than a dozen years since the first time I'd been here, and an age since I'd played with Max's soldiers and with the miniature tea-set. I felt my childhood cut off from me now by more than passing time.

Now I could just see the roof of the house. It appeared to grow out of the conifers and Scotch pines that surrounded it.

Heavens above, that was smoke coming out of the chimney.

I must be practical.

If anybody was there innocently they'd come

to my knock, so I'd knock first. If no one came I'd open the kitchen door and go in at the back. If I found Felix there I'd tell him I'd come for him. If Simon refused to let him come away with me I'd say the others knew where I was. Then I'd take Felix home.

What if Simon wouldn't let me, though — what would I do then? What if he kept me there against my will?

The main thing was to rescue Felix, never mind about Simon Voyle.

My mind went round and round like this till I found myself on the part of the drive that turned to the left to go behind the shrubbery to the kitchen door. I passed the window where Huntie had looked out at us playing that first time. There was no sound and no sight of anyone at the window at the back. Now I was in the courtyard. I took the key out of my pocket and went up to the door. Then I knocked, and thought the sound was no louder than the thumping of my heart, so I knocked louder. Nobody came to answer — yes, the door was locked; I put the key in the door, pushed it open.

The big kitchen had an air of neglect about it as well it might. There was a long range with a fireplace and a rack above with ropes to pull washing up and down. The pantry went off this room and I looked in before returning to the kitchen. It was very quiet.

Then I heard him.

'Simon — come and find me!' Felix's voice! A

great wave of relief overwhelmed me and I forgot everything else and shouted: 'Felix! Where are you?' and went into the hall that adjoined the kitchen. The green baize door was open and I went into the entrance hall itself.

Simon Voyle was standing there at the foot of the stairs.

For a moment we stood staring at each other until I found my voice. At first he did not move. 'Felix!' I cried again. 'Where are you? Where is he?' I asked him stupidly, as though it mattered. He was here somewhere.

'Why, hello, Hetty Coppen', said Simon Voyle. 'What are *you* doing here on a peaceful Sunday afternoon?' He drawled his words and I did not like the sound of his voice one bit.

'I've come for my little brother', I said, trying not to betray any fear in my voice, but it trembled in spite of myself.

'You mean your little *half*-brother, don't you? — or have they not enlightened you yet about our curious family relationships?'

'My half-brother then. Felix!' I called as loudly as I could.

Suddenly a little figure came running down the stairs which led from the hall and stopped at the bottom when it saw me. Simon had moved towards me, but I stood my ground. 'Felix, we've all been looking everywhere for you at home', I said. Simon did not stop the child as he came towards me.

'Hetty', he said. 'Have you brought me some

318

sweeties? Simon gave me some but I've finished them.'

I bent down and embraced him. He looked quite as usual except that there were shadows under his eyes as if he had not slept. 'You must come home, Felix', I said.

'What if he doesn't want to?' said Simon, staring at me with those cold grey eyes of his. So cold.

I was not going to ask Felix if he wanted to come home. The child was apparently unharmed and unsurprised to see me. Simon would not tell him he could not go home with me. He would tell *me* that. I said: 'They all know where I am, so Felix had better come back with me straight away.'

'If they all know, why haven't they "all" come?' said Simon. 'You can't fool me, Hetty Coppen.'

'Why should I want to fool you, Simon?' I asked ingratiatingly. 'Of course they didn't believe me when I said you'd be here', I went on, 'but I told them if I didn't return home this evening to come here for Felix.'

He said flatly: 'I don't believe you. And Felix is quite happy here with me — let your father come for him — or is he the coward I've always known him to be?' Felix was looking from one to the other of us. 'Felix likes it here, don't you Felix?' he said.

'Yes — but I'd like to go home now, I think, Simon', said Felix.

'I don't think that would be feasible', said Simon Voyle, and Felix looked blank.

319

'You can't keep him here for ever', I said, thinking I could go and tell the others where he was. I did not want to say that Ella was out of her mind with worry for that would only have pleased Simon and frightened Felix, once he realized that he could not go back with me, and the boy was not stupid, he would get the message.

But Simon now seemed quite prepared to frighten him, or at least confuse the child for he said: 'Felix has asked now and again for his mother — come here, Felix, tell your sister what a nice time we've been having.'

'Simon — it's nearly a week!' I said and could not help sounding angry, I suppose, for he turned to me and said: 'A week is not very long. To a child, I suppose, it might seem longer.' He sounded as though he were giving a lecture in a curious dry, formal voice.

'Well, I'm sure he has come to no harm', I said, attempting to sound bright and cheerful, as if taking a six-year-old away from his home was only a bit of fun. I had to try every approach to see which one might make him change his mind.

'It was clever of you to find us', said Simon, as though we were playing hide-and-seek. 'But you *are* clever, aren't you, Hetty?'

'Simon, I'm hungry — I want a biscuit', said Felix.

'I'm sure if we go into the kitchen Hetty will find you one', said Simon. 'And she can make us all a cup of tea in the room with the fire. Come, Hetty — see how comfortable we have been, haven't we, Felix?' He seemed quite normal when he spoke to him. It did not seem to be Felix himself whom he intended to harm. At least I hoped that was true.

He led the way into the sitting-room I knew so well where I found a smoky fire and a kettle. The dusty brown velvet curtains were still hanging and the original pictures that had been there on my first visit, and some still-lives of pheasants — not chosen by my cousin Max, I remember thinking. Perhaps if we drank a cup of tea this ordinary procedure might soften Voyle's resolve. Or was he mad? No, I did not think he was mad. Just very unpleasant and totally without a conscience. I hoped to God he hadn't brought drink with him or we should both be in danger. Whilst I was fetching water from the kitchen and rooting in a mouldy biscuit tin, Simon stood by the sitting-room fire and watched Felix who was playing with the tassel of the curtain.

'A nice place your aunt had here, wasn't it?' he said conversationally.

'Yes — I believe Max comes here now and then to see all's right', I replied, thinking, well, that's another lie, but it might frighten him.

'Oh, I wasn't thinking of staying for long. I thought we might go abroad', he said. Was he just trying to frighten me? I had to keep them here now or the trail would be lost. I ought to have waited for Gregory to come with me, I saw that now, but it was no use regretting my impulsivity.

'I'm surprised you came alone', he said conversationally. 'But you always were an impetuous creature, Hetty.' He had taken my own thoughts from my head and for a moment I wondered whether to stress our former acquaintance, talk about the family normally. But what he said next made my blood run cold. I had given him a cup of milkless tea, for I could find only an empty milk jug in the larder, and a tea-caddy half full of Max's favourite Earl Grey and a few cups that had clearly been already used on the draining board. I wondered where the biscuits were.

'I told you that your little *half*-brother occasionally asked for his Mama', he began. 'So did I ask at his age. But I got no answer.'

'The child should be with his mother', I whispered so that Felix could not hear.

'Children should always be with their mothers', he said in the same maddeningly rational tone of voice that yet had a charge of passion behind it. 'Do not worry, Hetty Coppen', he said. 'I have not hurt your precious sibling, but he is going to learn what it is like to be taken away from your mother at a tender age.' So he did intend him to suffer.

I said: 'But of course you had a father, Simon, to take good care of you. I met him not long ago — in Italy — you look a little like him!' If I'd thought that this would get him off the subject of mothers, I was wrong. Fathers too, it seemed, were also objects of blame.

'Oh yes, a *very* good father', he said, and put

322

down his cup. 'I'll have another cup, please. Not that it was my father's fault. Fathers can be hoodwinked, you see — unfortunately. But I mustn't grumble. I had a good adopted aunt to care for me, didn't I?' He said all this with such sarcasm. I felt more nervous than ever.

'I want a biscuit', said Felix suddenly.

'Where are they?' I asked.

'Felix, run upstairs and you will find a tin in my bedroom', said Simon. Felix ran out of the room without a backward glance.

'Now, Hetty, we are alone together and though I did not expect the pleasure of your company I think I must make the best of it. I might, just might, send Felix back where you think he belongs, but only if certain other conditions are fulfilled.' He was enjoying himself, I could see.

'Simon — what I told you was the truth. They will come for us if I am not back this evening', I began. It was almost dusk. I must get Felix away.

'I don't believe you — you never used to tell people what you were doing — it was never in your character to do that', he said.

'Well, choose not to believe me, but I am speaking the truth', I said, thinking in a weird access of childishness that I ought to cross my fingers at the half-lie.

'You might be speaking the truth', he said slowly, looking at my face, and I thanked my lucky stars I was such a good liar. 'But it's immaterial', he went on after a pause.

'If you'll let me take him back I'll give you a

good sum of money', I said. 'Then you will be able to get away yourself — abroad — wherever it was you intended to go.' I thought I'd struck lucky again, for I knew how keen he was on cash.

'Oh, Hetty — *you* haven't any money, have you?' he drawled. There he was wrong and I did not need to lie.

'I promise you I have — and that you can have it all if you let him come back with me', I said. 'And I keep my promises', I added, fully intending that I should give him my little fortune.

'What a heroine!' he said. 'And who gave you money, may I ask? That scheming aunt of yours, I expect?'

'No — her husband', I said boldly. His expression of incredulity changed to one of impending storm.

'No, that can't be — no! —' he said. I had surprised him. Then he went out of the room and called up the stairs: 'Felix, if you have found the biscuits you may stay upstairs and play with those toys, and then I shall put you to bed.' This was not at all what I wanted.

He came in again and said: 'Do sit down — I feel we could come to some sort of agreement, Hetty. I'll give the child back as you wish — I can't bear the sight of him — good actor am I not? — if you will surrender something belonging to you. No not money. Now, what do they call it — your "precious maidenhood"? There now. You can't refuse me that, can you?'

I swallowed and for a moment thought I *must*

be dreaming. What a fool I'd been. The man had no compassion, no honor, no shred of decency about him. But I could not really believe his words and gaped at him.

'Just a little "passion", Hetty', he said. 'I'm sure you have more in your little finger than your pretty sister has in her body — if it hasn't already been dissipated with those friends I'm sure your aunt has introduced you to?'

'How dare you bring Cara into this?' I said. 'You know she is your half-sister! You are disgusting.'

'But *you* are not my sister, Hetty, are you?' he said. Suddenly he seemed pathetic — dangerous, but pathetic. No sane gentleman would surely hint at such a thing. A fate worse than death, they called it. I was sure now he was capable of anything, but I must find his weak spot. The trouble was that Simon Voyle's weak spot had twisted him into this unfortunate, menacing individual who had me where he wanted me only on account of superior physical strength.

'Or do I disgust you, Hetty?' he murmured. 'It would be a good bargain — you can take Felix back with you if you give me what I want.'

I moved back a few steps, boiling with anger and shame, my brain paralysed by fear. 'Why should I trust you?' I managed to get out.

'Oh, you need not *trust* me', he said. 'Indeed your arrival has made things easier for me. I wasn't sure what I was going to do with the brat — but now you could take him back — at a price. I might as well revenge myself on your father's daughter as on my own mother's son. Otherwise I'll do what I was going to do in the first place — but my better self prevented me. How fortunate that you are here.'

I could not help, even at this point of a pointless conversation, thinking how like a stage villain he seemed. People surely did not talk like this. He was making it up, making himself into a villain. I *would* try to appeal to this better nature of his. How could such suggestions be made in this familiar room where I had played happily with Max?

'You could not allow a child to suffer, Simon', I said. 'I agree that you yourself probably suffered through the fault of your mother — but that was nothing to do with me. Remember, *I* lost my mother too.'

All he said was — 'If you don't agree to our little bargain, things will remain as they were — I shall take Felix abroad with me tonight or to-morrow — or perhaps give him on the way to a woman to look after in exchange for a little sum of money. Unlike my father though, unfortunately, I haven't very much money so I couldn't choose a very suitable person, I'm afraid.'

I knew I must play for time. It was the only card in my hand.

'If you will not let me take him with me then I shall go back without him', I said.

'Oh, no, I couldn't let you do that! — a young lady walking alone at night, wandering to the station where — incidentally — there are no trains till tomorrow. No, no, I couldn't allow that. I'm afraid you will have to stay the night here.'

'There *is* a train', I said. 'And I'm used to walking alone.' His brow darkened.

'It will be the worse for your brother then', he said. 'Think it over — I give you an hour.'

I was hungry and now it was getting dark.

'You can put the brat to bed whilst I have a bite to eat. Cold chicken in the pantry, but I'm afraid only enough for me — and a plate of porridge for Felix tomorrow.'

I remembered the apples in my bag. 'All right — I'll put him to bed', I said.

'And then come down and — talk,' he said. I can describe his expression only with one word — a 'leer'. 'I shall make sure the doors are locked', he added.

He went out of the room and I went up the familiar stairs and found Felix in the room that had been Max's so long ago. If only Max were here. If only *anybody* were here. I knew that Lucy would come or send help after midnight, but could I hold out till then, hold that twisted young man at bay? . . .

'Hello, Felix', I said brightly. 'Time for bed. I'm afraid we can't go home just yet.' He looked up and submitted to a wash. The water was icy cold. 'How did you meet Simon?' I asked conversationally as I dried his face. It was fortunate that the water had not been turned off at the mains. I felt very grubby myself and splashed my own face with it. Perhaps that sour-faced maid came now and then to see everything was all right. Perhaps she might come tomorrow. Perhaps a tradesman might call. But no, these were idle hopes. I gave Felix one of my apples and ate one myself.

'Simon was playing in the wood', he said. 'And he took me on a train. But I'd like to go home now to Alice and Papa — and Mama', he added. 'Will she be cross?' he asked.

'I expect she will be so glad to see you tomorrow', I improvised, 'that she will forget to be cross.' I thought, the child was always told not to go with strangers, but Simon is not a stranger to him.

'There are nice toys here', he said. 'Simon says they are his — it is his house.' I suppose it had been the only 'home' he had known, after all.

Max's old bed only had a blanket, and it was cold, so I searched and found another and lit a candle I found in a drawer, along with matches. 'No — Simon says I can't have a candle. He says I am too old for nightlights', Felix said in a piteous voice. Naturally — a light might attract visitors. The sitting-room was on the garden side of the house — but had he not thought of smoke coming from the chimney? I tucked my little brother up and said: 'Goodnight' to him and went downstairs to await my fate. I would hold out as long as I could. This would be the end of all my dreams of love, that was all. I would try to keep our conversation on a friendly footing, would promise him that if he allowed Felix back he would not be pros-

ecuted. I would ask him to sign my promise —
and then abandon myself to my fate. I wondered
what had been his final intention. Did he even
know himself? But when I entered the sitting-room
I saw to my horror that there was a large bottle
of brandy on the table and that Simon was sitting
by the fire with a glass already in his hand.

'Help yourself', he said. 'It will help *you*, I
think.' Then conversationally he said, 'I shall tell
your sister she's a bastard   won't she be pleased!
Her with her big ideas of marrying a rich man.'
Clearly he knew nothing of Max and Cara.

'I don't want any brandy', I said.

'You are cold', he said. 'Come and warm yourself
by the fire.'

I looked at him sitting there. He was not really
an ugly man, though not as good-looking as his
father Peter Voyle, but his face was red and the
backs of his hands bristled with ginger hairs. His
physical presence repelled me. I would try to get
him on to the subject of his work, anything that
would not start him off on parents and their in-
iquities. Could he once have been normal, or was
the nastiness there from the beginning? I would
try to sound sisterly, to put his mind away from
unsisterly thoughts, but realized that had not been
very helpful for Cara. If he'd kissed her against
her will in my father's house, of what would he
not be capable in this place with a weak woman
at his mercy? I hated thinking of myself as that.
He began to ramble on about his childhood and
I thought the best thing would be for him to drink

the whole bottle and fall asleep, but he must have seen this thought go through my mind, for he said — 'I can hold my liquor, Hetty Coppen. Come and sit near me.' Then he began again: his mother the whore, and his father her victim, and how he'd promised his father to avenge his honour.

'So your father would think your conduct that of a gentleman?' I asked.

'Oh, my father — none of them were a match for him! Spent money like water — hers and then the others — a ladies' man, my Papa.' I said nothing. 'Revenge', he said. 'And a piece of revenge I hadn't bargained for when you took the idea in your head to come here. How foolish you were.' He grasped my wrist and twisted it, and I thought, this is it, but then he released it and said: 'I shall revenge myself on you, Miss Hetty Coppen, in a most gentlemanly way. No fuss. All discreet and in the best of taste.' And then he laughed.

'And if I resist, what then? Do you intend to keep me here for ever, Simon?' I spoke as coolly as I could.

'Oh, it doesn't matter what happens to you', he said. 'I shall let the brat go when I think my Ma has suffered enough. Perhaps she'll think he's dead? Do you think she'll think of that? Eh?'

I could see as I looked at him why so many women were frightened of men, even ordinary men whom lust might fuel into monsters of repulsion. But his mention of death began to work upon my imagination. What if he killed us both? Felix and me. Was he truly capable of that? Better a fate worse than death itself. However could I escape now? I looked at the clock, but it had stopped.

'Thinking about your rescuers?' he asked unpleasantly. 'Oh, there's hours yet — time for you to take off your clothes very slowly — yes, I think I'd like that best, very slowly — it will be a moment to savour, Hetty Coppen, won't it? Not that I find you attractive — I don't — but as they say — any woman will do —' He laughed a short, sharp laugh. But he went on — 'Then when you are ready I shall ask you to bring the child down and watch.' I stared at him in horror. I could imagine he might rape me, but that he might want a child as audience, that was past comprehension.

'We shall make him watch', he said. 'As I watched my mother and your father, Miss Coppen, when I was even younger than that brat upstairs.'

I felt my heart jump and begin to beat irregularly, but I thought, would it be better to pretend to faint or would that just give him the opportunity he was waiting for? When I think of what I was feeling then, I am amazed I could think at all. But I was fuelled also by a burning hatred of this man. No more pity now. However awful his childhood, however guilty my father in the matter, Simon was warped — not mad, only bad. I should have to pretend I was going to do his bidding, and then get him drunk. But I wasn't certain how much it would take to make a young man really drunk and even if he were, that might not stop him from doing to me what he threatened. With another part of my mind I still could not

331

believe what was happening. I had the idea whilst he went on detailing what he was going to do to me, that I ought to play on the maudlin qualities I sensed in the man. Simon Voyle had always been sorry for himself; if he had turned that self-pity into anger, wasn't it possible that I could turn it back?

'How terrible for you', I said. 'How could anyone help being scarred for life if they saw such things as a child?'

'You don't even know what I'm talking about', he said. 'I wasn't just talking about taking off your clothes, you know!' He must think me ignorant of the basic facts of life — as I knew so many young women were. Should I pretend not to understand? I knew perfectly well what he meant. The idea in the abstract had in the past been both incredible and disgusting to me, but now that I had imagined being made love to by Orso Orsini I had realized why women did not always find it repulsive. I had felt it was my own little secret, and hugged it to myself. But I knew I did not have the physical strength to push him away, never mind the loss of virtue and honour.

'Why don't you have a drink?' he suggested once more. 'I'm being generous — then you can take off your dress — the way *she* did.'

'Have you *no* shame, Simon?' I said quietly.

'Oh, yes, if I wanted I could tear your clothes off you', he said brutally, 'but you are going to take them off yourself. You *want* to, don't you? Like *she* did.'

'I'll accept your brandy', I said. 'But I must fetch a glass.'

'Be quick about it then.'

I went into the kitchen and made a great noise opening cupboards — he was too lazy to follow me now. Swiftly I unbolted the door at the same time and returned to the sitting-room with a glass in my hand.

'I'm glad you're seeing sense', he said. 'You will enjoy what I do — as she did.'

I wanted him to forget this notion of fetching Felix down, so I poured out a very small quantity of brandy, wishing it were wine. Better I lose my virtue than he should harm Felix — but how would I know if he would let the child go?

'How do I know you will keep your word and let Felix go home with me?' I said. He was looking at me steadily as I drank, but did not answer. The brandy on an empty stomach, or one empty but for two apples, was burning my throat most unpleasantly. 'There is a soda syphon in the cupboard', I said.

'Get it then. You know you are not a bad-looking girl, Hetty Coppen — has anyone ever told you?' This was too much.

I squirted some soda into the glass and said: 'Not as pretty as your half-sister.' I knew he wouldn't care if I were the ugliest girl alive. This man wanted power, and indeed I wondered for a moment if he was even capable of passion. But he was impatient.

'Stand there then — let me see you — now,

take off your dress.'

I had a skirt and long white overblouse and many layers of underclothing. 'It is a strange sort of revenge', I said.

'What difference does it make to *you?* — your own mother, even *she,* would hide her face from you if she knew, but she is dead and can't help you!' he said. The thought came to me that he would dispose of me once he had raped me, so that nobody would know. Men who raped with violence had been transported at one time, or executed, but I was not sure what happened to them now. The fire was low and I was trembling from cold as much as from fear. 'I will take off my overblouse', I said — 'but will not take anything else off.'

He put his glass down and came up to me. His breath smelt of brandy and I shrank from him, longing to punch him on the nose. But I dared not anger him further. 'You can go and wake up the child now', he said in my ear and he put his hand on my arm — it was damp and I could smell his sweat.

'That I shall not do', I said.

'But you *will* — I like *my* revenge two-headed.' He twisted my arm back and I cried out in pain. Now I was at my wits' end. He started fumbling with the buttons at the back of my skirt, but they were too complicated for his clumsy fingers. He bent my head back and with a grunt bit my neck. If I could have remembered a prayer I'd have prayed, but my head was one cold block of fear

334

and loathing, and my knees like water.

Then I heard it — I was sure I heard a noise from the back of the house! Was it just the wind banging the door I'd unlatched? Suddenly I found the strength to push him away.

'There's someone there!' I said. 'Listen! I told you they knew where I was.' He still held my arm in a painful grip, but he looked up and it was true there *was* a noise. I lost my head then and began to scream as I have never screamed before. Even if nobody was there. It was not yet midnight, but Lucy might have decided to follow me anyway.

I screamed and, without knowing what I was doing, it was Orso Orsini's name that I cried, over and over, till Simon stopped my mouth with his hand. He released me for a moment from his grip, and took up a poker from the hearth. Then he grabbed me again and I went on screaming. Even as I yelled I remember thinking, — it will wake Felix. I was sure Simon was going to kill me now, but just as I had decided that this was the end, he dragged me with him behind the door and waited to attack whoever it might be. I screamed again 'Orso! Orso!' All this happened in a few seconds but they were also the longest seconds of my life. 'Help! Help!' I cried. Now I heard footsteps. 'In here', I screamed. Then, to Simon — 'Don't hurt Lucy, don't hurt Lucy!'

But it was not Lucy Little who burst into the room like a big angry bull, but Orso Orsini whose name I had cried in my terror!

Simon Voyle's blow glanced off his shoulder and Simon was sent flying by that most powerful right arm, an arm that had practised in operatic fights, an arm that belonged to a man who was not frightened of using force when necessary. Voyle picked himself up and was out of the room in a flash. All I wanted was for my torturer to go away and never to set eyes on him again — but what if he had gone for Felix?

'Ester! Ester!' shouted my saviour and took me in his arms. I leaned against him trembling for several moments. But then —

'The child!' I gasped and pulled Orso after me into the hall. Indeed when we got into the hall there was Voyle coming down the stairs holding Felix in his arms.

Orso went up to him. *'Lascialo'*, he said and punched Simon on the mouth. I ran up to Felix who had been suddenly dropped on the parquet. He began to wail and I took him on my lap. But Simon, though winded and bleeding, knew this house better than Orsini did and with a bound he was through the vestibule window and out on to the drive.

'Don't follow him! Don't!' I cried. 'What matters is the child', I said again. 'Come, Felix, I'll put you to rest on the sofa — then we're going home.' Felix was sobbing and hiccuping. But he had been half-asleep and soon put his thumb in his mouth again and was silent.

Only when there was silence outside too and I knew Simon Voyle was gone — not risking another hammer blow from Orsini's big fist, and when Orso had taken Felix from me and put him down by the fire, did I begin to cry uncontrollably. Orso had taken in the whole situation at a glance, for he took my blouse and wrapped it round my shoulders, and then he carried me in his arms to the sofa and knclt by my side murmuring things in Italian — '*La povera, la povera* — *mia piccina* — poor little girl, poor little Ester, never mind — it's all right now.'

Slowly I calmed myself.

'He will not come back', he said and took out a knife from his pocket. 'I carry this for robbers', he said. 'But I did not need to use it.'

Then the sheer impossibility of Orso's being there at last struck me and I sat up. 'Is it really you?' I said. '*È vero?*' He looked less like a bull now, more like a bear that has been disturbed, but seen off his enemy. His eyes flashed.

'We go home', he said then in English. He stood up and I thought how he not only sounded but looked like a natural force.

'I cried out for you! I cried out for you!' I said — 'But how could you know? — How did you know?' I looked at him in wonderment. Then I went up to Felix and sat him on my lap and Orso sat by me. I needed a few moments rest for my legs felt like water. He put his arm round me.

'I go to your address this afternoon and there is a kind gentleman who talks my language — and then a lady comes in and I say I come for Ester — and she says Ester is gone to look for a little brother who is taken away — '*rapito*' — how do you say? and if she don't come back it will be bad — and Ester think the boy is in the aunt's house with a wicked man who holds him there. I do not wait. She tell me all this and I get a carriage and the lady come too — and he drop me down there — near the road and I say, wait till I come back.'

'Do speak Italian, Orso', I said. 'Though I love your English.'

'Now we go home', he said in Italian.

'He didn't get what he wanted', I said in Italian myself, and he looked a long time at me, and then he kissed my cheek and it was the happiest moment of my life.

'It seems, Ester', he said in his own language, 'we are fated to rescue each other. Now take the *bambino* and you put on your warm coat and here is your bag and where are the *bambino's* clothes?'

Felix woke up again and watched in amazement as this big, dark man scooped him up and we all went out of the house at the back door and Felix was carried down the drive on Orso's shoulders. I walked beside them, feeling unreal.

'*Andiamo lentamente*', said Orso Orsini. 'You have had big shock — it is you I should be carrying.' I knew I could walk so long as there would soon be an end to all this and I could sit down and go to sleep. I was no longer hungry. I think the shock of what Simon Voyle fully intended to do to me had driven every other thought away. How to avoid thinking of it still? But the night air and the presence of this strong, cheerful man by my side made my heart steadier. 'Your friend is in the carriage — I tell her she must stay there till I come back', said Orso. Lucy had come too. The two people I liked best in all the world.

I saw that Felix was asleep, his head against Orso's shoulder and his arms round his neck, piggyback fashion.

'We take a carriage from London together and the driver is also big and strong', said Orso. 'But not needed now.'

'I wonder where Simon Voyle has gone', I said, thinking what expense — a carriage all the way here! I must pay, for Orso is not a rich man and Lucy certainly cannot afford carriages out of London.

'He will run away somewhere far', said Orsini whose English seemed to have made amazing strides since I'd last seen him, but I supposed that with an ear like his he could easily and quickly pick up sounds and meanings. 'You tell me all story later.' Then in Italian he said something like, 'I wish I had wrung his neck.'

The darkness at the bottom of the drive was illuminated by a few stars now we had come out of the trees and I saw a dark equipage waiting by the lane end and two figures standing by the horse who neighed as he heard our footsteps. Lucy turned at once and came up swiftly. 'Felix?' she exclaimed and took the child from Orso. He woke up again — poor child, would he ever forget this night? — and looked at her sleepily — 'Is it time for lessons then?' he said and promptly fell asleep again. We put him on the seat at the back and then Lucy put her arms round me. 'Hetty, Hetty, what happened? About twenty minutes ago a man came running down the drive — I was sitting in the carriage and he stopped for a moment on the other side of the road. I thought it was Voyle, but I dared not follow him.'

'Where did he go?'

'Towards the town.' We had both ignored Orso for a few moments and he was standing looking from one to the other.

'Lucy — this is Signor Orsini — I'm sorry I didn't ask your permission to give him your address —'

'Papa and Signor Orsini had a nice talk', said Lucy. 'And it was a good thing that you did give him it!'

I did not tell her anything of my ordeal until later, for now I felt unutterably weary and a little sick, the reaction, I expect, to all the horror and fear I had suffered.

'*Povera* — sleep', said Orso when I said I was tired.

The carriage jolted a bit and it was a long journey from Kent to New Cross, but finally we were going down Blackheath Hill and along New Cross Road and the Old Kent Road. I woke up then and Orso took my hand and if Lucy noticed she said nothing. I leaned against him. He felt like — like the Rock of Gibraltar, I thought dazedly. I must have fallen asleep again though, for the next thing I knew was we were outside the Littles' house and it was dawn. Orso paid the cabman and when we entered there was Lucy's father in the tiny hall looking very worried. When he saw us he said nothing but: 'Thank God!' There would be time enough for explanations later. Felix had behaved remarkably well; now he woke up and said he was hungry. Lucy fetched bread and milk for us all. I felt Orsini belonged here too. Lucy took Felix up to a little truckle-bed in her room, which she said was often used for a small cousin, and then came down to us.

'My *dear* Hetty', said her father. 'Your friend here seems to have arrived in the nick of time.'

This was an understatement, but I left it at that.

'He tells me he wants to improve his English', went on Mr Little seizing upon what interested him most.

'I shall leave Felix to sleep, and then take him home tomorrow along with myself who am going to your Papa's anyway. It is no use trying to tell them now, for the Post Office will be shut till eight and we shall arrive before a telegraph could. Now, Hetty, you sleep here and go home when you feel like it', said Lucy.

'Yes, get Felix home, that is the main thing. But just tell them he was at Zelda's — don't say too much about Simon', I said. 'I'll do that.'

Orso said: 'I sing tomorrow in rehearsal — but I come soon again, yes, to your house, this house?'

'Orso', I said. 'I have to see my Papa first, but then I think I shall come back here. When is your first performance?' I had realized that the poor man must be as tired as myself. I must not take him for granted.

'Next week', he said. 'But I come back here before that — and see you?'

'I shall have a lot of explaining to do to my father', I said. 'But will you say nothing of what you saw? I want to forget it — Papa need not know all the details.'

'Ester — I wait till you are asleep — then I go. But you all come to the first performance — front row — you do me the honour also, Miss Leetel, and Signor Leetel?' But Mr Little had tactfully gone to bed.

Before I went up to Lucy's room where I could share a bed with her, Orso took my hand and kissed it hard. 'Soon — soon', he said and then bowed to Lucy and was off.

14

I was young and so I slept soundly and woke late at eleven o'clock. I put on a morning robe of Lucy's and went down to the small dining-room where a breakfast was laid for me — toast and honey and tea in a large yellow teapot. Lucy had already gone to East Wood with Felix, as I had urged her the night before.

'He *was* excited', said the maid — ' "Will the dog be at home?" he kept saying?' How odd. We had no dog. I realized that Simon Voyle must have promised him one. I did not think Felix would be scarred for life by his abduction. Where was Voyle now? Perhaps we should have got the police to go to his Stepney lodgings while there was still time? But all I could think of was that Felix was safe — and that Orso Orsini had saved me. Yet Orso seemed like a dream I had dreamt, a dream arising out of a nightmare. *I* would never forget what had happened, even if Felix might.

Mr Little looked in as I was finishing my breakfast. Never had English toast tasted so good. 'Your family will alert the police?' he said. He was more agitated than I had ever seen him.

'Voyle will go abroad', I said. Lucy must have told her father yesterday afternoon about my all too well-founded suspicions. How wonderful to have a Papa to whom one might confide all one's fears and worries.

It was only as I began to dress in the little room that looked out over a quiet road with the Green in the distance that I saw the bruises on my arms. Great big purple bruises from Voyle's hands. It brought it all back. It had not been a nightmare, or an 'adventure', but a brutal and disgusting episode. I ought to have known better than to have gone alone.

'I had a short talk with your Italian friend', said Mr Little when I went down again. 'A remarkable man — and a follower of Garibaldi. It didn't take us long to connect you with "Ester", and the minute he realized you were in danger, he went off. I must say I didn't like Lucy going away like that, but I could see she was in capable hands. His English is coming along quite nicely', he added.

'He is a great singer', I said. 'We became acquainted in Florence.'

'He never said then he was a singer!' said Mr Little in surprise. 'He is here to sing in London?'

'Yes — at Covent Garden. But I must go home now, Mr Little.' I hesitated — 'May I return here soon to stay for a few days? It is so peaceful and I only came back to England for my little brother — now he's safe I can soon go back to Florence.'

'You will want to see your brother Gregory and your father', said Lucy's father. 'My daughter said your brother would know what to do — you must

344

find Voyle and prefer charges — but you are *very* welcome here, my dear.'

'If we can find him', I said. The one place Simon Voyle had never been was this safe haven in Camberwell.

Mr Little sent me back home in another cab. I must say I was glad not to have to travel alone by train. I kept expecting to see Simon Voyle round every corner, in spite of my belief that he would have disappeared, but such is human irrationality. In the middle of the journey I thought, I never thanked Orso, let him go away without even a 'thank you' — what must he think of me? And this thought led me to my growing conviction that he might think twice about getting to know a family where such things as the abduction of a child by a half-brother took place. It was just too operatic.

When I arrived home they were all in the drawing-room. Cara ran up to me in tears of joy. Mama had Felix on her knee though he was wriggling to get down. Papa looked even paler than the day before.

'The police are to come at two', he said. 'Your mother and I have already thanked Miss Little.' He bowed towards her and she tried to look gratified. 'It appears we have to thank you too — and a friend of yours, a Mr Cortini?'

'Orsini', I said. 'Oh, yes, you must thank *him!*' I did not want to say anything in front of Felix and Alice, and Papa saw this and said, 'Felix, go with Cara and play in the nursery — you are forbidden the garden.'

Felix went out with his hand in Cara's. He looked subdued. Perhaps he had realized that something awful had happened to him. Huntie came in with a tray of teacups and then Ella stood up. She had so far said nothing at all to me.

Now she turned towards me. 'We are waiting for Gregory', she said. Not a word of thanks.

'Ella', said my father. 'It is Hetty you have to thank, you know.'

Ella's face was a mask. 'Yes. Thank you', was all she said. Then she buried her face in her hands.

Gregory returned that same afternoon alerted by a message Papa sent to his chambers. To him I told everything, sitting on my old bed in the attic where he had told me about Mama when I was a little girl. He listened to me without a word, but his face was dark with shame and rage. I omitted no detail, but I played down my acquaintance with Orso Orsini, who I said I had got to know socially at Aunt's in Florence.

When I had finished, Gregory said: 'The police are to search everywhere for Voyle, but it will be too late if he has gone abroad — as you seem to think.'

'I believe he will go to his father', I said. 'Do you think his father knew what he was going to do?'

'No', he replied. 'I'm sure Voyle senior had no idea of his son's plan to steal Felix. Hetty, can you wait patiently until I have finished what I set

346

out to do last year? It is partly connected with Voyle.'

'I wish you would not be so mysterious — what else can there be now that the worst has happened? — and we know why he did what he did. I had a little compunction for him at first — but now I just want to forget the whole affair.'

He went on earnestly. 'Believe me, there are other things you will have to know. Does Cara know anything yet about her birth?'

'No — there's been quite enough to think about.' I felt I *was* living the plot of an opera. 'All I want is to have a peaceful few days before I go back to Italy', I said.

'Don't go back yet — please do not', he said.

I knew that I'd not been entirely honest with my brother so I could not expect him to tell me all that was in his mind. 'I want to go back and start my governessing', I said.

'You can do that here as well as there. Why not ask Mr Little if he would let you have his back parlour if you don't want to stay at home?' I said I'd think about it and Gregory said: 'Remember — it will not be long now, Hetty, and then you will be able to do whatever you want.'

He went into the study to tell the police what I had told him, omitting for Mamarella's sake the way her son Simon had dealt with me. I had not shown anyone the bruises either.

There was to be a big search for Simon Voyle — it even had a mention in *The Times*. I was sure that he was in Italy and I wrote to Zelda

347

in Rome and to Rosa in Florence without telling anyone.

Several days passed, but before I decided what to do and where to go I managed to have a talk alone with Huntie, who it seemed to me had been avoiding me. Surely she didn't think I blamed *her* for Felix's disobedience? No one had punished Felix, but he was not to be allowed out by himself anywhere.

'I knew it would happen, Hetty', she said in tears. 'But truly I never let him out of my sight more than a few minutes. Are they going to get rid of me?'

'No, they are not', I said.

'I thought my Auntie Daventry might tell your aunt when I was worried about your stepmother', she said. 'Then she could tell that Simon Voyle's dad and they could stop whatever it was he was going to do. *I* knew the mistress was frightened of the young man.' This was new. I'd thought Ella firmly opposed to any suggestion that Simon might do something unpleasant, and said so.

'No — she *was* frightened of him — but she dared not say so, not even to your Papa — I know that, I'm sure.'

'Well, Rosa did nothing — Peter Voyle came one afternoon — but I — er — didn't hear of any worry about what Simon might do.' I remembered though they had been talking of him, or I'd guessed it was him.

'I think my Aunt Daventry *did* do something', said Huntie mysteriously. 'I think she wrote to your Papa.' But she would say no more, though I pressed her.

The next conversation I had was with Cara. I felt increasingly awkward with her now that the danger was over. The poor girl would have to know one day the secret of her birth, but I did not want to be the one who told her.

As she came into my bedroom and sat in my one easy chair and looked at me with those big, blue eyes of hers and said: 'Oh, Hetty — I'm so miserable — and I'm ashamed of it now that Felix is back and everything is all right for Mama and Papa — am I *very* selfish?'

'Is it Bruno? Are you missing him?' I asked her sympathetically. I could understand that.

'No, no, it's not him — anyway when I don't see him I don't really think about him. It's Max.'

'But you saw him a week or two ago — you said — and you can't expect to meet him if he's away working.'

'No — it's Papa — he says I'm not to entertain the idea — of Max — that Mama doesn't want me seeing him at all, even with Miss Little. Why should I not? I like to talk to him — I know he was attracted to me in Florence — but *they* don't know that — it must be something else — and when people try to stop you doing what you want it makes you want it even more — and I don't see why I can't see him. We were going to meet next week when he came back — he said he'd take me to Covent Garden and Lucy could come too — you'd think all the business of Felix and everything would stop them being so — petty — and I was looking forward to going out — and now he says I must stop seeing Max.' There were angry tears in her eyes.

'Cara — just because Papa does not wish you to see him, don't let that make you feel more for Max than you really do.' I had not put it very well and there was silence for a time from my sister.

Then she said: 'I know he is only a boy, but — I *am* fond of him — and he of me, I know.'

'Then you can wait for him, Cara — there's plenty of time — I know you want to get married young, but believe me there are other things you could be doing.' I sounded very hypocritical, I know.

'Hetty, I'm not interested in the sort of things you like, but how can I go on living here? All they want is for me to meet some rich young man and then I'll be off their hands.'

'No — I think they want your happiness', I replied.

'I shall wait for him. I got him to write — addressed to Huntie — and he wrote today. He'd only just heard about Felix — it was in the paper — but he says he's looking forward to seeing me.' She burst into tears. That my little sister should go so far as to have her letters addressed to Huntie of all people amazed me. 'He says', she got out between sobs, 'that I could go back to Italy next summer and he'll be there. Why should they want to stop me? — they didn't mind before — I'm sure Papa had a letter about him — I've looked in his study, but I can't find it!'

'I think I know why they are against your seeing him — but it's a long story', I said. 'Let's just say that Papa — and Mama — don't like you to be involved in Papa's first wife's family.'

'What do you mean — Papa's first wife?'

'He was married before — and that's how I'm related to Zelda', I said quietly. She stared at me and then she said —

'But Hetty — *I* am related to Max? Is that what you mean? But it would mean only by marriage?'

I saw I'd have more explaining to do but was not sure how she would take it. I wished I'd told her before — it wasn't an ideal moment so I ducked it. 'He'll come round', I said. 'What do you think this letter said?'

'That he wasn't rich — I'm sure it must be that.'

'I *know* he will be rich one day', I said.

'But I don't care whether he is rich — I used to think it would be nice to marry and live in luxury', she smiled as she wiped her eyes. 'But now I think it's more important to marry a man who wants to work whether he starts off rich or not!'

'Cara — I'm sure they'll come round — and anyway you weren't thinking of marrying Max just yet were you?'

'No — and he's not exactly mentioned marriage — but I have a sort of feeling that I shan't ever meet anyone I like as much — I know I'm not clever like you, but I met lots of men in Italy

351

— not only Bruno — last summer and if I'd wanted to get married, well, I could have planned something whilst I was with you! And now I'm back here — and I'm trapped. Why did Papa ever let me go away if he won't let me out now?'

'It was to get you away from Simon Voyle', I said. 'And don't say "nothing ever happens here", because it just has.'

'I know, I know — but I knew you'd find Felix. Fancy Simon taking him away like that — wasn't it queer? — he did it to hurt Papa? — but why?'

'Well, yes —'

I had not told Cara everything about Orso's part in my rescue, but now I wanted to. She was not the only girl who nursed feelings for a young man. 'Orso Orsini came on from Lucy's when he heard I'd gone to The Laurels', I said. 'Without him we'd never have got Felix back.' I said nothing about the way Voyle had dealt with me.

'Orsini! How did he know — oh, I suppose you gave him the Littles' address — ? Clever Hetty. You do love him, don't you? I've been selfish talking only about myself. Does Papa know?'

'No — nothing about my feelings. But if you want to go to the Opera with Max I think I can arrange it. Lucy and I are to go very soon — I shall see Orso again before that, I expect, — but you can tell Papa — or I will — that we are all invited — and if he doesn't like the idea he can learn all the circumstances about how his precious son was rescued.'

'Does Orsini love you?' was all Cara said, but

she had a gleam in her eye.

'Oh, you know young men — at least he's not all that young — but we get on well — there were things that happened in Florence I couldn't tell you about — I will one day. The thing is, Cara, whatever I feel, I know I've got to be independent. I'm going to stay with Lucy and ask them if I can have a few pupils round there — it would be a start — and I don't want to stay here —'

'Why does he let *you* do what you want and treat me like a baby?' she said.

'You've always been their favourite daughter', I said lightly. 'I've been away too long for him to try to interfere.' I didn't want to mention my little income as it would entail even more awkward questions about my Mama and her sister. Yet Cara didn't appear to suspect anything. 'I don't want to feel that I'm under any obligations — because Orsini helped me in the matter of Felix', I said. 'He was under some sort of obligation to me before and I want to be free and independent — but yes, I do love him, Cara, in answer to your question.'

'Oh, Hetty, how romantic!' she said. 'Does he know?'

'You must never tell him! — he's the sort of man women swarm over, as you know, and it's only been pure chance that I've got to know him at all.' This at least was true.

'Max is only a boy', she said now — 'but I shall wait for him. In his letter he said he was fond of me.' She looked away shyly.

I was glad to get off the subject of my own feelings. How could I tell her that the fact of Orso's being in the world at the same time as myself was to me something incredible; that his beautiful voice gave me hope that beauty did count in that world? That it was like the pleasure of smelling the scent of a hundred roses together, something belonging to Paradise — but I had been afraid the world was no place for it?

'I can't always throw myself on male protection', I said instead. 'Our fate is in our own hands and I don't want to surrender my will to anyone's!'

'Oh, Hetty — you look so fierce', she said. 'Like when we were children and you used to frighten me when you got angry.'

I was surprised, could not remember being angry with her.

'You know — with Mama', she said. 'I think *she* was frightened of you too.'

How could I tell her then that Orso Orsini made me feel like the eternal woman, cherished and protected and wanting to exchange a mutual dizziness of the senses, not an angry independent woman at all.

'I shall tell Papa today that I intend to go and stay with Lucy', I said. 'I must see her first though. She will be in the schoolroom with Alice.'

Cara got up to go and I said: 'You can count on me, Cara — I'm sure in the end, if you want Max, you will be able to have him. And don't think of yourself as stupid — you're not at all stupid. It is I who am stupid with my dreams.' She said nothing and when she'd gone I looked at my face in the little pock-marked glass that was all I'd ever had to see myself in, and thought how one's expression can belie one's inner feelings.

Papa would see in my face what I chose to show him — a bluestocking desire for independence.

I spoke to Lucy and asked if her father might allow me to stay with them for a time before my return, as I'd already mentioned it to him. Lucy herself thought it a good idea. 'And we have the back parlour where you could have a small pupil if you found one', she said. She already knew of my ambitions in that direction.

Then I told Papa. 'I want to earn a little money to add to my allowance', I said. 'I shall soon return to Italy though.'

He had been very odd in manner towards me since the day I'd returned home to find Felix back safely. He'd thanked me, and seemed to want to say more, but I had the feeling he could not find the words. At least he'd thanked me, though he knew nothing of Simon Voyle's attack on my virtue.

'Papa', I added, 'I think Voyle will have left the country.' I wanted him to reassure Mama. 'And I am to tell you also that both Cara and I are invited to a production of *Rigoletto* in a week or two — I believe Gregory is to come too.' I said nothing about Max. 'It is at Covent Garden', I said. 'Perhaps you would like to come?'

'Oh, opera is not to my taste', he said, but did not ask from whom was our invitation.

'By the way', I said as I left the room, 'I'm sure that my cousin Max de Vere will one day be a very rich man.'

He looked up at this parting shot, but apart from giving me a most hostile stare, said nothing but 'Goodbye, Hetty — I hope you will be happy in Camberwell. Let us know when you intend to return to your aunt's, won't you?'

I'd like to have asked him from whom was the letter Cara was sure he'd received, but thought it politic to withdraw for the moment. As I came out, Felix came running up to me. He had never mentioned what had happened to him, but I asked myself if it would resurface later in dreams or nightmares. He had not appeared frightened of Voyle: I thought he must have put what had happened down to the strange goings-on of all adults.

'Hetty — why can't I go in the garden?' he asked now.

'You can go with me', I said and took him by the hand. We played ball on the lawn for a time. I needed the exercise. I saw Papa looking at us from his study window.

My principal reason, naturally, for going to Lucy's, was because Orso could come to visit me there. The next day when Lucy arrived to teach Alice — who had been rather clinging since Felix's escapade — she said that her Papa would be only too delighted to offer me his back parlour, plus the small son of a neighbour who was a little backward at his dame school in the matter of sums.

It was not ideal, but I reckoned my arithmetic would be adequate at this level, and departed for Camberwell, I must admit, with some compunction that I should have done more for Pooranna whilst I was at home. Our own backward child would never manage the simplest sums, but in Huntie she had a devoted nurse. I promised that I would see them all before I left for Italy. Mamarella actually came down to say goodbye, which she had never done before. Holding Felix by the hand she said: 'You have my gratitude, Hetty.' I kissed her on the cheek — which I had also never felt like doing before and she returned my kiss. But she never mentioned Simon and so I did not either. None of them but Gregory had any idea what I'd been through. I wanted to forget it myself.

Lucy and I took the usual horse bus. 'Your friend is coming tomorrow evening', she said, once we were safely away from East Wood. 'He is to bring six tickets for *Rigoletto* — Papa had a note, so we are all invited.'

'Gregory and Max and Cara and I', I said. 'I didn't tell Papa that Max would be there too!' I was nervous about seeing Orso.

She said: 'He is a very nice man, I think — when I consider what would have happened if he had not come to find you in Camberwell! — You never told them? — your Papa and your stepmother?'

'I can't bear being seen as a victim', I said.

Later that evening, before we had a simple supper and after I'd unpacked my bags, she said: 'Your Papa has accepted you are independent, Hetty — he said to me how grateful he was for what you did — I think he finds it hard to appear in anyone's debt — he is a little like you.'

I digested this. 'Signor Orsini was once indebted to me', I said. 'So now I suppose we are equals. But they say that Italians don't like independent women.'

'You are in love with him, are you not?' she asked.

I took my time in replying. 'I was — am — in love with his voice', I said. 'You will understand when you hear him sing yourself. And, yes, I love him — though I don't know him very well. Circumstances brought us together.'

'Do you think that love is bred out of knowledge then?'

Lucy did not usually indulge in this sort of conversation and I was a little shy of talking about love with her. She was so composed and cool and rational, but I supposed she was made of the same humanity we all were.

'Father liked him', she said. 'And my father has good judgement of people.'

'I *like* him too', I said. 'But he is also a great singer — and artists have to put their work first.'

But any imaginary reservations about Orso vanished when I saw him, though I tried not to let my feelings for him show. I received him in the little back parlour already put at my disposal after Mr Little and Lucy had greeted him. Lucy led him in, and left us together.

'Ester', he cried and I was enveloped in those immensely big arms and hugged like a long-lost friend. I felt myself melt like an ice crystal at the first touch of sunlight. He wanted to know how I was and apologized for not coming again sooner.

'I was at home — I wish I could take you there, but they don't realize that you rescued *me* as well as Felix', I said. 'I might tell them one day, but I am to stay here for the present and then return to Italy.'

'And I am to go and sing everywhere!' he said. 'Invitations from Vienna, St Petersburg, Warsaw — New York even — you will come to hear my wicked Duke? — you have the tickets I sent?'

'Of course I shall —'

'Oh, Ester, you cried out for *me*', he said. 'In that brute's arms you cried out for *me.*' Then he put his arms round me again — I was standing near the small fire and there was a mirror above the hearth. 'See, Ester — you are still pale', he said. I wanted to cry; it seems absurd but I wanted to cry there in his arms in Mr Little's back parlour. Because he hugged me as I had not been hugged since I was a child, when Huntie had done any hugging that was needed. Except that Huntie had been bonier than this big man and had not smelt of a mixture of sun and grease-paint. The beard he had grown for his new role tickled the top of my head. I felt like his child, but I was not his child. Why had I shouted for him that awful Sunday? I had not shouted for Gregory, or Max, or

359

even Papa. Out of some depths I had not known existed in me I had shouted for Orso — and he had miraculously arrived.

'You rescued me by magic', I said. 'I didn't know I was shouting your name — truly I did not. But now *I* am in *your* debt — and you are released from the debt you said you owed me — so now we are equals.'

'Equals — yes — but do not be proud, Ester. I am glad I was in your debt and you are *not* in mine — no! no! — I did only what any man would have done — have they found him yet, that animal?'

I moved away, glad that we were to have a proper conversation before I lost my head completely. I told him that nothing had been seen or heard of Simon Voyle since Lucy had seen him running away down that dark road.

'I am staying in London only to hear you sing — and then, because my brother also has asked me to stay for some business matter. So I am going to teach a child here at my governess's house — and then I shall go back to Florence', I explained.

I sat down in the chair near the fire and he sat down opposite me. 'It is true', he began, 'that we do not know each other in the ordinary ways — but they are not the only ways. When I return from my tour I shall take you to meet my family near Bologna — you will come? I should like to show you my city.'

'Tell me about your family', I said.

He began to describe to me one of those large

Italian families where everyone knows everyone else's business — a family who had a little farm in Emilia Romagna, the same province whence came Verdi himself. Brothers and sisters, and not much money, but all of them musical. 'But I am a modern man', he said. 'I need to stand on my own feet, one day make my own family. My sister Aurelia — a very good soprano by the way — carries on looking after Papa and Mama, and my grandparents are there too. I left home young to sing how long it takes to learn! — one is still learning — a whole lifetime is not enough. Now I can travel, do what I want, and send money home as well. I am a very lucky man, very lucky.' He beamed.

'It is not just luck to have a voice like yours', I said.

'Is luck', he said in English. 'Yes — partly luck. Chance — fortune — fate — same as when you hear those two fools plotting in Florence — to luck we add intelligence — and work.'

'Your voice sometimes seems separate from you', I said, hoping he would not take my remark amiss. I so wanted to get to know him.

'Is a gift', he said simply. 'But it is also *me* — like when you are ill — hurt your finger, bruise your hand — and it seems apart — you look at your hand, you cannot make it better from force of will alone. Or a woman, say she is beautiful. She did not make herself, but if she is disagreeable then beauty is no longer important and disappears with frown on face.'

'You mean your voice is part of you and you

361

can improve it, but the power to do so is not yours alone?'

He switched back to Italian. 'I mean that we are not in charge of ourselves all the time. If I do not work and practise, then my voice is not good. But *I* did not make the voice. So it is sometimes my enemy and sometimes my friend. My enemy because it makes me work when I am tired, and my friend because it makes ladies come and love me.' He gave a great big laugh and beamed at me. I supposed it had occurred to him that it was his voice that had attracted me to him in the beginning. I ought to put him straight over that. Yet where did the voice end and the power of personality begin? He was all of one piece, it seemed to me.

'Orso — I love your voice', I said. 'The very first time I heard it. But you are both more and less than your voice.'

He thought a moment, digesting this. 'You are very clever — it is that exactly', he said. But I knew that I adored the man who possessed that voice without knowing whether the two things were separate or fused.

'We must not become too philosophical', I said, and fortunately Lucy came in then to call us to eat some dinner. Mr Little enjoyed himself airing his Italian at table, and Orso was the perfect guest. Only afterwards when for a moment I was at table with him alone, Mr Little having limped away to find the cat who was mewing outside, and Lucy fetching the pudding in with the help of the maid,

362

did he say to me in quite a different tone of voice, 'You 'ave the little MIZPAH I give to you — send it to you — on an impulse — you know?'

'It is round my neck', I said.

'Oh, then that is why I came to rescue you', he said.

He was so simple and direct, the same quality that was in his singing, I thought, along with a beautiful 'tone' and that magical quality I had noticed when I heard it first. A less exceptional person could not produce such singing as I had heard, and yet he had himself confessed that the 'voice' was also something apart from him. He was looking at me with that honest gaze of his, so I said quickly: 'I want to know what others say about your voice — I am so looking forward to hearing it again.'

He looked, I thought, a little put out. It must be hard to be doubly judged — as a person and as a singer . . . Yet if I had not heard that voice would I feel as I did now about him? I was sick and tired of analysing my feelings, longed just to give myself up to them.

The tickets were for next week. 'Now it is rehearsal — rehearsal, and I cannot come to this little house', he said. 'But before I go we will arrange things — yes?' I wasn't sure what he meant. I longed to tell him exactly what I felt. I'd had a lifetime of dissimulating, it seemed, when I thought about it later.

I resolved to work and teach and improve my

363

mind whilst I was in Camberwell, and try to give my heart a rest. So much had happened. I began to read Lucy's father's copy of Vasari's *Lives of the Painters*, but found it difficult to concentrate. My pupil, one Herbert Frederick Squibb, was a lazy, pleasant, but seemingly empty-brained boy and I despaired of teaching him very much. Still, it was a start.

I had a letter from Gregory. No news of Voyle, but he had seen my cousin Max. 'Max has told me of his feelings for our little sister', he wrote. 'And I have counselled patience. I expect Cara told you of that letter she claims came from Italy to Papa? I have a good idea who wrote it — our old friend Rosa Daventry! Thank you for the ticket for *Rigoletto* — at last I am to hear the famous Orso. I believe you will shortly be able to return to Florence, by the way. By the end of April I should be able to acquaint you with the matters of which I spoke earlier. It involves Max — and others too — so await my summons, will you, to my chambers here? Say nothing of this when we meet at the theatre. Ever your Gregory.'

It was no good replying to say what I'd already told him — that I wanted to put the past behind me, so I composed myself to wait. Once Orso had gone away again though, I knew I would not want to spend what was left of the spring and the early summer in London, even if Zelda was not to open up the villa before the end of June. I had heard nothing from her at all, though Cara had been told to send on any letters for me.

Well, we did go to hear him and he was even more wonderful than in Florence. Here in the great Opera House with a critical audience, Orso Orsini gave one of the greatest performances of his early career the night I sat there with Lucy and her father and Gregory and Cara and Max (who had eyes only for each other). Other pens, more acquainted with musical hyperbole than my own, have described the effect the wicked Duke of Man tua had that night on an audience who knew the music well. I imagined, as he sang of his love being torn away from him, that Orsini was thinking of how he had torn me away from my intended seducer, and then when he was singing to his *belle figlia d'amore* a song of pure lust, I imagined too that one day he might sing it to me and that love and lust might be joined. Yet over and above all this was that soaring voice. In the duet with poor Gilda I felt real tears spurt from my eyes. Though the Duke was faithless and the girl deluded, it seemed that he did sing of true love. After the end of the opera we were invited round to Orso's dressing-room, already filled with bouquets; Cara curious, Max impressed, Gregory looking at me rather than at Orso, and the Littles sincerely congratulatory. I had eyes only for Orso. I could see he was tired, but he looked splendid. It was not the time or place for anything personal to be uttered. All I said was: 'The drink you drank in the First Act was this time a magic potion, "Signor Orsini", for your voice came from heaven.' But

365

I said it in his own language and if Mr Little understood, he gave no sign.

It was a short season and Orso was off to Vienna in a few days. I realized that such would be his life in future, a travelling life which would lay him open to every temptation. My emotions were still in turmoil and hearing him had made them no easier to bear. Were they one and the same, the man who possessed the voice of an angel, and the man who was in every respect my ideal, yet who was of common humanity, not an idol or a god?

I knew he might not be able to see me again before he went away. He had hundreds of things to do — costumes to fit, rehearsals, agents to see, travel arrangements — and I sank back into my humdrum life during the next few days and told myself I wanted nothing else. Yet he had said he would see me before he departed.

The day we heard news of Simon Voyle was also the day I received a letter from the man I now adored in full recognition of our differences. I had felt I could never surrender my independence for anyone but a great man and a great and mutual love. Orso was a great man and I knew I loved him greatly, though I felt that the struggle I was having between my feelings and my reason would never be settled, indeed was impossible of solution in our time; I felt that the world would have to wait hundreds of years before men and women could know each other honestly, so that a woman might feel both free and accepting of love. At other times I berated myself for imagining that Orso felt anything for me but a mixture of gratitude and protectiveness. Why should he? *I* was not a genius. I had no special gift to pour upon mankind! And yet it seemed that he did feel something for me.

The news of Simon Voyle came from Italy, from Zelda herself. A body found on the main railway line out of Rome was that of Peter Voyle's son. His father had identified it and then Peter Voyle himself had disappeared. This was her first paragraph. The second was that she was to accept the offer of marriage she had received from Count Carlo Belotti Donatoni.

'Dear little Ester', the other letter began, in Italian.

'I am off to Vienna and I have not seen you to tell yell what I must write. Then I go to Warsaw and Prague and Russia and after that perhaps to the States. I was frightened to say things last week at the house of Mr Little and his clever daughter because you might have misunderstood and I was also nervous because of the work I was doing. I did not know and do not know what *you* felt — Ester. Perhaps I should not have sent that small MIZPAH to you, but I felt these things even in Italy and it would do no harm, I thought. You know a little of my life and that I am dedicated to it because my singing is a gift from God and I must do the best I can with such a gift. But I have decided that I can no longer wait to tell you what you must surely know — and I apologize if you do not and if my words seem to you impertinent because they cannot be responded to in the same way. I love you little Ester. When I first saw you on the bridge I thought, that is a girl I would like to get to know, but it is impossible. A girl who walks alone with a book under her arm and is not coy and answers directly the stranger who speaks to her. Then I saw you at that party in the villa and you looked so beautiful and shy and sincere among all that crowd of hangers-on and pushers and shovers. Then to cap it all, when I had said to myself, 'Luigi — no more nonsense — you are a singer not an intellectual', then you overhear that couple of rotters, and you understand, and you make it your business to tell me. I think — what can it be but the hand of God? I am not a good Catholic. I believe in fate. You saved my voice, Ester, and so you saved my life, for whether I like it or not I am a slave to this voice of mine. Usually I like it, but often I do not. Finito. End of chapter. Then I send you the little remembrance, a little daringly I think — but it is also a badge of friendship. Then I come to London and I think, she said she would be in London one day soon — perhaps it cannot do any harm if I go to see? So I go to this Camberwell and I find your governess in tears and her kind father who tells me you may be in great danger, that your little brother has vanished into thin air and you have gone to look

for him in the house of your aunt. Alone —
and there may be a bad man there. I cannot
believe it! And then I take this long journey
on the cobblestones and Miss Little sits by me
and tells me what a clever young lady you are
and not happy at home, but willing to take risks
for the little brother. And then I walk up under
those dark trees and it is like the setting for
Il Trovatore and I approach this dark house and
try the door at the back so sure am I that you
are there. I feel it in my bones and in my heart.
And then I hear that terrible sound, that scream
and it is *my* name you are screaming! *My* name
— Orso! Orso, my singing name. I am filled
with anger and I dash to that voice and there
you are with your little dress half off trembling
before that tall man who hits me with a poker
and I smash at his face — and I like even now
to remember it — I am sorry, but I do — and
then you fall into my arms. I cannot tell you,
Ester, what it was like to have you fall into my
arms. Just for a moment before we go to look
for the little boy.

I do not know what you feel, Ester, but I
know you will tell me the truth. You will have,
alas, too much time to consider before I return
to Italy. You will think about it though and
please give me your answer one day when you
have thought. Do not write — I shall move everywhere. Just think of me and tell me when
I come. My question is — Will you marry me,
Ester? I do not know English customs, but I

can ask your brother for permission — or your father, though I have not met him. But I am asking *you* and I shall abide by your answer, and you will, if you say yes, have a man who adores you and who will wish he could spend more time with you! But you are a woman, I think, who also wishes to have a life of your own and so you will not grieve too much when I am away!

Your devoted and for always your 'Orso Orsini' — Luigi.

I do not ask for betrothal — these things are stupid, but to marry you. I shall think of you every day till we meet again.

The police in London closed their file on Simon Voyle.

Ella, my father's wife, was ill for many weeks when the news came to East Wood.

As for me, I had the biggest decision of my life to make alone. I told nobody. It was shortly after this, when my whole life was in the melting pot, that my brother Gregory Coppen called me and my cousin Max to his chambers one April day in the year 1879.

15

It was a mild London spring morning when I made my way to Gregory's chambers in the Middle Temple. Gregory wanted to see me, and Max had also been summoned, but Cara was to meet us later.

I walked through the Temple — and saw Max waiting outside my brother's stairs. I knew he was newly returned from yet another trip to a large auction, in Wiltshire this time. There was the smell of spring in the air, a mixture of violets and grass. I never saw the violets; perhaps they were pinned to the bosoms of the wives of clients who continually came in and out of the place with their barristers.

'Hello, Hetty — how are you?' It was the first time I'd seen him since *Rigoletto*, though I'd heard of his doings from Cara with whom he corresponded regularly now through Huntie. Lucy knew about that too, and since she thought my father was being most unreasonable, was on Cara's side, though I believe she thought my sister should wait before making up her mind that Max would one day be the man for her.

'I like your cousin', Lucy had said. 'He is not a fortune-hunter.'

'What do you mean, Lucy?'

'His *taste* is his obsession and he will make his own fortune, I don't doubt, by applying it', she replied.

Today I thought him grown a little less thin, and even handsome in a Maxish way, with still the same easy manner and friendliness towards me.

'And how is your tenor?' he asked mischievously. He had now heard the story of my romantic rescue.

'Singing far away', I replied.

He said nothing to that, having glanced at me to see that I was not eating my heart out at Orso's absence.

'Cara is to come at two', he said. 'Old Greg is being very mysterious, isn't he? What can he have to tell us?'

'I think it will be something important', I said. 'He's been — "investigating" — odd things — has he said nothing to you?'

'Nothing — are we in for unpleasant surprises, do you think?'

'I expect there will be surprises', I said as we went up the stairs to the first floor.

A clerk let us into an anteroom and took my umbrella, and Max's case which he always carried with him. I guessed it was full of catalogues and reproductions of what I always called his bric-à-brac.

'Mr Coppen is waiting for you', the clerk said in hushed tones. I almost expected to see an old family solicitor instead of Gregory, and when we went in my brother did not look unlike one, sitting at a desk facing two comfortable-looking chairs. He shut the window and gestured us to be seated. Max looked at me with a slight smile, meaning 'how self-important he looks, but we know old Gregory'. Max and I had not yet spoken to each other about Simon Voyle, though we had corresponded on the subject of his death, Max having had the details from Zelda. *I* was trying to forget him, and Max had told my sister he could find no pity in his heart for him. I had not thought that Cara had ever told Max exactly what Simon had tried to do to me, or that she had ever spoken to him in detail of Simon's former unwelcome attentions to herself, but when I saw Max's face after my brother's first words, I realized that she must have done so. We sat down expectantly and Gregory began by saying, 'I have to start by bringing up a subject which I know is painful — that of Simon.' Max flinched and looked out of the window.

'We have all suffered from the actions of Simon Voyle', he said. 'Possibly he was brought up by his father to believe that his mother was a wicked woman who had abandoned him when he was five years old. In fact Ella wanted to take the child with her, but Peter forbade it, and took him instead to Italy.'

I wondered whether Gregory was sure of that.

He went on. 'When he came to live with you, Max, he was seven years old. Do not the Jesuits say — "Give us a child until he is seven and we can guarantee that by then he will have the faith for life"? The boy had been turned in a certain direction by his mother's divorce, and then by his father's attitude, and finally by his father's own disappearance. He left him in your mother's charge, Max, as you know —'

'Gregory, we know all this', I said uncomfortably. I did not want to think about the reasons for Simon's conduct. I might forgive it, but would never forget it, and Gregory seemed intent upon digging it all up again. And after all, it seemed that Simon had killed himself. What immense despair could drive anyone to do that?

'Believe me, Hetty, it is all part of the story I am about to tell you', said Gregory. 'We will leave the subject of Simon Voyle very soon.' He went on —

'His father, Peter, had always been a womanizer, but he loved money more, and ran through Ella's fortune once he had married her. As you know, a woman has as yet no right to property or money of her own once she is married. He was also, I believe, unfaithful to her — many times. Our stepmother was as much a victim of Peter as our own mother was a lesser victim of our father', he added, turning to me. Max frowned.

He probably found washing dirty linen in public distasteful.

'Yes', I said. 'I have often thought that.'

'I'm afraid there are details which, as a lawyer, I have to go into with you that would not normally be revealed in mixed company', said my brother. 'But we three know each other pretty well and it is absolutely essential that I speak of them.' He turned to Max. 'You have told me that you are in love with our half-sister, Cara Coppen, and hope to marry her one day. It is partly because of your feelings — which you have avowed in all honesty and sincerity — that I decided to call you here with Hetty.' He coughed slightly. My brother Gregory was nervous.

'Hetty will explain to you that Cara was born illegitimately', he said — 'Since her father was still legally married to his wife Maria, our mother, and was not free until she died —'

'Yes, I'd worked that out', interrupted Max, 'it doesn't make the slightest bit of difference to me, I assure you —'

'Far more important', pursued Gregory, and I could not help feeling as he spoke that he gave less the appearance of a young man than that of a prematurely old one — 'Far more important is something else that appertains to you.' He paused. Max looked slightly bored. 'I will speak plainly', Gregory went on, 'you have been brought up in the expectation of inheriting a fortune when you come of age. I believe that fortune cannot come to you!' Max and I were both silent. Gregory said: 'To explain why is a very complicated story that has taken me a long time to piece together. When I started my enquiries I had no idea where they would lead — your financial portion was none of my business — but what I have unearthed is a far-reaching and long-standing "plot" — there is no other word for it, I'm afraid — on the part of' — he paused — 'Griselda de Vere.'

Max, who had not reacted to the momentous news of the loss of his future fortune with any visible indication, now looked directly at my brother.

'It is a *very* long story', said Gregory. 'Do you want to hear it?'

'Does it concern Hetty too then?' asked Max after a pause.

'Yes. It concerns all of us to some extent.'

'Then does Hetty want the details?' asked Max. He turned towards me and I saw that old mocking look in his grey eyes.

I sighed. 'Gregory knows that I expressed no interest in his digging up the past', I said. 'Except as far as it concerns our Mama.'

'It concerns our mother', said Gregory.

'Then tell us, Greg, but spare us the melodrama', said Max. Then he added in a queer sort of way: 'I could believe anything of *my* mother.'

There was a knock at the door and the clerk came in without waiting for an answer. 'Tea is ready, Sir', he said. 'The boy will bring it in, if you wish.'

'Yes —' said Gregory, and we waited whilst a diminutive boy staggered in with a tray on which there stood a silver teapot and three cups and saucers, milk in a jug and sugar in a bowl.

'I will do the honours', I said hastily and the boy went out. The next few minutes were taken up with my pouring out the tea and Max examining the teapot.

'Fake Georgian, but quite a nice little piece', he said. I thought he was overdoing it rather. We drank self-consciously and then Gregory rang for the tray to be taken away. Then we prepared ourselves again to listen. I think Max was more nervous than he wanted us to think, for he shifted in his chair quite a lot before he settled. I did not know what to expect.

'Well, then', said my brother. 'I am sorry I plunged in the way I did but I thought it better to get that over first, Max. Now I can give you my reasons for believing — nay — *knowing* — that you are not the legal heir of Basil de Vere.' Max looked out of the window and Gregory cleared his throat before continuing. 'Peter Voyle went to Italy to avenge himself upon my father, Leo Coppen', he began. 'I do not know how he did it, but he managed to make the acquaintance of Zelda de Vere and her husband and of our poor mother, Maria, who was out there, as Hetty knows, to recover from Hetty's own birth. Hetty was there too as a baby and until she was nearly three, remaining there whilst much of my story took place.' I felt a cold premonitory shudder go through me quite involuntarily.

'Peter Voyle intended to seduce Maria Coppen', Gregory said baldly. 'But he found her sister more attractive. Zelda, by all accounts, was married to a nice old buffer who had inherited a fortune from his father — from a plantation in the West Indies. Peter Voyle, as I have said, wanted to punish the man who had stolen his wife from him — a wife

377

whom, as I say, he had ill-treated and bled of her own fortune. But to Voyle a man's wife was his property — not that that ever stopped his own habit of stealing other men's wives. He went to Italy to seduce my mother, Maria, who was on the way to full recovery from the illness that had come upon her after Hetty's birth, an illness which is, I believe, more common than we are led to think. *He* was the person who told her of the details of her own husband's conduct and thereby wormed his way into her favour. Maria was a gentle person who, once recovered, would as soon have thought of being unfaithful to Leo as robbing the Vatican. I expect it took time, but Voyle had plenty of time. He had with him his son Simon, and Maria had her and Zelda's old nurse, Rosa Daventry. Rosa saw the way things were going and warned Maria against Peter, but Maria, still not quite well and in a nervous state of mind, thought Peter was only being kind. I had this from Rosa herself. So he went to Italy to seduce our Mama, Hetty — I have the dates if you want to see them. Eventually he did so, but it took rather longer than he had imagined and in the meantime, whilst making up to Maria — so that he could then write and tell his rival what he had done — he dallied with her sister Zelda. I'm sorry, Max, but you will forgive me in a moment.'

I had been thinking of my Mama — not that I could remember anything much about her — but suddenly I interrupted Gregory and said: 'The dead baby! The grave, Gregory! — so it was Voyle's child?'

Max looked baffled.

'You see, Max', I explained, 'she had another child — but he died — Gregory found the grave — not in Florence but in Como — I always remembered a cradle with a dead baby — I dreamed it over and over when I was little — it terrified me —'

'But, Hetty', said Gregory, 'that was in Como — you were never there — only Rosa was there — she told me. You were in Florence with your aunt, and so was I.'

Max was looking from one to the other of us.

'Tell me then, tell me now!' I cried, and it seemed that we were children again and Gregory was telling me that Mamarella was not my Mama. 'It is Max I have to tell', replied Gregory slowly and fixed his eyes on our cousin.

'I have to tell you, Max, that Zelda de Vere had a son by Peter Voyle.'

'Oh, I always suspected that Basil de Vere was not my real father', said Max with an appearance of nonchalance. I couldn't guess what his real feelings were.

'But I also have to tell you that the son Zelda had with Peter Voyle died when he was a few months old — just after Basil himself died. They called him Max.'

Max was now looking open-mouthed at my brother.

'This child, whose little body Hetty saw taken out of a cradle, is buried in the garden of the Villa de Vere — at the bottom of the garden by the wall, under a carpet of wild violets. She planted a little cypress there too —'

'Behind the pool?' I cried.

'Yes, Hetty. And there was no death certificate.'

I waited. Max looked about to pinch himself to assure himself that he, Max, was not dead.

'You remember', Gregory went on, 'I said it is what is not there that gives a clue to the truth? No death certificate for that little Max.'

'But if the *other* baby died too? — then did Zelda have *two* children — and Max here is Basil's son!'

'Think, Hetty. I assure you — I have checked all the dates.' Then he paused and shifted his gaze to Max. But he seemed to be speaking to me. 'Our mother, Maria Coppen, was also seduced by the same man who seduced her sister. Maria died giving birth to his son. But she was buried alone. *There is no dead child in that grave.*'

The hairs rose on my head. Had he even had the grave exhumed?

'And', he added in a normal voice, 'there is no death certificate for that baby either, not in Como, nor in Florence. The little dead baby that you remember, Hetty — shall we call him The First Max? — died, as I said, just after Basil de Vere had died of a heart attack. Zelda was out of her mind with grief. But she was also aware that all her husband's fortune was entailed upon his son, with Zelda herself having only a life interest. If their son died —'

'But he was *not* Basil's son, was he?' interjected

Max who had been silent, digesting all this information. 'He was Voyle's — you said "The First Max" ', he went on. 'Then if you are right, who am I? Two dead babies *and* a second Max?'

Gregory ignored Max now for a moment and said to me: 'Our mother's grave, Hetty, has no dead baby buried there for the simple reason that he did not die. And Zelda had only one son and he *did* die.' Then he turned to Max who had lost his customary ironic expression. 'I am sorry, Max, but you are the son of our mother Maria Coppen and Peter Voyle. You are half-brother to Hetty and to me.' Max was searching Gregory's face with a look of bewilderment.

'Zelda substituted her sister's son for her own dead child and also called him Max — naturally. There were only a few months between them — Voyle was a swift seducer. There is no death certificate when there should have been for the first Max.' I shuddered. 'You see, Hetty? — these "absences" — but we know how often children fail to be registered in Italy. Her friends never knew Zelda's baby had died but those who were in the know about Mama's pregnancy — Mrs Holroyd for example — were told that Maria's baby had. Who do you think brought that baby, the second little Max, back to Florence after burying its Mama?'

'Rosa', I said dully. 'Rosa — she knew it all.'

Max still said nothing. Gregory went on as if to convince him — but I knew Max believed him — 'Her little dead Max was Zelda's Achilles heel, the sorrow of her life. Voyle had abandoned her, and her husband had died, and so she buried the child at night so that nobody would know. She knew her sister's child was due in a month or two and was already planning that if it were a boy she would ask Maria to allow him to be brought up as Basil's son. Unfortunately she never could ask her, for Maria died. Rosa can give you all the details.'

'Surely, brother, you did not dig up the grave in the villa garden?' I said.

'No, I went to the villa alone when I fetched Cara back last time and I looked round the garden and asked myself where I would bury a small child if I did not wish the grave ever to be found. I walked down past the pool almost to the wall where there is a lot of undergrowth. There I pulled out the flowers and plants. Underneath was a simple stone bearing only the name *Max* and the date, 1862. I had always thought that baby cypress was there for a purpose.'

'Like a dog's grave', I said, and the tears came to my eyes. 'But why did she go to all that trouble? Just for money?'

Suddenly Max roused himself. He said slowly, 'Then I am your mother's son and my father was Voyle? Zelda is not my mother?' He said it again, 'Zelda is not my mother', this time as a statement rather than a question.

Gregory said gently, 'Yes, Max, I assure you, it is the truth.'

'Oh, I believe you', said Max. 'I always felt she

was not a motherly person to me. I learned early to fix my mind on other things. But she would get the interest on the fortune in any case! De Vere did not know that her son, who died later, was not his?'

Gregory went on implacably — 'She knew that Basil had made a second will after her child was born. He must have suspected something, but had no proof, and he was old and ill. The second will, a copy of which he lodged in Florence in the *Offici* said that if his son should die the fortune was to go a different way. Zelda destroyed the original and looked for the copy. When she discovered it she told the clerk to file it under D not V. I expect some money changed hands. That copy was "lost" till I discovered it in Florence filed under "D" as *"Devere"* — one word, Italian-sounding. Another "absence" you see. Zelda went by the London will, made before she had any children. Peter Voyle came back asking for money — he always needed money, and I believe she loved him — he must always have attracted women. So she used some of the capital, not the interest, to pay him off and keep him quiet about the substitution, provided he went away for good. She managed her husband's estate, but she was careful not to allow Voyle too much. In any case you, Max, were not her son so she cared less what you were left. I have that second will here.' Gregory opened a leather case and drew out a yellowing piece of parchment, stamped with some complicated arrangement of eagles and vine leaves. 'I shall read

383

from it', he said. 'It is quite legal. ". . . that in the event of the death of my son Maximilian the monies held in my name at Coutts Bank, London S.W. and all investments . . . etc. etc. shall be left solely and exclusively to".' He paused and looked up at us both. ' "To Hester Johanna Coppen, niece of my wife Zelda de Vere, when she attains her majority or marries, whichever is the sooner . . .".'

I gasped, stared and stared at Gregory. This was something that had never entered my head. But perhaps it would not be very much when Zelda and Peter had taken what they needed? The thought was consoling.

'Hetty — !' Max was actually smiling. '*I* can make my *own* fortune', he said. 'But you!'

'I don't want to be left a fortune!' I cried. 'If this is true I cannot take it! But surely it is not much?'

Gregory did not answer my question but said: 'He was fond of you, Hetty — I remember him talking to you — you used to sit on his knee —'

'The cradle with the blue ribbons then, that was *after* he died — they put the new little baby there?' I was remembering now from the mists of the years the kind old man with whose watch I played as I sat on his knee . . . Mama was there, and a baby in the cradle. Then the old man went away and I was sad, and later Mama went away too . . . Mama kissing me goodbye dressed in a billowing grey coat — and another lady — Rosa — coming in. I had jumbled up the months, but there had been a cradle before she went away, that cradle where I'd seen a dead baby lifted out. Mama never came back, but then there was a baby in the cradle again and blue ribbons, and I asked for Uncle Basil . . . The times were all confused. I said: 'I have — you say — gained a fortune — and a new brother — but poor Max has —'

'Lost a fortune, but gained a brother and sister', said Max. 'Discovered a mother I never knew. And another brother! For if I am the son of that bounder Voyle, Simon was my half-brother! I'm sorry, I can't take it in. Never mind about the money — never mind — but I don't need a father now.' He stood up and looked out of the window. I think he was crying.

'How much is it, Gregory?' I said.

'Half a million', he said and looked down at his papers. There was a stunned silence, and Max turned round.

'Then I shall share it with Max and Cara and you', I said. 'It is too much for anyone — even divided up — he must have been very rich if Zelda has already spent some of it — and Voyle.' My voice trailed away. 'I'm sorry', I said and went up to Max and put my arms round him. I turned to my other brother. 'What does a fortune matter when you have undermined our whole conception of ourselves? Did you need to do it, Gregory?' I said. I was angry.

'Yes, he needed to do it', said Max. 'My — Aunt — I suppose I must call her now — stole money that was not hers by right, thinking she would never be discovered. But I'm not so un-worldly as you, Hetty. You must take it — I suppose I must get *some* of my character from my adopted Mama? But by the way, where is Voyle — my father?'

'Disappeared. He was sticking close to Zelda, I think, hoping to blackmail her into giving him more, but then she produced the Count who has friends in high places. He's lost one son and I don't think he'll want another.'

I remembered what I had overheard and told them. ' "You took one of them off my hands in exchange for my saying nothing about the other".' He had been referring to Simon and Max.

Gregory went on, 'I have written to Zelda de Vere. She covered her tracks well, but I interviewed Rosa who was so jealous when Zelda left her for the Count that she was willing at last to confess to her part in it. I think it was her "Miss Maria" she was most fond of — she thought she was doing you a good turn, Max, as Maria's child if *you* came into a fortune.'

'Did Huntie know some of it?' I asked.

'Huntie knew Zelda's baby had died, but she thought she'd had another child later — she suspected he was Voyle's. They were both loyal to Zelda, not to Peter Voyle. See, the papers are all here — certificate of exhumation — will signed in London 1855, and another 1862 in Italy —'

I didn't want to look at them just yet.

'Thine, Mine, and Ours', I muttered.

'What?' said Max.

'Five couples', I said. 'It's the expression used for children belonging to a wife and a former husband and a husband and his former wife and their children together — but we've gone two better. The abandoned husband has a child with the abandoned wife — as well as seducing her sister. I'm sure Voyle's intention would be to use you, Max, to make trouble for my father — but he couldn't stay around to see you do it. Pressing financial problems, I expect.'

I had suddenly seen where Peter Voyle might have thought he could use his third son. What if that son seduced and then abandoned Leo and Ella's beloved daughter Cara? But Max resembled his father not at all and had fallen in love with her. What a Pyrrhic Victory for Voyle. That part of the plan had never been put into action.

'Our Papa knew *none* of this?' I said to Gregory.

'No — if he'd known our mother had succumbed to Voyle he still could not have got his divorce in time for Cara. Peter promised Zelda not to inform him though, in exchange for more cash.'

'Hetty is welcome to her money', said Max. 'It gives me great pleasure to give away a fortune to which I never had any claim!'

I looked at the two young men sitting there in that pleasant old room. It was all incredible — like something out of one of Zelda's novels. But it was *true*. They did look alike, Gregory and Max — I always thought so, and the resemblance was even more striking now. They must both resemble our mother, as sons so often do.

'None of it would have happened this way if Mama had had another *daughter!*' I said. Then another idea struck me. 'Do you think perhaps Zelda was going to give me my fortune in any case when I was twenty-one?'

'She'd have enjoyed telling me I hadn't one', said Max.

'Then I'll pretend she was. I don't hate Zelda — it's a man's world — and she did give me what *was* to me a little fortune, you know — and she was kind to me when I was little —'

'She likes you', said Max. 'And she likes Cara too.'

'My brother might one day be my brother-in-law', I said aloud as the thought struck me. Max blushed. I had never seen him blush before. 'Poor Max', I said. 'You are the loser in all this and none of it is your fault.'

'It's odd to know that Zelda is not my Mama', he said. 'But it is far too late for me to have a father. I hope I never meet him.'

'It will take us time to adjust ourselves', said Gregory. 'But you agree I was right to try to find it all out? I did not do it for a fortune — or one for Hetty — I was as surprised as she is when I discovered that. I did it for our Mama, so her other child would know who she was when he grew up.' There were tears in his eyes. My poor brother, who had suffered more than any of us.

'Now you have done it and it cannot be undone, Greg', I said. 'Let us resolve to forget the past. Why need Papa and Mamarella know? It is nothing to do with them now. Cara must know of course, I agree.'

'You were right to do it — and very clever', said Max. 'Shake hands — yes?' There was that little Italian sound in his voice, but apart from that my big brother and my little one were similar in ways other than looks. I saw both had the driving force of ambition — hidden in Max's case by a graceful demeanour. Peter Voyle had never acknowledged Max so he need have no fears on that score. I knew Zelda might deny it and go on denying it except to us three.

'Was it my father who prevailed upon — Zelda de Vere — to send Simon to the same school as you?' Max asked suddenly. There were to be many more questions answered and unanswered in future, but this one Gregory did answer.

'Yes — I think so — and Simon proceeded to bully me all the time I was there.'

'You never admitted that!' I said.

'No — it was a matter of schoolboy honour, but I vowed to get my own back one day.'

'How can we blame him? — he inherited the worst of both parents!' I said.

'Oh, Peter was a fortune-hunter — Ella's money, other women, Zelda duped too when he took up with her sister. Maria seduced. Charm in every pore', said Gregory.

'His charm was lost on me', I said: 'He made Simon what he was too.'

'You are independent, Hetty — and you would never fall in love with a bounder', said Gregory.

But I was thinking furiously. Did I want to tell Orso that I was to be a rich woman one day? I must immediately make proper arrangements to divide this money when I was of age. After her little son died Zelda must have tried to cut herself off from Peter, when she discovered her sister was expecting his child too. How strange that the weaker sister's child should have lived and strong Zelda's die. Fate was indeed unaccountable.

Max must have been thinking on the same lines for he said: 'She did look after me — what would have become of me otherwise? She did not allow Voyle to have me, did she?'

I thought, Peter Voyle would not even bother with his own legitimate son, never mind his by-blow — but better let Max believe his adopted mother had shown compunction. How would he see Zelda now? I suspected that for some time he had been distancing himself from her and so it might not be too hard for him. Zelda would soon be leading a different kind of life with Count Donatoni. I wondered, as we sat there and waited for the teapot to reappear before Max went off to meet Cara, whether maybe Peter Voyle had done Papa's dirty work for him. If he had not divorced Ella and thereby made Papa feel he would have to marry her, Papa and Mama might have got together again before Mama was laid siege to by Voyle. I thought of that poor abandoned ailing woman, only twenty-three years old, and utterly dependent upon the men in her life. No wonder a stronger woman made the best she could out of the situation. But, if Max did one day marry Cara, my mother and Cara's would be reconciled through their children. Leave the men out of it now! even if it had been men who had set it all in motion.

'You mentioned Mrs Holroyd' I said to Gregory. 'Did she know Mama well?'

'Netta Holroyd knew Peter Voyle in the old days', said Gregory. 'Another of his victims.'

Poor Mrs Holroyd. How many other women had he seduced and cast off or bled for their fortunes? All he had wanted, once he'd had the women, was their money — Ella's and Zelda's and probably countless others. Except for Mama — that had been for vengeance against Papa. 'Voyle would deny everything — and we wouldn't want to drag Zelda through the courts — *has* she admitted it?' I asked Gregory.

'There is an injunction out against Voyle for fraud and sundry other matters', replied Gregory calmly. 'And Zelda has confessed about the second will and thrown herself on your mercy!' I was silent.

'What, as a matter of interest, did Voyle — my father — do for a living? Has he ever worked?' asked Max.

'You won't like this, Max — but he was a dealer — in fake antiques!'

'Oh my God!' said Max. 'Let us hope I am more successful than he ever was — and with genuine ones!'

I think this was the worst thing he had heard that morning.

Other questions came to mind and we three met once or twice to talk them over. Max acquainted Cara with the facts and I suppose with the one concerning her illegitimacy, but she never said as much to me — only said she knew now that we were half-sisters. Cara was going to have the problem of getting permission to be courted by a young man who was the son of her father's ex-wife, though Papa did not know that, and also the son of her mother's ex-husband, though Mamarella did not know that either. I thought money might help them over this little hurdle, money I would give them both when they married. Greg told me that I could borrow on my 'expectations' if I so wished. I talked it over with Lucy and her father to whom I told some of the story. They said it was up to me whether to take out an injunction against Zelda de Vere and I assured them I had no desire to do so, but that I'd like to start a little school soon in Florence. I would certainly go back there soon, but I had to write to my Aunt before I could return to Italy. I had not yet congratulated her on her forthcoming marriage. Now I could afford to be generous. She knew I knew everything. It was a strange feeling to have some other person in my power, but I did not relish it. I was tired of the whole thing. I was sorry for her because she'd lost her own baby and I imagined that she must have loved Voyle. And since she had always protected my mother, I owed her something. I wrote her a short letter, making all this quite plain.

Gregory was to see more Italian lawyers very soon. This I told Zelda. She would not now oppose the implementation of her former husband's second will 'misfiled' by a clerk — and I did not want that clerk subpoenaed. I said I had never expected to be rich and that I did not blame her for concealing it. I said: 'Tell me about it, tell me about my Mama. Tell me all that happened and then we will never refer to it again'. For although I knew my brother Gregory had discovered the truth, 'truth' always looks different through another's eyes, and I wanted to know more about Mama's own feelings. I ended my letter as follows:

It is my fondest hope, Aunt, that we shall be reconciled through the marriage of my brother Max and my sister Cara. What was put apart through divorce and death will be brought together through love and kindness. My father will be unknowingly 'reconciled' with my mother if his daughter marries her son; Ella will be confronted with her own past and her taking a woman away from her husband when she sees her own daughter marry into the same family. Even Papa and Voyle, one who abandoned a wife and the other a son, will be linked if Max and Cara one day have children of their own. The sins of the fathers will be redeemed by their children . . .

Only her own dead child and dead Simon Voyle

could not partake of this healing. But Gregory and I, the original children who had been formed and shaped by our mother's unhappiness and death, and our father's adultery — could *we* be healed? I would be rich even when I had given two-thirds of my inheritance away, and I hoped soon to leave the scenes of my childhood for happier and sunnier ones. But my brother Gregory, old before his time, Gregory who had implacably sought the truth — could money make up to him for his unhappy boyhood? *I* would make it up to him, I thought. I would find him an Italian wife and he could settle, perhaps, in Florence and see to the needs of the British community. I was full of plans.

Not for a moment had all Gregory's revelations and my ruminations made me forget Luigi Orsini — 'Orso' — who earned every lira by the sweat of his own efforts. I could now, if I wanted, give him a life of luxury. But somehow I knew he would not accept. Money would give me the opportunity to be independent, for money always does that. Would Orso accept that I could have the life I wanted and yet look to him alone for love? He was a proud man and I was frightened of what his reactions might be.

Palazzo Donatoni, Venezia.

Dear Hetty,

This is the last letter I shall ever write to you. We may see each other now and then — I have no objection to that — but confession is not my *forte*. You tell me you 'know everything', and you say you want a new perspective on what I did. Or do you mean perhaps that you do not trust 'facts' and would prefer a description of *feelings?*

There was never a certain moment when I decided to cheat you out of what poor old Basil wanted you to have. It was just how it happened, and who knows but I might not eventually have let you have the money, 'found' that will of his which I managed to persuade someone to file under Devere, pronounced *à l'italienne,* in the labyrynthine depths of the Palazzo Vecchio! Every time you went with the Pontraven girl to look at pictures I would reflect that somewhere in the same building in the Offici, or in the next one, was proof that you were an heiress. When my husband died I declared only the will Basil made in London when we married. Nobody in Italy ever knows what to do with copies of official documents or how to file them, so it could very well have been lost with no ulterior motive. And, after all, I treated you well, didn't I? I took you from that cold fish of a father of yours — cold except in one regard, I'd imagine — and put a bit of colour in your life? And I did give you an advance on Basil's money, you must agree.

I was married at twenty-two. I was two years older than your mother, my sister Maria, but twenty years older in common sense. Except concerning Voyle. There you have me. Why did I let him do it? I was sorry at first for what his wife had done to him, running off to Maria's husband, and I was on Maria's side, but I saw quickly enough that he used women. I was desperate for a son for Basil and pretty sure that Basil would never give me one. I didn't know what he'd do with his fortune if he had no heir, and as it turned out I was right to be worried.

Rosa always had a good idea the way the land lay — I didn't have to tell her. But Rosa preferred your mother in her heart. On that subject, Rosa will stay on here if you wish her to and the apartment here will shortly be put in your name.

Well, I have said enough before I begin at the beginning as this letter should have done.

Your Mama married your Papa because he was crazy about her — he wanted her and, if we are to be crude, the only way to get her was to marry her. I was too strong-willed for Leo even then, and he didn't like me much. Then I married Basil who was staying at the house of friends in Kensington after his first wife died. He had no children. I married him in 1857 and we went straight out to Florence. I loved it there. He had also bought a villa, hoping his first wife would enjoy summers in the country. Well, you don't want to know all the tedious details of my marriage, but Basil was a good husband — and he adored children. Your mother had married your father in 1856. He was twelve years older than her. Basil was *thirty* years older than me! Both the Hartley girls married older men — odd wasn't it? Your brother Gregory was born nine months after Maria's marriage and your Mama recovered physically quite quickly, but she was always the sort of woman who fell easily into low spirits and I think she hadn't realized what babies do to a woman. I sent for Rosa's little niece to help her. She was only young, but a sensible girl, and your Mama was grateful. Then you were born, in December 1859. I wasn't there, but I soon had a letter from your father who said Maria was much worse this time. Huntie had had to take you over, and see to little Gregory too. Maria wouldn't allow anyone else. I suggested my sister should come out to me to regain her strength and she could bring you out with her. Rosa came to fetch you and I must say when I saw your Mama I thought she'd become another person. Your father was impatient, couldn't understand why his wife was so depressed, and I suppose he found consolation in the first woman who was sympathetic, as so many men do. They were still living in Ealing then — you don't remember it. The new neighbours in one of those big houses on the common near where we'd lived ourselves as children were Peter Voyle and his wife Ella. I heard some of this later from Peter and some from what Huntie told me. According to Peter, his and Ella's was a case of love at first sight — if you can call it *love*. Your future stepmother, Ella, was a beautiful woman, some years older than my sister, and from what I know now she'd come to Peter with a fortune which he'd proceeded to spend — investing in some rackety business of his, scouring old castles and such like for antique objects, and then copying them in great quantity. Ella came to hate him — Peter didn't tell me that, but I read between the lines. Later I found what a womanizer and general cad he was, though he could be charming. Ella was frightened of him for some reason, though not too frightened to deceive your father *chez elle* whenever Peter was away. (I believe Leo and she had met at some neighbour's dinner-party.) Peter found out and she ran away to Leo. Peter'd had most of her money, and the rest he had his hands on, so when she came to your father, who was distracted over Maria, and lonely, with only Gregory for company, Peter told her she couldn't keep Simon with her.

I don't suppose Greg remembers that time? He spent most of his time with Huntie. She was the one who told her Aunt Rosa the way the land lay. There was a friend of theirs, maid to Mrs Holroyd, who was going out to Italy and she told her to tell Rosa and me, and to keep it from Maria, that Ella had seemingly 'come to stay.' There'd be a lot of puffing and blowing and threats from Peter, I expect, before he decided to divorce Ella. Your father didn't know what to do. There he was, expecting his wife back any minute as far as he knew and with a lovely woman staying in his house with whom he'd become infatuated. All Leo did then was to tell Maria to stay abroad until she was better. He couldn't marry Ella unless he were divorced himself and he could hardly divorce a wife for being ill. Maria was getting better and asking to go home and we tried to put off telling her, but in the end she had to know, which made her worse. She finally had a strange letter from Leo. Then, who should arrive, full of sympathy and grief, in the summer of 1860, but Peter Voyle with his son Simon. His wife was a wicked woman, we were told, and he was inconsolable. Huntie was sent for and came out with your brother to try to cheer up your Mama. By this time — it must have been the spring of 1861 — your father had moved to East Wood with Ella who was already expecting a child. Voyle had started divorce proceedings for adultery — he got the divorce in 1862 — these things take time. But by then I'd given birth to my son earlier that year. Basil was delighted at first. How was I to know that Peter was intent on seducing my sister? — that was his plan all along. The poor girl was amazed anyone could still want her and he told her he'd marry her if she divorced your father. Then Basil took ill and died in September 1862. He'd often played with you and talked to you — you were his favourite — and I think he'd put two and two together and had doubts about our little Max being his. I know he'd warned my sister against Voyle. I expect he was a bit sweet on her himself. She was a real man's woman. But hardly had we got over Basil's funeral when my poor little Max died too. I found him in his cot one morning, lifeless. I was mad with grief. He hadn't even been ill, nobody knew why he should have died. After all I'd gone through — and the birth was not easy; nobody tells you what a terrible thing childbirth is . . . You were there in Florence that morning. I hadn't seen Peter for some time and to tell the truth had no desire to see him ever again. Your Mama was now expecting, and the idea came to me — I must have been really out of my mind with sorrow — that I'd persuade her to pass her baby off as my own if he were a boy. I couldn't let that money go away from me. I'd been a good wife to poor Basil, except for my one lapse with Voyle. Rosa and I took our little dead boy and we buried him at the villa and put just a simple stone there in the garden where I'd used to sit with him in the sun that summer. They don't bother much about death certificates over here, all they mind about is that babies are baptised Catholic, and we hadn't even had the child baptised with all the terrible sorrow of Basil's death and my finding that second will of his, afterwards.

I'm sorry I'm not telling this at all well. I've tried not to think of it for years. I knew I could persuade Maria to let me bring up her baby

— he was due to be born in November — because Voyle had disappeared again. Maria was now less inclined to believe his protestations of undying affection and wanted to go home to Leo. I suppose I should have let her go. Your father could hardly blame her when he'd done the same thing himself. But the world is not fair on women. I thought Leo probably loved my sister more than his new woman, but he could never abide 'nerves'. I believe he was already regretting what had happened, but what could he do? He knew I'd look after Maria, and Ella had nobody but him to look after her. He never came out to us, not once. I think at first he was frightened of finding a mad wife — and then he was too ashamed.

I sent Maria off to Como with Rosa, and you and Gregory stayed with me at the apartment. Peter was somewhere with Simon — we didn't know where. He knew perfectly well that the child Maria was expecting was his, but he never saw her after the summer. My own Max had been gone from us only a few weeks when your Mama gave birth prematurely to a boy. Rosa did not expect the child to survive, but he did, thanks to her. Your mother died at his birth, though I'd given Rosa the money for the best doctor in the district. I'm sorry I lied about that. I went to Como and found them, Rosa and the baby, and your mother laid out, and I took the child. Basil's will had not yet been proved — they are very slow with these matters — and

I'd produced the first will he'd made when we married, in order to settle the estate, and burned the other one I'd found in his desk. I knew I'd have to check later to see if there were a copy. Then I put Maria's little baby boy in the cradle where my Max had died, and a few months later when, against all the odds, he did live, I got a priest in and told him the child was older than he really was, but had been ill and I was a Protestant, but now my child had survived I'd decided to have him baptised in the Faith! Such lies I told, thinking all the time of my sister dead in that beautiful place by the lake. Rosa and I had seen to the funeral and we'd told them to dig a grave for a woman with a dead child. As we were Protestants I got the coffin closed up and the minister came from over the lake for the funeral and then we ordered a gravestone. I don't know how I managed it all, but I did and nobody suspected there was no dead child there at all.

Then just when everything seemed rosy, Peter Voyle came back and wanted to know what had happened to Maria. When he saw the baby he knew it was not our child — though he had taken no interest in him before, so I had to tell him our little Max had died and that this baby was Maria's. I suggested we passed him off as mine and Basil's. I told him about the will. I had to bribe him with money and with the promise that I'd take Simon off his hands. He was tired of trailing the child round with him. Simon got in the way of his own life and no servant would stay long with him. Huntie took you back with Gregory to London, to East Wood, and nobody but myself and Peter and Rosa and Huntie (though I was never sure how much she knew and how much she suspected) were the only ones who knew whose the baby was. But Voyle knew my secret and left Simon with me and went off God knows where — I believe at first to South Africa, and then to Sydney. I knew that I'd have eventually to go to England to settle the probate of the will Basil had left there and I thought it better to leave Florence for a time so that people — if they suspected anything — would take it for granted when I returned that I was with my own son. But how I longed to go to the villa and to sit by my own little one's grave. I knew I'd done wrong, but I wasn't frightened of Voyle. I was aware of certain financial peccadillos of his he'd been unwise enough to confide in me when he was wooing me and trying to persuade me to become his mistress. He was a triple-crosser, Hetty, and I sometimes ask myself how he could have had a child as honest as Max. And I wonder whether I'd have been as lucky with my own Maxie or whether he'd have taken after his father, as poor Simon did.

You know most of the rest. You may wonder if Peter Voyle asked me to marry him after Basil died and when his baby son was still alive, and the truth is he did, but I refused because I knew what he'd do with my fortune. By then I was free of the spell of his passion. Before, it had been exciting, after being married to an old man, to have the attentions of a comparatively young one, but now I detested him, though I took good care not to let him see. Peter always knew how to cut his losses, and moved on. But I had to keep him sweet — and he was grateful I'd taken Simon off his hands. He's probably got other children elsewhere — men like that don't change.

When I returned to England semi-permanently in '67 your father allowed you and Gregory to see me since he had a guilty conscience about Maria. I was a respectable widow. Rosa stayed on to oversee my possessions over in Italy and I decided Max had better be brought up English, which he was. Rosa wanted her beloved Miss Maria's son to inherit — she didn't know the second will had left the money to you if my son died, for she never saw it.

Your stepmother was also guilty about her precious Simon and asked me privately, without Leo knowing, to send him to the same school as Gregory. Which I did. I don't know why — I suppose I was sorry for her as we'd both 'lost' our sons. But Simon had been well drilled by Peter to take revenge on his mother. I'm sure that Peter knew nothing about the Felix affair though. Violence wasn't in his line, though Ella concocted a cock-and-bull story about his beating her and the child. Simon came to see

Peter this spring after what happened in London — I had the details from Gregory — but Peter wouldn't have anything to do with him. Any idea Ella had that *Peter* was going to return and wreak vengeance on Leo or his children was the fruit of Ella's imagination. She always moped after her first son, according to Gregory, but I am afraid Simon was born a bad boy and his mother's conduct made him into a criminal. I knew that Max had suspected for a long time that he was not my husband's son from the kind of questions he asked me, but I flatter myself that he never thought he was not *mine!*

Gregory tells me that you are to divide your inheritance — when you are of age — between you and him and Max, and that Max intends one day to marry Cara Coppen. Take my advice, Hetty: think carefully before you do that. People come and go, but if you are prudent a fortune stays. Cara is a pretty and nice child, but I hope Max is not making a mistake. He has none of his father's ruthless nature with people, but is it not ironic that he is passionate about antique *objets d'art!* Max has the ability to make money, which you will think pleases me, but he will not need to think about *me* for I shall be well provided for.

Perhaps when you have thought it over you will not judge me too harshly, Hetty. Do not judge your mother either. *She* had no idea that my little baby was Voyle's and was distraught over your father's conduct. Voyle went from me — a willing and passionate woman — to my sister who was passive and sweet — and ill. I was four months pregnant when he seduced your mother. For that I shall never forgive him. You, Hetty, I believe, take more after me than after your own Mama. You will not need to marry for money, but take care you do not marry a man who wants yours.

You may think I am a hard woman, but after the death of my baby, I grew a shell that nothing could crack. The day he was found dead was the worst day of my life. I remember how after I'd found him I wrapped him in a shawl and laid him back in the crib. Maria had been preparing for her own child before she went north and the cradle had blue ribbons — for she was sure she would have a son. I wanted an artist to come and paint my Max, for he did not look dead, only sleeping, but I dared not. You were in the apartment all the time. I wonder if you remember anything of my grief? You may remember your mother and how ill she was in her pregnancy — three months of morning sickness the poor woman suffered. Voyle took no further interest in her once he knew she was expecting, but I often wonder if he wrote to your father to tell him about her. He only wanted her so he could punish Leo, and I can't imagine he thought *I* would tell him. Max from being a weak little boy soon grew much stronger. But he is so young, Hetty, and your father will never consent to Cara's marrying him. She will have to wait almost four years if she wants that when she is of age.

All I have told you is the truth, but you cannot understand my feelings and they are always part of the truth, are they not? I do not expect you to 'forgive' me — but I remain now devoted to your interests. Let me know, or Rosa, when you wish to return to settle the estate. Gregory tells me you have some notion of starting a small school, but maybe once you taste the fruits of wealth you will decide to enjoy life. The apartment in Florence will be yours.

Your Aunt,
Zelda de Vere

This letter left me with conflicting feelings. I cried over her description of the death of her son and marvelled at her self-justificatory tone, but more than anything I was amazed that she never once mentioned the effect my brother's revelations might have upon Max. To lose both a fortune and a mother in one morning is not a common occurrence, even if one gains a sister and a brother in exchange. No mention of Max's feelings, only her own, and several discrepancies between her account and Gregory's. But it was all now water under the bridge. Some mornings I woke up determined to give *all* my money away; at other times I remembered the kind old man. Why should I go against his desire? Orso was not a fortune hunter, of that I was certain. I worried only that he was the very reverse.

16

I read Zelda's letter many times, full of special pleading as it was. She later wrote formally to Gregory to resign all her claim to Basil de Vere's fortune. I let matters rest there and when I finally replied to her only wished her happiness in her new life.

Gregory and I returned to Florence in June and the long process of sorting out Basil's will, which Gregory had begun in London, continued. We stayed at the villa for a time. I had had the idea that I might one day use it for a small school for girls but many repairs were needed. Gregory showed me the tiny gravestone, now hidden under ivy. I had promised Zelda I would look after it, the least I could do, for I knew she would never return there.

When Gregory went back to London I moved into Zelda's old apartment where Rosa still was. She refused at first to consider rejoining her newly-married mistress, but by October she was weakening in her resolve. Apparently Zelda had pleaded for her to try it out for six months and see how she liked it. Eventually she decided to go, for, as she said — 'Miss Zelda can't manage without me.' I had not 'had it out' with Rosa, but I think she was a bit wary of what I might think about her keeping so many secrets from me.

Two maids stayed to help me when Rosa left one morning to take the train to Rome where Zelda was now living. I had already assembled a small group of girl pupils of several nationalities, mostly about twelve years old, who I hoped might form the nucleus of my future school. For the time being we were to meet each weekday morning in Zelda's old sitting-room. In the afternoons I prepared my lessons or read the novel I had bought on my last day in London, the new Hardy — *Return of the Native* — in which I saw a little of my aunt Zelda in Eustacia.

I had heard nothing from Orso since I had written to him to tell him about the changes in my fortunes, but I consoled myself that he was moving from place to place, country to country, and might not have received my letter. In it I said I knew I wanted both love and a certain independence. I awaited his return to Italy and to Florence with a mixture of longing and excitement — and apprehension — for he might not still want to ask me the same question — never mind my answer. I guessed he would be singing very soon in charity performances to assist the victims of the Po Valley floods, and in December, on the day of my twentieth birthday, I passed the Opera House and saw the *Requiem* billed for just before Christmas, the music Verdi wrote for the same Manzoni whose long novel in Italian I was still trying to finish.

: Luciana Pietrangeli was billed as soprano
: Orso Orsini was to sing the tenor part

409

I bought a ticket immediately. I had known when I returned to Florence that I was still in love with a voice, but that I loved more the man whose voice it was.

He came for me in the evening of 18 December. I had ended my morning lessons early, for there was a light powdering of snow, unusual for Florence. At about four o'clock in the afternoon, I was sitting marking exercises, and about to plan my Christmas shopping. The maid had gone out to the restaurant for one of their 'meals on charcoal' and it was the other girl's evening off. I had loosened my hair and put my slippers on, but had not yet lit the oil lamps. I had left the outside shutters open and only the inner windows closed so that I could see the snow and the silvery sky where already stars were shining . . .

'Did you think', he said, when I had opened the door to loud knocking — 'Did you think I could lose you, little *Salvatore?*' and he swept me up in his big arms and hugged me, and lifted my feet off the ground. I buried my face in his smart new velvet collar that smelt of cologne and snow and then he put me down, stood back, and said: 'I love your hair like that.'

'Are you going to ask me the same question?' I said, and sat down, and Orso sat down opposite and we looked at each other.

'No! *You* can ask the question!' he replied. 'I am tired of asking questions!'

'Do you still want to — marry me?' I said in

410

a trembly voice and never took my eyes off his face.

'Of course, Ester — that *is* a silly question — but now I must ask *you*, now that you are an heiress —'

'You don't mind then — about the money?' I asked timidly.

'It is your money, Ester — you can spend it how you like — have this school you say you are planning, live where you like – but marry me, Ester! — and be with me when I come home from all the other places —'

'But where will be "home"?' I asked him.

Just to hear his voice and see the possessor made me so happy I did not care what he said so long as he wanted me.

'Home is wherever we are together — you and I —' he answered. 'Carissima', he added and he came over to me and kissed me and then buried his face in my long hair.

'Don't cry', he said later. 'I am here. Please stay with me — yes?' I could not speak. 'I only got your letter yesterday — waiting for me in Bologna', he said. 'Oh, it has been so long — but now I am famous! — everywhere, not just here!'

I laughed, then kissed him back, and the past melted away. Later he said, 'I only want you to want me the way I want you, Ester.'

I knew I did.

'*Ti voglio bene*', he said.

'*Ti amo* — I love you', I said, in Italian and in English.

He said it many times after that, and he sang for me too, just for me. I always asked him to sing *La rivedrà nell 'estasi*, and my heart always lifted whenever I heard his voice, whether alone with him, or when I was one of a large audience. Whenever I heard him sing I would touch 'the sky with my finger', as the Italians say.

We went to other parts of Tuscany on our *luna di mielo* before going to see his family. I enjoyed it all, just to be with him, wherever it was. Everywhere he went, wherever we travelled — past the wooded gorges of Tuscany and its battered old red-roofed farmhouses, or outside the cities of Emilia with their cabins and broken down old huts and swarming children, or, later, in the Veneto with its ubiquitous vine-poles and curiously shaped rocks, glades and greenery, and ranks of poplars . . . and in Rome before St Peter's — and later back in Florence and in the summer at the villa — everywhere was home, for he was with me. But I knew that we could not always be together because of his work and I gathered myself up whenever he was absent and planned my school.

Later we were to buy a small palazzo in Florence for the winter, and we let the old apartment. We moved to the villa the next summer. There our first child was born, whom we called Maria . . .

But I did get my school in the end in spite of everything, and he said: 'You are too busy now to get into mischief.'

So long as I know he loves me I am content.

Love always gives hostages to Fortune, and the way we love each other is also full of the pain of knowing that, unlike the music he sings, neither of us is immortal.

Ella did thank me when I gave Cara her share of my fortune, but there was a sting in the tail of her thanks. 'It is good to see, Hetty, that you are no longer jealous of your sister', she said. Another time when I was in London with Orso who was singing again at Covent Garden, she warned me against the love of men. 'It is women's ruin', she stated solemnly. I did not reply.

She seemed happier as she grew older — but kept my sister Alice at home once Alice had finished her studies at the new high school in Parkheath.

Papa unbent a little towards me, though his manner was never easy. To my husband he was always frigidly polite. Orso called him the English icicle. Papa was just as constrained and polite to my brother Gregory who never married but stayed in England and became a country solicitor. Only a few people know what a clever — and loving — man Gregory is. Country solicitors know many secrets, secrets of damaged lives. Gregory knows many, I suspect, though he keeps them to himself.

Gregory and I and Orso visited Mama's grave in Como soon after my marriage. We never had the headstone altered.

Peter Voyle never reappeared in our lives. I imagine he is probably in America's Far West making money and losing it, and breaking hearts . . .

Eleanor Pontraven married her Laurence and settled in Boston. I hear from her now and again. She has heard Orso sing in New York — she says the women all spoil him there.

What happened to Mrs Holroyd we never knew. She disappeared completely, so that we were never invited to her 'At Home'.

Little Paolo Bassano to whom I had once taught English became later in life Italian Consul in Liverpool.

Herbert Frederick Squibb became a very successful grocer in Camberwell — I never understood how he managed to add up his customers' accounts.

Zelda lost her freedom when she married her Count. What is a rich husband when weighed in the scales against financial independence and freedom of manoeuvre? I doubt if she enjoys her new life as much as she once enjoyed her freedom bought at my expense.

Huntie came to live in Italy with us eventually and brought Pooranna with her, which was a relief

414

for Ella. Pooranna alone remains unchanged, but I think she likes it here. She loves to lie in a hammock in the garden of the Villa de Vere.

Rosa went back to London in the end to die and was buried in Ealing.

Max made a lot of money, as he had said he would. He is now the director of a large auction house and writes books on the Italian quattrocento. Cara managed to be patient and wait for Max for two years. Papa finally relented when she was twenty when he realized that my promise to give them a third of my fortune was meant in earnest. Max insisted that half the money should be in Cara's own name, and would not touch it himself. The Married Women's Property Act came along the year after their marriage, but Cara said she trusted Max more than the Law. Their children, Barnaby and Quentin de Vere — for Max kept his old name — have united all of us, even Papa and Mamarella, for Cara is the head of a very happy family.

Felix became a rather restless fellow, but redeemed himself as an officer in the British Army, and much later fought the Boers in South Africa — and was killed out there.

Lucy Little became an Honorary Fellow of the Royal Society for her research on lichens. Mr Little died at a great age in spite of his rheumatism and left all his books to my school.

I said farewell to my childhood the day I pledged my troth to Orso Orsini. I have never since dreamed of the dead baby.

We have been so happy — I believe I am still known as Orsini's funny foreign wife. If I am ever low-spirited — for humans are not meant to live on the mountain peaks every hour of every day, and we have had our sorrows as well as our joys — I just ask him to sing, or go along to wherever he is singing or rehearsing. I am especially fond of the opera *La Favorita* in which he sings of the Ghosts of Love — *larve d'amor* and the thought of past unhappiness is enough to restore my own spirits.

For my Orso was to become the greatest tenor of the age. But, when we celebrated our silver wedding he asked a new young tenor to sing for me. His name was Enrico Caruso and Orsini said he was an even better singer than himself. Personally I prefer Orso.

I often think of my mother as I become middle-aged, which she never was. I am sure that she loved Gregory and me, as I now believe Basil de Vere loved her, though he may never have spoken of his love to her. Instead he left to her daughter a memory of affection, a prize more valuable than money, the memory of a kind old man with a child on his knee who played with his watch-chain, in Italy, long ago.

416